ONE FOR OUR BABY

ONE FOR OUR BABY

a novel

JOHN SANDROLINI

MYSTERIOUSPRESS.COM

OPEN ROAD

INTEGRATED MEDIA

NEW YORK

To Lt. John Donald "Pete" Petersen, KIA 13 Nov 1944,
who remains at sea

1

PALM SPRINGS, CALIFORNIA 1960

Normally, I didn't do Frank's "Angel Flights"—that's what his regular pilots were for. Our understanding was different, and I reminded his valet of that when he phoned.

"No, George, I will not be able to fly Mr. Sinatra's lady friend into Burbank this afternoon. He knows the rules."

Then I hung up.

I stood there a moment watching the sun ooze down toward the top of Mt. San Jacinto as I measured the remaining daylight, faint glimmers of the South Pacific arcing across my mind. I enjoyed the memory for a few seconds and then got back to work unloading my airplane.

The hangar phone rang again thirty seconds later. I eyed it warily for several rings before walking back and picking it up. He began speaking before I could say hello.

"Joseph, it's Francis. I've got something cooking here with a dazzling young lady and I'm gonna need your gossamer wings for a quick trip to the moon."

The song lyric shtick was standard Sinatra, but the "Francis" routine meant he really wanted my help. She had to be someone special.

"She better be Rita Hayworth dazzling, Frank, and it wouldn't hurt if she's shtupping William Randolph Hearst's ghost too, because I've got to fly five thousand of his papers up to Oakland tonight and I can't be late."

"That fascist? Nix the papers, dago, this is much more important than a few yellow rags. My new girl has a screen test at Fox tomorrow morning at seven."

Frank was used to people steaming at flank speed to come kiss his ass, but I couldn't be bothered. "How would that affect me?" I replied, smothering a yawn.

"Come on, they just called me—they had to move it up a day—it's gotta be tomorrow. Do you know how long it takes to drive from Palm Springs to Burbank on a Sunday night? It's wall-to-wall weekenders on the 10."

"You better get a head start then."

"Hey . . . paesan . . . you're not gonna make my baby run that gauntlet, are you? She's gotta meet with Zanuck tomorrow. You know, Zaa-nuck."

He was almost pleading now. I ginned up a grin, having him over a barrel for once. "Last time I checked, you had a snazzy DC-6 at your beck and call with two aero-cabana boys to jock it. Aren't they up to it?"

"Those mammalukes? They're as likely to jock *her* as the airplane. Besides, they aren't good enough. I need someone I can trust like my own brother, and that's you, pally."

"You don't have a brother."

I heard him grunt. "For Christ's sake, Joe, help me here!"

I was busting his balls and he knew it, but he liked the game. Besides, he knew his insistence would wear me down, as it always did. And his protectiveness told me that she really had him right in the old *bra'zhol'*. She must have been top shelf.

Now I was leaning. "Gee, Frank, I haven't seen you this squirrelly over a skirt since the last time Ava was in town."

"Let me tell you something, Giuseppe, this one, she makes Ava look like a Hoboken housewife. Screws better than Ava, too, if you can believe that. Ring a ding, ding!" He held the last note a good five seconds.

That did it. I was hooked. He'd never put anyone above Ava before—in any category—let alone beauty and bedroom.

"Okay, goombah, you win, but I'm leaving as soon as I get this order for Chi Chi's unloaded. I want to get through the pass before sundown. And how the hell did you know I was here, anyway?"

"Thanks a million. We'll be right over—fifteen minutes. Lucky I caught you!" There was a click and the line went dead.

"Lucky . . . yes." I said, eyeing the heavens with suspicion.

I'd known Frank Sinatra for eight years, ever since I saved his ass in that casino jam in Havana back in '52. They had been eight wildly entertaining years—how could they not have been—especially with those women? Through Lana and Ava and Marilyn and a dozen others, two things about Frank's lovers were inarguably true: They were all drop-dead gorgeous. And chaos followed them every step of the way.

I'd learned to be ready for trouble whenever he fired up a new torch. At first mention I should have taken wing back to my hangar in Long Beach, or headed up to Lake Arrowhead for some fishing, or down to San Diego to visit old navy buddies. I should have done anything other than staying put. Instead, I let my curiosity lead me down an old path.

With unfortunate results.

2

I had the Electra unloaded and ready to go when the black Eldo pulled up. Frank bounced out, arm fluttering as he strutted over toward me. He was sporting a bright orange golf shirt and a mood to match.

"Hello, pally, how ya doin'?" he chirped, squeezing my hand.

I looked over toward the car, where George was opening the passenger door to let Frank's inamorata out. "Let you know in a second, chum."

"Hold on to your bird, Joe; she's a fucking knockout!"

He was positively giddy with excitement, and it was beginning to rub off on me.

The door opened and two lovely legs floated out. That was nice.

As she took George's hand and climbed from the recess of the car, Frank announced, "Joe, meet Miss Lilah DeHart, Fox's next big star!"

I leered just a little in anticipation and stepped forward, my eyes scanning her entire figure as she rose, taking it in nice and slow like good bourbon.

I started with those legs that went on for a week, then followed to the hips that Monroe could only dream of. Working my way up, I surveyed the full, round breasts, fighting for attention. I could feel the smile breaking out on my face.

Over that supercharged body, she wore an emerald-green crushed velvet dress that hit every curve doing seventy. It must have set Frank back at least a hundred bucks at Neiman Marcus. Her face was hidden beneath a white, wide-brimmed Ingrid Bergman hat with green trim that just nailed the look.

She raised her chin as she approached and the shadows retreated. I looked upon the face that emerged.

It was a beautiful face. Pillow lips, celestial nose, Everest-high cheekbones—all framed by cascading waves of chestnut hair. Men killed for a woman like that.

But as her features sharpened, something stopped me cold, an unsettling feeling welling up in my gut and moving north fast. Then I stared directly into those eyes of a singular green fire and the world just faded out. I could feel the shock setting in as the realization struck home like a bosun's fist. It was Helen.

She carried it off better than I did, quickly adjusting her hat brim over her rapidly expanding eyes and clearing her throat with a little cough.

The enormity of it was staggering. Nothing, not one damn word for five years, and suddenly she was here, now—and with Frank Sinatra. I listed back on my heels, stunned, silently cursing every god in the pantheon as I gaped at her.

Helen. My ex-fiancée Helen.

"Hey, paesan, take it easy," Frank said. "You've seen gorgeous women before. Stop staring—you'll frighten her. Please excuse him, Lilah, he spends too much time up there in all that thin air and not enough down here where the real angels are."

He laughed and slapped me on the back. I barely heard him. Notes of bergamot and sandalwood came dancing on the air then, wafting by like an early summer day. *Chypre. Her scent.*

Man, the knife was really turning now.

George gave me a long look before getting back into the car. Frank hugged "Lilah" and wished her luck, promising to meet her in Bel Air in a couple of days. He kissed her good-bye and winked at me before bounding back into the Cadillac. Then he rolled away on a wave of cool, a snap-brim hat in the rear window slowly fading from view.

I just stood there, eyes down, hand on my forehead, as the last remnants of my soul tumbled to the tarmac and shattered at my feet.

3

We hardly spoke as I closed up the plane. I don't think either one of us knew what to say. Finally, I offered, "I'll get you into Burbank right away. I know a good taxi driver I can call."

"No thanks, hon," she replied in that smoke-wisp of a voice that always sent me. "Frank's got a limo waiting for me."

I got the picture. But quick.

I stared at her, seconds ticking by, the words not coming. Finally, I managed, "Helen . . . you're more beautiful than ever."

She smiled. "Thanks, Joe."

I started to say something else, then turned and walked toward the cockpit.

~

Squinting into the dying afternoon sun, I scanned the horizon for air traffic, refracted sunlight bouncing off the mountains and radiating back into the sky in brilliant red rays. Normally, I would have appreciated the beauty, but this was no normal day.

It was a short flight into Burbank, maybe thirty minutes, but I wanted to get it done quickly. I still had to make a bounce into Long Beach and a night hop to the Bay, and now I had two tons of granite on my shoulders.

Helen sat alone in the back of the Electra, just staring out the small window. She'd taken her hat off, her long, dark hair spilling down and blocking my view of her face.

But I'd seen too much already.

By the time I reached San Bernardino, I'd missed two radio calls and forgotten to close the cowl flaps. I couldn't think straight. If he's lucky, one time in his life a guy gets a woman like that. I had—then I'd lost her.

And now she was back.

4

We met back in '54 at a Chet Baker show right after she arrived in L.A. She was a typical fresh-faced kid from Bumfuck planning to make a big splash in Hollywood. I was an ex-fighter pilot trying to close some dark chapters of my life and make a new go of it. She had dreams, I had nightmares. We hit it off.

We'd have dinner on Saturdays at the Starlight Club and then go dancing, or catch Frankie Laine or someone at the Hollywood Bowl. We both loved to bet the horses over at Santa Anita and watch those beautiful beasts run—she always seemed to pick the winners. Sometimes we'd just knock around the beaches in Redondo or go deep-sea fishing off Newport. She was easy to be with, dressed up or down.

Over time, I began to leave my past behind me and look toward a future with her. I was still flying night and day trying to get my freight business up and running, and she always had an audition to attend, but we found time to be together. It was hectic, but we were holding on. One day on Catalina Island I asked her to marry me. We both had a shot at what we wanted.

And then my past came calling.

Having to go to Southeast Asia to settle an old score with Chinese mobsters wasn't exactly the kind of thing you can explain to your fiancée in one hour, which was all I had. Not when all she knew about your time in the Pacific came from an old squadron photo on your desk and a faded *Chicago Tribune* article recounting how you won the Navy Cross at Midway.

But there was more, much more, about my time over there that very few people knew. I gave everything I had in that war until there was nothing left and still came back in one piece—but I didn't make it all the way home.

Soon enough, I wound up back in China, where it all began. While I was there, I fell in with some of the people your mother warns you about, and I did some things I regret.

The kinds of things that follow a man the rest of his life.

So I went to Macao to make things right, but Helen wasn't around when I got back a month later. She left a note—and the ring. I threw them both off the Seal Beach pier. I gave some thought to going in with them but dove into a bottle of Old Number 7 instead.

~

I was still lost in the past when that forgotten aroma came floating into the cockpit. Before I could turn, she slipped into the copilot's seat. As she squeezed past me, breasts brushing my arm, I thought I felt her breath on my neck. I closed my eyes as memories of her lying next to me flooded in.

A honeyed voice cooed, "Whacha know, Joe?"

"Mmmmm . . ." I mused. "Guess, why don't ya?"

The dulcet tone climbed an octave. "Honey, is it supposed to be going up like that?"

"Like . . . what? . . . Oh . . ."

As I slipped into my daze, I'd tightened my grip on the yoke, pulling the Electra into a climb. I smiled in embarrassment and brought the plane back to altitude, both of us laughing at the moment.

That broke the ice.

Then I turned to face her, struggling to conceal my amusement. "Lilah?" I intoned, raising an eyebrow.

"Hollywood name," she said, smiling. "You know."

"Do I?"

I kept on staring, doing my best deadpan to keep from cracking up. She looked over at me, then away, then back again.

"What?" she said, throwing her hands up. "Okay, I got it out of some New Orleans romance novel I read when I was a kid. Satisfied?" She slapped my arm, trilling through a laugh.

I let the moment ride, but then I cut to the chase a little too soon.

"Helen . . . what the hell happened with us?"

She looked at me for a long, agonizing moment, her smile fading by degrees. "Why did you have to go away, Joe? Why did you do that to us?"

She made a small, pained sound, gazing away toward the window. As she turned, I thought I saw tears welling up in those gorgeous green eyes.

I didn't say anything for several minutes, just sat there hating myself. Helen stared silently out the window, wiping her cheeks a couple of times.

When enough time had passed, I tried a different tack. "Hey, there's the Rose Bowl up ahead. See it?"

She nodded. We both followed with "Remember when we . . . ?" and slipped into another giggle.

That did it—she owned the world when she smiled. Right then I'd have given ten grand to have never met Frank Sinatra.

"I'll have to start down soon for Burbank," I said. "You'll be home in no time."

"Shall I sit down in back, hon? I know you'll be busy." She started to get up.

"Don't go, baby, stay until landing. Let's have that, just that much time."

She nodded, then settled back in her seat, maxing out a Hollywood smile as she beamed in agreement.

I radioed Burbank tower, reduced power for the descent, and rolled in toward the field. For those seven minutes, Smilin' Jack Martin had nothing on me.

5

I taxied clear of runway 26 and brought the plane over to transient parking. The lineman marshaled me in and signaled a stop, then I cut the throttles and the fuel levers, killing the engines. As the magnetos wound down with a whine, I looked over at Helen, her face radiant in the twilight glow. She had an air of serenity about her, or maybe it just looked that way to me.

I stepped off the aircraft, chocked the left main tire, and then hustled back to the cabin door to help Helen down, feeling the cool clutch of the L.A. evening as it enveloped the field.

Helen was waiting at the door, looking back over her shoulder when I returned. I planted the wooden step beneath the doorway and offered her my hand. She took it, then stepped down to the ramp, taxiway lights glowing blue in the incipient darkness around her as she descended.

The limo hadn't arrived yet, so we sat down in the charter lounge to wait.

After an awkward moment, I blurted out, "Baby, I didn't think I'd ever see you again."

She reached out, rubbed my knee ever so gently. "I didn't think I'd see you, either, but I'm awfully glad I did."

"Me too. Of course I was a bit stunned—dumbstruck really—but I'm starting to get my bearings back. This whole thing with Frank—"

"You never told me you knew him. Why?"

"We had a chance meeting in '52—I don't see him all that often. And when we were dating, I obviously had better things to do."

It wasn't all true, but it was cover enough for the moment.

"Hmm," she said, drawing out the word while measuring me with a stare. "Well, Frank spoke of you like a brother on the way to the airport today. He said you've been a real lifesaver for him on a few occasions."

"Yeah," I said, nodding, "coupla times."

"Of course, how could I suspect you were the guy he was talking about? This is all confusing the bejeezus out of me, Lieutenant Commander Buonomo." She placed her hands on her hips, tilted her head. "Just what goes on with you two?"

I grinned. "Not much—besides you. We're just a couple of guys from different parishes who look out for each other."

"Joe . . ." she chided, her voice trailing off as a dark blue Lincoln pulled in, glided to a stop, and dimmed its lights. A uniformed driver stepped out and stood at the passenger's door. He wore an impeccably pressed dark suit that showed a good deal of cuff. Very Frank Sinatra.

Neither of us stood. I just stared into those emerald eyes, wanting them to ensnare me again, newly aware of a feeling long dormant inside me.

"Honey, there's so much I want to say to you. I know you have to go—"

"Listen, you, I live at the Regency Court Apartments, 399 North Palm Avenue in Alhambra—across from the park. If you're not there at eight p.m. sharp to pick me up, I'll never speak to you again."

"Tonight?"

"Tonight, Einstein."

"But it's seven oh five already."

"You'll think of something, I'm sure. You're good like that."

She rose and motioned through the window. The driver snapped to attention and opened the car door. I quietly noted her regal air and poise. The farm girl was long gone.

I swung the lounge door open and leaned back to let her pass. As she did, she pressed against me, kissing me full on the mouth, her long lashes fluttering like butterfly wings before my widening eyes. A wave of heat rose on my lips, crested at my temples, and then washed straight down over me. I almost pulled the doorknob off in my hand.

"See you later, flyboy," she purred, then turned and sauntered off toward the limo.

I watched every step.

6

It took some doing but I finally convinced the charter company's manager to let me borrow the airport car they kept on hand for local runs.
The fin I gave him didn't hurt, but I think the eyeful of Helen that he
got tipped the scales in my favor.

The car was a '49 Stutz with rust in the wheel wells and a large dent
in the front quarter panel—no radio, either. It could just as well have
been Ben Hur's four white stallions, all trimmed and brushed for the
big race for all I cared, as long as it got me to 399 North Palm Avenue
by eight p.m.

I shot down San Fernando, cut back up 66, then ran south on Fair
Oaks to the park doing a good sixty most of the way. Nobody died,
but there were a few close calls in there. I pulled up in front of Helen's
place with a whole minute to spare.

I had to fly later, and I also had some qualms about keeping her out
when she had a screen test in the morning, but no way was I going to
miss the chance to talk with her, to find out where she'd gone, to just
be near her again—if only for an hour.

As I drove, I sang a few bars of "Stars Fell on Alabama," amusing
myself by inserting Alhambra into the lyric in place of Alabama. The

sudden nearness of her had filled me with powerful emotions, the good ones overwhelming the bad. I was as stupidly giddy as a young sailor on shore leave. I realized then that I still loved her—that I always had.

Jesus, that girl could twist me in knots.

$$7$$

We went over to The Hat on Garfield to grab a sandwich and a soda. Helen had changed into a cashmere sweater and capri slacks that went a whole lot better with my flightsuit and boots than that velvet va-voom number of hers. I still wasn't going to pass for Fred Astaire, but we weren't exactly dining at Ciro's anyhow.

As we sat there on our stools, the wonderful scent of warm pastrami and mustard wafting up, it almost felt like it was 1955 again, that we were still together.

But it wasn't, and we weren't. It was 1960 and Elvis Presley was on the jukebox, not Frankie Laine. This kid Elvis wanted to know if we were lonesome tonight, were we sorry we'd drifted apart. A real tearjerker, that kid. What timing.

After some small talk, I got right down to brass tacks.

"Helen, how did you fall in with Frank?"

She sipped her soda, pursed her lips a moment. "We met in Acapulco about a month ago. I was visiting a friend who knows Bob Mitchum and we got invited to a party on Bob's boat. Frank was down fishing with Jimmy Van Heusen and they crashed the party. It was just, you know . . ."

"One of those things?"

"Yes, I suppose so. Look, he's been very good to me."

I took a bite of my sandwich, wiped my chin with my napkin. "I know. He's good to all of them—three or four weeks at a time."

Her eyes went wide. "My, my. Aren't we a bit catty? And he's a *friend* of yours?"

I smiled, picking a fleck of pastrami from my teeth with a thumbnail. "Look, honey, he *is* a friend of mine, but you're someone I was madly in love with, and I just want you to see all the angles in play here."

"*Was?*"

I didn't bite on that one.

"Just keep your eyes open, Betty Boop. I've seen some rather mercurial behavior from ol' Frankie now and then."

She went suddenly serious. "Look Joe, I'm meeting with Darryl Zanuck tomorrow morning at Frank's request. If I get nothing else out of this deal, that's the chance of a lifetime. I plan on knocking their socks off at that screen test."

"That sounds a little calculating, darling. Surely you care for our Sicilian friend just a little, don't you?"

"I don't know what I feel, but I've been pounding these streets for six years. My shelf date is just about up, and I am not going back to America's Dairyland to cuddle up with some farmer and bang out a brood of Beaver Cleavers, thank you very much."

"Wow. You've acquired a few sharp edges to go along with those curves, baby."

She didn't say a word, just narrowed her eyes halfway down like an angry cat and put on a pout that could have broken Rodin's heart. I felt an unpleasant wave of déjà vu and began to recall the *other* Helen who had popped up from time to time when we were together—the sullen one.

"Can we go have a drink together?" she asked. "I've got another hour or so still and I wouldn't mind a belt."

She hadn't said things like that when we were together. Now she was talking like Frank, a change I didn't care for at all.

"I'm flying tonight, no drinking for me. But . . . I'll go with you if you promise me a dance."

She perked right up, red lips parting into a matinee idol smile.

"I know a place around the corner where they pour 'em tall and strong. Let's hit the bricks, Lindbergh!"

"He wouldn't drink with you either, lady."

"I know, lover, but he wouldn't be sitting here with mustard on his face, trying to make time with an actress either—the stiff."

～

We buzzed over to the Sapphire Room. The place was fairly lively for a Sunday night, patrons lined up and down the bar and filling most of the tables. I wedged my way into an opening along the rail and ordered a Manhattan and a cup of coffee. I got a look from the bartender, but he took my buck fifty just the same.

We found a spot in the corner at a small table and sat down. Helen took a cigarette out of a small gold case and I lit it for her with my worn silver Zippo.

"Still got that old thing?"

"Had it since the war. You know how I'm sentimental, hon," I said, looking directly into her eyes so she'd know how I meant it.

I pulled a Lucky out of a battered pack for myself and torched it, still grinning at her.

We swapped some catch-up stories and shared a few good chuckles. She told me about the parts she'd scored in some movies I hadn't seen, and a relationship with a movie star that ended abruptly when she caught him wearing one of her dresses. I laughed out loud at the thought of the All-American heartthrob in polka dots.

I filled her in on the semiepic affairs of my freight business, but steered clear of my occasional adventures with one Francis Albert Sinatra. There was no point in showing that card yet.

While we were talking, I noticed a stocky guy in a Hawaiian shirt at the far end of the bar, dark eyes peering out from beneath a heavy brow. Helen was a stunner, all right, but he seemed a little too interested in us just the same. The first twinge of wariness sprang up deep inside me.

The next time I looked up, he'd moved on down the line somewhere so I let it go. That's the thing about a girl like her, though. You think every guy in the world wants something from her.

Some dinosaur popped a nickel in the jukebox then and pushed "Moonlight Serenade." I caught the first few bars and closed my eyes reflexively. It took me back—way back—like it always did, the personal Movietone reel replaying memories of flight school, wild nights on Oahu, and good buddies—some long dead.

Helen saw my fade and stopped talking. I always loved that about her, the way she didn't mind my occasional drifts or intrude on my reminiscences. She understood that we vets had some places inside where others couldn't go.

"Begin the Beguine" came on next. Jesus, the guy was wallowing in it, but I seized the moment. "Let's dance, cutie."

"Let's," she said, her eyes shimmering in the dusky room.

We joined a few other couples on the small dance floor and began swaying to the infectious Artie Shaw rhythm. I held her close, letting the nostalgia sweep over me, damn near bathing in it.

Patsy Cline's "Just Out of Reach" followed. We danced to that one and one more, then sat a few out while Helen had another drink. We shared more stories and laughs, all smiles and sunshine. I ate my heart out the entire time.

That could only last so long. Both of us had questions we needed answered. It didn't matter how it ended up, we needed to clear the air. It wasn't the setting for me to delve into my past, but I hoped she would tell me her side. I'd been through too much not to ask.

Helen had moved closer to me throughout the evening, our chairs now touching. When I looked down, her hand was on my arm. She had a look of longing in those exquisite eyes.

"Honey," I said, closing in, "I hate to bust up the ice cream social, but I have to know what happened between us. Tell me where you went—and why."

She moved into close range, ran her finger across my chin.

"Not here. Let's go back to my place, we can talk there."

"Talk?"

An iniquitous smile bloomed on her face.

"I can't do that. You're with Frank now."

"Yes, you can," she said, willing me with those eyes, that voice. "Joe . . . we left a lot behind us a few years back. I'd like to try and find some of it."

My pulse raced at the words. I leaned in toward her until I was almost touching her glistening lips, feeling the pull of the current as I drifted into dangerous waters.

"How much of it?"

She just grinned at me, bedroom eyes narrowing. "All of it."

I stared back, trying to grasp what she said, but knowing full well exactly what she meant. A voice inside me protested but was drowned out by my overwhelming desire to hold that woman close through the long, dark night.

A thin smile rolled onto my lips, a smile five hard years in the making. "Let's go."

8

We started off toward her place, both nervous but bubbly. Things were moving fast—way too fast. I knew that I loved Helen—but she wasn't my girl anymore.

More to the point, she was my buddy's girlfriend. I just wasn't that kind of guy, even at my worst.

I took my foot off the gas, let the car coast to a stop sign while I decompressed. When I realized that I wouldn't be going in with her, I exhaled with relief. Then I crossed the intersection, pulled over to the curb, and parked.

"What's up, lover?" she asked with a smile. "Are we going to start right here?"

I made a small shake of my head, shifted around to face her, resting my arm on top of the seat. "Baby . . . you know that I still love you, don't you?"

"Yes, Joe. It's as obvious as that wonderful Roman nose on your face."

"Thanks. You also know that if you tell me you love me, I'll believe it."

"I do. Always have."

"Then . . . we can't do this, honey. Frank is my friend. I know how crazy this situation is, but . . . I just can't do that. I couldn't face him again, and it would ruin any chance we had to ever make this work."

"Well, you can be sure he hasn't made the same choice when faced with it," she said, her lips curling up.

I sat up. "That doesn't cut any ice here, baby. This is about *me*, not him."

She went back to that pout again, crossing her arms and staring out through the windshield. An oncoming headlight rose up, bathing her face in light, then plunging it back into shadow when it passed. As I went to turn the key in the ignition she spoke, surprising me with the calm, measured tone in her voice.

"You're right. Not tonight, but he's got to know. Something's gotta give here."

I gazed into those eyes, for the first time not intimidated by them.

"Are you sure? You are intimately involved with Frank Sinatra, the number one music and movie star in the world, who just happens to be nuts about you. You better think this one over long and hard before making any decisions, honey."

"I already have," she declared, her voice cracking.

First a tear, then a river followed. "Can't you see how much I still love you, Buonomo," she cried, reaching out.

Slender arms wrapped tight around me as she began sobbing.

"If you only had any idea what I've been through since I last saw you . . ."

9

I held her several minutes while she wept, her tears dampening my flightsuit. It was cool outside, but the windows began fogging up, so I rolled mine down halfway. Helen looked up as a nip of night air crept into the car.

"I'm sorry," she said, easing away.

We sat there while she composed herself, dabbing her eyes and sniffling a bit. I brushed those long locks away from her face, stroking my fingers through them several times. She started to speak, but I put a finger to my lips, then touched it to hers.

"Helen," I said, weighing my words, "let's take the night to think this thing over. You'll get some rest, and I'll get my newspapers up the coast then fly into Burbank and sack out in the Electra—I'll be up by ten. How about we meet for lunch someplace and you tell me how your screen test went?"

"That would be nice," she said, wiping away a final tear stealing down her cheek.

"Good. The charter company's number is on the car door here, THorndike 3-5200. You just ring them up when you're done and they'll grab me. Deal?"

23

"Deal," she murmured low, almost with resignation.

I pushed back the last few tear-dampened strands of hair, hooking them over her ear. "Don't throw in the towel just yet; maybe there'll be some way to work this out."

I turned the ignition over and the Stutz rumbled to life. I checked the rearview mirror, slid the transmission into first, and eased away from the curb.

As I pulled out, I caught a glimpse of a man shuffling down the sidewalk in our direction. He stopped and stared at us, hands on his hips. He was too far away to recognize but looked too much like the guy in the bar for my liking.

As we drove the remaining blocks, a wave of uneasiness came over me. I knew I hadn't done anything wrong, but I wondered just what in the hell I was getting myself into.

~

Helen asked me to stop a few doors up the street from her building since she had a busybody neighbor who'd just love to tell the whole neighborhood that she'd been out late with another man. I told her I'd watch her go in, then drive past to make sure she got into her apartment all right.

"This is a very nice neighborhood," I said. "I guess one gossip isn't too much a price to pay for these digs. But aren't you rather far from the studio scene out here?"

"Yes, thank God, but they usually send a car for me. I lived in Hollywood for several years, over on Afton with my girlfriend Betty, but that part of town was knee-deep in shady operators. A girl could find all sorts of trouble down there if she wasn't on her toes."

"Really?" I asked, feigning surprise.

"Really. Just ask Betty when you meet her. She'll tell you."

I leaned back, crossed my arms. "I can only imagine."

"She's made some questionable decisions, but she's a true friend. She loaned me the most beautiful dress the other day for my audition. You'll see it when we meet for lunch."

"I'm looking forward to it."

"Okay, gotta go."

Helen leaned over and hugged me, then kissed me on the cheek.

"You be safe up there tonight, Buonomo, I need to see your handsome face across from me at lunch tomorrow. We've got a lot to talk about."

Her sultry tone had returned. I liked that. I liked that fine.

"Just make sure you call me no matter how your screen test goes," I said, shaking a finger at her. "I don't want to go chasing all over the world to find you again."

She got out, closed the door, and pattered around to my side. Then she leaned down into my open window, flashed her perfect teeth at me. "But you would, Joe, wouldn't you?"

"Bet your life on it, bambina."

She smiled again, then turned and walked off.

In ten seconds she was gone.

10

I hustled on over to the airport and cranked up the Electra, then zipped over to Long Beach. I caught a break when I saw my partner, Roscoe, hanging around. He'd blown a jug on the DC-3 and was waiting for the mechanic to finish the repair. He helped load my plane while I checked the weather and filed a flight plan.

It was just after one when I took off. I hugged the coast until I was north of Los Angeles then began a climb at Malibu, up and over the hills. Along the way, I cadged a radio signal from KNOB on the direction finder and dialed in some Big Bill Broonzy. That was good.

After that, they played an album side from trumpeter Clifford Brown. That was great. Helen and I had seen him play back in late '54, so it seemed like a good omen.

As the Electra droned on, Cliff's aching version of "What's New?" cut through the heart of the night over the gyrating hum of the props, the soulful notes and the dull buzzing blending into a relaxing rhythm. I leaned back, letting my mind unwind, drifting through the day's dizzying events.

The shock of seeing Helen, her love affair with Frank, the rush I got when she kissed me in the doorway, the way she wept when she said she still loved me—all these events played out again for me, the woman in the middle of them whirling and weaving like Salome as she danced through my mind.

A squall line, rare for the season, boiled up ahead in my windshield. I was so busy daydreaming that I damn near plowed right into it before altering course out to sea to avoid it.

Brown's trumpet stayed with me as I flew on amid the lightning flashes, interference slowly enveloping the signal in fuzzy static. I rotated the dial a couple of times, but Cliff faded away, then he was gone. But I didn't really notice.

I was still thinking about that kiss.

~

I finally dropped onto the runway back in Burbank around five thirty just as the first shafts of morning light began creeping above the San Gabriels. Venus shone like a beacon as she shimmied above them in the dawn sky.

"Good morning, doll," I said, giving her a wink she didn't return.

I taxied back into "Transient," cut the engines, and threw a pair of chocks around a tire. Then I pulled the foldout bunk down, slipped off my boots, and draped my leather jacket over my chest. The sandman had me under in thirty seconds.

My dreams were entirely about Helen. They were vivid and sensual and very, very real. None of them would ever be described in *Ladies' Home Journal*.

11

The cabin door creaked open with a metallic groan, the woman I was holding fading away into the gloom as I raised my head to see who was at the hatch. The dark shadow of the lineman's head appeared, framed by white light in the opening.

"Mr. Buonomo? You've got a call inside. Someone says it's urgent—he's very insistent."

"Who is it?" I rasped, my fingers still clutching for the vanishing wisp of Helen.

"He didn't say, but he threatened to have my legs broken if I didn't wake you up. He's real worked up about something."

Frank. It couldn't be anyone else.

I sighed and checked my watch. Eight thirty.

"Tell him I'll be right in," I said, the words tripping across my tongue.

I pulled on my boots and combed my hair back with my fingers. The morning sun was bright, so I slipped on my Ray-Bans to ward it off and stepped down from the plane, trudging off to the lounge toward God knew what.

~

I picked up the receiver, stifled a yawn, and opened with, "Morning, Frank."

"Did you screw her?"

"*What?*"

"Lilah. Did you screw her? Where the hell were you last night? And why are you still in Burbank this morning?"

"Whoa, easy. I'm not one of your boys, Sinatra, don't talk to me like that. And I was in the skies over California until five a.m. so, no, I didn't screw her—but screw you, pal!" I started to hang up.

"Joe," he blurted out, "she's gone. She didn't show for her screen test and she's not answering her phone."

I felt my heart skip a beat.

"Gone? Nobody's seen her? Could she be running late?"

"Nobody in Hollywood misses a screen test with Zanuck, not one that Frank Sinatra sets up! She would've called them anyway. You gotta get over there right away; something's not right here."

"Why don't you call the police?"

"Do you remember who you're talking with here? Ten minutes after I call, that piece of shit at *Hush-Hush* will be asking me for ten thou to keep it quiet—you know the cops tip those guys off. I need one of *my* guys, Joe, and you're the best. There's got to be an explanation, but I need to know something soon."

Silently, I agreed. I was starting to feel alarmed, too, as I woke up. "Okay, Frank. I'll do it. Where's she live?"

He gave me the address I already knew, begging me to hurry.

"I'll call you from there as soon as I know something. Good-bye." I banged the phone down, grabbed the Stutz keys off the wall without asking, and headed out.

"I'll be back in an hour," I shouted over my shoulder as I ran for the parking lot.

12

I kept my cool as I drove, but just barely. I hoped I'd find her at home, maybe asleep, maybe drunk. I wanted her to tell me that she just didn't want to do the screen test and hadn't wanted to talk to Frank about it, or that she was sick, or jittery, or anything at all—just so long as she was there.

I parked right out front and double-timed into the foyer. She didn't answer her bell after three rings, so I punched all four second-floor bells on the intercom, pushing the door open as soon as I heard the buzzer.

At Helen's door, I stopped and listened for several seconds, then knocked firmly. Nothing. I knocked again and called her name, scanning the hallway in both directions, listening for any sounds. Twenty seconds passed. Just to be sure, I waited twenty more.

Then I pulled my knife.

I stuck the blade into the jamb and jimmied it around a couple of times. The bolt slid back easily, but the door chain caught firm. I slipped that, too, with a gentle flick of the blade and the door swung inward quietly.

The place was dark, curtains drawn and all lights out. I closed the door behind me, switched on a table lamp, and surveyed the room.

A large one-bedroom, neat and well appointed. The furniture was streamline style, black lacquer with green cushions. Chromium lamps capped with dark green shades dotted the room. They looked expensive—and new. It was a smart place.

A sleek bureau edged out from the wall on the far side of the room. Half a dozen pictures in silvered frames rested on the embroidered silk cloth on top. I recognized the one of Helen's parents, and one of her and her sister. Several other people looked vaguely familiar from Hollywood. A large autographed picture of Frank from about 1949 stood prominently in the middle. He still had most of his hair in that one.

I called her name in a low voice, but she didn't answer. Then I made my way across the carpeted floor to the kitchen. Everything was in order, not even a dish in the sink. A copy of *Variety* and a pencil lay on the small Formica table next to a bowl of fruit. The back door was locked, but the chain wasn't hooked.

I walked back across the living room, toward the open bedroom door. She wasn't in there, either. The bathroom was more of the same, the sink and bathtub bone dry.

I returned to the bedroom. Last night's velvet dress lay on top of the still-made bed. One of the foldout closet doors on the near side of the bed was full open, but the reams of clothing inside hung in neat, orderly rows on their cedar hangers. When I closed the door, the garment hanging on the knob caught my eye—a spaghetti strap navy dress with white piping on a knitted hanger, a laundry tag for Betty Benker pinned to the fabric.

I "hmmmmed" audibly as I added that number to the equation, then turned to survey the rest of the room.

A large vanity dominated the space on the far side of the bed. I walked over, then bent down to inspect it, my hand coming to rest on a pair of lavender silk pajamas that lay on the cushioned chair back. I knew them well. I bought them for Helen in San Francisco while we strolled through Chinatown one day after lunch. They weren't cheap, but she loved them and wore them every night.

I picked up the top and breathed in deeply. Chypre. I closed my eyes, recalling that day on Grant Street, the silk cool and smooth between my fingers.

I gave the vanity a good looking-over. Bird's-eye maple inlaid with marquetry and banded with mahogany on the edges—not something you'd buy at Woolworth's.

But the top teemed with life like their lunch counter on a Saturday: small glass bottles with French labels nestling amidst a troika of tortoise shell cases in front of a gilt mirror, a silver ashtray, a cut-glass lighter and black cigarette holder, a jade Bakelite jewelry box brimming with enough baubles to send a crow into overdrive, and a pair of ebony hairbrushes with mother-of-pearl inlay, random strands of dark hair protruding from the brushes. It might not have done for Coco Chanel, but just about any other woman would have been thrilled to have that vanity. Hollywood hadn't been too bad to Helen.

I moved across to the bed, sitting down on the mohair quilt and scratching my chin with my palm. Nothing seemed amiss, but she clearly hadn't spent the night, nor had she taken Betty's dress for her tryout. Yet I had seen her go in the front door last night. Everything had been fine then. So where the hell had she gone?

I glanced over my shoulder at the nightstand closest to me. A pale yellow Crosley clock and a leather-bound black-and-white photograph sat topside. I took a good look at the man in the picture: leather jacket, sunglasses, dark hair slicked back in waves—the guy had an air about him. And the way he leaned smiling against the side of a polished aluminum airplane brought a smile to my lips. He reminded me of myself years ago.

Probably because he was me.

~

I made a second sweep of the apartment but didn't turn anything up. Then I went over to the telephone nook on the wall and flipped through Helen's address book in search of Betty's listing. An L.A. exchange appeared next to her name, along with several men's names, most of which had been lined out. Hunter hadn't made the grade. Neither had Johnny, Henry, or Ace. *Ace?* Some guy named Carmine seemed to have boyfriend duties this week.

I dialed the number. Someone picked up on the fourth ring.

"H-hello," a woman said.

The voice was small and fragile—it might have broken if you spoke too loudly to it. It sounded shook up.

"Hello, Betty?"

"Yes?"

"Betty, I'm a friend of Lilah's and I'm trying to reach her. She's not at home and I was hoping she was with you."

There was a long pause, then, "No. No, I haven't seen her all week. Sorry."

"Listen, this is very important. She missed her screen test this morning. I'm worried about her. Do you have any idea where—"

"I'm s-sorry," she stammered. "I can't help you."

A man's voice mumbled in the background, the words fuzzy.

"Betty—"

"Good-bye," she said. "Please don't call back."

There was a click, then a C chord hummed on the line. I cradled the phone.

Now I was fairly certain something was up. Carmine, or whoever that was in the background, was just going to have to wait for his Cream of Wheat this morning because I was going to speak with Betty Benker just as soon as I could get to Hollywood, and that was going to be pretty damn quick.

I dialed the operator, but her number was unlisted. Ditto the address. Betty Benker was a ghost.

But a ghost who sent her laundry out.

Back in the bedroom, I lifted the navy dress off the closet door and held it up. The tag read Chin's Hand Laundry, address on North Gower, in Hollywood. That checked. It would be my next stop.

The laundry slip in my pocket, I took a last look around the room, feeling faint stirrings of Helen's presence in the familiar objects. I wanted things to be all right for her. For us.

I snapped off the light, set the lock, and pulled the door gently behind me until I heard the lock click into place. Then I hustled down the hallway and went out the front door.

A set of eyes followed me as I strode across the porch. When I turned my head, I caught the quick fall of a Venetian blind over a side window. I smiled cheekily in the direction of the busybody neighbor and turned front again. Then my smile just evaporated.

Two police officers were coming up the walk as I went down the stairs. I nodded smartly and wished them a good morning as I neared.

Maybe it was their great police instinct, maybe it was just routine, or maybe it was my flightsuit, boots, uncombed hair, and two-day stubble, but something tipped them off that I might not have been a resident of the Regency Court Apartments.

"Hold it, pal," the first one said.

"Yes, Officer?"

"You live here, Jimmy Doolittle?"

I made a head shake. "Just visiting a friend."

"Who might that be, Baron von Richtofen?" He smiled at his partner like a kid who made a funny in math class.

It's always the same with cops, always the wiseass for thirty bucks a day. But I wasn't going to let on about Helen—that could put Frank in it. So I did the best thing I could—I grinned and said nothing.

That went over like a one-bladed prop.

The second bull said, "Listen, Jimmy D, you tell us who you were visiting here or you're going in on a burglary beef, get me? We've got a report of an intruder here."

This cop was older and meaner than the first, probably because he knew that patrol sergeant was as far as he was going to go in life and there wasn't enough booze in all California to help him forget it anymore. He was heavy and tired-looking with blotchy gin-mill skin, the kind of guy who went to work solely to fill the hours between his tours of duty on the barstool. He vibed Fatso Judson, the sadistic guard in *From Here to Eternity*, all the way.

I gave up. It was going to happen anyhow.

"Actually, guys," I said, "I came to meet Howard Hughes; he wanted to sell me the *Spruce Goose* for two thousand bucks. I told him to throw in Jane Russell or it was no deal. You would have thought he'd live in a bigger place, wouldn't you?"

Two minutes later, I had a comfortable seat in the back of their nice patrol car, handcuffed to a rail.

The cops came back to the car in five minutes, talking to someone who looked liked Central Casting's idea of a landlady—thin, spinster-ish, hair in a bun. Even the cat-eye glasses.

She took a long look at me through the car window. I smiled—it seemed like the thing to do. She shook her head back and forth several times and mouthed the word *no* to the officers. They thanked her, dropped into the car, and let her return to whatever landladies do.

Fatso glowered at me and poked me in the chest with a sausage link finger. "You're going down for some questioning, Doolittle." Then he pulled his jowls into a grin. "And I think I'll do it myself."

I shrugged. I was too worried about where Helen was and what kind of trouble might be brewing to give a damn about him. As the car pulled away, I saw the busybody's face in the window again. I shot her the bird, drawing just the tiniest fraction of satisfaction when the blinds banged shut.

13

Fatso leaned in close, squeezed my cheeks in his weathered paw, and said, "Listen, guinea, we're going to keep going over this until you give us something. We got a report of a prowler, and we got you, Wrong Way Corrigan, in the same complex looking like he just fell to Earth without any explanation for being there."

I stared straight ahead at the wall, his words beating down like someone kicking a washboard over and over.

"You got a private detective's license in your wallet, but you say you ain't working on a case. You also have a chink laundry ticket for a Miss Betty Benker of Hollywood in your pocket, but apparently you don't know her and she said she never heard of you, either. That don't square, brother."

I flexed my lips, cracking the blood dried in the corner, said, "You bore me, Fatso. I went to see a friend and had a wrong address. I'd have found him by now if you hadn't shanghaied me. I already told you that."

He snarled, said, "Tell it again, then. It's gonna go a lot easier if you stop holding out on us."

"You've been at this for at least two hours already. Really, don't you have some hopheads to shake down, or phone calls to make on behalf of the reelection campaign of Chief Pissant? Anything to earn your shit salary today other than knocking the paint off my fenders?"

This time he only hit me with an open hand, but it stung just the same.

"We can play this game all day, pal. I don't get off 'til five," he said, chuckling with self-gratification. "Besides, the chief is appointed in Alhambra, not elected. Guess that proves you ain't from around here."

"The only thing you've proven all day, Mr. Holmes, is that you're a disgrace to that uniform."

He pulled back his hand again, then stopped and looked toward the door.

Footsteps sounded in the hallway, growing closer. I could hear two men speaking in elevated tones as they approached. One sounded familiar, an East Coast accent.

"Lieutenant, that's my man you have in there and I want him released right now."

Frank. I shook my head, made the wryest of little smiles.

"Listen, Mr. Sinatra, this man is under investigation for breaking into Miss DeHart's building. And if I understand you correctly, she's unaccounted—"

"*I* sent him over there! Are you paying attention, Lieutenant? If your idiot goons hadn't pinched him, he might have found her by now, and I wouldn't be wasting my goddamn time talking to you—I might be holding her instead. Get him out of there. *Now!*"

Frank burst into the interrogation room and announced, "C'mon, Joe. Grab your stuff; these Harveys are gonna cut you loose. I already spoke to Gene Biscailuz. He still runs this county—all of it."

I turned my head toward him, raised my hand the four inches the chain allowed, and opened my palms upward in the universal *whaddamigonnado?* gesture.

He looked at me, saw the blood on my face and the welt under my eye, and just stopped dead.

"You fucking gorillas," he said, his face darkening. "You roughed up *my* guy? Which motherless bastard touched my man?" His fists came up, his eyes bulging like a gargoyle's. "Who *was* it?"

No one ever did incendiary like Frank Sinatra.

Fatso stood up and stepped forward, posturing with his chest out and his hands on his hips.

"Hey, buddy, I don't care who you are in Hollywood, you watch yourself in here or you'll get some of your own."

Frank hit him running, a good right cross to the eye. The blow sent Fatso staggering backward into a corner table with a coffeepot on top. He pancaked down on top of it with a heavy groan, pot, mugs, and muddy water raining down on the checkerboard floor amid the clatter of breaking objects.

It was a Pier Nine brawl after that. Fatso went for his gun, but I kicked it out of his hand as he cleared leather. Then a wall of blue wool surged into the room and fell on us. It took the lieutenant, a sergeant, and two other uniforms to keep them separated, Frank screaming the entire time that he was "gonna kill that sonofabitch!"

It ended when the station captain stormed in, gun drawn, and grabbed Frank by the neck, pulling him out of the room. Thirty minutes, two calls from the DA, and one from retired L.A. County Sheriff Biscailuz later, Frank and I walked out of the station like two kids who just dodged detention. As we passed through the opaque glass doors, Frank cut loose with a yuk.

"Did you notice that goon I popped looked like Fatso Judson? Ha! Maggio finally gets even! That was beautiful."

"Tough Monkey," I quipped.

He looked at me grinning, that sparkle in his eyes. Then we both broke up.

We walked over to Frank's Dual Ghia and climbed in, still chuckling. Frank left a foot of rubber in the chief's spot when he pulled out.

"Fucking hayseeds," he said as we zoomed away. "I hate small-timers!"

As soon as we'd turned the corner, he went stone solemn. "Have you got anything, Joe? Where's Lilah?"

"I don't know, but she might be in trouble."

"What do you mean, *trouble*?"

"I don't know, just a feeling. I spoke to her girlfriend Betty and I got a funny response when I asked about Lilah. I'm pretty sure she lied to me."

"Jesus, what's going on?"

"I don't know yet, but she didn't spend the night at home. She might have stayed at Betty's, but I don't know why. And how did you know I was in the tank down here anyway?"

"When I didn't hear from you, I called the Alhambra PD, I couldn't wait any longer; it's killing me not knowing where she is. I told those idiots I'd sent you over there to check, but someone dropped the ball."

"Yeah, right here," I said, touching my swollen cheek.

"And these hicks are telling me that she isn't missing yet, that she could be sleeping one off. Can you believe that shit? What am I gonna do now?" he demanded, shaking both hands above the wheel.

"You're going to run by Lilah's and we'll ring her bell again. If she doesn't answer, you're going to Beverly Hills to cool your heels, Marciano. I'll take the airport car to Betty's apartment—she knows more than she's telling. Do you know her, by the way?"

"No. Just heard Lilah mention her name once or twice."

"All right. I'll find out what I can and call you as soon as I have something." I laid a hand on his shoulder. "One more thing, Frank . . ."

He glanced over at me. "Yeah?"

"Try not to deck any more patrol sergeants, okay?"

Frank murmured his consent and took a deep drag on his cigarette. I caught a glimpse of his blue eyes in the rearview mirror. There was a hint of anguish in them.

I wondered about my own.

14

Frank dropped me at the car and went inside, but he came out shaking his head two minutes later. We said good-bye, then I got in the Stutz and hotfooted it over to Hollywood. It was pushing one o'clock when I reached the Chinese laundry.

It was an open-air job like most of the others, only just a bit shadier. The pink exterior had turned a swarthy salmon from decades of accumulated smog, and the weathered marquee above had a few cracked and wayward characters that weren't toeing the line. An Oriental woman, somewhere between sixty and six hundred, stood at attention behind the counter staring down the building across the street as if she thought she could make it blink.

I waited until the single departing customer took his wrapped packages and left before I approached the counter.

"He'p you, sir?" she said through an accent as thick as a banyan tree.

"Yes," I said, holding up the ticket. "My girlfriend works with Betty over at Columbia. You know Betty Benker, right? She's an actress, probably comes here a lot. Always wants to look nice."

The old woman just stared at me, her black eyes giving away nothing.

"Well, I've got a bit of a predicament, you see. Betty needs this dress today for an audition, but she left it at my girlfriend's place by accident. I told her I'd run it over to her, but I forgot the address and Betty doesn't have a phone."

I feigned sheepishness, turned up my palms.

"Lilah—my girlfriend—is on a soundstage all afternoon and can't be reached. All I need is Betty's address—I know she's on Afton, here in Hollywood. Can you please tell me?"

It was a fairly convincing story, I thought, since I had her name and her street. To help sell it, I put on my most obsequious face and pulled out a two-dollar bill, then plaintively mouthed the word *please.*

The woman munched on her lips a few seconds, stealing glances back and forth. Then a hand shot out quick as a viper and snagged the deuce from me.

I watched her eyes snake downward as she consulted a worn black ledger. She stopped abruptly, looked up, and said, "6344 Afton," then nodded.

Before I could thank her, an angry voice cut loose behind her in Chinese. I looked toward the sound as a man in a Mandarin coat appeared in the roiling steam cloud at the laundry room entrance. He was young and lean, and he was glowering at me through coal-dark eyes. He ordered the woman to leave the counter, telling her not to say anything else to me.

"What goes here?" I muttered, utterly mystified by his broadside.

His eyes marked mine, lips wrinkled up. I stared back, searching his face for recognition, but getting none.

I had what I'd come for anyway, so I just shook my head and turned to leave. The man continued to berate the woman as I walked away. He couldn't have known that I understood a fair amount of Cantonese— but I'd seen enough of that world to let the past stay in the past.

15

I shot on over to Betty's place in two minutes and parked out front. As I yanked up the parking brake, I noticed a newer black Mercury in the rearview mirror. The car was double-parked and idling at the far corner of the block. I hadn't seen anyone following me, but I knew that car hadn't been there when I drove past twenty seconds earlier.

It wasn't overly suspicious, but it didn't feel quite right, either, so I leaned back against the driver's seat and dug out a smoke. I took my time lighting it to see if anyone got out of the Mercury. The car was just out of range. I could tell that someone was in it, but nothing more. No features, just a smudge.

I waited a reasonable amount of time for someone to get into or out of the Merc, but no one did so I stubbed out my cigarette in the ashtray and got out of the car. I faked a stretch and took one more long look at the idling car, but it remained dark and quiet. I shrugged and walked toward Betty's place.

It looked a lot like every other decorative-era apartment building in Hollywood—pastel paint over stucco and wood—but it was dressed out in a faux nautical motif, right down to the porthole window on the front door. Might have been a cute idea in 1930, but who in their right mind would sign on to a ship in this grimy corner of town these days?

Two young girls in tennis whites with rackets in their hands burst out the main hatch as I approached, tittering down the gangway as they darted past me. Probably actresses too green to know what Hollywood had planned for them. I doubled my pace, just catching the door as it swung back before it could lock.

"Permission to come aboard, sir," I said aloud, just to be a smart-ass.

Inside, brass ship's lanterns gave off just enough light to illuminate the area around each door in the gloomy corridor. I'd never been on a boat with carpeting before, but I appreciated the silence offered by the faded sea-foam pile as I inspected each brass-handled door. The architect was a stickler for authenticity, but he'd wasted his pearls on this dive.

Some serious Charlie Parker bop swirled out from one of the units as I walked the hallway checking the little engraved nameplates. A familiar sweet smoky scent swirled out along with it under the door bottom. It seemed to fit—the place just had that certain edge to it.

Betty's name was on number four. I stopped in front, listened awhile, then knocked firmly enough on the hardwood door to fleck off a piece of the peeling paint. There was no reply.

I tried twice more, then went to the knife routine again. This lock gave even easier than Helen's. I never knew how easy it would be to be a burglar in Los Angeles—none of the locks were worth shit.

The door swung open with a creak when I pushed it. I waited a beat, looking inside, then eased into the darkened apartment, pulling the door closed behind me.

"Hello? Betty?" I called as I moved in.

Sunlight filtered through the thin navy blue curtains, bringing some light to the murk. As my eyes adjusted, I noticed an upended high table and a broken planter lying on the floor, a bamboo stalk and a healthy amount of dirt fanning out across the carpet. Some picture frames lay a few feet away, one facedown, one faceup.

In the hallway I spied a single high-heeled pump. I walked toward it, then peeked into the bedroom. Empty. The bathroom was the next room over. Its door hung partially open, but I couldn't see inside. I stood there a moment listening to a faint echoing sound, making it for water dripping nearby.

As I walked toward the door, the plopping sound of water falling in a full bathtub became clearer. My nose also began picking up a cloying scent I couldn't quite place, but didn't like. Some kind of cheap cologne or incense. The whole setup didn't jibe.

Just as I reached to push the door open, the telephone let loose with a shrill *rrrrrring*. I stopped, let it repeat a good five times, and then violated the very first commandment of breaking and entering.

"Hello," I said.

Silence on the line.

I said it again, louder.

"Joe?" a voice asked in disbelief. "Is that you?"

"Jesus . . . Helen? Where are you?"

"I'm close," she whispered. "I think I'm in trouble. Come get me, baby, I'm—"

Suddenly, but far too late, I felt a presence behind me.

I turned, saw a shadow scything across the wall, and caught just a glimpse of a large man with granite blocks for a face. There was a *whoosh* and then the boom came down on the back of my head. I lurched sideways and down as blackness flooded in.

16

I felt the pain before I opened my eyes. Throbbing, jolting, call-for-your-mother pain. I lay on the floor for a minute, rubbing the knot at the base of my skull before rolling over to stare at the ceiling. You never really get used to blackjackings no matter how much practice you get.

The room was gloomy and appeared empty. I sat up slowly just in case it wasn't, focus coming in grudgingly as I scanned the room. The phone was on the floor, but someone had racked it. Nothing else looked different.

There wasn't a sound except for the destroyer firing salvos in my ears. No telling how long I'd been out. I sat still another minute, choked down a little nausea, then collected myself and stood up by degrees— it didn't take any longer than it did to build the Hoover Dam.

I trudged to the kitchen, opened the cold-water spigot, and stuck my head under the faucet. A hundred little icy daggers stabbed me. It was bracing but brought me back around. I leaned against the sink for a long time with my eyes closed, rubbing my temples and examining the walnut on the back of my head, small waves of pain radiating irregularly from its center.

I gathered that either I'd interrupted someone's exit or Betty had one hell of a hard-assed housekeeper. Grabbing a dishtowel, I dried myself off, then ran my fingers through my hair several times until I looked just like Cary Grant.

The thought that I should check the place over bored slowly through my lead-lined mind. I went about it slowly, checking behind me every few steps. I didn't know what I'd do if I found someone, since they were apt to be armed, but I usually thought of something.

I looked under the kitchen table and in the pantry. Empty. I peered around the corner into the living room. Clear. Then I checked the front closet. Same. After that, I ducked into the bedroom and gave it a once-over. Still nothing. The bathroom was the only room left, but now I was sure I was alone.

Turned out I wasn't.

I opened the bathroom door and leaned in. There was a woman in the bathtub. She was partially naked.

And completely dead.

Her body lay on the bottom of the full tub. Long, dark hair sprang from the depths, floating up to the surface of the still water. I couldn't make out her features, but the body was all business. I felt a chill as I approached, wondering if it was Helen.

I knew that she'd spoken to me earlier, but irrational fear blossomed in my mind as I moved toward the edge of the tub. I took a deep breath and swirled the cold water with my hand, the small eddy carrying the hair away in gentle ripples. As the water calmed, I made out the features of a very attractive face—but not Helen's. I closed my eyes, exhaling deeply.

I looked her over from above. She hadn't been there too long, but her skin was bluish and already beginning to puff up. Her round eyes were wide open, pale blue irises staring without focus at the ceiling. She looked for all the world like a Siren, lolling listlessly in the waves, waiting for some doomed sailor to happen by. I shuddered at the sight.

The woman had several scratches on her chest and some deep purplish bruises on her neck and throat. Someone had drowned her in the tub, sure enough, but for what reason I didn't know. I assumed it was Betty, but couldn't really be sure.

I scanned the rest of her body and the pink-tiled bath area. My eye caught a black object on the bottom of the bath between her outstretched arm and torso. I rolled up my sleeve and stuck my hand in to retrieve it. It squirted away, so I reached under her rib cage to fish for it, grazing her cold, firm flesh in the process. That sent another chill through me.

I noticed her arm then. Something didn't look right. Grimacing, I pulled it gently from the water to examine it. A half-dozen small red areas and twice as many tiny scabs covered the inside of her lower arm—track marks. The girl had been on China White. Somehow, that made it just that much sadder.

Holding her cold arm out a moment with one hand, I plunged my other back in, hunting anew underneath her for the dark object. Grasping it, I pulled my hand from the tub, then let her arm fall quietly into the clear water, where it sank below.

I examined the item. It was a cuff link, two half-size black dice, face-on but offset, each showing a four.

Eight the hard way.

There were no initials or markings of any kind on the dice, or on the gold post. Somewhere, I thought I might have seen one before, but I couldn't recall where. I wiped the cuff link off, then dropped it back in the tub. It landed on the bottom with a *ploonk*.

I checked the apartment over. It bore the signs of a struggle, but it hadn't been tossed. There were several photos of the deceased woman on a dresser, as well as a glossy of a guy who'd borrowed his chin from Mt. Rushmore. An inscription was scribbled across the bottom. *Forever* was misspelled, but he got *Carmine* all right. It was a fair bet that he was the brute who'd sapped me.

The facedown photo on the floor featured the late, great Johnny Stompanato and the dead woman in a clinch. It was now obvious that the Siren was Betty. I didn't like the mob connection at all. How Helen figured in, I hadn't a clue.

I rifled through Betty's address book and mail but didn't come up with anything—no notes or numbers stashed away anywhere. I picked up a few books and leafed through them, but without anything to go on, I was just drawing dead. From time to time I looked at the telephone, hoping I could make it ring again, but nothing happened.

Figuring that I'd just about used up my quotient of good luck for the day, I decided to punch out before anybody else saw me. I needed a shower—and a drink.

I wiped down anything I'd touched with my handkerchief and headed out the back way. Then I cut down the alley and looped the block, planning to come up behind the Mercury, but of course, it was gone.

I took a final look at the ocean liner parked at 6344 Afton—home to bobby-soxers, jazz hopheads, and dead starlets—then sped away at a good clip.

On Sunset, I pulled up to a drugstore, dropped into a phone booth, and pulled the door shut. I threw a Roosevelt in and dialed CRestview 4-2368 in Beverly Hills. Frank answered on the second ring.

"Hey, it's me."

"Whaddya got? You find her?"

"No. You sitting down?"

"Don't tell me . . ."

"It's her friend Betty. She's dead. Drowned in her bathtub."

Silence.

"Frank?"

"Yeah, Joe?" His voice was thin, far off.

"This is bad. Real bad. I've got to call the cops, too—it's murder now. And when I do, they'll put me in hack on Suspicion if they find out she and Hel—uh—Lilah were friends. You want me out, you better get your best lawyer on this."

"Mother of Christ. The press will devour this."

"That what you're worried about—or Lilah?"

He didn't answer.

I gave him the quick lowdown on what I'd found and described the cuff link to him. He said he'd make a few calls to Vegas and Tahoe to check it out. We hung up.

Then I decided to get my plane out of Burbank and back down to Long Beach. There was a chance Helen might have stopped by my hangar, and I was fresh out of leads in L.A. anyway.

I put another dime in and called my hangar. After ten rings, Roscoe picked up.

"Goldbrickin', partner?"

"Like hell. I was up under the DC-3, changing out an oil sump. It's always something on that Gooney Bird, you know."

"Anybody stop by today?"

"Like who?" he said, his natural skepticism coming through the line.

I shifted the receiver in my hand, leaned back in the booth. "Oh, I don't know, say a very beautiful woman, dark hair, green eyes."

"You mean the one from the picture on your desk?"

"That would be her."

"No chance. Stop dreaming, hotshot."

I exhaled, then paused a second before continuing. "Brother, I'm going to need a favor again."

"Let me guess, you need ol' Roscoe to pick up your routes for a couple of days, right?"

"You got it. I'm helping out you-know-who again—and myself as well this time. I'll pick you up double when this deal is over. Just keep taking them until you hear back from me."

"Couple of days, no more, Joe. Wanda Mae's gonna have my ass. And someday you're gonna tell me what I actually get out of this partnership."

"Thanks, Roscoe, you're all aces, brother."

"I was once," he laughed, then hung up.

I replaced the receiver and headed back to the car. It took me an hour in afternoon traffic to reach Burbank.

17

I pulled into the airport about four thirty. To my surprise, they didn't have me arrested at the charter office. The Electra had been topped off and serviced, but there was no bill, so I knew that Frank had called them and smoothed it out. He probably sent about five hundred bucks over just to be sure.

I grabbed the slacks and shirt I kept onboard and headed to the pilot's ready room to take a shower.

A haggard face stared at me in the mirror—it looked like someone had made a carrier landing on it. My nose was reddish, and a discolored welt was spreading beneath my eye. Fatigue had left deep creases in my cheeks, and gray stubble speckled my beard. I felt every bit of forty, maybe fifty. It occurred to me then that I hadn't eaten all day.

The long, hot shower helped. I even tried feeling my nose for the first time since Fatso had socked me. It wasn't broken but it hurt like hell. When the steam loosened up the clot in it, blood began trickling down my face, pooling below on the shower floor. I watched it mix with the water and whirl down into the drain, shaking my head at the number of times I'd seen that before.

I toweled off then reached for my razor, pulling out the small hip flask from my shower kit instead. It was a happy mistake and I took a long drink of the whiskey, a surge of life shooting through my veins when the rye sank in. I scraped my face with the blade, ran some Vitalis through my hair, and got dressed. The Ray-Bans did a decent job of covering up the welt, but I did get a couple of *who the hell do you think you are?* looks for wearing them inside.

I didn't file a flight plan, no point making it easy for the police. Those small-timers in Alhambra weren't very likely to make a connection, but they would go all out for me if they did. They didn't have much to tie me to Betty, but I'd be back in the tank for a couple of days thanks to that laundry slip they'd found on me. That wasn't going to work if Helen was still missing. I needed a day or two.

Outside, I struck a Lucky and grabbed the pay phone on the wall. I got the number for the Hollywood Police Department from the operator and rang it.

A put-upon voice answered, "Hollywood PD, Sergeant Cooley."

"6344 Afton, number four," I said. "You got a dead mermaid in a bathtub."

I hung up the phone—they weren't going to get a trace on that one. Then I walked back through the lounge and headed out to my plane.

~

I made Long Beach in twenty minutes, rolled off 25 Left, and coasted up to my hangar. My best hope was that I'd find Helen inside, or at least a phone message or a note from her on my desk. I got exactly nothing.

I sat down on the swivel chair, closed my eyes, and put my hands over my face, decompressing, trying to make a few connections.

I didn't know Helen anymore, didn't know her habits or hangouts, and I had no idea how well she had known Betty, but the facts strongly suggested that Miss Benker had some rather unsavory playmates. Helen had always liked excitement, but she wasn't the kind of girl to mix it up with the bad boys. No, she didn't fit in this puzzle at all.

The phone rattled and I snatched it mid ring. It was Frank.

"Buonomo, that you?"

"Yeah, just got here. Whaddyagot? Anything?"

"The cuff link. Jack Entratter just called me from Vegas, says cuff links like those are given out to high rollers and VIPs at the Stardust. Maybe a dozen or so a year. Pretty exclusive, only been doing it a year or two."

"Would these VIPs include guys like Johnny Stomp and his cronies?"

"Could be, Joe; you know as well as I do who runs the Stardust, and it's not Estes Kefauver. But Johnny took the knife from Lana's kid two years ago, remember? If he's wearing them, it's in an upholstered box over at Forest Lawn."

"I recall. But I saw him in a picture with Betty at her place, and they were making time together and then some. I'm getting a bad feeling here, Frank."

We compared notes. Helen hadn't contacted Frank or any of his friends. She hadn't contacted me, either, but I didn't go into that. Helen had to know that Frank and I would be together and was bound to call one of us soon.

I asked him point-blank if he had any idea what Helen might be into that could cause her friend to be murdered.

He paused a little too long for my liking, then said, "I've known this girl for less than a month. How much is a guy supposed to know about someone's past after that much time? What are you driving at here?"

It was the first time I ever felt that Frank hadn't leveled with me. He seemed to be holding something back but I wasn't sure. It had been one hell of a long day. I let it pass.

"I don't know, Frank, it's just an awful big mess for someone as sharp as she seems to be. It just doesn't add up."

"Look, she's a good kid. She drinks a little, but who doesn't? Let's just find her and then worry about the details later."

"That's what I'm trying to do, buddy."

"What happens next?"

"You're gonna sit tight here in L.A. That puts you close in case she turns up. I'll be back tomorrow night."

"From where?"

"Las Vegas."

"*Vegas?*"

"Yes, Vegas. As in the Stardust Casino. Whoever killed Betty is somebody important there."

"Yeah, but Lilah's down *here*," he said, frustration creeping into his voice.

"Yes, Frank, somewhere in the midst of three million people—and hiding. If I can find out who that cuff link belongs to, I'll be a lot closer to finding out what's going on with Lilah. There's no way her disappearance isn't tied to Betty's snuff."

"Ohh, easy. Do you have to talk that way?"

He was right, that was out of line. "Sorry, pal. Now, listen, in the meantime, there's a very good chance she'll call you and we'll get this whole thing cleared up."

"I sure hope so," he said without any conviction. The famous voice sounded weary and flat. He was all torn up.

18

I had a load of showgirl costumes to take to a guy in Henderson and fifty cases of Hawaiian beer for some bullshit Bali H'ai joint on the strip, so I took the DC-3, which is bigger than the Electra—but slower. The trip took almost two hours. Every minute crawled.

Frank set me up pretty good in Vegas, though. He had a new suite at the Sands just for him, which he made sure was ready when I arrived. A limo met me at the airport and took me to the hotel.

Jack Entratter, a Sands exec and close friend of Frank's, was waiting at the door when I arrived. He promised me any assistance I needed. I told him I was going it alone but asked if he'd take all calls for Frank's room personally.

I also told him I'd need a car. He offered a Lincoln Continental. I told him I'd need a little less car. He said he'd take care of it.

Frank's suite was about what I'd expected—not quite as large as the Vatican but plenty big and well appointed. Walnut furniture, plush orange carpeting, velvet drapes, a full bar, and a television in each of the five rooms. It would do for a weekend.

The valet knocked while I was fiddling with the remote control. He brought in two Saville Row suits and Frank's personal Vegas tailor.

Room service arrived ten minutes later with rations for the Russian army: a New York strip steak, baked ziti and eggplant Parm', accompanied by steamed asparagus, a baked potato, and a Caesar salad. A bottle of Chianti, a six-pack of Ballantines, and a magnum of Dom Pérignon were presented for my consideration. I told the tailor to give me an exta half inch in the waist after surveying the feast.

I put a sizable dent in most of it. While I was eating, the valet returned with both suits and two pairs of shoes. They were all perfect fits. Thirty minutes later, a masseuse arrived and worked over my weary bones until I was nearly asleep on the table.

I was beginning to realize how good it was to be Frank Sinatra.

Jack called and gave me the name of the manager to ask for at the Stardust in the morning, Wally Raspiller.

I looked over at the sunburst clock on the wall. It was eleven thirty. Some days you do more living than others.

A sleek silver dish atop a big walnut credenza caught my eye. The dish contained a couple dozen Camel cigarettes, stacked up neatly in a little pyramid. It was a nice presentation—pure Frank. I snatched one off the top and lit it with the accompanying gold lighter. I burned the smoke and looked out the window at the strip beyond, letting fatigue have its way with me.

When the cigarette burned out, I headed to the bedroom and undressed. I turned out the light, lay down in Frank Sinatra's bed under Frank Sinatra's silk sheets, and thought about Frank Sinatra's new girl until I faded away.

19

I hit the ground running at seven. I showered, then threw on the tan suit and maroon tie, choosing the brown lace-ups over the black wing-tips—an easy decision. They don't tell you in *Esquire* how to stash a .45 under your arm so it doesn't show but I made it happen. It was a lot of gun, but I'd learned during the war that too much firepower was something you never regret. Based on what had already happened it seemed like a smart play.

I went down to the lobby at seven thirty, walked up to the jazzy modern counter and floated my name. The desk clerk nodded and handed me a set of car keys with the Cadillac logo on the fob. He told me the car was parked right out front in Mr. Sinatra's space. He asked if I needed directions to the Stardust. I shook my head, thanked him, and headed out.

The morning air was cool. So was the car: a '59 Fleetwood, champagne with a brown top and beige leather interior. Tail fins like a B-25. So much for subtlety.

The engine growled when I turned her over then settled into a subdued chuff when I put her in gear. But the big Caddy simply glided down the Vegas streets, the V-8 purring like an iron tiger the whole time. It was a helluva nice car. It was a Frank car. I made the Stardust in four minutes and parked out back.

I walked around front, beneath the hideous astro-marquee, and pushed through the revolving door. Inside, I adjusted to the unnatural light and smoky air, then made straight for the cashiers' cages, catching the eye of a plump, middle-aged woman under an enormous blond beehive. Her name tag said Edna.

I asked Edna where I might find Mr. Wally Raspiller. She said he was somewhere on the floor but she'd call for him. I thanked her and leaned against the wall, watching the winking lights reflecting in the empty eyes of the all-night gamblers. They looked like extras from *Invasion of the Body Snatchers*.

A minute or so later, a gelatinous form approached and officiously announced himself as Mr. Raspiller, the morning manager, how might he help me? He gave me a gassy smile that was just the cat's ass with his horn-rimmed glasses and awful pencil mustache. Then he held out a pale hand that could have passed for mashed potatoes. I took the measure of the man: 38 Short, all the way.

I gave him my name and nodded toward the front of the casino, suggesting we talk alone. Then I made for the doors, Raspiller following dutifully behind me.

Once outside, I made a quick scan then bored right into his black-framed eyes.

"I understand that the Stardust gives custom cuff links to certain favorite customers."

"Yes, Mr. Buonomo, that's correct. Black onyx dice on a twenty-four-carat stud. A pair of fours. Eight—"

"The hard way. I'm familiar. Do you have a list of who you've given them to? I understand you've only been doing it for a couple of years."

He broke into a disingenuous smile. "Well, that's confidential information. The casino likes to respect the privacy of its clientele, you know."

Then he folded his arms and gave me his very best ballsy look—had to have practiced that one in the mirror a few times. I went for the jugular.

Narrowing my eyes down, I scowled, "Mr. Raspiller, you are aware of who told me to contact you here, yes?"

"Uhh, ahh, I believe that would be Jack Entratter."

He was waffling already.

I raised my voice. "That's right. And you are, of course, aware of whom Jack Entratter is close personal friends with, and on whose behalf he's asking?"

"I, uhh, I imagine that would be Mr. Sinatra, wouldn't it?"

Here I went soft and low. "Yes, it would." I let the words hang there, like straight razors, watching his face as it twitched. I leaned in, put my arm on his shoulder, and squeezed just a little. "Wally . . . work with me here, brother."

I stared into his horn-rims for a good ten seconds. He swallowed a few times, blinked some more, then broke.

He told me there was a jeweler in town, Murray Fine, who made the pieces for the casino upon request. He said if there was a list, he'd have it. He recited the address for Fine's Jewelry and told me they opened at ten. I checked my watch—it was 7:55.

I thanked Mr. Wally Raspiller for his assistance. He smiled disingenuously again, straightened his tie, and then mopped his forehead before heading back into the casino.

I had some time to kill so I walked down to a coffee shop and downed some eggs and hash. I leafed through the newspaper awhile and managed to drink a second cup of coffee without doing any permanent damage to my digestive system. I asked the waitress if she'd ever seen anyone in there with black dice cuff links but got nothing.

It was a long shot.

～

I swung by the Sands to check on messages but there weren't any. It was going on nine thirty so I headed over toward the jewelers, figuring I'd catch him when he opened up. It was a fifteen-minute ride in morning traffic over to Freemont St. I arrived at a quarter to ten and parked across the street, half a block down.

Fine's Jewelry stood in the middle of a typical commercial block in outlying Vegas. All the buildings were brown stucco with glass doors. A rather nice neon sign set the jewelry store apart from the beauty parlor and pharmacy that bookended it. As I crossed the street, a wiry man in a busy suit exited Fine's and strutted off. When I reached the store, I saw the hours of business painted on the glass door. It said they opened at nine thirty. I gave that and the wiry man some thought as I pushed the door open.

A thin, middle-aged man with a jeweler's eyepiece on his forehead looked up from a desk as I entered. I took a wild stab and asked if he was Murray Fine. He said he was and that he had a fine selection of opals on sale.

"I didn't come here for jewelry, Mr. Fine." I replied.

"Well, this *is* a jewelry store, sir."

I minted up my very best million-dollar smile. "Can we talk?"

He gave me the once-over, then motioned me to sit down with a small gesture of his hand. I did so. We made a little small talk, then I flashed him my P.I. license and put it away. I didn't really care at this point if anyone knew I was asking questions. So far I was in the dark and Helen was still missing, and I needed to make some connections.

"Mr. Fine, I understand you make those fancy cuff links that the Stardust gives to big shots and high rollers, the black dice on the gold studs."

He hesitated a second then said, "Yes, I do. Would you like to see one?"

"Please."

He reached down and opened one of the desk drawers, fished around a bit, then pulled out a small plastic case. He opened it up, took out a cuff link, and handed it to me. It was identical to the one I'd seen at Betty's. I gave it back to him and he put it away.

"Nice work," I said. "I don't suppose they give those out to just anyone."

"No, I don't suppose so," he said, sounding rather tired of the whole affair.

I leaned toward him, my hands gripping the edge of his desk. "Would you happen to know who gets them? Any of them personalized?"

"No, sir. I make them special order for the Stardust. What they do with them is their business." He flourished the statement with a hand swoop, further distancing himself from any possible state of interest.

"But I was told you might have a record of those clients."

"Oh no," he said, "I don't. Never have. I'm just a jeweler, I have no affiliation with the casino whatsoever. It's a business arrangement. Now, really, sir, I have to get back to my opals here."

I stared at him intently, watching his eyes.

"So you have no idea who they give the cuff links out to?"

He didn't bat an eyelash, said, "No, sir, I don't. Why would I?"

I whistled out loud, sat back in the chair, and mouthed the words *You don't say?* It was just beginning to hit me that I was the guy P. T. Barnum had been talking about.

I sat there a second, waiting for the light to come on. While I did, a faint, almost imperceptible odor caught my attention. A cloying scent, like cheap musk cologne. The store was empty except for Fine and me. I swiveled my head a few times, spotted an open transom over the back door, and felt a bit of a breeze coming through the store from that direction.

Then the connection clicked in my mind like a generator kicking on-line. It was the same smell I'd picked up in Betty's place the day before. The flashy guy who left just before I arrived was probably shadowing me, and he, or a partner, was hiding out back, maybe listening in.

I stood up. "Mr. Fine, has anyone else been in here this morning?"

"Ahh, no, you're the first person." His eyes darted as he spoke, his head making an involuntary turn toward the back of the store.

"What's out the back door?" I whispered.

"Just an alley. Runs behind all the stores—no one's ever back there. Hey, where are you—"

I was already on my way. I slipped the Colt out of the holster and held it under my suit coat as I turned the handle on the heavy door and pulled it inward. I made a quick scan, then stepped out into the alley. I looked to my right past empty boxes and several garbage cans but didn't see a soul.

As I turned, the door slammed shut behind me. Half a beat later the deadbolt locked, then the sound of a weapon being charged clicked in with chilling finality. I winced as that *oh shit!* feeling arose, then dove toward a steel dumpster several feet away.

The report of a large-caliber pistol ripped through the alley as I hit the asphalt behind the trash bin, the gunshots echoing like a howitzer in the narrow lane. Pieces of stuccoed plaster erupted from the wall and fell on me, followed by a powdery brown dust that filtered down on my face like it was Ash Wednesday in a shooting gallery.

I flicked the safety off my .45, pointed it in the air, and squeezed off several shots. The booms rang loudly in my ears, punctuated by the *pings* of the shell casings as they hit the asphalt and spun away. There wasn't any return fire.

Then I got up into a crouch and pressed myself against the dumpster, breathing fast and peering through the narrow gap between the metal and the wall. I didn't see anybody, but I could hear the sound of footsteps clattering out of the alleyway and fading.

After several beats, I eased out into the open, gun first. The smell of gunpowder was heavy in the air as I stood and pointed my weapon down the alley. As much as I wanted to wring Mr. Murray Fine's neck, I decided it might be in my best interest to make myself very scarce at that moment. I'd already found out what I wanted to know anyhow.

I glanced behind me at the wall. The bullets had chewed nasty holes in the stucco where my head had been a few seconds before. It was safe to say it would have been a closed-casket affair if they'd hit me. I brushed some plaster off my jacket and moved out.

At the end of the alley I stopped, poking the .45 out before edging onto the sidewalk. Walking quickly, I eyed each entranceway on both sides of the street, holstering the pistol before turning down Freemont and making for the Fleetwood. I crossed the street before reaching Fine's but I couldn't see him in the store when I glanced back. Chances were that he was halfway to Carson City by then anyway.

I fired up the Caddy and pulled right out. Several people were standing around in front of their stores, but no one seemed to make me for anyone other than another bystander. The wail of a police siren howled in the distance as I made the corner at Las Vegas and zipped away. Exhaling deeply, I pulled a cigarette from the pack, my fingers shaking with adrenaline as I reached for the lighter.

20

I made for the Stardust. That worm Raspiller was on the hook now.

The tumblers clicked in as I drove—it was a setup all the way. Raspiller had tipped off whoever tried to shellac me. He'd had half a day to do it since Entratter had contacted him. Somebody knew that I'd found the cuff link in the bathtub and made the pieces fit. And that person had already seen me at Betty's, but at that point he didn't know who I was, so I got a knock on the block instead of a shell. That was his mistake, but he was working hard to correct it.

~

They told me at the Stardust that Mr. Raspiller had gone home early due to illness. Two bucks and a bullshit story about us being old army buddies got me his address from a kid I saw in the break room.

Army buddies, right. I had Wally for 4F all the way.

His place was a fleabag apartment complex off Las Vegas Boulevard, a two-story catwalk job with a postage stamp–size pool in the front. Other than a hooker meandering the weed-pocked sidewalk out front, the place was deserted. She gave me a hopeful look when I pulled in but I didn't have the time.

Raspiller's place was number nine, on the second floor. I took the stairs two at a time and stopped just short of the picture window in front. The curtains were drawn, but there was a small gap between them. I listened for voices, then peeked in. He was inside, cooking eggs and bacon on a small stove. He was alone.

Part of me felt sorry for him. A much bigger part of me felt like kicking the shit out of him. The big part won.

I leaned back, then put my foot to the door with everything I had. It flew open, banged off the wall, and ricocheted back toward me. I stopped it with a forearm shiver as I burst through. Raspiller turned at the sound and dropped his spatula. I'm pretty sure he wet his pants on the spot when I pointed the gun at his head.

"M-M-M-Mister Buonomo," he sputtered, "what, what are you doing here?"

"I'm going to kill you, Raspiller," I announced as I crossed the room.

Before he could reply, I backhanded him across the cheek with the Colt. He went down like the Hindenburg, bouncing off the stove and crumpling down to the linoleum in sections. The skillet clanged down a half second later, followed by the eggs and then the bacon, a spray of grease splotching Wally's rayon slacks. That was going to call for some dry cleaning.

I stood over him and looked down, seething.

"Wally, I don't like being lied to. I really don't like it when the lie gets me into a setup. And I really, really just fucking hate it when the setup has some goon trying to finish a job Japan's best fighter pilots couldn't."

I reached down and grabbed his shirt, yanking him back up to his feet. He slipped on the bacon grease and fell against the stove, scorching his hand on the burner. His yelp sounded like a dying hyena.

I tossed him against the refrigerator to prop him up. Things fell inside it and broke as it rocked back and forth like a pinball machine. Wally went on *tilt* himself, his eyes blinking rapidly several times then fixing wide open.

I leaned in close, bracing him with my forearm and pressing the gun into his bleeding cheek. "Wally, you are in a world of hurt right now, but you still have this one last chance if you do as I ask, okay?"

He nodded his head up and down several times, his lips convulsing as he tried to form words. He just hung there quivering and staring, sagging like *The Blob* in my hands. I was already feeling a little guilty for pistol-whipping him.

"Wally, who tried to take me out over at Fine's?"

"T-take you out?"

I cranked up the thermostat. "Wally," I shouted, "somebody tried to shoot me over there. Used an elephant gun, may as well have been a bazooka. Who was it?"

He made wild eyes back and forth to nobody then began hyperventilating a little, but he didn't say anything.

I casually slid the safety to *off* with my thumb, dropped my voice an octave. "Someone very close to me is missing and that man has something to do with it. Now, you are going to tell me exactly what I want to know right now or, so help me God, I am going to unload this entire magazine into your head."

His mouth dropped open. Something dark oozed out from the refrigerator onto the floor.

"But, Wally," I said softly, "I do have some good news."

"Y-y-yes?" he stuttered. "What?"

"The last six shots won't hurt."

As bluffs go, it was a pretty good one. I wasn't going to kill that wretch but he didn't know that. Wally sucked wind several times, slid his hands in his pockets, and squirmed a little bit more. Then he gave them up.

"Carmine Ratello and Johnny Spazzo," he said in a tiny voice.

I'd heard the first name before. The second guy didn't jibe.

"Carmine the Rat?"

"Yes, yes, that's him."

I relaxed the gun, resting the barrel on his temple. "And who are they to you? Does either of them qualify as the kind of VIP at the Stardust who'd get a set of those cuff links?"

Wally's face was warped, his eyes fixated on the pistol alongside his head.

"Oh, sorry." I took a step back, then lowered the weapon to the ready position. That seemed to improve his diction.

"Yeah, Carmine got a set last year. He moves with a lot of the right people around here. He's wearing those things every time he comes in. Johnny's his pal. They're thick as thieves."

"They *are* thieves. What's your angle, Raspiller? Why did you tip them off about me and send me over to Fine's to get scalped?"

"I guess I was just trying to make a little noise for myself, get noticed by them. Guys like that can put you in with the girls, or get you a front-row seat at the big shows."

"Hey, chumbolone, don't you *work* at a casino?" I gave him a playful slap, but he flinched like I was swinging a sledgehammer. I couldn't suppress my smirk.

"Yes, but they're somebodies; I'm just Wally Raspiller. When I heard that some buddy of Sinatra's was flying in to ask about those cuff links, I figured it was something they might wanna know. They just told me to send you over to the jewelers . . . but I didn't think they were going to kill you. Why would they? What do you have on them?"

"Wally," I chided, patting his shoulder, "best not to ask those kinds of questions."

He didn't flinch that time. I safetied the weapon and holstered it. Wally Raspiller exhaled deeply, his shoulders slumping down in relief. His hands shook as he reached for a cigarette from his shirt pocket. Pall Malls—I could've guessed.

I held up a light. He whiffed three times before he got the nail over the flame.

"These guys come to the Stardust every night?" I asked as he sucked in a third of the cigarette.

"No," he whispered in an inhalation falsetto, "the Flamingo, too. Sometimes the Tropicana and the Dunes." He blew out several ragged smoke clouds after he spoke, regaining a touch of composure with each herky-jerky puff.

I placed my arm around him, went friendly. "Listen . . . they don't know I was here—and they don't have to. Don't contact them again, they're wrong numbers, savvy? They won't give you the chance I just did."

"What, what am I supposed to do now?" he asked, his voice sharpening. "Carmine will kill me on the spot if he finds out I gave him up."

"Take a week or two off. Go visit your aunt in Elko or blow off some steam at a cathouse. You look like you could use it, brother."

He just shrugged, raising his palms helplessly.

I soft-punched his chest. "Don't lose any sleep over Ratello . . . I really don't think you'll be seeing him again."

He half nodded in nervousness, but his eyes betrayed him.

"And Wally . . . ?"

"Yes, Mr. Buonomo?"

"Sorry I hit you."

I handed him a dishtowel and some ice for his cheek, gave him ten bucks for the busted door, and trudged out, feeling like a total shitheel with every step.

21

I drove back to the Sands and parked nearby at the Desert Inn. Then I walked across the street and took the side entrance up to the suite. After listening outside the door a minute, I slipped the key in.

Once inside, I loosened my tie, took my shoes off, and sat on the bed. The telephone message light was blinking so I called the desk.

There were five messages from Frank. The first asked me to call him when I got in. The second said don't bother, he didn't have any news. The third said Betty made page three of the L.A. *Examiner*, but both our names were out of it. The fourth said Alhambra had called the Hollywood police about Betty and that HPD was looking for me. The fifth said he'd spoken to his lawyer—they thought I'd make bail, no problem.

That did it for the messages. I'm pretty sure the sixth would have said the empire of Japan was suing me for destruction of government property.

It was nearing noon. I started to go downstairs to grab some lunch, then thought better of it and ordered up some room service. It was just as well that I stayed out of sight now. I dialed again for the valet, told him where the car was, asked him to return it to the stable and get me something a little less conspicuous, maybe a solid-gold Rolls-Royce.

~

The waiting was the worst part. It always is. I had the whole afternoon to kill before hitting the casinos in the evening to find Ratello and Spazzo. It was frustrating sitting around doing nothing, but it was my only play.

At one o'clock Frank called. I detailed my morning's adventure and gave him the names. He said he'd heard of Carmine but never met him. I told him I could use a little help covering the casinos but recommended we not send in the cavalry, just a man at each place to keep an eye out and place a phone call. Frank told me not to kill them before he got his hands on them.

I reminded him that we still didn't know where Helen was and Ratello probably didn't either. But it also occurred to me that he could have killed her already if he'd found her, something that would account for her continued silence. That sent a cold chill through me from the back of my head on down to my heels. I didn't offer this thought to Frank.

Twenty minutes after we spoke, Jack Entratter came up to the room. His face was balled up with worry, as if he'd just found out that Eliot Ness was the new head of the Nevada Gaming Commission. He said Frank had asked him to get any info he had on Carmine and Johnny up to me ASAP but hadn't said why. He shook his head disapprovingly over the request.

"What's eating you, Jack?" I asked.

"I don't like it. Carmine Ratello is a bad hombre. He's a small fish, but he's on a fast burn to move up. Some people who crossed him out here have gone missing."

"That makes him a standard-issue Vegas thug, doesn't it?"

"A little more. He's not that bright—and Spazzo's a bona fide idiot—but Ratello is wild, and he's mean, even by mob standards. He put one of our showgirls in the hospital last year, busted her up pretty bad."

That was ugly news, but it didn't surprise me.

"Sorry to hear that."

"Why is Frank asking around about these schmucks? They couldn't wipe his ass."

"I can't discuss it—it's just better all around if I don't. But trust me,

Frank doesn't want anything to do with those jamokes—they're crashing his party."

Jack crossed his arms and shook his head, anxiety lines creasing his face.

"Can you tell me what they look like?" I asked.

"Ratello's built like Chuck Bednarik and twice as ugly. Big guinea nose, heavy brows, mean dark eyes. Jaw like an alligator. Maybe thirty-five. About five nine, two twenty—a real steamroller."

It sounded a lot like the sandman who put me under at Betty's place.

"And Spazzo?"

"They call him Johnny Spazz. Good-looking fucker—tall, dark, wiry. Thirty-three, thirty-five. Slicks his hair back, wears suits with big lapels. Looks like a goddamn pachuco—no one ever told him the forties are over. Total clown."

The guy I saw ducking out of Fine's in the morning. It was my turn to shake my head.

"I understand they're bookends, is that right?"

He nodded. "Yeah, find one of these guys, you'll find the other. Like Heckle and Jeckle with heaters."

"They ever come here?"

"No, not anymore. Ratello pissed Frank off at the craps table a year or so ago and we threw them out. Frank was really bent over it. They are officially barred from the Sands from here until the resurrection, my friend."

I made a sour face.

"Frank just told me he doesn't know those two guys. What gives?"

"Joe, Frank was hitting the gasoline pretty hard that night. He wouldn't remember if it was Jackie Gleason. Besides, the list of guys who've pissed off Frank Sinatra would run out the door and wrap around the casino two or three times, dontcha think?"

I managed a smile at that. He smiled too, then walked to the door and opened it. He leaned against the frame and looked back.

"Be careful, Joe Bones, we don't want to lose you."

"Promise. Say . . . Jack?" I said, turning toward him.

"Yeah?"

"No one told me, either."

"Told you what?"

"That the forties are over." I winked once and flashed a grin.

He shook his head and went out, pulling the door shut behind him.

22

My plan was somewhere between mediocre and piss-poor. At five o'clock, Frank blew it all to hell. He called me in the room. He'd been drinking.

"Joseph," he began, "I can't take this not knowing. I think you should get out and start checking those casinos right now."

"That's not a good idea. Guys like that don't show before sundown. Asking around now will just cause someone to tip them off. They'll blow for sure, then we've got *niente*."

"Yeah, but you might get the jump on them when they come in."

I made a fist with my free hand. "I don't want to get the jump on anybody. I want to watch them quietly and pick off whichever one I can, preferably Spazzo, when I get a chance. We're trying to do this thing low profile, remember?"

"Well, my girl is still missing, remember?"

I gripped the phone a little tighter as my blood pressure came off simmer.

"Yes, I do. But these guys are a direct link. Let's not screw the pooch here by being too anxious."

"Anxious? Lilah's missing, her girlfriend got deep-sixed, and these guys tried to clip you. Am I anxious? You're damn right I am, Joe! I want her back."

"Let me handle this thing. You sing, I fix shit—it's been working. Let's keep it that way."

"Well, I already sent a few boys out."

"*What?*" Now I was positively choking the orange handset as my pulse hit full boil.

"A couple of Johnny's boys are at all their usual hangouts. You can check with them when you get to each place."

"Roselli's boys? Mobsters? Jesus H. Christ. Those idiots will blow the lid off this thing. They don't fix things; they break things and kill people. I said send a man or two out, not an army of goons."

"Hey, listen, she's my girl. What are you—?"

"Goddamn it, Frank, this isn't going to help. I'm out the door. I'll make the rounds, but have Roselli call his dogs off. We do not want to blow this chance, okay? Good-bye."

I banged the phone down in its cradle.

"*Figlio della puttana!*" I shouted out. "Why did he do that?"

I balled up both my fists and whacked the credenza a good one, the little pile of Camels spilling over both sides of the dish and rolling across the countertop.

I stewed for a whole ten seconds. Then I shifted gears—there just wasn't time for hand-wringing or histrionics. I threw on the midnight-blue suit and the dark wingtips, strapped on the holster, and blew out of the room.

This time they gave me the Lincoln. Dark blue, black top. Straight eight, easy on the chrome. An evening car, as Frank might say, something to match the suit. I swear to God he probably called it that way. Him and his fucking rules.

I mashed the pedal leaving the parking lot, whipping the car onto Las Vegas Boulevard so hard that it skidded sideways a good two feet, my arm waving in the air like a lunatic as I tore off into the evening.

23

The Flamingo was my first stop. God only knows why I drove—it was right next door. But I was so bent about Frank calling in the goon squad I wasn't thinking straight. It felt good to burn a little rubber anyway.

Keeping to the corners, I worked my way around the rooms. I didn't really expect to see either guy, but hoped I might turn up something about them by chatting up a few dealers and bartenders. Five bucks well played can buy a surprising amount of information in Las Vegas and is a damn better bet than trying to fill an inside straight.

I pulled up a seat at the bar in the Tropical room and struck a Lucky. The bartender came over, said, "What'll it be, son?"

His craggy, weathered face told a tale of long years in the desert sun, lots of busted plans, and too many ugly women. It was all there for the reading. But he looked like he might know a thing or two about Las Vegas, like he might have worked this bar for a few years, like he might have served Lewis and Clark somewhere along the way. I ordered a whiskey sour.

When he returned, he pushed the drink toward me and I threw a bill on the bar. I was halfway through the first word of my first question when a side of beef in a pale-blue sharkskin suit enveloped the chair next to me.

I gave the mauler the fish-eye, but I already knew who he was. I'd seen him before behind the scenes at some private affairs in town. He was muscle, worked for Roselli. Name of Sal or Nunzio or something.

I tilted my head, took in his dimensions. He was a good three hundred all the way—neck like a capstan, hands like hawsers. The mitts were tanned, gnarled, and folded together on top of the bar, one of them crowned by a pinky ring that checked in at maybe a pound and a half. Subtle.

He gave me a knowing look, rasped, "Joe Bones," in a voice like gravel in a cement mixer.

I looked up, waited until Methuselah walked away toward the cash register, then acknowledged him.

"Yeah. Got anything?"

"They ain't been in all day. Usually come in around ten. Like to show off at the craps table."

No shit, they haven't been in. It's six p.m. I grimaced internally, said, "Thanks. Drink?"

"Blatz."

I signaled the tender, called out the order.

"You guys pick anything up, I'll be at the Frontier next. Or call the Sands, leave a message with Jack E. I'll get it."

I wasn't going to ask the barman any questions now, not with Tony Galento next to me. It was just too obvious. I tossed back the whiskey, threw down another buck, said, "See ya."

He nodded. I got up and walked out of the bar, cursing Frank Sinatra out loud.

~

The Tropicana was more of the same. I played some craps, made some small talk, ventured a few questions. Got nothing. Lost twenty bucks, too. Next to the slot machines I saw a couple of Outfit boys having drinks together. When I walked by, I nodded at one of them. He shrugged, mouthed the word *nothing*, and went back to his story.

Around seven, I headed over to the Dunes. Things were still fairly slow. I talked to a couple of blackjack dealers, got my twenty dollars back, made ten more. No one from Roselli's crew showed his face. I hoped that meant those hounds had finally been kenneled.

On my way out, I bumped into a guy coming through the door. He was Oriental, but other than that, looked like just another Vegas tourist, right down to his Stacy Adams shoes. I said I was sorry and started to move on. The guy gave me the once-over, however, when I apologized. I took another step then looked back.

He was still standing there, looking at me. I didn't know him from Stacy or Adam, so I left. He was going to have to start a fight with somebody other than me tonight. Must have been related to the guy at the Chinese laundry—what was it with these Asian guys all having a hard-on for me lately?

Next I tried the Stardust. I learned, to my relief, that Mr. Raspiller would not be in that evening. In fact, he was off all week. I didn't get anything else on Carmine or Johnny other than a few employees saying they knew them. I waited around, caught a show. I waited around some more, then gave up.

I got in the car and drove a little. I knew that the whole night was a prick-pull, but I decided to hit the Flamingo once more. Along the way I stopped at a pay phone and called the Sands because I was still too pissed to speak with Frank. Jack said he had reported "No news" thirty minutes earlier. I slammed the phone down in frustration, then punched the brick wall it hung on. That hurt. I decided I wouldn't do it again.

~

Back at the Flamingo, I stopped in the dining room for a cup of coffee. I dropped down onto a stool, lit a smoke, and reached over for the newspaper on the countertop. It was the evening edition. I grabbed the front section and snapped it flat, then said, "Fuck me," under my breath.

In block type above the fold the headline cried out: "Local Jeweler Shot to Death!" A picture of Murray Fine accompanied it. I ran my fingers through my hair, let a deep breath out, and read the story.

Mr. Fine had been found dead in the back of his store with two bullet wounds in his back. The front door was unlocked and no jewelry or money was missing so robbery was not a motive. The police had no suspects, but a tall, dark man in a beige suit who left the area in a late-model Cadillac shortly after shots were fired was listed as a possible suspect. His identity was as of yet unknown.

The shooter's rounds must have penetrated the wall behind me and caught Fine as he turned away from the door. Tough break; he probably didn't have anything to do with Ratello and Spazzo, even if he was a bit of a weasel.

I folded the paper and put it on the counter with the story facing down, shaking my head in disbelief. Odds were ninety-nine to one in favor of Ratello and Spazzo being long out of town. Funny thing about wiseguys, they're usually pretty caught up on the local news from killing time watching TV in bars. They would've known. I should've, too.

I decided I should get myself the hell out of town as well. Vegas was a dead end now anyway—for me and Murray Fine. I stubbed out my cigarette, eased off the stool, and headed for the front doors. I made a final, futile glance for Carmine and Johnny, then walked out of the casino into the neon night.

~

Dejection gnawed at me as I headed for the Sands. I'd connected Ratello and Spazzo to the case but I didn't know what their in was or where they'd gone, and I still had no idea where Helen was. Oh, yeah, I was wanted for another murder now, too.

I parked in front of the hotel, tossed the keys to the valet, then headed upstairs to gather my things. From the ruins of the pyramid I scooped up several Camels and put them in my pocket. They still smelled fresh—it probably would've made the evening newspaper, too, if they weren't.

Twenty minutes later I spun the number one engine on the DC-3. Four minutes after that, I pulled the old bird into the sky as runway 1 fell away below in the dark, the lights of the strip blazing beneath me as I pitched up into the night sky and rolled into a thirty-degree bank to the west.

I'd pretty well crapped out in Vegas, but I did get two new suits out of the deal. At least they'd have something nice to bury me in after the hanging.

24

It was just after eleven when I touched down in Long Beach. I whipped the Gooney Bird around in front of the hangar and cut the motors. Down the ramp a ways, several huge DC-6s sat silently in the dark. They were slumbering elephants now, but I knew they'd be waking up for night hauls within an hour.

I turned my key in the lock, pushed my hangar door open, and stepped into the oil-soaked darkness. A pull on the light chain threw a pale yellow circle on the floor, enough to lead to the office area in the far corner. I made my way across the hangar toward it, my heels clicking emptily on the concrete as I walked.

Once inside the room, I snapped on the lamp, powered up the radio on the invoice-layered desk, and spun the dial until it locked on Cannonball Adderley. That was a start. Surveying the various bottles of hooch that adorned an otherwise empty shelf, I decided I was a little long on Old Overholt. I poured some into a paper cup from the water cooler and ambled over to the carpeted "living room" Roscoe and I had set up against the far wall, pausing along the way to spark up the cigarette I'd stuck between my lips.

I dropped into the ridiculously out-of-place Eames recliner that

Frank had given me, put my feet up, and threw back a swallow of the rye. Its smooth fire burned just right with the cool rush from the Camel. I closed my eyes and pulled some smoke in.

Helen had been missing for two days. Her girlfriend was dead and somebody had tried to send me over today, too. Forty-eight hours earlier I was a guy jocking boxes around for good money and hanging out with Frank Sinatra for laughs. All I'd done was give some girl a lift as a favor to a friend and I'd been ducking haymakers ever since. I never even heard the opening bell.

I blew the smoke out and drained the cup. "Goddamn you, Helen Castano," I said. "What the hell are you doing to me?"

25

I sat there for a long while trying to make the pieces fit, playing back the events from Sunday night forward in my mind, searching for some clue to where Helen might be or what might have taken place. Nothing clicked.

I'm close, she had said. *Come get me, baby . . .* Come to where? Close could be anywhere in Southern California: Los Angeles, Hollywood, Burbank, Santa Barbara. Where?

I poured another slug of the whiskey, leaned back in the chair thinking, thinking.

~

Her face came to me slowly, in soft focus. There was fear in her eyes, but also faith.

"Helen," I said, "tell me where you are. I'll come to you."

Yes, I know you will.

The background looked vaguely familiar, shapes moving in rhythm behind her. There might have been a note of music. A trace of recognition dawned on me. She smiled at me then.

Yes, Joe, now you know. I'll be—

Something ground in my ears. A faint scuffling sound—a shoe on concrete, then the *ca-chuk* of the light chain. I awoke with a start, staring into the dark depths of the hangar, the empty paper cup falling from my hand.

A shadow stirred in the darkness. I struggled to focus on it—then detected rapid motion near the shape. I flung myself clumsily to the side and out of the recliner as something whooshed past me and thudded home in the chair back. I made out another shape moving toward me as I hit the concrete.

My holstered gun lay on the desktop, maybe ten feet away. I rolled once, then sprang up and lunged for the weapon as phantoms closed in on me from the dark.

I got to the holster and ripped the .45 free. As I swung my arm toward the emerging shapes, something barreled into me at high speed, propelling me into the desk, the impact launching the gun into the air.

It was a man, thin but powerful. We hit the floor together, along with the swivel chair, the lamp, and the radio. I felt a sharp pain as a blow landed on my neck, then another on my shoulder.

In the half-light I could see now that there were two men, one pinned to my side by my arm and another raining blows on me from above. I threw my forearm up, blocking another strike with my right arm while holding the other man tightly around the neck with my left.

The standing man got too close in the scrum and I snapped a leg out toward him, clipping him right in the crank. He dropped with an *ooof*, just as the other attacker slithered out of my grasp and slipped on top of me.

It was a good move, but I was a light-heavy and he was a welterweight all the way. He struck me a glancing blow on the cheek before I rolled and tossed him clear. Even in the blind confusion I was beginning to draw a bead on who I was up against—and didn't like it one bit.

A high-pitched "Haiiiiiiii" cut through the air behind me as I rose to one knee. I grabbed the upended swivel chair, then spun and swung it in one motion at the wiry man bounding toward me like a frenzied panther. I caught him flush in the chest, smacking that cat yowling over a workbench.

Then the other assailant struck me in the back with what had to be a karate kick. I staggered forward, lost my balance, and fell down, rolling onto my back as I landed.

He was upon me in an instant. As he dove down, I coiled my legs, grabbed his wrists, and kick-flipped him over my head into the wall ten feet away. He hit hard and rattled down in a heap.

There was a creak at the far end of the hangar, and then I saw that the first attacker was at the door and already slipping through. I leaped up, reaching for the one in the corner, but he lashed out with a quick foot-sweep and tripped me. By the time I scrambled up, he was already halfway gone. I'd only made a few strides when he reached the door and thrust himself through it.

Outside there was a muffled thump. A half second later his limp body flew backward into the room and accordioned to the floor, out cold. I stood there, slack jawed in the dim light, wondering what to expect next.

Then the glowering face and cocked right fist of Roscoe Montgomery appeared in the doorway, demanding, "Just what in the *hell* is going on here, Buonomo?"

26

Roscoe Montgomery was my partner in Nighthawk Aviation, the freight company we formed after several years of beating each other's brains out competing for the same customers. It wasn't that tough of a decision since we'd always been friendly rivals and shared some common history, having both been fighter pilots during the war.

The similarities stopped there, though, since I was Navy and Roscoe flew for the Army Air Corps's 332nd Fighter Interceptor Group. And whatever my issues had been, I always knew that I'd served a nation that respected me and was grateful for my service. Roscoe had volunteered knowing full well that America and the U.S. Army didn't give a damn about him or any other Negro servicemen, regarding them as too dumb, too lazy, or just too unskilled to be of any value to the military.

During the last six months of 1944, nine German pilots had found out in the hardest way possible that Roscoe Montgomery was neither too dumb, nor too lazy or too unskilled, to man a P-51 Mustang in combat. He was brave, tenacious, and unflappable, and he had bailed me out of jams on more than one occasion. A guy could do a lot worse for a partner.

We stood there together a moment and looked down at the unconscious Asian man at our feet.

"Someone you shot down who's got an ax to grind?" he asked with a smirk.

"No, much worse I'm afraid. Close the door quick, he's got a partner who might be back."

"I don't think so. That little man tore out of here like he'd met the *devil* in this hangar," Roscoe said, lowering his eyes just a little, giving me that dubious glance of his.

"He's running in bad luck today—he got me instead. Step back out of the light, buddy, I have to see something."

I bent down toward the battered little man, lifted his right arm, and pushed back the sleeve of his tailored suit coat. The one thing in the whole world I least wanted to see at that moment was etched in green on the inside of his forearm: a tattoo of a phoenix and the Chinese characters for *integrity*, *wisdom*, and *honor*. The markings of the Ching Hwas.

In truth, the Ching Hwas had none of these attributes, but that didn't make them any less dangerous or stop them from being a never-ending pain in my ass.

I dropped the sleeper's arm to the floor and took a deep breath, running my hands over my face and back through my hair. Down at the far end of the ramp, the sound of the big freighters firing up for their long-haul runs rumbled through the air.

"What's this all about, Joe? This fellow isn't dressed like some common thief."

"He's not. He's *Ching Hwa*."

"Uh-ohhh."

"Yeah. Check him for weapons; we're going to be asking him some questions when he comes around."

Roscoe propped the small man up against the hangar door while I walked over to the office to retrieve my gun and the Old Overholt. When I returned, he'd amassed a collection of two throwing stars like the one stuck into my recliner, a nasty little curved knife, and a garrote, all spread out behind him on the hangar floor. Probably not the arsenal you'd take out for a night at the movies, but standard issue for the Hwas.

"Goddamn, this little man is armed to the teeth!" Roscoe said as I neared. "I thought your troubles with these guys were all settled."

"So did I. Here, take a drink," I said, handing him the bottle of rye. "We might be here awhile."

I seldom involved Roscoe in my affairs since he had a wife and two children at home, but this time the affairs had invaded our hangar and he'd just coldcocked one of the goons, so his ticket to the rodeo was already punched.

I looked down into the face of the Chinese thug and slapped him twice. His head lolled from side to side a few times, then he looked up toward me slowly through vitreous eyes. I grabbed his bruised cheeks in my hand hard enough to make him wince, then spoke to him in broken Cantonese.

"What are you doing here?"

He eyed me with surprise but didn't speak. I pulled the .45 out and cocked it, laying the barrel alongside his nose. I stared into his widening eyes for several seconds, long enough to know that he wasn't a hard case.

I pushed the muzzle against his eye socket, drove it in. "You've heard enough about me to know you won't be the first Ching Hwa I've killed—or the last. What do you want with me now?"

"The film," he said in English, his voice a sliver. "We want the film."

"Film?" I asked, looking back toward Roscoe for confirmation.

That was a mistake.

His hand shot out and pushed the gun away, and then a foot struck me in the chest with a snap-kick, knocking me backward into Roscoe. We both tried to lunge for him but blocked each other, and he slipped away through the door, slamming it behind him.

"Stay here, Roscoe," I said as I reached for the handle. "They might be back."

I yanked the door open and tore after the assailant as he ran wildly across the flightline. He was fifty feet ahead of me, but I knew the layout. Darting left and right like a wild rabbit, he ran down the taxiways looking for an exit, with me gaining a step on him every time he reversed field. I knew there was no opening without a fence to scale, and I'd have him easy if he tried that.

It was dark, but the lights of a half-dozen DC-6s warming up their engines at McBride Worldwide seemed to draw him as if he were a moth, and he headed toward their gathered masses near runway 7 Right, with me just thirty feet behind and charging hard.

I had no idea what the Ching Hwas wanted with me now—I sure as hell didn't have any film—but with this guy in tow I could call for a sit-down to straighten the whole thing out. Otherwise, the Hwas would just deny it all and pull some of that inscrutable bullshit. I just couldn't let their man get away.

Ahead of me, the Chinaman rounded an opening in a cyclone fence and broke right, into the field of parked transports that rose in the dark. I vaulted the low fence as he ran underneath one of the planes, made a half turn, and scurried forward toward the next. I only needed another ten seconds to catch him.

The plane ahead had been idling its engines for warm-up before taxiing out. Just then, the pilot brought the propellers to high speed for taxi, their arcs spinning almost invisibly in the dark, the blue wicks of fire licking back along the exhaust pipes from each of the four engines. I was just a few feet behind him as I saw it unfolding.

"Look out!" I shouted at the top of my lungs, but my warning was lost in the bellow of the 2,500-horsepower engines.

The Hwa cut too close to the exhaust flames, throwing his hands up to ward off the unexpected searing heat. He covered up then spun around, and I watched, aghast, as he sidestepped into the whirring blades.

For a second, it looked like he'd lived the myth of walking through unscathed. Then he simply sheared diagonally into two distinct pieces, a scarlet fountain erupting from his body and vaporizing in a whirling cloud around the propeller.

His head and arms fell straight down to the ramp, but the rest of him kept walking. I stopped cold, transfixed with horror as I watched his legs and lower torso stagger forward several steps before collapsing.

Grasping the trailing edge of the flaps for support, I fought off the shock wave of sickness that washed over me. My face felt strangely damp. Then I tasted something warm and salty on my lips.

Even in the dark, I knew it wasn't sweat.

The engines were already retreating as the pilots realized what had happened, but there was nothing to be done for the little guy now. It was horribly gruesome, but almost everyone who flew off carriers saw it at least once.

I took stock of my situation as I stood there: I was within twenty feet of a freshly bisected man, and I was bathed in his blood. Any basic investigation by the police would determine that he was a Chinese mobster, and that I had a long history in his country.

It was no good.

I wanted to tell the pilots it wasn't their fault, but that would have to wait. Getting as far from that asphalt killing floor as fast as I could was my only move. Turning from the corpse, I ducked away and fled, weaving beneath the other aircraft as voices called out behind me that someone was down.

I stole away swiftly across the darkened tarmac, blood stinging my eyes as I ran.

27

I made the hangar in two minutes, slamming the door shut behind me as I rushed in. Roscoe was inside, policing up my mess. He looked me up and down as I approached. Anyone else would have burst out screaming or asking if I was all right. Roscoe didn't faze.

"You're covered in blood, Buonomo."

"Yeah."

"And you're getting it on my hangar floor."

I looked down. "Yeah."

"So get your ass in the shower and give me those clothes. I'm going to burn them."

"But it's a Saville Row suit, from Frank."

"Have his tailor make you another one—they can send it to San Quentin. Now give me the goddamn suit, Joe!"

I gave him the goddamn suit and jumped into the work shower. When I got out, he was gone. A shirt and a pair of slacks from my locker were on the chair close by, along with a note that read, *Call me if you need me. Be in tomorrow night. R.M.*

I had only one option. Things were spinning way out of control. I'd gone from looking for a missing girl to colliding with the mob in

Vegas to running a member of L.A.'s most notorious Chinese crime clan through a blender.

I needed help. I needed a friend. I needed Sam Woo.

28

The cool night air flowed over me as I cruised north toward L.A., the gray Long Beach freeway playing out in front of the nose of my LeSabre like a storm-studded horizon. I hadn't bothered to make a phone call. Sam would be in. He was always in.

Sam Woo and I went back to 1942. He was a member of the Chinese resistance who rescued me after I'd been shot down over Japanese-held Nanking. Later, we battled the Communists in service to Chiang Kai-shek, all the way to the disastrous end. Then, in Taiwan, we fell into some rather lucrative business together in our own enterprise. Things like that tend to build a bond between guys—and Sam Woo was a guy you wanted a bond with when the Ching Hwas were your enemy.

His name wasn't actually Sam Woo—Chinese for "Three Harmonies"—that was the name of his restaurant, but everybody, even the locals, knew him that way. Sam had continued the activities we began together while in exile, moving on to the States after I left for the Caribbean. And he had done spectacularly well in my absence.

Sam didn't command the street gangs, drug peddlers, and heist mobs that slithered through nocturnal Los Angeles, but he was so well connected to so many people, with so much muscle at his disposal, that no one did anything in Chinatown without getting his okay.

In China, he'd been a warlord. In America, they called him a kingpin.

~

It was past two when I arrived. I pulled short, made a U-turn, and pointed the car toward the West Gate for a speedy exit. You just never know.

SAM WOO blazed in red neon letters against a green background as I approached the restaurant. A gaggle of ducks hung by their necks in the window, their roasted brown bodies dripping grease into catch pans below.

I peered through the glass door for a second, then pushed it open, locking on the half-masted eyes of Lo Chi through the kitchen porthole. He leaned halfway out, yawning, a clutch of feathers in one hand and a dead bird in the other. I gave a faint head nod toward the back, and then he disappeared silently through the swinging door behind him. Mama Chu gave me a seat at a table along the far wall then brought me some tea. I poured a cup and looked around the room.

Two elderly men with white beards sat quietly near the window playing mah-jongg and sipping tea. Closer to the door, two young toughs with furtive eyes spoke in dialect beneath their breath, the occasional angry glance cutting the air. From the looks they were telegraphing, they either didn't know Sam or they didn't know me. Since I was the only person in the room who wasn't Chinese, I figured the stare-down was definitely all mine.

I ignored them both. Predictably, this only incited them. Vague curses about white devils and the chosen profession of my mother flew across the room. Mama Chu told them to behave.

The old men kept to their game. I sipped my tea. The minutes crept.

I don't know, maybe it's my face. There must be something about me that invites this shit. Finally, one of them got bold, stood up, and advanced toward my table, accusing me of committing immoral acts with a dog, or maybe a pig's head. I couldn't be sure which—my Chinese wasn't that good anymore.

It had been a long day, and I was tired of beating up Moo Shu Cagneys, but this was a threat.

I put down my tea.

Mama Chu stepped behind the counter and the old men looked up. I steeled my guts and put my fiercest stare on the lead guy. His eyes dilated with fear, but he wouldn't meet my glare, looking beyond me instead. Then he shrank visibly and bowed low, his partner doing the same. Even on my best day I wasn't that tough. Leaning back, I glanced sideways in the direction of the thug's genuflections.

Fire burned hot in two dark eyes set deep in an iron face. From the recess of an open door, Sam Woo stood beaming molten fury across the room, his narrow mouth turned down, his body rigid.

Shot through with terror, the young men spouted multiple apologies, bowed repeatedly, and then fled from the restaurant. Sam never said a word.

When they were gone, a small smile cracked beneath a steel-gray mustache. "Can't you go anywhere without busting up the joint, Joe?"

"Don't blame me, it was your tea they were bitching about."

He shook his head, pointed toward the back room. I followed him in. Two guards started to frisk me as I entered, but Sam waved them away with a flick of his hand. One of them dared to give him a surprised look.

A torrent of furious words tore from Sam's mouth in a dialect I couldn't cipher. As he spoke, he rat-a-tatted his finger against a large glass frame on the wall. It contained a Flying Tigers leather jacket along with the "blood chit" that American Volunteer Group pilots had been instructed to show Chinese locals if they were shot down.

It was mine.

I'd given it to Sam as a gesture of thanks after he'd helped hide me, and he'd prized it all these years. A curious bit of hero worship from a godfather, but Sam and I had gone through a few walls for each other in the late '40s.

Anyhow, it was a trump of a talisman to have in a place like that. Both guards and two other men left the room quietly as Sam finished his tirade with a pointed "you sons of whores!"

The door closed behind them with a dismissive click.

"You get any of that?" he asked in heavily accented English, his face drawn up in a mischievous smirk.

"Yeah. The sons of whores part."

We took seats across from each other at an old mahogany table inscribed with Chinese characters and adorned with red tassels at each corner. Sam lit an elaborately carved ivory pipe and drew in some smoke.

"What brings you to my world, old friend? You didn't come in at this hour for the slippery shrimp."

"No."

He saw the look in my eyes and sat back against the padded back of the bench. "You got trouble?'

I zippoed a cigarette, sucked in some smoke. "Like Custer."

He scrunched up his face, wrinkles binding as he searched for the reference, but he got the point just the same. "Bad, huh?"

I nodded.

"Somebody dead?"

"Yeah. A Ching Hwa."

His face fell. "Oh shit. What is it with you and those guys?"

"I don't know, Sam. I made a clean break from them in Taiwan. They dragged me back once for that little dustup in Macao, but that was my last tea ceremony with them. It's all over, *finito*, *zai jian*, baby, and goodnight."

He exhaled sharply through his nostrils, his eyes contracting until they were just slits in the mask of his face. He said nothing for quite a while, contemplating the complexity of the machinations that would surely follow now.

"Tell me," he said finally.

"Two guys. They broke into my hangar tonight. I don't think they expected me to be there, but they sure as hell tried to wipe the floor with me just the same," I said, rubbing my sore neck at the memory.

"Go on."

"We reenacted the Boxer Rebellion—you guys lost again. One got away, but Roscoe came in and flattened the other."

"He would appear to have a talent for that."

"Yeah, I've seen it before. Anyway, I slapped the guy around a little and he said they were looking for a film. I have no idea what he was talking about. You got anything on it?"

He just shook his head and pulled down the edges of his long mustache with his fingers. "Take me to the dead part, Joe."

"Well, he broke away from me and took off down the ramp. I chased him because I wanted more answers. I've made my peace with the Hwas—they've got no cause to be hounding me again."

"They *didn't.*"

"Right. Well, the guy ran under some parked planes warming up. He never knew what hit him—right through the blades—I couldn't stop him. It was an awful mess."

"I imagine so," he replied, puffing out a curl of pungent smoke.

"That takes me to here. They're going to blame me, of course."

"Of course."

I ground my palms together. "Sam, I can't afford another war with them. They're not too bright, but they outnumber me about two hundred to one. Besides, I'm in another deal up to my neck."

"Which is?"

"I'm looking for a missing girl. Unrelated."

"You sure?"

I thought a second about the scene at the laundry in the afternoon, then asked, "Do the Ching Hwas run a laundry over on Gower and Sunset?"

He closed his eyes a moment, then opened them again while nodding his head down twice.

I swallowed hard. "Do they move heroin out of there?"

He paused, and then replied, "Yes," with a gravity that fell like a boxcar of pig iron upon the room.

"Sam," I said, "I've got a real problem here."

∼

I told him what I knew. It was a tough decision to bring Frank's name into it, but Sam would have known soon enough anyway. He said he'd take care of things, but reminded me that the Ching Hwas were getting bigger and more difficult to control. I didn't find that terribly reassuring.

I thanked Sam for his help and bowed to him. To my surprise, he stuck out his hand, a first. I took it and held it tight, feeling the strength still in his grip.

"Careful, Sam, you're becoming more American."

"And you, my friend, want to be a little less Chinese, but we must all follow the paths we have chosen for ourselves."

I grinned as his words sank in, recalling his wisdom, his hypnotic power over men, our friendship forged in fire. Remembering what was best from a very dark time.

"Thank you, Sam. Goodnight."

Sam's steel eyes met mine, perhaps a trace of sadness in them. "Goodnight, old friend."

I turned and walked through the door. On my way out, I said goodnight to Mama Chu and waved at Lo Chi, then nodded to the old men. They barely looked up from their game.

I went outside and headed down the street toward my car. A man was leaning on the driver's door smoking a cigarette, watching me as I approached.

I kept walking, closing the distance, while he sat there flicking ash on my seats. It was one of the toughs from Sam's, apparently not smart enough to take the warning to heart. Not a Ching Hwa or a mobster, just a dumb kid heading down the wrong path in life.

I heard the scrape of a heel behind me as I passed the darkened alley twenty feet from the car. That was his wingman, coming up behind me for the squeeze play.

Number One Wiseass smiled at me as I neared, said, "You in the wrong part of town, buddy," then flicked the cigarette into my car.

That did it. I was just all done with *Fuck with Joe Buonomo Day*.

"Nuts to you," I said, swinging my fist up and out. I caught him flat-footed, plastering him with the blind left hook that nobody ever expects.

His head went back and didn't come forward, then his knees buckled and his tent just folded up. He dropped straight down, bouncing off the car door and crumpling onto the street.

I pivoted on my right heel and launched a roundhouse kick in the direction of the hard breathing behind me. It wasn't quite a clean blow, but it put him down on his ass. I had him then.

I just hauled Number Two up and tossed him onto the sidewalk, then into the chain-link fence that ran alongside.

Before I could reach him again, he scrambled up from the weeds and broken glass and lit out down the alley. I turned and stormed back toward the driver's side.

Number One was parked on the pavement, leaning up against the front tire with his hand jammed up against his nose, trying to stanch the red river flowing out.

I leaned into the car, plucked the burning cigarette off the seat, and knelt down next to him. With a grunt, I ripped the hand from his face and then buried the butt in his palm. It made a *tzzzzzzz* sound as it sizzled out in his blood.

"Next time use the ashtray."

I climbed into the car, cranked it over, and yanked the shifter into first. Rubber shrieked against asphalt as I mashed the pedal down, a whimpering Chinaman tumbling down in the street as I sped away from the land of paper dragons.

~

I went back to the Nighthawk hangar. Police lights flashed away over at McBride, but it was quiet at my end of the field. I went inside, searched the whole place twice, then took a long drink from the bottle of Old Overholt and yanked back the covers on the cot I had in the back. There was work to be done, lots of it, but none tonight so I decided to steal a few hours of sleep.

Darkness enveloped the cavernous space when I pulled the light chain down. This time I was all alone—except for the .45 under my pillow.

29

Morning broke hard. I rolled over a few times, but I was up by eight. My neck was a little stiff from my workout with the Peking Circus, my hand hurt from decking the punk outside Sam's, and my head was throbbing from the acute lack of caffeine in my bloodstream. Other than that, I was serviceable.

I climbed out of the rack, put a pot of coffee on the hot plate, and cleaned myself up. The java was oil black and nearly as heavy. I downed it in a few slurps, then realized I was hungry as hell, so I jumped into the Buick and headed over to Curley's. Near as I could tell, no one followed me.

I hammered down a plate of biscuits and gravy, some eggs, and two more cups of coffee. Over my second cigarette, I started to feel like a human being again.

I thought about the last crazy couple of days while I sat at the bar. This affair was beginning to have more players than a Sousa march— but those weren't piccolos in their hands. Now there was some film in the mix, which Betty may have died over. And, of course, there was Frank—and his girlfriend.

I called him up in Bel Air and told him we needed to talk face-to-face. He agreed. Five minutes later I was northbound on the 15 again. Frank's place was my destination, but I had another stop to make on the way first, a hunch I wanted to play.

It took me a good forty-five minutes to get up there, but I scored a great parking spot just off Vine, which helped.

The Brown Derby in Hollywood lacked the ridiculous hat shape of the one on Wilshire, but more than made up for it with its wild cast of characters inside, one of whom I'd come to see.

They were in a slack period between breakfast and lunch and no one came to greet me at the podium. I stood around awhile, scanning the waiting area, taking note of the large photo of Betty on the wall along with the newspaper article about her murder, taped right on top of the many caricature drawings of celebrities. I guess they meant well, but it played like another one of the cheap exploitations the movie industry makes of its own, even beyond the grave. They still lined up by the thousands for a shot.

From the corner of my eye I saw the woman I'd come to speak with, so I just seated myself at a booth in her section and waited for her to walk over. She didn't make me until I looked up at her.

"Hello, Ida."

Her face fell upon recognizing me, which was an accomplishment considering how much it had already fallen over the years.

"Try another section," she said, acid eating the words.

Ida Brügger had harbored Hollywood ambitions twenty years earlier, but her looks had been just south of attractive and she couldn't act well enough to get the *hard-luck girl* parts. Eventually, she settled into the role of mother and mentor to dozens of young actresses, most of whom still came in to see her regularly.

Helen had been one of her favorites, and Ida blamed me for derailing her career after our breakup. She told me so in no uncertain terms when I made the mistake of bringing another date to the Derby a couple of years later.

"Ida, it's about Helen. It's important."

"Well, you're five years too late for that," she snapped. She stared me down for several seconds through steel-gray eyes, then demanded, "What is it? Out with it, Hamlet."

I looked around the room. "She's missing, Ida, and she's very likely in trouble with the people who murdered Betty Benker."

Her hand flew to her mouth. "Oh, dear God."

"Have you seen her in the last few days? Please tell me if you have."

She shook her head slowly, said, "No," her face ashen in the sunlight streaming through the window.

"Well, if you do—"

"I might have known you'd be responsible for getting her into something else like this. You're the worst thing that ever happened to her."

She'd found her footing and was back to throwing spears. Ida was overprotective of all her "girls," and I could respect that, but I was in no mood to be taken down a notch by the Crone of Hollywood. I got a little tough.

"I'm not responsible for getting Helen into anything. I'm trying to find her before something bad happens to her. Can you help me, yes or no?" I demanded, pounding the heel of my palm on the table so hard that the silverware rang out in a two-note clash symphony.

She looked me over, stone-faced. "I'm sorry, she hasn't been in. I'll make some calls to the girls when I go on break to see if she's staying with any of them."

"Thanks. Call me at any hour if you have any information. There's an answering service when I'm out." I wrote my number down on a napkin and handed it up to her. "I don't know what you think I ever did to Helen, by the way, but I loved her very much. She left me, you know, not the other way around."

"Yes, but you broke that girl's heart when you went away. She needed you then, and you disappeared on her. She wound up in some very dire straits after that, Joe—all thanks to you." She began aiming a chubby finger at me as she drove home her point. "Helen idolized you, Mr. War Hero—and you let her down *flat*."

"Listen, Ida—"

"You shuddup, I'm not finished yet. You may be a big deal to some so-called glamorous people who keep you around as some kind of a curio, Buonomo, but I see right through you. You're a crash-out bum, just like me. What have you ever been good for anyway—besides killing people?"

The speech was high Hollywood, but it bit deep just the same because it was true. Our eyes met for several seconds, cold fury brimming in hers. I thought about responding, but she'd already won the round. I let her keep it.

"I'll call you if I hear anything, okay?" she said icily. "Now get the hell out of my booth."

She turned and stormed off, a Valkyrie triumphant.

30

I brooded as I drove. Nothing much had gone right these last three days, and now I was even getting told off by the waitresses.

What have you ever been good for anyway—besides killing people?

The words burned in my ears. Involuntarily, I conjured images of men dying at my hands. I recalled something an overeager navy PR officer had said to me once.

You're a born killer, Buonomo, like Achilles or something. It's like they created you for this war!

I was still feeling sorry for myself when I noticed the car following me—a brown Chevrolet, three cars back, with me light for light. I made a few lane changes and varied my speed to confirm it, but someone was definitely on me.

I continued west on Sunset for several blocks, marking him in my side mirror. At Laurel Canyon, I spun a hard right and punched the pedal down, picking up speed as I soared up the steady incline toward the hills where the moguls looked down upon the world.

The guy in the Chevy was game though, and, sure enough, he came flying out of the turn behind me, now a good quarter mile back. I overtook a Deville doing seventy, scaring the matching white hair off some dowager and her poodle as I swung past them just inches away.

The Chevy came on but was losing ground rapidly to the big eight I had under the hood. I almost had to slow down to let him catch up again.

At Wonderland, I whipped a left, then made a series of turns until I lost myself amid the half-million-dollar homes nestled in the cool, green hills, following the meandering curves past castle-massive Tudors worthy of Henry and French Provincials so large that you half expected to see Marie Antoinette sunning herself by the pool.

Finally, I rolled back onto Laurel Canyon, stopping a hundred feet from the corner. I waited several minutes for the Chevy driver to pass by, but he was nowhere in sight. He might have been arrested for simply having the audacity to drive that car in those lofty Olympian heights of the beautiful and the ascotted.

With a shrug, I put the car in gear, made a right at the corner and rolled back down the hill toward the hoi polloi.

～

Frank's L.A. place was in Coldwater Canyon, another hike up into the hills, but only a few minutes away. It was Japanese but also contemporary, and just cool as all get-out, with push-button panels hiding every modern convenience imaginable. It was every man's dream of a bachelor pad, right down to the starlets who hung out there.

The problem today was the one who wasn't there.

I honked when I arrived and Frank waved me in. He led me through the house to the patio area out back.

Some untouched breakfast sat on a tray drying in the sun. Scattered song sheets lay on a table. Several pages had fallen to the cement flooring, where they sat in arrhythmic flux. A cool puff of wind spun across the patio, rustling Carmichael and Kern against the chair legs.

Frank took no notice, looking up at me instead, a hint of desperation on his face. He wanted me to tell him something encouraging, but I had only bad news.

I surveyed the expansive downhill view of Bel Air, and below that, Los Angeles, befouled in smog but still striking in the late-morning light.

"Frank, things are really going south here."

"Yeah, I noticed that's not a leg of *prozhutt'* you're carrying under your arm there, Joseph," he said while nodding at my weapon. "What's going on now?"

"It got worse last night. Much worse."

He pulled his lips in tight, sucked in a breath.

"This isn't just about Lilah or Betty," I continued. "Those B-team hoodlums want something. So do a bunch of scheming Chinese mobsters, and I think Lilah is somehow connected to what they want."

Frank drilled holes through me with his stare, slowly assessing what I'd told him.

"Oh, yeah, the owner of the jewelry store in Vegas is dead, too. Took a stray one when Ratello tried to clip me. I'm a suspect, of course."

"Any reason I shouldn't bring the police into this right now?"

"None. I've been at it three days, and all I know is that our girl is missing and Ratello probably doesn't have her, the Chinese don't have her—and we don't have her."

"Our girl? We? You're a wonderful pal, Joe, but please don't forget that she's *my* girl. There'll be a finder's fee, brother—but she ain't it."

He forced a smile to soften the words, but his world-famous jealous streak was showing itself, even in a crisis.

I thought about spilling the whole kettle of fish concerning Helen and me right then but decided it had to wait. It was all going come out soon enough anyhow, but I'd had it up to *here* with the whole stupid charade. It was going to have to wait until we found her—but not one day more.

"Sure, Frank, sure," I said. "I just feel responsible because I flew her down and left her with the limo driver. I should have taken her home myself."

It was a crummy little lie, but it was all I had in me at the moment. I stomached it, then refocused on the issue at hand.

"Did Lilah ever say anything to you about a film of any kind?"

"She's an actress, I'm an actor. We talk about movies all the time."

"No, not a movie, a film of some kind. I don't know exactly what, but the kind of thing underworld goons would want."

He looked straight ahead, massaging his chin, while he thought it over. Then those cornflower blue eyes widened visibly for a second and his face tightened a notch.

After a lengthy pause, he shook his head and said, "Nothing outside of studio work. What could she have that some mobsters would want?"

"Dunno. I was hoping you could tell me."

He didn't respond. He seemed to have thought of something, something that concerned him greatly, although he appeared to be covering it up.

"Frank?"

"Uh . . . yeah?"

"Anything? You had a look on your face there, buddy."

He stared at me. "I thought I had something there for a second, but it was nothing."

I arched an eyebrow.

"I tell ya, it's nothing."

"Okay, Frank."

I had to accept that, but I wasn't crazy about possibly being kept in the dark. I scratched my head, took out a smoke.

Frank pulled out a gold lighter, waved it under my cigarette, then leaned back against a railing.

"Joe, do you think it's possible she just ducked out somewhere with a guy and doesn't know anything about any of this? I mean, I'd much rather deal with that than the other scenario."

I blew out a funnel of white smoke, fixed him with a look.

"No, I don't. This is all related, I'm afraid. I've been around this stuff too long to see it any other way. I didn't have any connection until a Ching Hwa mentioned a film to me."

"A Ching-who?"

"Ching Hwa. A bad bunch of operators from Taiwan. They made landfall here about five years back, been spreading like the Asian flu—only deadlier—ever since."

"Well, why don't you ask your buddy the Chinaman what in the name of Confucius this film is, and how it involves Lilah?"

"Can't do that."

"Why the hell not?"

"Because he's dead."

He threw up his hands. "Sure are a lot of people dying around you."

I flicked some ash over the patio into the crevasse below and looked out. "Yep."

"Well, please, don't let Lilah be one of them—or me."

I just eyed him for that one.

"So what do we do now, Joe?"

"I think I smoked Ratello out of Las Vegas, and I'm willing to bet he's down here somewhere. Can you call some of your guys up and see if they have any idea where he hides out in L.A.?"

"Right away."

A moment later, the doorbell rang. There was some conversation inside, then Sanjee, the houseboy, walked out and said that Mr. Sinatra's lawyer had arrived. Frank said to show him on back.

I took this as my cue to exit. I wanted to make some calls, but not from Frank's house—I wasn't going to connect the dots from Frank to Sam Woo if the feds were tapping his line, which was a fairly good bet given some of his friendships.

I said hello to the lawyer. He said we should discuss my turning myself in over the Benker snuff. I told him he was going to have to cover for me for a few more days. Frank said he'd explain it all to him. I nodded and made for the front door.

Before I left, I turned to Frank and said, "Have you discussed this matter over the phone with anyone other than me?"

"Only in the vaguest of terms. Why?"

"Because it just occurred to me that you might have a party line here with the feds already. You can probably just pick it up and get J. Edgar Hoover anytime you want them in on this thing."

He didn't find anything inherently funny in that.

Neither did I.

31

There's a small store where Coldwater Canyon forks into Mulholland Drive. Outside of that small store, near the road, there's a phone booth—at least there used to be. It was only a few minutes away from Frank's house the short way.

But I went the long way out Bowmont and snaked around until I reached Mulholland. Then I made a left and rolled on a half mile until I reached the store on my right. It was as good as any place to phone Sam, and the view of the canyon was nice. I figured I owed myself that much.

I parked the car, gave the lot a good once-over, and walked over to the booth. I pulled the door shut behind me and put some coins into the slot. My first call was to the hangar. I caught a lucky break—I was due.

"Good morning, Mister Bwoh-noe-moe," the girl from the answering service cooed. "You have three messages. Shall I read them to you, sir?"

It was Simone—English for sure, knew diction like nobody's business. If she wasn't bucking for a part in the next remake of *Wuthering Heights*, nobody was. Everybody's after something in L.A.

She read the messages. The first was from Mr. Rising in Florida about an engine invoice. The second was from Sean Parker, a young pilot still looking for work in night freight, poor bastard. The third was from Ida. She said I should call Millie at MAdison 6-3747 regarding our conversation. The old battleaxe had come through—and quick. There are many ways to send information in this modern world, but I've never seen one yet that could match the speed of the old lipstick wireless.

I pulled the rack down and released it, fed in a pair of nickels, and dialed MAdison 6-3747 before my short-term memory could betray me. After four rings, I could feel my heart sinking a bit, but she picked up a moment later.

"Hallo," she said, the voice a nasal vibrato.

"Millie. Hi, it's Joe Buonomo."

"Oh, hi, Joe. How ahh ya? Lahng time, no heah."

The *R*s were falling like dominoes—the Boston was never going to leave that kid. Millie was another one of Helen's Hollywood gang perpetually hoping for that big break, and she just kept throwing herself into the fire in the hope that one of these days someone was going to catch her. She sure as hell wasn't going to make it as a voice coach.

"Millie, I'm trying to find Helen. Have you seen her?"

"Oh, that's sweet. She told me she sawr you the other night."

"When did you see her?" I demanded, my pulse surging.

"She came by real late a couple of nights ago, asked could she stay with me. Of course I said yes. But, Joe, she was real scahed—didn't have no clothes with her or nothin', just what she had on."

"Was she okay?"

"Oh, shu-uh, just upset, I guess. She wouldn't talk about what it was, though."

"Do you know where she is now?"

"No. She made some phone calls in the mornin'. Somethin' spooked her again and she said she had to get away. I thought I heard her mention your name on the phone. That wasn't you?"

I nodded as the tumblers lined up in my mind. "Any idea where she went, Millie?"

"Said she was headed toward Lahng Beach; I thought she was goin' to see you, the way she was mentionin' your name. That's the last I seen of her. You ain't seen her neither? Funny, huh?"

"Yeah. Funny. Thanks, Mill."

"Shu-uh. Say, Joe, if you two don't make a go of things, why don't you give ol' Mill' a call someday. Ya got my numbah now."

I frowned. "Gotta go, Mill'. Thanks, doll."

"G'bye, Joe."

It was the closest thing I'd had to a lead in a while. In Long Beach I could find Helen, or she could find me when she was ready, but L.A. was another story. There were three million indifferent people marking time in the smog grid below, along with one rather interested party in a brown Chevy.

That reminded me that I needed to check in with Sam to see if he'd brokered some kind of a truce with my old enemies.

I fished in my pocket for some more change and dropped it in the slot. That pleasant ding sounded twice more as the phone determined the coins weren't slugs. I dialed Sam's number, waiting for the wheel to *clack-clack* all the way back after each of the nines.

I never made it through the last one.

A thunderclap exploded in my ears, then the glass above me disintegrated, the booth shaking like the Big One had hit. My hands flew to my head as I covered up, hunching forward and low beneath the phone.

There was another detonation and Ma Bell took one right in the gut, the coin box bursting open, a metal storm of dimes and nickels raining through the air amidst the pulverized glass.

Despite my shock, my numbed brain made a grim connection— someone was using the phone booth for shotgun practice.

I scrunched down on the floor and kicked at the door, which slid about one inch before jamming on a buckshot-mauled track. A dirty brown haze began to fill the cloistered air in the booth, the reek of gunpowder and scorched aluminum stinging my nostrils.

A third explosion punched a hole through the metal frame a foot above me.

I curled up in a defensive position as twisted shavings of hot metal and a thousand shards of shattered glass pelted me. Somewhere along the way, the severed receiver fell upon my head with a *thok*. It was hell in a tin can.

And I had had my fill of it.

Drawing my weapon close to my chest and cocking it, I twisted my head around to see who was blasting chunks out of my world.

There was an Oriental man at road's edge. He was sporting a tan suit, a short-brim fedora, and a very large pump-action shotgun. White teeth shone beneath black sunglasses as he advanced.

The shotgun clicked loudly as he racked it. It was an awful sound. I had maybe one second to get off a shot—but I didn't get the chance.

The roar of a speeding vehicle filled my ears. Twelve-gauge Charlie turned toward it and froze.

There was a brown blur of a car, a splattered watermelon *thump*, and then Charlie wasn't there anymore. I didn't even see where he landed.

The shotgun came down from the sky a second later, clattering down on the gravel in front of the booth, brakes shrieking around the corner as the car skidded to a halt.

Seizing my opportunity, I grabbed the folding door and slung it open. I turned, gun drawn, and spotted a black Mercury across the street—just like the one I'd seen on Afton two days earlier.

Two suited Orientals occupied the front seats. The passenger swung out onto his door and pointed a pistol across the roof at me. I didn't wait to see if he just needed directions.

I squeezed off a round as I dove onto the gravel, poorly aimed shots whistling through the air above me.

A dust tornado kicked up several feet away from a bullet impact as I hit the ground, lunging for the fallen shotgun. I kept firing with my left hand as I reached out with my right.

Another bullet zinged into the gravel, rock fragments stinging my cheek.

Then I had the shotgun.

I rolled right, bracing the barrel with my left hand, then pulled the trigger.

Somehow I hit something. Not much, but enough.

Double-ought shot blew out the top of the driver's window, shredding the roof above his head. The shooter panicked and slid back down inside. A second later, the car lurched forward. I sat up, swapping hands on the weapon and pumping the action back hard.

This time I saw it before I heard it—a brown Chevy cruiser with a smear of blood on a wrinkled fender—barreling down hard from my right then absolutely plowing the black coupe in the driver's-side door.

Car pieces flew in all directions amid the crunch of rent metal. Both vehicles careened sideways, the Merc slamming to a stop against a guardrail along the canyon's sheer edge thirty feet away.

A lone chrome hubcap spun crookedly away from the crushed cars as busted glass tinkled down to the pavement in small *plinks*. A radiator hissed a dying breath. Someone moaned inside one of the cars. Then nothing.

A grinding whine spun up suddenly as the Chevy flew backward toward me. I dove away in confusion as it drew back a good fifteen feet then surged forward toward the stricken Mercury, smacking into it like a wrecking ball hurtling down.

The wooden guardrail snapped with a *crack* as the black hulk of the coupe was driven within inches of the abyss.

The Chevy squealed into reverse again.

I could see the Merc's dazed driver trying to right the steering wheel as the passenger gestured wildly with his arms, hunks of rock and dirt spraying out beneath the rear wheels as they dug into the loose shoulder.

The brown battering ram surged forward as the coupe's passenger looked on in terror, hauling himself onto the doorsill, trying to climb out while the driver struggled desperately to open his crumpled door.

Neither guy made it.

The Chevy hit the black coupe square, punching it through the splintered guardrail and clear off the edge of the cliff.

It seemed to hang there just a moment, its wheels spinning uselessly in space. Then it plunged out of sight, a fading scream trailing out as the car dropped away.

An echoing *thud* of breaking metal issued from the depths of Coldwater Canyon moments later. I winced at the palpable finality of it.

The Chevy was already in gear and pulling away as I neared the road's edge, mesmerized, but I still got a long look at the driver as he flashed by. The recognition astonished me. It was Lo Chi, the sleepy-eyed cook from Chinatown I thought I'd known all these years.

It was immediately clear that he did a whole lot more than pluck ducks for Sam Woo.

I shook my head several times in disbelief at the nightmare that had just unfolded before me, then backed away toward my car. I got in and made fast tracks out of the area before any witnesses could creep out from the store.

I looked back reflexively as I sped away. The view of the canyon was just as striking as it had been five minutes earlier—but I wasn't ever going to think of it in the same way.

32

I just drove. Straight down Mulholland, westbound and fast, up into the hills and the hell away from Los Angeles.

The world was coming apart at the seams. It was all gunfire and corpses and blood—and I had no idea why.

Radiator pipes were clanging in my head, iron fingers clutching at my chest. I was having trouble breathing, started hyperventilating. Blood shot in surges through my heart as that old shuddering dread rose up inside and began to overwhelm me.

I tore open my shirt and opened the vent windows, letting the air rush over me as I fled down the road. I needed to get away. It didn't matter where—just away.

I drove for miles and miles on Mulholland, twisting around curves and switchbacks, running up and down through the hills. Gradually, the houses came less frequently and other cars not at all. I could feel my chest unwinding, realized I wasn't laboring as hard to breathe any longer.

At some point, I turned onto Topanga Canyon. I didn't have a plan, just let the car go. Something inside was driving me now—I couldn't fight it.

Eventually, I pulled into a state park, far, far away from anything. There were quiet places there, hiking trails. I took to one, began to walk.

The path wound up into the hills, past a thicket and out among the Santa Monica Mountains. The air felt good. Sea air, even several thousand feet up.

The trail wrapped around the hilltops, bathing me in bright sunshine one moment and plunging me into dark shade the next. The views were spectacular, I knew that, but it could have been Gary, Indiana, to me for all I noticed.

After forty minutes of walking, I realized that the trail was familiar to me, that I'd been on it before. None of my thoughts were coalescing, though. Too much wild energy was still coursing through my head.

An hour in, I crested an incline and looked down to the end of the dirt path, which dead-ended on a cliff facing the sea. I shambled down the last two hundred yards, stopping at land's very edge. A strong wind blew off the ocean over the scrub and low grass, carrying the chill of autumn on its swirling currents.

I sat down on a boulder, staring at Malibu's beaches far below. Farther down, beyond Point Dume, the great expanse of the mighty Pacific thundered, sweeping out and away from Los Angeles and its horrors, rolling six thousand blue miles toward another world I knew a long time ago.

~

I don't know how long I sat there, but the sun was slanting down in the west when I shook free from my memory sanctum.

Nothing had changed while I was melting down. Betty was still dead. Ratello and the Chings were still on the loose. Helen was still missing. And the only guy with a hope in hell of finding her was burning daylight on a hilltop sanitarium. *Jesus Christ, Joe.*

I dropped out of the clouds, reacquainted myself with the planet. Cupping my hands against the wind, I flamed a Lucky, took in a drag, my mind drifting through my night with Helen. I started at the airport, moved on the bar. One cigarette later, I still had nil. Then I walked myself through her apartment again, culling my mind for details.

I remembered the pleasant sensation the scent of her pajamas gave me, and the feeling of nearness the hairs in her brush brought me—a nearness from another time, not the present.

Other observations came and went: Betty's dress, the mohair quilt, the Crosley clock. There was something about that picture on Helen's nightstand. I framed it up in my mind, turning it around once or twice. It surprised me that she would still have a photo of me next to her bed, still carrying the torch five years on.

She'd taken that picture, giggling as she did because she couldn't figure out the shutter speeds on the Voightlander I'd picked up in Germany after the war. I recalled telling her she needed to reduce the light because there was less haze than on the mainland.

And then I had it.

So goddamned obvious—and literally right in front of me.

I stole a glance to the south, through the glare of the falling sun. There it was, forty miles away, jutting dark and remote out of the sparkling sea.

The place where we'd taken that picture.

The place where I knew she was.

33

Santa Catalina is one of the Channel Islands that lie hard off the Southern California coast. Just twenty miles out at its closest point, Catalina rises steeply from the ocean in several uneven hills along a central spine. Avalon, the only town, is a sleepy place most of the year, but comes alive in the warmer months. Thousands of visitors come by ferry on summer weekends to dance at the Catalina Casino at harbor's edge, or to enjoy the island's many other charms. Sailing, swimming, sunbathing, salooning—Avalon's got something for everybody, sober or torched.

It was a regular stop for me since they needed all sorts of things on a time-critical basis. Helen and I had spent many nights there dancing, strolling the waterfront, or shutting down the bars. We both loved the place and knew it well.

What clicked for me when I thought of us on the island together was the memory of the night we stood on the Casino balcony, watching the ocean swells cruise by under a bright harvest moon. It was just before I had to go back to China. We were taking a break from dancing, grabbing a little air.

Out of left field, Helen had said, "This is a special place. I feel safe here, like I could always hide away from my worries."

It was almost as if she knew our time was near its end. There was something unnaturally serious in her eyes as she spoke.

I said something dumb like "Wrap your troubles in dreams, huh?" and didn't think anything more of it. Went back to dancing a few minutes later.

When I came back from China and read her note, I thought that she might return soon, or at least contact me, but she didn't. Then I recalled her words and her face that night at the Casino, decided I had nothing to lose, and caught the next boat over.

I searched for her on Catalina for several days, walking the few small streets of Avalon, riding up and down the hills on my motorcycle. Every afternoon I checked the waterfront and the pier, looking for her face among the many. I asked about her in all the shops and bars as well. A couple of friends pulled me aside and told me I was just hurting myself.

In the evenings I'd go to the Casino and wander among the dancers on the curved balcony high above the sea, watching, waiting for her. Every night the surf rolled in and broke over the rocks, the people danced the old dances, and the moon bounced cold light upon the dark water—but that was all. She never came.

That was five years ago. Time and grief helped suppress the memory, and it was just as well buried anyhow.

But this time was different. I *knew* I'd find her there. I just couldn't believe I hadn't figured it out sooner. Might have saved a hell of a lot of trouble—and a few lives—if I had.

Always the hard way, Buonomo, always.

～

My first impulse was to run all the way back to my car, but then it hit me that I was about as far away from Long Beach as I could get and still see it with the naked eye—a good two hours of walking and driving, maybe more.

Now I knew why Helen had gone to Long Beach from Millie's—to hop a ferry—but the last one for the night had already sailed, so I would be flying myself over to the island.

It was well after sunset by the time I'd worked my way down the hills and onto the coast highway. At Santa Monica, I cut across on 66 and joined the 405 southbound toward Long Beach. There were a couple of wrecks. It was a slog.

I finally made the hangar about nine. The DC-3 wasn't scheduled out that night so I grabbed her. She was a beast but she'd do. The tanks were pretty low, too, but there was enough gas to get over and back. I didn't bother to phone anyone, either; I just wanted to get there. Took me less than ten minutes to get her in the air.

34

The sea was black, but the lights of Avalon were visible at altitude by the time I crossed the coast outbound. I dead-reckoned the heading toward Catalina's only airfield, the Airport in the Sky, which was in the center of the island and flung right on top of a 1,600 foot mountain. They'd chopped it out of the rock in 1940 to make a small private strip, but the government shut it down during the war and kept it that way for many years. It opened again as a civilian field in 1952—for those daring enough to land there.

The field was short, poorly lit, and sloped down dramatically on the south end. The winds usually came shrieking in off the open Pacific, skipping off the mountaintops in treacherous, swirling gusts. Landing short or long was a sure ticket to the undertaker as the terrain fell away precipitously at both ends of the runway. Even veteran pilots got their lunch handed to them at Catalina on occasion.

The moon was nearly full, so I was able to locate the field about fifteen miles out, but there was a west wind blowing, dropping in a marine layer as the island cooled in the night. Sea smoke was already slinking down the hills, obscuring visibility near the ground. And when it came, it came for the night. It looked like I'd get just one shot at a landing.

The field was legally closed after sunset, so I knew I couldn't get the wind report or the local altimeter setting. I'd been up all day, wasn't on top of my game, and didn't have an instrument approach available to guide me down. Other than that, it was a walk in the park.

I turned down all the cockpit lighting, slowed to 70 mph and lined up on 22. At three miles out I dropped the gear, flicked on the landing lights, and began a shallow descent toward the field.

The runway was just a smudge in the moonlight, a negative space outlined by fuzzy edge lights magnifying by degrees in my windscreen. It reminded me of those night carrier landings I'd made during the war—a tiny landing strip against a dark ocean, a one-way ride to Poseidon's palace waiting on all sides if you screwed up.

I squinted hard to focus on the numbers as I drew closer, blinking repeatedly as I bit off on false depth perception cues created by the fog. As I neared the field, the wind sheared away to port, striking the aircraft with several unpredictable gusts that rolled off Mt. Orizaba like rogue waves. I gripped the throttles tight, prepared to cob the engines up for a go-around at any time.

On short final, a wicked downdraft pushed the lumbering DC-3's nose below the end of the runway, down into the marine layer. Haze enveloped the aircraft, a thick mist wiping out my forward vision.

And just that fast I was in the hurt locker—below ground level at night and in the soup.

Instantly, I fed in back pressure on the control yoke and ramped up the power toward the firewall, pulling the aircraft out of the fog and back on glide path, squeezing the throttles hard enough to choke 'em.

It was a white-knuckler all the way.

The field boundary flashed beneath me, and I chopped the power as the aircraft entered ground effect and began to float. Then the wind swung full-around behind the tail, and the plane took off like the 20th Century Limited toward the far end of the short strip. For good measure, I sank into the scud layer again as I neared the ground. My brain said go-around, but my gut said wait one more second. My gut won, but it was the longest second of my life.

Just as I reached to push the power up to reject the landing, the plane shot through a break in the fog and I got a visual with the runway. I double-checked the throttles to idle and pushed down hard.

The wheels hit the pavement with a screech, and I jumped on the brakes. The big bird tried to skid on me twice, but I reeled her in both times by backing off the brake pressure as much as I dared.

When I got below 20 mph, I pushed in left rudder and led her off the runway. As the Gooney Bird sloughed through the turn, the end of the strip appeared in the mist barely a hundred feet ahead. The cliff edge lurked unseen just beyond.

I exhaled heavily and whistled low when I made the taxiway, calculating the seconds I'd had to spare on one hand and hoping that wasn't a harbinger of what lay in store for me on Catalina.

~

I parked the plane in front of the only hangar on the field, then took off my holster and stashed it and the .45 ACP under my seat. I couldn't take a gun into Avalon, not with Sheriff Ruggles on my ass every time I set foot on the island.

I stepped down to the ground, slid into my flying jacket, and made for the brown corrugated steel building thirty yards away, the peeling paint letters that spelled SAGEMAN AVIATION coming into view as I approached.

Clint Sageman took care of the field and maintained the motorcycle I kept on the island. It was a pretty good deal—Clint kept it gassed and running, and we both had something to knock around with on the wild switchback roads that encircled the island. It was a good bike, too, a war-surplus flathead Indian, with a whole stable of horsepower.

Nobody locks anything on Catalina so I called Clint's name a few times, then strolled right into the hangar. The bike was right where it always was, in the back corner, behind an unskinned Jenny that Clint had been refurbishing for about twenty years. I brushed off a few cobwebs and wheeled it out. After three kicks, the engine roared to life, found its timing, then settled into a throaty *ummmmm*.

I switched on the headlight, shifted into first, and goosed the throttle. The bike lunged forward, and I burned a quick figure eight on the tarmac to get the feel, then rolled her over the wooden bridge at the field boundary and set off down the mountain road, spinning around the bend toward Avalon.

Catalina's roads are unlit and feature the same widow-making drop-offs as the airport. I checked my watch and saw that I wouldn't have to risk my neck like I did on landing to make the ten miles to my destination by closing time.

The salt air was brisk as I rode. I flipped the collar of my jacket up and gave the zipper a quick yank, then lowered my head and set my chin for the ride ahead.

The road was empty but familiar, and a comforting feeling settled in me as I zigzagged down the hills. I recalled the many nights Helen and I had ridden this same motorcycle along this darkened highway, her hair blowing wildly in the wind.

I cracked open the throttle subconsciously and leaned into the turns, the bike picking up speed. I could almost feel her holding on to me the way she used to when there was nothing but us, the moon, and the muffled exhaust of the Indian on this winding asphalt strip far above the sea.

35

It was past ten when I pulled into Avalon. Most of the bars were closing due to the hour and time of year, but a few stalwarts manned the stools at scattered saloons along Crescent. Small clusters of people were wandering the streets as the night wound down, their laughter blurring with jukebox music as I zoomed by. They were in search of any open gin joint, but I had just one in mind—Barbi's.

I made a right on Catalina Avenue and pulled up several buildings in on the left side. The lights were still on, as I knew they'd be. I parked the motorcycle and headed toward the entrance, Barbi's voice audible long before I reached the door, telling some rummy to shut up and pay his tab.

Barbi Bettendorf had been on Catalina as long as anyone could recall. She'd been running her bar since she won it in a poker game back in '46. She kept late hours and mixed company, chain-smoked her Viceroys, and had been arrested at least once, on a charge of indecent exposure. She swore better than any sailor and didn't shy away from their brawls, the tattoo bearing her first husband's name flashing through the air on her taut right bicep as she flailed away with an old Shore Patrol nightstick.

Four Stack Jack had been her only true love, but he went down on the *Reuben James* back in '41. There was talk that Barbi had once slugged a tourist who said that our own navy—and not a German sub—torpedoed the destroyer.

She had the cut of a warship herself, sporting a body that could have sunk the *Bismarck* and looks that had been hot enough to melt steel about the last time the Cubs won the pennant. The years and the booze had taken their toll, but even today, that face could still put a solid hurt on better grades of tin. Barbi was no Emily Post girl, but everyone on the island loved her, and if anybody knew anything, or anyone, on the island, she did.

I wanted to slip in quietly and ask her if she knew anything about Helen's whereabouts. That plan got as far as the threshold.

As I stepped into the pub, she shouted out from behind the bar, "Joe Bones, how in the hell are you, honey? Come over here and give Barbi a kiss."

Every face in the joint looked over at me. Quietly was no longer an option.

A whiskey shot hit the bar before I reached the rail. Barbi leaned over and hugged me until I thought my ribs were going to break. As she did, she whispered, "Let's talk . . . five minutes," into my ear.

I smiled in acknowledgment and picked up my shot glass.

Barbi made the usual sailor's toast: "To our wives and our lovers," she said, "may they never meet!" following with a smoker's guffaw that could have doubled as a foghorn.

I drank the shot, caught the bottle of Anchor Steam she threw at me, then walked toward the open shutters at the front of the bar. I put the beer down to let the foam subside, lit a smoke, and leaned against the corner door post, staring out into the darkened streets of Avalon.

Two cats were reenacting the Battle of Guadalcanal in the adjacent alley, their growls and shrieks gouging pieces out of the still night air.

When the cigarette was gone, I stubbed it out and took a pull of the Anchor Steam.

"That fucking Tommy," Barbi said as she walked up behind me. "He's clawed up every other cat on the island. Christ, he's tougher than Patton! Hey . . . did I ever tell you about the time the general and I—"

"Yeah, honey, you did." I smiled at her, did a double swivel of my head out of habit, then said under my breath, "Barbi, I'm looking for Helen—my Helen. Can you help?"

"Angel Eyes? Some hot number arrived in sunglasses yesterday morning. Dark hair, great gams. Tits like *this*," she said, holding her hands out to make the point.

"Sounds about right," I said, smiling in recollection. "Face?"

"Hard to tell under the sunglasses. She did seem familiar but that dish looked a little too spicy to be from the Midwest. Tell you one thing, that gal was spooked. That was *Helen*?"

Relief flooded through me. I was sure it was.

"I don't know, sweetie, but I hope so."

"You hitting that again, Sky King?"

"Honey, this is serious."

"Yeah, I can tell. You gonna start all that 'I Cover the Waterfront' shit again? What goes, Joe?"

"I don't know, Barbi, but it's bad and getting worse. I've got to find her—she's in trouble."

She raised an eyebrow. "So you *are* hitting that again. Thought so. Doc Walling's still—"

I grabbed her hand. "Not that kind of trouble. Real trouble. Bad guys, guns."

She gave me a knowing smile, intoning, "Ahhh. *Buonomo* trouble—that checks. One of my spies told me someone was asking about you today down at the Marlin Club. That's what I wanted to tell you."

"You don't say? Friend or foe?"

"Dunno. About forty, stocky, loud Hawaiian shirt. East Coast accent. Some kind of William Bendix wannabe, God help him. Didn't sound like he was one of your closest friends."

This didn't come as a big surprise but was disturbing just the same. Somewhere a faint memory of a guy like that struggled to surface in the black pool of my brain, then drowned.

I managed a profound, "Hmmmm," took another swig of the beer.

She shrugged, turned her palms up. "That's all I got on him."

"Let's go back to the dish. Any idea where she's staying?"

"She got off the ferry alone and sashayed out of sight. Not many places to hide that body on Catalina, though. You try the Wizard?"

"No, you're always my first stop. I'll head over there next. Think he's in?"

She stared at me as if I were a five-year-old.

"He's been in for fifty years, Joe. He spends all his time in that castle making that crazy goddamn artwork. Yeah, I think he's in."

I wiped my mouth, parked the beer bottle. "Okay, I'm off. I'll be staying at Clint's tonight. You let me know the second you see her—and don't let her move an inch if you do."

"Okay, hon."

I had a flash of inspiration. "They still have a late feature at the Avalon?"

"Think so. Nine thirty. Be over soon."

"What's playing?"

She gave me a look. "Who am I, the *L.A. Times*?"

I shrugged. "Just a thought. Thanks, baby." I started to leave, then paused. "Say . . . Barbi?"

"Yeah?"

"I love you."

I grabbed her cheeks and planted one on her. She actually blushed. I'd never seen that before.

"Get outta here, you crazy guinea," she said, swatting my arm.

I stepped outside toward the motorcycle, feeling pretty good about things on Catalina so far.

I made maybe three steps before it all went into the spittoon.

36

The saloon shutters were still swinging when a voice behind me boomed out, "Hold it right there, Buonomo!"

I didn't have to turn around. It was Sheriff Ruggles.

There was no such thing as a good time for running into him, but this was easily a personal worst.

I kept my hands down at my sides as I turned to face him.

"Sheriff," I said through gritted teeth, nodding slowly.

"Rink" Ruggles stared at me, but he did not smile. Instead, he spit a little tobacco juice into the street, wiped his mouth with the back of his hand, and puffed out his barrel chest, marking me with the small dark eyes commonly seen on raccoons.

He was wearing his trademark flannel shirt and yellow-striped ranger pants. Those pants were fully bloused and tucked smartly into his highly polished cowboy boots, one of which was propped up on a bench, his crossed hands planted on the raised knee above it. He had a look of restrained malice on his face, and I could tell that he was just dying for me to make some kind of move, any move.

We were five hundred miles from Tombstone, but there was little doubt that Hubert "Rink" Ruggles fancied himself the toughest sheriff in the territory, a territory that consisted solely of Avalon, winter population one eighty, and the village of Two Harbors at the far end of the island, numbering between seven and thirty, depending on how many boats were tied up that night at the marina.

Rink had been on me for years, ever since a barroom brawl got a little out of hand at Barbi's. He regarded me as an undesirable "provac-a-teer," although I'd always suspected he was jealous of my war record since he'd spent his time as a machinist's mate, third class, repairing motor launches in San Diego.

He told it differently, though, painting himself as a member of the 1st Marines when they stormed Peleliu. I'd lost too many good friends in the war to suffer through a bullshit artist glomming on to the suffering of the men who died on that miserable rock. I knew the truth about Rink—and he knew I knew.

We had an uneasy truce wherein he hassled me only so much as he needed to look tough and I didn't tell anyone on Catalina what a complete fraud he was. Something in his face told me that tonight he felt like pushing the ball across the fifty-yard line.

He stepped toward me, a smirk bending the corners of his lips.

"I see you're about to get on that motorcycle of yours after leaving a drinking emporium," he said, grandstanding loudly enough for anyone on the street to hear. "The citizens of Avalon expect me to keep their streets clear of drunken yaa-hoos. You want to play Marlon Brando, son, you'd best do it over in that cesspool they call the City of the Angels."

I just didn't have the time or the inclination.

"Sheriff," I said without emotion, "how about you and I go sit down there in Barbi's with those two merchant marines drinking cheap whiskey. I know you know Jimmy in there—the guy who lost an arm when his freighter was sunk in the Formosa Strait. Let's have a drink with them and discuss the attack you led on Japan—from a whorehouse in the Gaslamp District. What say, Hubert, shall we?"

He stiffened visibly, then his face fractured into a scowl. He leaned in close enough that I could smell the Brylcreem. "Listen, Buonomo, you'd be wise to fly on offa my island while I'm still smilin'."

"You're not smiling, Sheriff."

He reddened.

"I'm gonna be watching you. I'm up for reelection in a couple of weeks and I'm not going to have any hooligans like you running around town makin' me look impotent."

I just smiled at that one.

"If you're still here tomorrow," he sneered, "you're going back in the can."

"Charges to be determined?"

"You're goddamn right. I got enough on you right now to hold you for a week. Consorting with coloreds, mafi-atin' with that Sinatra fella, busting air traffic regulations—"

"Air traffic regulations? Aren't you a little out of your territory, Rink?" I asked, grinning. "And, by the way," I continued, waving my arm toward the waterfront fifty yards away, "doesn't your 'territory' pretty much end at those floaty things at the beach there?"

There was a little growling noise in his throat, and I saw his fists tighten at his sides. Then he puffed up his chest again and planted his hands on his hips, above where his riding gloves stuck out of his pockets.

"Don't push it, tough guy. Now get out of my sight and remember what I told you—any trouble whatsoever and you're going down."

I matched his stare for several seconds, then climbed onto the motorcycle and cranked her over.

Somewhere in Hollywood, a studio was missing a cardboard sheriff.

37

The Wizard lived up a dark road at the back edge of Avalon. Children said that he'd been there since the island rose out of the sea, maybe longer. Truth was, he was an artist named Wes who had come to Avalon around 1920. His actual age was a mystery, but he was eighty if he was a day, and he had the history of the world in his eyes. If he had a last name, I didn't know it.

Wes's home wasn't so much a house as a series of open terraces strewn across a high ridge, each one a work platform for one of his different artistic talents. From the road, it resembled a series of fortress-like bulwarks sloping down the rock outcropping. The lighting was by torch or oil lamp, and the plumbing was outdoors, fed by a trickling creek that ran down the hill and meandered through the ramparts. I suppose he had a bed somewhere, but I'd never seen him sleep.

Of all the very unusual people I'd encountered in my travels, Wes was the most arcane—and kindest—with a long-standing reputation for taking in society's flotsam and jetsam. Helen didn't know him as well as I did, but I guessed that she might seek him out for shelter.

After I put the sheriff behind me, I cut down Tremont, made a left on Avalon Canyon, and drove out past the ball field, out toward

Divide. Small piles of leaves kicked up as I whooshed by the corners, fluttering crookedly through the air around me.

Nearing Wes's place, I ran up the speed, cut the motor, and let the bike coast the last two hundred yards until the incline of the hill slowed it. I parked on the side of the road well short of Wes's property, scanning the wooded hillside while my eyes adjusted to the dark. Out of habit, I patted my chest with my left hand to confirm that my weapon was secure, which it was—under my seat on the floor of the DC-3. I gave that some brief consideration, then pressed on.

Ordinarily I wouldn't have been so cautious, but the Bendix thing didn't play well. I wasn't even sure that Helen would be there—let alone any heavies—but it wouldn't hurt if I surprised anyone.

I crept up toward Wes's, avoiding as many of the curled leaves under my feet as I could. A few torches glowed at the higher levels, but I couldn't see anyone on the decks. The gate was unlocked, as always, so I raised the latch and slipped in.

The staircase to the second level was at the far end of a stone walkway. I took a few steps toward it, then stopped cold at the sight of a pair of luminous green eyes blazing in the reflected light.

I squinted to focus on them, then recoiled when I realized they were not human, not by a long shot. I reached again for the weapon that I wasn't wearing, then just stood in place while trying to determine what I was up against.

A broad smile broke across my face when I realized it was Mars, a black cat that Wes kept as a talisman, one of seven or eight on the property. I rubbed his chin a little and then moved on toward the staircase ahead.

The hand-hewn oak steps were well worn, each one emitting a small creak as I took them. Swinging my eyes back and forth, I crept upward, stopping at the top step to inspect the second level.

Nothing moved, the only light the flickering of a torch against the rock wall. I called Wes's name a couple of times, but there was no reply.

The stillness wasn't unusual as I often found him quietly immersed in his work in some recessed nook of the property. Peering into the shaded corners, I strode slowly across the wooden decking, then wound my way up the iron spiral staircase to the third floor. Again, I paused at the top to look around. This time it seemed like I was in luck.

At the far end of the level a man was bent over a stone brazier, poking at the coals with a thick iron rod. Wes was a metalsmith, of course, and I smiled in relaxation at the sight. I ambled over toward the brazier, casually regarding the dozens of his Gothic candelabra, weather vanes, and lanterns that cluttered the workspace.

He was busily at work as I approached, his back to me.

"Hello, Wes," I called out. "It's me, Joe."

He turned toward me then, a black welder's mask pulled low over his face, a slate-gray smock shrouding his body. He was holding the long, hooked poker down by his waist, its end shimmering white hot in the night.

I hadn't seen Wes in quite a while, but he looked larger than I was expecting, even with the gear on. He stepped toward me, making no attempt to lift his mask. A very bad feeling came over me as he approached.

"Wes?" I asked, stepping backward.

Wordlessly, the faceless man drew back the rod in his hand, raising it over his head.

Then he lunged toward me.

I turned to duck away—and banged into a candelabrum. My feet got crossed and I tripped, crashing hard onto the metal-plated wooden timbers, the heavy iron candlestick holder thudding down a second later, just inches away.

He was on me in a second, brandishing the superheated poker over his head, waves of heat dancing off the tip. He held it there for a split second, then slashed down with a savage thrust.

I grabbed the candelabrum with both hands. It was heavy as hell, but my adrenaline was locked on max. Rolling flat onto my back, I heaved the pole up and over my chest.

The poker came down an instant later, pranging heavily off the candleholder with a ringing metallic clang, flaming sparks erupting from its end. The shock wave coursed through the bar, the reverberations numbing my hands as falling metal flakes bit my cheeks.

Black Mask dropped down on top of me, slamming a knee into my thigh. Grabbing the candelabrum with one hand, he yanked it down toward my stomach, leaving my face unprotected.

He drew back his other arm, then came spearing down with the poker, ramming it toward my throat.

Shifting my weight, I slid away and shoved the candlestick one-handed across my chest, just barely deflecting the poker as Black Mask drove it home. It slammed into the steel plate next to my face, shrieking with resistance as it skidded forward several inches amid another shower of sparks.

Its awful heat radiated out next to me as the man in the mask struggled to rake it across my face while I fought against it with the candelabrum.

Black Mask had me by weight, weapon, and position. I was in a terrible spot, but I still had physics on my side. When he brought both of his hands to his weapon to outmuscle me, he gave me an opening—and I took it.

I swung my free leg up and buried my knee in his ribs, then nailed him in the side of the head with a forearm shiver, pushing the metal mask sideways across his face.

The blows were just enough to knock him off balance. As he fell off to one side I rolled into him, then spun onto all fours, bearing down on him with my shoulder, keeping him on the defensive.

Then I brought my fists together and hammered them down on the back of his neck. He let out a convulsive *ooof*, the poker slipping from his grasp and falling underneath him as he collapsed onto one forearm.

I fell on him for all I was worth. He was strong, but I had him now. Forcing all my weight on him, I pushed him toward the floor, ratcheting him down by degrees over the burning iron.

Closer and closer he went, thrashing like a roped longhorn.

I could smell the asbestos-lined smock as it began to smolder, hear the fear in him as he struggled in desperation.

He let out a grunt, then a moan, and finally a full-fledged scream as the poker began digging in, incinerating the flesh on his convulsing chest.

I held him there a second, then leaped up, crouching above him as he rolled writhing onto his back, clutching at the hook shape branded into his chest and grimacing in agony.

I kicked the poker away, then grabbed one of Wes's lanterns and flung it down hard on his masked face.

I thought that would finish him, but by the time I had snatched up the candelabrum again he was staggering to his feet. He was a bull, that guy.

He steadied himself, then chucked the mask off and glanced at the smoldering wound, rage contorting his features.

But I could still recognize him as the guy from the Sapphire Room on Sunday night—had to be the Bendix dupe Barbi had mentioned.

I didn't waste a second.

Swinging the metal stand up like a lance, I charged into him, jamming the business end of the candelabrum into his breadbasket and shoving him backward, my feet pumping like pistons as I drove him toward the low log railing at the edge of the work area.

The big man staggered into the rail, grabbed emptily for the last post, then tumbled over the top, flailing away as he fell from the platform down into the pine trees below. A heavy crashing, thrashing, breaking sound rippled through the air as he plunged through the branches. There was a dull thump when he hit the needle-carpeted forest floor below, followed by a grating clang as I dropped the candelabrum on the plating. Then it was tomb quiet.

I rushed to the rail's edge and peered down through the darkness. His still form was just barely visible below, but he wasn't moving.

Two thoughts immediately rose in my brain. The first was that I needed to find out what had happened to Wes, and the second was that I had better damn well tie up that wild animal before he got loose again.

Wes was going to have to wait.

I took a running step as I turned to hit the staircase—and looked straight into the reddest eyes I'd ever seen.

38

A man in a flowing white robe was standing in front of me on the platform, holding a broken lantern in weathered hands.

His long gray hair fell in tangles about his sloped shoulders, half-closed eyes lined with red spiderwebs peeking out from behind. Beneath those eyes, a pair of chipped half-moon glasses rested upon a short, hooked nose, and beneath that, a benign smile creased the wrinkled corners of his dark, leathery lips. He might have passed for King Lear on the heath, except for the scent of marijuana that permeated the air around him.

He was old—and he was hopped—but mostly he was old.

"Hello, and peace to you, my friend," he said as if he were speaking to a child.

"Wes," I blurted out, "am I happy to see you. Are you all right?"

"And I you. I'm fine, quite fine. I've just been lying down in back meditating."

"That what they're calling it these days?"

He smiled. "Yes. I had some amazing visions."

"Yeah, me too—a mad ironworker."

I glanced behind me then, leaning back down over the rail. Bendix was still laid out below like a palooka at a Friday night smoker. If he wasn't dead, he was out cold. I reached down to pick up the candelabrum, hoisted it back upright.

"I heard some banging sounds out here, Joe. Have you been testing out your artistic abilities at the forge with that big fellow? Maybe we could all make something together."

"That's not gonna happen."

"Why not? Did your friend fly off already?"

"Oh, he flew all right—like Icarus."

His face went perfectly blank.

"Wes," I said, jabbing my thumb toward the railing, "that man is a mobster. I just shoved him off your terrace. We've gotta talk—right now."

"Oh my. Let's sit then and have some tea. It's chamomile, very calming."

I stole a nervous look toward Bendix again, decided he would keep, and then followed Wes across the decking to a covered alcove at the back corner of the terrace.

I grabbed a seat near the rail on one of the heavy wooden benches where I'd passed many a night. Wes picked up a kettle from the fire, poured two cups of tea, and set them on the table. Then he sat down across from me and removed his glasses. I drew a bead on those ancient eyes in the wavering light.

"I've come here for Helen," I said. "Have you seen her? It's vital that I find her."

Wes sipped his tea, then lit a hand-rolled cigarette with a wooden match. He inhaled deeply, holding the smoke in a good ten seconds before purging it through his nose. The smell was unmistakable.

"Joe," he began paternally, "Helen came here seeking sanctuary. She asked me not to tell a living soul she was here—except you."

That was the best thing I'd heard in three days. Now I knew she was near.

"Is she still here?"

"Not at this moment. Would you like to wait for her to come back?" He waved the cigarette toward me. "Here, I've got some boffo Mary Jane. We could meditate together."

The thought of waiting there, drifting on reefer clouds and contemplating eternity while some thugs were trying to take Helen to it was a bit much. I reached across the table, grabbed both his shoulders, and shook him.

"This is very serious business—Helen's life is in danger. That big guy's not an autograph hound—he's a killer! I've got to know where she is. Please!"

"But I can't tell you where she is."

"Why not?"

"Because I don't know," he said, giggling just a little. He was totally stoned.

"*Madonn'!*" I exclaimed, shaking my hands in frustration. "When did you last see her?"

"Oh . . . hours ago, I guess."

"Did she say where she was going?"

He shook his head. "Maybe she took the ferry, maybe she'll return. She didn't say."

"Look, I've got to find her before anyone else does. Do you have any idea where she might have gone if she's still on the island?"

"No, I'm only the shepherd here at my home. I don't follow the flock when they roam."

I thumped my fist on the table. "Shit, Wes!"

"Please calm yourself, my friend. Clear your mind, then search within. Maybe you know where she is—the connection between you two is unnaturally strong. Look inside yourself, my friend, you've come this far."

Ordinarily, it might have all been amusing. But in the last thirty hours I'd been through a lifetime of misery. It was the wrong week for deciphering the psychobabble of Catalina's own Sal Paradise.

"Joe," Wes said, his voice floating like incense through the air, "Helen needs you. Go to her. Don't think—follow your heart."

I looked straight at him, nodding but saying nothing. I wasn't going to get anything more of use from him. The more he smoked, the more he summoned Wes the Mystic. He sat there, beaming at me like the Buddha, then closed his eyes and folded his hands on top of each other across his chest.

I stood up. "Thanks, Wes. I gotta go. Sorry about the lantern."

"Follow your heart," he repeated as I walked away, the words echoing in my ears.

It was starting to sound like good advice—but I'd probably been sitting too close to the ashtray.

39

On the way down I thought about Bendix lying there in the woods. Doubling my pace, I bolted down the stairs, grabbing one of Wes's big wooden walking sticks on the first level before I shot through the gate. If the big guy put up any more of a fight, I'd crown him once and for all.

I hustled around the side of the property and made a beeline for the pine tree stand, approaching Bendix with the stick cocked above my head.

Only he wasn't there anymore.

I stared wide-eyed into the dark a good three seconds, then shifted into reaction mode. Ducking my head, I dropped to one knee and swung the stick full force—into nothing. Then I cut it back the other way, whiffing again like the mighty Kluszewski.

Leaping up, I flattened myself against a tree, then spun my head around several times, certain that I'd pick up that wounded ox as he lumbered through the forest. I watched and listened for better than a minute, but he was gone.

I searched the whole area twice without seeing any sign of him. I didn't think he would return, but I couldn't take any chances, especially since Wes didn't have a phone. For all I knew, Bendix was after me, not Helen, but I couldn't risk that either. If she was still on the island, I had to go find her before he did.

I went back to my bike, kick-started it, and spun a quick one eighty in the road. I made the turn on Avalon Canyon and headed back toward town, stopping at the traffic circle at Tremont while I tried to decide whether to ride into the hills or work my way back through the streets.

A flash of movement from the park caught my eye. I thought it might be a man, lurking back in the tree line. When I turned my head, he was gone—if he'd been there at all. Probably just a deer or a dog. I had that Bendix guy on the brain too much. He was probably curled up in the woods somewhere nursing a terrible burn and one hell of a splitting headache.

I sat there another moment, staring at nothing. Then I spied the small movie marquee for the Avalon Theatre in the middle of the traffic circle. At first it didn't register. Then it clicked: the poster was for an old Orson Welles/Rita Hayworth flick. A rerun, but a nice taut mystery—exactly the kind of movie that would pique Helen's interest.

"Why not?" I asked.

The theater was a three-minute ride away, and I had nothing to lose by going by. It was late, so I gave the shifter a kick and headed for the waterfront.

"*The Lady from Shanghai*," I mused. I'd seen it years ago. Fell asleep in the middle, never did find out how it ended.

40

The Avalon Theatre was located in the base of the Casino Building, an immense Venetian palace of a dance hall that old man Wrigley had built back in the '20s for two million bucks.

Built on a spit of land at the northwest edge of town, the Casino abutted a rounded stone jetty that doubled as a seawall for Avalon's small harbor. The seven-story-high dance hall featured a stunning ballroom on the top floor encircled by a massive covered terrace. Both the Casino and the theater were finished in an extravagant Moorish style, heavy on dark woods and richly colored friezes. Each could hold at least a thousand people at any given time.

It was a hell of an impressive work. Like the pyramids, no one really knew why it existed but everyone was glad it did. Chewing gum—who knew?

Helen and I had enjoyed many hours in the Casino together. A tingling of anticipation stirred in me as I rounded the corner on Crescent and caught my first glimpse of it. I gunned the throttle, whipping through the turn as the brightly lit edifice rose out of the night sky before me.

I passed several couples walking back from the theater as I rode but didn't see a soul after the Yacht Club. The movie had apparently been over for some time.

Nearing the end of Via Casino, I slowed, then stopped underneath the stand of palm trees that fronted the theater. The Casino's upturned floodlights bathed the building in yellow light, but the high balcony and the massive buttresses that supported it were lost in deep shadows fifty feet above the ground.

I stood and took a few steps toward the theater, then paused, listening for voices or any footfall. Other than the small waves lapping the beach, all was still.

Moving slowly, I walked toward the darkened box office, my steps echoing in the damp air of the high vaulted chamber as I neared.

Four twelve-foot-high sets of glass and walnut doors flanked either side of the ornate aluminum ticket window. Beyond them, stone hallways ran off in opposite directions, disappearing into dark corners.

I stepped into the center of the chamber, listening, watching, the decorative glass chandeliers above yielding just enough light for me to see into the empty corridors. I tugged on one of the theater doors but it was locked. They all were. Then I leaned up close to one, staring beyond my reflection into the foyer. Could have been a funeral parlor as dead still and quiet as it was.

Stepping back, I gazed up at the beautiful nautical murals painted on the chamber walls above me. Flying fish, crabs, and seahorses frolicked in muted colors beneath fading waves. In the central panel, a forlorn mermaid stared longingly out at the world with the sad eyes of one who'd seen too much. I wondered if she'd witnessed the things I had.

I walked away from the theater, across the jetty, surveying the town. The beach and the marina were quiet, and all the houses on the hills that ringed Avalon were dark. A single light shone on the water in the distance from the back of the Tuna Club, but that was probably just some old fishing buddies burning the midnight oil.

Nearby, an eighty-foot schooner bobbed at anchor, the stern lantern swinging back and forth rhythmically with the waves. As the faint yellow light seesawed across the transom, I made out the name *Kingfisher* in worn letters. It seemed like it should mean something to me, but it didn't tumble.

As I stood there, a feeling came over me—a tingling of recognition from old memories—and I began to gravitate toward the end of the jetty. I suppose I planned to circle around the building, or maybe just stare off into the night from water's edge and look for that mermaid—I don't know—I was feeling more than thinking at that moment.

As I walked, I peered into the many arched recesses that encircled the base of the Casino. They were steeped in shadows, but all appeared empty. Rounding the midpoint of the walkway I stopped, looking out toward the dark water. In the distance, the Chimes Tower sounded on the hills, then fell silent.

The sea breeze gave off a faint chill that clung to my face. Moonlight fell in shards through ragged clouds and bounced off the undulating water, the silver-blue haze washing out all color. A single long shadow from a gas lamp darted across the concrete and ran up the side of the Casino. I traced its path with my eyes up the wall to the balcony above that loomed over me, quiet and austere. There was no light, no sound other than the water.

I pictured Helen standing high above on the parapet, laughing and glowing as we took five from dancing, her arms around my waist. I stood there a long time with her image in my mind. It hadn't been so long ago.

The acrid smell of a cigarette cut the cool air. Shaking from my daze, I turned my head to find the source. As I did, a woman spoke.

"Hello, Joe," she said in a velvet tone as she stepped out of a darkened archway into the bluish light.

I just stared at her. I couldn't do anything else—it just didn't seem real.

She looked at me for what felt like minutes, her lips trembling.

"Helen," I said finally, then broke forward, flinging my arms wide to embrace her.

41

I held her for ages—not daring to let go—running my hands through her hair, then caressing her cheeks, just reveling in the feeling of her. She looked up at me, and I kissed her lightly on the forehead. A heartbeat later we were locked in a passionate kiss—I just couldn't stop myself. Then I drew her close, fading back into the archway, blending with the shadows, our lips enmeshed.

My brain kept trying to make sense of it all, but the rest of me didn't care. Everything else in the last three days had been disturbing, painful, or both, but this was wonderful. I wanted it to continue, I wanted to let go, I wanted to have her—and I didn't give a damn where we were.

And yet.

And yet, I had to know.

Nudging my head to one side, I pressed my lips to her cheek, then opened my eyes. Her breath was hot on my neck as she kissed it. I could feel her heart pounding in her chest, thrumming against my own, the smell of citrus and sandalwood suffusing the damp air around us.

I stood there silently, catching my breath, hating myself for what I was about to do.

"Helen . . ."

"Let it wait," she implored, her voice quiet, desperate. "Kiss me."

I hesitated.

"Joe, make love to me. I need you," she whispered, running her hands up my chest to my shoulders, pulling me close.

"Baby," I said, "I want you. I want you like nothing I've ever wanted in this life before . . . but I've got to know what happened and why you're here. And I've got to know right now."

"Not now. Please."

I put my hands on her cheeks and raised that fabulous face up toward mine. I kissed her again, looked directly into her smoldering eyes. "Helen . . . people are dead; I almost joined them three times, and Frank Sinatra—your boyfriend—is beside himself with worry about you. What in the hell is going on, baby?"

That did it. The spell was broken.

She sighed deeply, eyes and arms dropping in resignation. We stood there in the shadows for the longest time, our exhalations the only sound in the dank chamber as the heat slowly left our bodies.

Finally, she looked up, her eyes laced with sadness. "I never meant for any of this to happen."

42

I walked toward the edge of the jetty, tugging Helen's hand as she trudged behind me like a kid on the first day of school. We sat down on top of the crumbling concrete that covered the wall, overlooking the water that slapped off the rocks below.

I surveyed the Casino, the jetty, and then the shore in both directions, searching for any sign of anyone, anyone at all.

When I was sure we were alone, I turned to Helen and said, "Give. All of it."

"God, where do I begin?"

"Try the beginning."

She started to speak, then paused and pulled the gold case out of her purse, extracting a thin cigarette and holding it out with a shaking hand. I lit it for her and she took a deep drag, holding it in.

She drifted briefly into thought, arrived at some decision, and then exhaled the smoke through her nose.

"I made a film," she said quietly.

"Must be a smash. People all over Los Angeles are dying to see it."

"Don't do that to me. Not now." Her voice was steel hard.

"Well, what kind of film is this, hon, some top-secret Hollywood thing?"

She waved her hand. "No. It's a burlesque film—plain and sleazy."

"You?"

"Yes. It's not *that* kind of film, though, just something we made at Frank's."

"*Frank's?*" I could feel my eyes enlarging as I spoke.

"Slow down, sailor. Frank was having a party in the desert. He likes to film those events—he's into Super 8 movies, you know. Everybody got pretty bombed, and Lana and I started to do a burlesque dance for Frank. Just for laughs."

"Lana?"

"Lana Turner. Not exactly a Vassar girl, you know."

"No. More of a Varga girl."

She made a face. "Anyhow, we got a little carried away and stripped naked and danced with Frank and Peter Lawford. That's all."

A pair of headlights popped up around the far corner on St. Catherine's Way, wending their way down the coastal road. I marked them as they drifted toward us, my natural wariness rising.

"Helen, if that's all, why is so much unchecked mayhem erupting around it?"

"Betty . . ."

"She's dead, you know."

She cringed slightly but nodded her head. "Yes, I know. I saw it in the paper," she said, her eyes glossing up.

"Did you know that she was involved with Carmine Ratello?"

"Yes."

"And that he was something of a mob meteor?"

Pause. "I knew he was trouble, if that's what you mean."

I leaned in. "Did you know she was on the junk?"

Here her eyes flashed genuine surprise. "No, I didn't know that."

The oncoming car made the bend at Descanso Beach. We were almost invisible in the dark, but I leaned over, reducing our exposure to a sliver. I looked up at Helen's face as I moved toward her. It was seamed with worry.

Tumblers began falling into place for me then, taking me to conclusions I didn't want to make.

"Honey, did you tell Betty about this film at any time?"

"Umm, yes. We are—were—good girlfriends. She's the one who told me I should get it from Frank to protect myself."

"Protect yourself?"

"A lot of careers have been ruined by that sort of stuff, you know."

The car passed behind the casino, out of sight.

"But Frank would never—"

Then it hit me, my jaw dropping open as I made the connection. "Baby, you didn't take that film without telling Frank, did you?"

She lidded her eyes, put on a *kid who broke the lamp* look. "The other day. Just before we met you at the airport. I slipped into the library while Frank was outside."

She bit her lip when she finished speaking. That was a nice touch.

I shook my head in disbelief. "Oh, Christ. Let me guess, Ratello's behind this. He wants to shake down Frank and Lana."

Beyond the Casino, I picked up the car moving down the road. It was white, with some kind of markings on the door. There were only a few dozen cars on the whole island, and just one with markings on the door—Rink's.

A bright red blur bloomed on the back of the car then as the driver hit the brakes.

"Shit!"

Helen looked at me, alarm flooding her face. "What is it?"

"The sheriff. Must've seen my motorcycle. He's busting my nuts as usual."

The car was flying backward now. It came to a halt with a screech just out of sight in front of the Casino. A door banged shut a moment later.

"Come on," I said, lifting her up. "He's dying to toss me in the can. There's at least one bad guy on this island looking for you, and I can't protect you if Ruggles locks me up. We've got to get off this rock."

We tiptoed across the jetty, pressing up against the stone side of the building. The sound of boots clacking on the concrete rang out around the corner, still a ways off. Rink always was a study in the obvious.

Helen clutched at my arm, whispered, "What are we going to do?"

"I've got my plane at the airport. We just have to slip ol' Sherlock here and we can split."

She beamed at me then. "The Electra? The one we took the other day?"

"No, the DC-3." I wrinkled my mouth in curiosity. "What does it matter? Neither one has a first-class section."

The footfall came clearer. I put my hand up to silence her before she could respond. Rink was coming up the near side, maybe halfway around already.

I turned to Helen, pointing aggressively with two fingers toward the far edge of the building. "Step lightly," I whispered.

Then we snuck away in the dark, holding hands as we ran like young lovers in Dutch.

43

We made the bike unseen. I rolled it up the hill, hustled it down the road a bit, then cranked her up. Helen jumped on back and we were gone—scot-free.

Only I didn't want to get completely away. Rink was just cagey enough that he'd probably head straight up the hill to the airport, blocking my access to the DC-3. I had to get him to chase me, and then shake him. So I headed into Avalon, laying on the throttle and making a racket like hell's bells ringing out as I tore down the street.

I blew through downtown and swooshed around the bend at Wrigley, cutting back down through the alley behind Barbi's, almost flattening a yowling Tommy as we zipped through the narrow passageway. The whole thing was kind of fun, almost exhilarating, and I'm pretty sure I heard Helen giggling at least once as I ground through the gears.

I jerked the bike to a halt behind the Marlin Club. While we waited, I wrapped my leather jacket around Helen. It wasn't quite the Hollywood style, but I thought she looked terrific.

When Rink's car buzzed by on Crescent doing fifty the opposite way, I knew we had him beat. I took one more alley and launched for the airport.

We cleared town in ninety seconds, then began scaling Chimes Tower Road, the Indian's exhaust backfiring once as we roared up the steep grade. Helen shimmied down low against me as we accelerated, her arms locked tight around my waist.

Up and up we went. At each hairpin curve I glanced back, catching fragmented glimpses of her face. A hint of a smile through sienna lips, a gleam of light in electric eyes, ribbons of chestnut hair flowing in the air in wild tangles.

I started to get that feeling again.

The wind picked up steadily as we climbed, and Helen kept scrunching down closer to me to ward off the chill. You couldn't have gotten an atomic particle between us at that point. Then she leaned forward suddenly and bit my ear—I felt that one way down inside.

I suppose I was cold, but I couldn't tell. Like I would have said anything to break that rhythm, anyway. There we were, back on the Indian, running free under the night sky above the sea. Just like old times on Catalina—if you didn't count the fact that she was my buddy's girl now and bodies were piling up all around me again.

153

44

Halfway to the airport I saw the headlights, maybe a mile and a half back, winding up the S-curves behind us. I was well ahead, but I put on some speed just in case.

We rolled through several tight switchbacks with no further sign of the lights for several minutes. I started to ride a little easier and reached down and patted Helen's hand.

Then the lights shot out of the black, maybe a mile back and coming on quick. The car was speeding, going way too fast for the conditions. A lifer like Ruggles would know the roads well enough to go that fast at night and he was just crazy enough to do it. Ten to one it was him.

I gunned the engine and opened her up as fast as I dared.

"Aren't we going a little fast, Joe?" Helen shouted out, a shrill edge sharpening her voice.

I didn't want to worry her, but I had no choice. I jerked my thumb behind me and yelled, "It's Ruggles. He's following us."

It went like that, minute after minute. The bike was quicker, but if I missed a turn we'd crack up, so I could only go so fast, especially with a rider. The driver of the car didn't seem to care, barreling forward and narrowing the gap turn by turn.

My pistol was still under the airplane seat if it came to that, but I had no desire to engage Ruggles in a gunfight. He might have been a nutcase, but he was still the law. I'd wind up shot or in jail if it came down to gunplay and I couldn't afford either.

After a gut-churning five minutes, the airport emerged just ahead, the flash of the beacon skipping off the low cloud bases and radiating into the night, backlighting Clint's hangar and the terminal building in white, then green hues. I steadied my grip, told Helen to hang on tight, and opened the engine all the way up when we hit the straightaway that ran the last mile.

But the car stayed right on us the whole way, the twin yellow beams matching my turns, then coming on like hellhounds when they reached down the final drag.

We struck the raised railroad ties that broach the gulley at the field entrance doing sixty and the bike went airborne. That old Indian flew a good twenty feet before landing front wheel first on the asphalt. The bike wobbled beneath me back and forth and I nearly lost it, down-shifting twice as I fought for control, Helen clinging to my chest like she was a part of me.

I leaned hard left and made straight for the Gooney Bird. The car had eaten up more ground when I slowed and was streaking across the ramp just a few hundred yards behind us. I circled around the left wing and locked her up, skidding the back end in front of the aft hatch. Helen was off and moving before I had the kickstand down.

"My gun's under the left seat," I shouted. "Anything happens to me, you protect yourself, baby."

She already had the hatch open and the stairs down. By the time I got off the bike, she was slipping through the doorway.

Then brilliant yellow-white light flashed against the side of the plane, outlining me against the polished aluminum. A car screeched to a halt on the asphalt behind me, ending any chance we had of getting away.

I turned to face the car, the headlights blinding me. The car was white—as I'd expected—but I couldn't see much else. A man got out and strode forward into the aura cast by the headlights. His figure was a blur, but I could tell he was holding a gun.

A big gun.

"You've really lost it this time, Ruggles!" I yelled.

Then he took another step forward, and I got a full look at him.

He had a face like a foot. Beneath it he wore a hideous Hawaiian shirt, the unbuttoned red-and-blue obscenity flopping back and forth in the gusty plateau wind, flashing a savage red burn underneath.

Bendix.

"I'm here for the dame," he said in a big-city voice.

The hammer clicked back on his revolver. "But first I'm gonna shred you, boy. Nice and slow."

45

I stood perfectly still, focusing on Bendix and his three feet of gun. His features were as cold and heavy as a sarcophagus, his soulless eyes marking me vacantly.

It might have been the last moment of my life, but the only thing I could manage to say was, "That's a really ugly shirt."

I waited for the impact.

The rolling rush of a sliding window whooshed out from the cockpit. Then a big .45 came dancing out of the dark opening—in Helen's hand.

"Stand back, Frankenstein, and drop the gun!" she shouted.

I was amazed—but impressed.

Bendix took a step back, still drawing down on me.

"No, honey, I don't think I wanna do that. I think I'm gonna keep pointing it at Tokyo Joe here. You shoot, he dies. Your move, sister."

I drew a bead on Bendix, looking for an opening. His eyes were darting back and forth between the cockpit and me. He was too far away to bum-rush but way too near with that cannon in his hand.

I crouched down, hands primed, preparing to pounce if I got any kind chance at all. He'd surely blast me, but at least Helen could fire freely then.

Tough break for me.

"Listen, lady," Bendix said, "I'm gonna blow a hole right through this guy in about three seconds if you don't put that gun down."

"To match the one I'll drill through your forehead, asshole. You think the only thing we did at 4-H club was milk cows? Just try me!"

The tension was epic, every fiber in my body rigid. Something was going to give—and fast. I just didn't know what.

When it came, it took us all by surprise.

A piercing beam from aft of the airplane cut through the darkness, bathing Bendix's face in light. Then an amplified voice rang out across the ramp. "Put that gun down, boy! This is Sheriff Rink Ruggles of Avalon and I've got the drop on you! You move and I will blast you clear off this island."

Astonished, I jerked my head toward the sound. It was, indeed, Ruggles, kneeling behind a sidecar motorcycle and bracing a rifle across the seat, a police spotlight on the handlebars stabbing out toward the gunman. The sheriff must've followed the crowd up the hill and coasted in behind the DC-3 during the standoff.

"Come now, boy," he added, "don't make me shoot you. I'm a marine marksman."

Bendix thought it over a second. Then he unsheathed a great big carving knife smile and tossed the gun to the ramp.

Sly like a fox, I thought. He made a simple calculation and determined there was nothing here worth dying over. That was cold comfort after all I'd been through.

Ruggles advanced in grim determination, holding the rifle in a shooter's position, almost the way a marine might. I had to admit, he looked good doing it.

"You there, in the airplane," he yelled. "Put that gun away, little lady, and come on down! Buonomo, you and your playmates here are in trouble—bigger than Dallas!"

"Wait a minute, Rink," I protested. "I don't even know this guy."

He grinned at me, then looked at Bendix, then back at me again. "That's the dirty bastard who stole my cruiser at the Casino!"

Bendix made a play. Lunging sideways, he hauled another pistol out of his waistband and swung it toward the sheriff. I dove for him but was half a beat late.

Gunfire whistled through the air, then Bendix spun around, grabbing for his arm as his pistol discharged into the tarmac, a lone bullet ricocheting away across the darkened taxiway.

Then he was down, rolling over and clutching at his shoulder as blood began to seep out, doing absolutely nothing for his luau attire.

I swooped down on him, ripping the gun from his feeble grasp and tattooing him on the beak with a straight left. His head banged off the asphalt, then his eyes rolled slowly upward into his head as the lids came rushing down. That was the end of William Bendix's performance for the evening.

While Rink was ratcheting the cuffs on that fallen ox, Helen stepped down from the plane—but without my gun. Smart girl.

Rink did a double take when he saw her, then raked me with an envious look. "She's the gal from *Nightprowler*! She played the gun moll." Then to Helen, he added, "You were terrific, young lady."

Helen's smile lit up the darkness. "Thank you, Sheriff. At least somebody here has seen one of my movies."

Then she gave me a look that could have doubled up Captain America. I grimaced in mock fright as she stared me down.

"Help me wrassle this guy into the car, Buonomo," Ruggles said, "And would you please get me a sheet or something, Miss . . . uh, Miss—"

"DeHart. Lilah DeHart."

"Of course. Please, Miss DeHart, bring something so he don't bleed all over my cruiser."

"Certainly, Sheriff. I'd be glad to help you," she said, half curtsying, still flashing the red carpet whites and just burying ol' Rink with Hollywood glam.

Then he and I each grabbed an end, lifting the battered bruiser up.

"Nice shooting, Rink," I said, bestowing my first-ever nonsarcastic smile upon the sheriff of Avalon.

He mumbled something that might have been a thank you and then shuffled off toward the car.

Rink kept looking back at Helen, then me, while we walked.

"Some guys have all the luck," I heard him muttering under his breath.

~

After we got Bendix into the car, Rink said he had to hustle him down to get medical attention. I was expecting him to order us along for the ride, but he didn't say anything else. When I started to offer some bullshit excuse for what had gone on, he just waved me off.

I looked at him with curiosity. We both probably had a sense that our uneasy truce had been bolstered by this little engagement, and I could tell he was starstruck by Helen. She'd come back from the hangar with Clint and some shop towels for Bendix's wound. Clint had his arm around Helen's shoulder, his yellow teeth glowing in the night. "Don't you ever lose this little gem again, Buonomo. Lightning doesn't strike twice."

I patted him on the shoulder as I pulled her away and tucked her under my own arm. "Maybe just this once it did, barnstormer, but I do have to get her out of here tonight so she can be on set in the morning. We'll come back soon to spend a couple of nights up here with you. Whatsay?"

"I'd say it sounds like bullshit . . . but I'll make up the spare room just in case." He gave Helen a big wink and me a long, skeptical glance.

I asked Rink if it was okay if we left and promised to give him a full statement by telephone within a day.

"No problem," he said. "Please do come on back soon to visit, Miss DeHart; we'd be honored to have you in Avalon."

Then he asked Helen if she could get him a cameo in a western with his hero John Wayne sometime. She said she'd look into it. I said I thought that was fitting. Clint just laughed. Then we all actually shook hands and said goodnight.

It had been a very strange day.

~

The plane was empty so the takeoff roll was short. The marine layer still shrouded most of the field, but finding the sky above is a helluva lot easier than finding a runway below.

We punched through the clouds, then I made a lazy climbing turn to starboard, laying the nose on a heading for Long Beach. As we rounded the island, I dipped a wing down and Helen and I both took a last, long look at Catalina, our island of lost dreams. Neither one of us said anything as we flew over the black hilltops that lurked quietly in the dark like brooding sentinels.

Beneath us, the narrow highway we'd just raced up shone inky black through the gaps in the cloud base. Far below, a white ring of surf broke against the forbidding coastal rocks as we pulled away toward the mainland.

I glanced across at Helen as she stared down in quiet detachment, wondering if I'd ever be back there with her after all.

46

We made Long Beach in fourteen minutes. There was no time for conversation as I was throwing levers or talking on the radio almost the entire time. I settled for a few smiles flashed in my direction.

Helen looked just a bit tight. She was probably thinking about what she was going to say to Frank. I hadn't given it any thought at all; I'd been too busy finding his girl to figure out how I was going to tell him she still loved me. I don't know what good it would've done anyway; things like that can be thought out half to death but the telling doesn't get any easier.

It wasn't going to be pleasant—for any of us—but it had to be done. Helen was going to have to spill the whole story to Frank and me, and she was going to do it tonight come hell or high water. For her sake I hoped it checked.

~

We touched down just after one thirty. Two minutes later I shut the plane down in front of the Nighthawk hangar.

The palms were starting to bend a bit in the wind as we walked across the ramp. It was kind of balmy for an October night in Southern California, but I had no complaint with that.

I stuck my head inside the hangar door, pulled on the light, and gave the whole place a long once-over for high-flying Chinese or anyone else who might be on the hunt for the world's deadliest stag film. The Lockheed was parked and chocked inside, but otherwise the place was empty. I stepped in, Helen close in tow.

"Oh, the Electra is here," she exclaimed. "Thank God."

I turned to face her. "And Roscoe. He brought her back early, I guess. What's the big deal about that old freight queen anyway?"

She slipped an arm around my waist, cinching herself up close. "Well . . ."

She was trying to be charming, but she was laying it on a little too thick. I held out a gentle stop sign with my hand. "Out with it, lady."

"Okay. I kind of hid the film in the back of it the other day."

"*What?*"

"Honey, don't get mad. I didn't want to take it home any longer—I just got a bad feeling about everything after we saw each other."

"That's encouraging," I said, crossing my arms.

"No, I mean seeing you made me realize I'd made a terrible mistake."

"I've always thought so, too."

She slapped my hand. "You know what I mean."

"Yeah. Okay, let me call Frank and then we'll go get that damn movie—but I'm gonna torch that thing in the ashcan. It's already caused a lifetime of heartache."

I walked over to my desk and Helen followed, watching nervously as I began to dial the number.

"I'll just let him know we're coming up. He'll be awfully relieved to hear your voice."

She reached out with a crimson fingertip, depressed the phone hook, then placed the finger under my chin, lifting it up.

"Joe, darling," she said, "please don't put me on the phone with him. I'd like to think a few things through before I speak to him. You understand, don't you?"

I understood that she was working me, but I let it go. "Not really, but I've got to call him either way, then we're heading up to his place, *capisce?*"

She got my best stare after that so she'd know I was serious. Then I dialed Frank's place in Bel Air.

He wasn't in. The houseboy said Mr. Sinatra had rushed out to Palm Springs a little earlier and that he was probably still en route. Now we'd have to fly out to the desert to see him. But that was a day at the beach compared to everything else that had gone down.

I tapped the hook and massaged the stubble on my cheeks back and forth a moment, the dial tone buzzing in my ear. Then I began entering the number for my message service but stopped middial when I looked over at Helen. She was fidgeting like she'd swallowed a sparrow, already burning her second cigarette since we landed.

I tilted my head, made eye contact with her, teased, "You really want your film, don't you?"

"Yes," she said, her eyes pleading. "Can't we please go check for it?"

"Yeah. We gotta take that bird out to Palm Springs now anyhow—Frank took a ride out to the dunes. Let's saddle up, Pocahontas."

I replaced the receiver. There was a message from Frank about Ratello's whereabouts I might have wanted to hear, but I didn't get it until I called again two days later—by which time I no longer needed it.

47

The hangar door let out its familiar groan as it rolled unhappily on rusting tracks. I let out one of my own as I muscled the Electra out onto the ramp with the tow bar, pushing it out into the alleyway between the hangars. Then I clanged the doors shut and locked them and marshaled Helen over to the plane.

A rogue palm frond went skidding by as we walked.

"Getting windy, isn't it?" Helen remarked.

"Little bit."

I opened the airplane door carefully so the wind wouldn't snatch it, then held out a hand to help her up. She ducked her head and climbed onboard. Her eyes went right to the spot where she must have stashed the flick. Then she looked back at me for reassurance.

"Go ahead, honey," I said. "I sure as hell haven't been fishing around back there."

She reached between the seams of the wainscoting, moving her hand back and forth several times. She started to give me a panicked look, then just as fast broke into a triumphant grin.

"Oh, here it is!" she exclaimed, retrieving a small metal movie canister from behind the fabric paneling.

I didn't have the inclination to go back and open the hangar again just to destroy the damn thing. It was late and I wanted to get a move on. Long Beach, Palm Springs— what did I care where it burned—just so long as it did.

"Enjoy it, hon," I said, "'cause that's going to be its last showing ever. That thing dies when we land."

"Fine, Joe," she said absently, her eyes riveted on the pale-green aluminum can she held in her hands.

~

We sat down and buckled in. I listened to the field report and reviewed my charts, checking the elevations of the mountains that rise steeply on either side of the only pass through the San Bernardino range. The highest, Mt. San Jacinto, rises more than eleven thousand feet out of the sands at its peak. Hitting that could ruin your whole night.

I hustled through my preflight checks, cracked the left throttle open half an inch, cleared the prop arc, and turned number one. When it stabilized at idle, I reached for the other starter.

As I did, a kid in an Earl's Flight Services cap ran to the front of the aircraft and waved for my attention. He was pointing to a clipboard and holding a pen. I snarled at him, reduced the propeller pitch to Low, then thumbed him on back.

He came up to the cockpit, apologizing between gasps for air, and said no one had signed for the fuel bill when the plane came in. Over the exhaust of the engine, I told him I ran an account with Earl and paid by the month. He gulped upon hearing the words.

Normally I'd have taken a good-size chunk out of his ass, but he was clearly new—just a kid. Looked like Mickey Rooney with his jug ears jutting out from under the cap. I suppose I'd been like him once about a hundred years ago.

I signed the bill anyhow just to get rid of him. He apologized again and disappeared aft into the dark recess of the cabin, taking way too long to latch the door. Fucking new guys.

I taxied out quickly, advancing the throttles for a rolling takeoff. At seventy miles an hour I hauled back on the controls and pulled the plane into the air. It hesitated just slightly, so I gave it an extra yank. Then the earth began dropping away beneath me and I brought the landing gear up.

At five hundred feet I signaled my luscious copilot to raise the flaps. She gave me a knowing nod and flipped the lever up. Then I rolled the plane into a shallow bank, feeding in some rudder to keep her from slipping through the turn.

As we climbed away, I thought over the sluggish takeoff. The Electra had made several flights since I last flew her so she may have developed low cylinder pressure again, although Roscoe hadn't mentioned anything about it. Both engines checked within limits, though, so I pressed on, making a mental note to do a full engine run-up before leaving Palm Springs in the morning.

But morning was still a long way off.

48

Helen didn't say much as we climbed up to cruising altitude. Her face was a study in solitude, and I could see she was immersed in thought. Given the circumstances, it was hardly surprising.

The ride was rougher than I expected so I dialed up an en route weather frequency. The broadcast said a ridge of high pressure was flowing through the west, channeling strong desert winds through the mountain passes. These were known locally as Santa Anas but there was nothing heavenly about the scalding winds that came howling through Southern California every fall, tearing down trees and breaking windows with their vicious gusts.

After we leveled off, anxiety began creeping into my bones. Maybe it was the challenging weather ahead, or maybe I was just coming to grips with the vice and violence I'd been surrounded by for three days. Either way, I could feel a tide of uneasiness rising in me as we bored on eastward.

"Joe," Helen said quietly, almost inaudibly above the wind noise and the engines.

I glanced over at her, saying nothing, my eyes inviting the question.

"What *do* you do for Frank?"

I looked out into the night, corrected the flight path, rolled in some trim.

"You really want to know?"

"Yes."

I thought about what I was about to say for several seconds before speaking. Then I tore the lid off an old can of worms.

"I fix things."

"Fix what? How?" she asked, uncertainty spreading across her face.

"Just exactly what you think, my dear. I know my way around in the dark, and Frank's famous, wealthy, and a bit careless. Every now and then some grifter tries to put him in a tight corner—"

"And you help him out?"

"Yes."

"But he's got an army of agents and assistants, some of them with pretty broad shoulders."

"They can't do what I do, not quietly at least."

She gaped at me, shock and disbelief flooding her face. "Dear God, you don't kill these people, do you?

I gave her the full eye roll for that one. "No, I do not kill people, Helen. Did you really just ask me that?"

"But you are some kind of a troubleshooter, aren't you?" she asked, turning cool as she spoke.

"Not exactly. I'm a licensed private detective—fair and legal. Frank's my only client. I rarely do anything for him and I don't accept any pay for it. I help him because he's my friend, okay?"

"Is that what you've been doing this week, fixing something for Frank? Just tying up another loose end?" Her eyes were glimmering in the dark now like the northern lights—intensely green and glacier cold.

"You know better, Helen. Do you think I'd go through all this for anyone else in the whole world? I do help him, but I have a personal stake in this case—a huge one, one with emerald eyes and a beautiful smile."

"Thank you." Her voice was softer, her face warmer. "But why do you feel you have to help him? Is this about your buddy Pete? Do you look out for Frank because of what happened to him?"

I shrugged, deflected the question. "I've never really thought about it."

She touched my hand, held it. "Yes, you have," she said, her tone low and soothing. "That *is* why you do it, and we both know it. You've got to let that go, honey. It was a long time ago."

The props were out of sync. I bumped up the left one just a hair, merging the vibrations into one sound, thinking about an old friend while I did.

I could see his face as I told her, "It was forever for Pete."

~

Several minutes passed before either one of us spoke. Helen looked at me then, tension marring her features.

"Baby, what are we going to do?"

"About?"

"Us."

"I haven't figured that out yet, but I'll know by morning." I floated her a smile but she wasn't buying.

"Seriously. What about all this?" she asked, gesturing between us with an open hand. "What are we going to tell him about us?"

I thought that over for a second. "I don't think Frank's gonna handle it well no matter what I say."

"I wouldn't expect him to."

"Most guys would understand—but it's been a long time. Things change."

"Do they?" she replied, piqued. "Are you saying you don't love me now?"

"Whoa, Silver, who said anything about *that*?" I could hear the incredulity rising in my voice as I spoke.

"Well, what's all this about things changing then?"

The plane hit a dip then, dropped a few feet. I leveled her back out, gave Helen a *what the hell?* look. "You *are* Frank's girlfriend, honey."

"Now there's something we can talk about changing."

I cocked my head, making sure I'd heard her correctly over the props.

"Just what exactly are you saying, that you don't want to go back to him?"

"I'm saying that you and I had something once, something wonderful, something I've never felt before—or since. And if you aren't willing to fight for that, Joe Buonomo, you aren't the man I thought you were."

I sat there, trying to get my head around the idea that she wanted to be with a freight jockey instead of the most famous and wealthy entertainer on Earth.

"Well . . . ?" she intoned.

"You've got to give me a second here . . . Frank is my friend . . ."

"And I want to be your lover. Besides, I didn't hear you calling Frank's name out in the dark when you were kissing me at the Casino."

"That was different . . . I was just so happy to see you."

She laughed, then smiled at me. "Yeah. Don't think I couldn't feel how happy you were."

I grinned back. She had me but I had to try. "Helen . . ."

"Yes, love?"

We hit another, bigger air pocket then, the plane shuddering as it bounced through the increasingly rocky sky.

"Look, darling, first we have to work this whole—"

"Let me make it easy for you," she said, a huntress's look gleaming in her eyes as she unbuckled her seat belt.

In a flash she'd slithered over to my seat, straddling me in the confined space, pinning my wrists to my sides. The top button of her blouse had come undone, things beneath brimming near the opening.

"Goddamn you, Joe, you want me, you know you do. Don't deny it," she whispered, pressing her face against mine, staring deep into my eyes.

I leaned back, struggling to resist her, turning my face away. She stayed on the attack, sliding sideways toward me, soft fingers caressing my cheek.

I started to raise a hand in protest. Then I just gave in to her. She pounced at the opening, smothering me with deep, lustful kisses, a low moan tickling my ear as the Electra rolled into a bank, curving off course and down in the angry night sky.

Palm Springs was suddenly far away. Very far away.

49

I loved every second of it—all seven of them. Then the sheer, insane danger of what we were doing shook me from my stupor. Entering mountainous terrain at night—and in rough air—was no time to re-up our membership in the Mile High Club. I just couldn't let it go on.

Reaching around her, I rolled wings-level and pulled back on the controls with one hand, clasping the other around her back. Well above us, the moon shone bright and clear, its luminous beams bathing the cockpit in silver light, painting Helen's face pale blue as she gazed hungrily into my eyes.

My head was spinning—and it wasn't from the turbulence. A gorgeous woman, one I'd risked my life over repeatedly, one I loved madly, was sitting in my lap begging me to take her. And what was I doing? Taking her to somebody else.

I had no idea what I was doing any longer, whether keeping her or giving her back made me the bigger fool, but I knew if I kept forging ahead to the airport I could sort it all out on the ground.

Somehow I got myself together in the midst of the emotional tempest she had conjured within me. I sat up and slung her across my seat, wiping away beads of sweat that had broken out on my brow. "Helen, listen to me. I know what we talked about, I know what we had and I want that back—but not this way."

She pressed her hand to my cheek again, stroking it. "Baby, turn around, fly us away. Anywhere, anywhere at all, let's just go away together—please."

I grabbed her hand, pulling it down to her lap. "The only place we're going is to Palm Springs. We're going to clear up this entire mess—and it's going to involve the police, I'm afraid. Then we'll see about us, but Frank is my friend, and I am not going to steal you away in the night like a Trojan bride."

"But Joe—"

"But nothing. You want this to work, you do it my way. Okay, lady?"

Her face drooped a little, then she forced a bitter smile. "All right," she said in resignation, "if that's how you want it."

"Yeah, that's how it's gotta go down."

She just looked at me, flummoxed, bemused. "It's never easy with you, Buonomo, is it?"

"Never."

~

The worn tops of the San Bernardino range began creeping into view as we approached the Banning Pass, a narrow channel cut through the black-brown crags that guard the entrance to the Coachella Valley beyond. The visibility was great, but the continuous thumps and unpredictable jarring were going to demand all my attention on the way down.

"Honey, I'm sorry but playtime's over. We've got to start down—better take your seat . . . and button up your blouse, for Christ's sake."

I pulled back on the throttles, initiating a slow descent, my eyes locked on the path ahead—sort of.

"Like what you see, don't you?" she teased, bending down enticingly as she sat across from me.

"Ave Maria," I said, shaking my head.

~

Passing seven thousand feet, I began picking up the lights of Palm Springs and the other smaller communities scattered across the desert floor. I located the airport a few seconds later, the dim outline of the runway glowing murkily through the wind-borne layer of dust. Just then, Helen touched my hand. When I turned toward her, she was staring at me, her face pulled tight, her lips pursed.

"Baby . . ." she said.

"Yes?"

"There's something I have to tell you . . . about the film I took. There's more."

The turbulence had increased dramatically as I navigated through the pass, which was a natural wind tunnel even on the best of days. Heavy jolts were rocking the Electra repeatedly now, the airspeed fluctuating 10 to 20 mph in the gusts.

"Sorry, darling," I said. "It's going to be ugly from here on in. I want to hear, but it has to wait until we get on the ground. We're only fifteen miles out."

"Do we have to land there?" She was pleading, not kidding.

"Yes."

The aircraft hit another pocket then, dropping a quick hundred feet. We both lurched forward as the plane dove down the invisible gulley, then jerked sideways in another brutal gust.

I heard a distinct metal pinging sound, followed by another, and caught a blur of metallic green from the corner of my eye.

"Oh shit!" Helen said. "The film fell out of my purse."

"Don't sweat it, baby, you can grab it after we land," I said above the noise of the screeching wind outside.

But she was already up and moving past me unsteadily in a crouch.

"Honey, if it unravels, it'll be a mess. It's just out of reach here; I'll have it in a second."

We hit a nasty updraft at that moment, the nose of the aircraft pitching upward abruptly. I grabbed Helen's waist to steady her and, in a *what the hell* moment, pulled her onto my lap and kissed her. I shouldn't have done it, but for all I knew it was for the last time. We locked eyes for several seconds, sinners' smiles on our lips.

I heard a few more pings as the film canister banged its way toward the back of the aircraft. I laughed at the sound; what did I care about that damn film anyhow?

Helen squeezed my lips with her fingers, grinning at me as she pulled herself free. "You just hold this crate steady for ten seconds and I'll get that film. I am *not* going to have you looking at those frames while I roll that thing back up."

She grabbed the handhold next to the bulkhead and stood up.

Then she didn't move. Not one inch.

I checked the flight path through the windshield then looked up at her. Her eyes were transfixed, her features wooden. Before I could say a word, a voice boomed from the cargo bay, "This what you're looking for, honey?"

50

Primal reaction gripped me instantly, before my brain could even process the situation. A jolt of cold adrenaline shot through my body as I turned to see a brick wall of a man lurching forward with a film canister in his left hand and a very large pistol in his right.

The moonlight blued his hard features and nickel-plated gun. He was grinning like a court jester—a cold, ugly smile. In that millisecond, I picked up a whiff of his awful cologne and recalled that lantern jaw from our previous encounter.

Carmine Ratello.

He started into some standard bad guy speech. "Flyboy, you just put this thing down easy or the broad is—"

I didn't hesitate—just too many years of combat flying. That perfumed *pagliaccio* got the blackjacking and the jewelry hit, but this time I was calling the play.

I snatched Helen by the waist and pulled her down while grabbing the yoke and hauling it back hard. The plane's attitude shot up twenty degrees in an instant, shoving the gravity load downward and aft.

Ratello careened backward, half off his feet, discharging his cannon into the aircraft ceiling several times as he went, flashes of white lightning searing the cabin as the explosion of gunfire reverberated throughout the confined metal shell of the Electra.

I released the yoke then and brought my hand to the butt of the .45, yanking it free from its holster and flicking the safety off in a move practiced ten thousand times.

Arching over my seat, I windmilled my arm over my head and down in one fluid motion, craning my neck back until I picked out the bulk of his thick, stumbling body.

I fired three times.

The first shot was high. The second blew off an ear. The third hit him in the throat.

His head jerked back and his hands flew up involuntarily with the impacts, a dark spray of blood issuing from his neck as he staggered back in shock, his finger squeezing the trigger of a gun he no longer held.

Ratello's dying eyes met mine momentarily then rolled into his head as his legs gave way, an awful, gurgling hiss escaping from his mouth as he tumbled down. He crashed heavily to the floor and slid downhill, folding up against the aft bulkhead like a runaway barge on a bridge piling.

I twisted around, pushed forward on the yoke to get the nose down, and reached for Helen's arm to help her to her seat. Fear distorted her face as she looked up at me, but she gathered herself quickly and sat down as I stowed the gun.

The plane had banked sharply and shed thirty knots in the sudden climb, putting the aircraft close to an accelerated stall. We were coming back down through the horizon now, but still nose high. The altimeter blurred through 4,300, then 4,200, then 4,100 feet in a steady plunge. That was not good.

I rolled wings level and gave the control wheel a shove full forward. The plane mushed down, the airspeed picking up a bit, but she still handled like she was on the ragged edge.

Ratello again.

It had to be his dead bulk, two hundred twenty plus pounds, at the most rearward part of the aircraft, pushing the center of gravity out of limits.

"Helen," I said, "I need you to take the controls for a minute while

I pull him forward. His weight is making us tail heavy. Keep the nose down and watch the airspeed—I'll be right back."

She just stared at me a second, then said, "Okay," without much conviction.

I released my seat belt, swung around, and raised myself into a crouch.

A fist rocketed out of the darkness and exploded against my jaw, an eruption of stars obliterating my vision as a man yelled out, "Muthah-fuckah!" in a Brooklyn accent.

I collapsed backward across my seat against the sidewall of the cockpit, banging my head hard against the window frame. I heard Helen shriek as I struggled to sit upright, still recoiling from the pain and shock.

Then Johnny Spazzo leaned down toward me, snaked his arms behind my neck in a hammerlock, and wrenched me toward the back of the seat.

"I'll kill you, you son of a bitch!" he shouted, hot spittle flying out of his mouth onto my neck and face.

He pulled my arms backward until I felt they were going to snap off, at the same time shoving my head down and away with his forearm.

Helen turned to face Spazzo, looking like she was going to take a swing at him. He gave her a vicious kick across her upraised arm that sent her sprawling as she let out a banshee wail of pain.

Her leg flew up against the throttle quadrant as she fell, knocking the starboard engine control to idle. The plane yawed immediately to the right and dropped a wing, racing back toward a stall. Despite my struggle, I could feel the airframe tremble and roll over to one side as the lift decayed.

Spazzo, blind with rage, either didn't know or didn't care what he was doing, but he was on the verge of killing us all. He tightened his grip on my neck and laid the weight of his body against my shoulders, pushing me toward blackout as his arms mashed my arteries.

Helen grabbed at the controls, but she was a hair too late. The Electra shuddered heavily once, then snapped over into a violent spin entry, wrapping up tight as she began slicing downward in asymmetric arcs.

Spazzo and I fell sideways against the copilot's seat, but his grip held firm. Thrashing against his crushing hold, I tried to call to Helen to push the control wheel forward but could only summon a grunt.

Down we spun, the groaning airframe and the piercing yowl of the stall warning horn unleashing a hideous sound as the aircraft corkscrewed wildly toward the granite peaks below. The noise finally distracted Spazzo from his maniacal intent, and he loosened his grip as fear began to overcome the murder in his brain.

As soon as I felt his hands slacken behind me, I flippered my left elbow up and back into his face. I hit him with everything I had left, raking him across the eye socket and schnoz, breaking his nose and maybe more. I can't remember anything ever feeling as good.

He went down like Gene Tunney, dead to the world. If he got back up, he'd just have to take a number.

I spun around to assess the position of the aircraft, sucking wind and blinking away stars. Helen was still fighting with the controls, but she was pulling back on them, actually causing the plane to wrap up tighter in the spin.

"I've got it," I shouted, seizing the yoke and neutralizing the inputs while closing the throttles. I verified the spin direction from the whirring city lights and then mashed the left rudder pedal to the wall.

After an eternity of several seconds, the nose swung left as the airplane wrenched free from the spin. A split second later I buried the yoke to the forward stop, pouring on power to break the stall.

The plane recovered rapidly and transitioned into a steep dive, the airspeed running away like War Admiral toward redline.

I glanced at the altimeter. We were below two thousand feet and still dropping like a battleship anchor.

What I saw next was worse.

As I searched for the horizon, the lights of Palm Springs abruptly disappeared from view, leaving a field of black emptiness in the windscreen. My blood froze as I realized we were now below the level of the hilltops that surrounded us.

Helen gasped then, sucking her breath in with fear. A moment later, I saw it too: a dark form rising up in the indigo gloom. It was a ridgeline, well above us—and close in.

Instinctively, I gripped the yoke and reefed it full aft while slamming my right hand against both throttles, shoving them halfway to Bakersfield.

The engines surged with power, the propellers groaning in protest from the heavy torque load driven back on the camshafts. The aggressive pull-up tripled the g load on the plane, my vision fading for several seconds as I held fast on the controls in the blind.

As my eyesight returned, I saw that the aircraft was edging up, the nose pushing through the horizon, then soaring above the dark outline of the hill just a hundred feet away.

We almost made it.

51

The Electra cleared the hilltop by a good fifty feet, but as we shot past, a blur of Joshua tree flashed by on the starboard side, bashing into the wing.

The sound of shearing metal filled the cockpit as the aircraft whip-sawed to the right, skidding upward into the sky. As the right wing dipped, I caught a flash of city lights again in the distance.

In gut reaction I stomped on the left rudder and pushed the nose down below level, struggling for control of the yawing aircraft as she staggered through the air like a drunken buzzard.

"What do you see out there?" I shouted. "How much damage?"

Helen peered out her window and yelled back, "Part of the wing is torn off, it's bent all to hell . . . and I think we lost the right engine. Oh, God, it's on fire, too!"

A quick glance at my instruments verified what Helen had said about the engine while the seat of my pants told me about the wing. Another glance outside confirmed the rest. We weren't just on fire, we were blazing—a full-on flying bonfire, arcing down through the night like a flaming arrow.

Even worse than the fire was the windmilling propeller, which was causing crippling drag. Eliminating that would get me down to the lesser problem of flying a transport aircraft with part of a wing shorn away, a burning engine, and an angry mobster somewhere behind me.

What I did next was all rote response, deeply ingrained by years of emergency training.

I looked over at Helen, spoke in a firm voice. "Honey, push the right engine Feather button and pull the mixture to full lean. It's the big red button on the instrument panel right in front of you."

She knew enough of the basics of flying the Electra that she could do it, and I was too busy trying to control the plane to attempt it anyhow.

Helen jabbed the button, then pulled the mixture control to full lean, simultaneously reducing the propeller angle and cutting off fuel to the engine. That eliminated enough drag for me to pull the wings close to level, but the fire didn't go out.

I analyzed our situation. We were about ten miles from town now and clear of the last of the hills with nothing but sand and scrub between the airport and us. I checked the altimeter again, we were maybe eight hundred feet above the ground and still sinking. It was easy math—we had no shot.

The only variable I still controlled was how smooth the crash would be. I turned toward Helen, looking deep into wide emerald eyes. My words were hard and clear.

"Honey, we're not gonna make it. I've gotta put her down out here. Strap yourself in—all the way—and lock your harness. Put your head down and cover your face before we hit. Understand?"

"Yes, Joe," she replied with odd detachment. She was a cool one, that girl.

"We've got about fifteen seconds. Do it now."

There was no time to buckle my own harness. It took all my efforts just to hold the attitude near level.

I looked out ahead at the landscape. It was mostly smooth sand with a few gentle dunes and occasional clumps of vegetation, but it was hard to tell for sure in the flying dust and darkness. I picked the clearest spot I could see, turning the aircraft into the wind that was blowing like hell out of the southeast.

At fifty feet, I closed the left throttle and shut the fuel off. I stole one last glance at Helen. She was staring directly at me, her face a mixture of hope and grit and fear—at once as courageous and as lost as anyone I'd ever seen. I'll never forget that look.

I pulled the nose up just before impact, wrestling the wings toward level, but we still went in cockeyed and low to starboard.

We punched in hard and bounced up, the burning wing digging a furrow into the ground, spinning the aircraft around. A halo of sand and brush fanned through the air as the Electra chewed into the Sonora, skidding sideways toward her ruin.

The rest of it is a blur. We struck something hard on the way, probably a boulder. I think we lost the tail then.

I don't remember anything else after that.

52

I came to slumped against the cockpit wall, one hand still clutching the yoke, the other hanging limply at my side. The reek of aviation gas hung thickly in the air even as the scouring wind swirled through the open cargo bay. Blood, salty and raw, permeated my gums, trickling down my thickening lips.

My left eye wouldn't open. I raised my hand to check it, but a searing pain in my ribs cut that short. I tried the other hand, dabbing at my forehead. It was slick to the touch, and there was a large lump above the swollen eye. I looked at my fingers—they were damp and dark.

Then I rubbed my cheek and felt another knot toward the back, where Spazzo had belted me. I wiggled my jaw back and forth a few times to see if it was broken. It wasn't, but it still felt like I'd gone fifteen rounds with Joe Louis. My earlobes didn't hurt, so at least I had that going for me.

Having ascertained that I was more or less alive, I looked across the cockpit to check on Helen.

She wasn't there.

I shook my head several times to clear the fog, but she still didn't appear. Grimacing from the pain in my side, I put a hand on the glareshield, pushing myself up from my seat. I called out several times as I steadied myself to walk.

There was no response, only the wind on the desert and the crackle of fire.

The fuselage was a wreck. Electrical wire harnesses dangled from the ceiling and the wainscoting hung down like rotted palm fronds in several places. The cabin was tilted a good twenty degrees down to the right on the sloping terrain, moonlight flooding in from where the tail should have been.

Bracing my right hand against the ceiling, I hobbled toward the back of the aircraft, looking for Helen as I went. Neither she nor Spazzo were in sight, but what was left of Carmine Ratello lay twisted beneath the fold-up bunk halfway back on the right side. A dark stain surrounded his body on the aluminum floor.

I stepped through the gaping hole in the back of the plane, snagging my pants on the jagged metal, slicing my calf. I grunted from the pain but didn't even bother to check the cut—it just didn't rate. My boot sank into the soft sand an inch or so as I lowered myself from the shattered airframe to the ground.

"Helen," I called out. "Where are you? Can you hear me?"

Nothing.

Thirty yards away, the wreckage of the tail section sat upright on a rise, the twin rudders jutting up like tombstones, backlit by the burning right engine that lay behind in the trench gashed in the sand.

I couldn't have been out long, five minutes, maybe ten. I checked my watch: 2:44. Even if Helen had started to walk away, she couldn't be far ahead. I felt my chest pockets for the penlight I normally kept there, but it was gone. Then I checked my holster.

Empty.

Wary of Spazzo popping out with a gun, I circled the remnants of the aircraft searching for Helen. Desperation began clutching at me when I couldn't find any sign of either one of them.

I climbed a low dune on the port side and peered into the murk toward the crown of light above the city. I spit out some blood and sand, calling Helen's name again and again. A wave of shock-induced nausea welled up. I dropped down on one knee to let it pass. For the first time, I became aware of the throbbing pain in my head, to go along with the dull stabbing sensation in my rib cage.

I knelt in despair, watching, the flickering flames glinting off the wreck of the Electra and dancing across the sand in irregular patterns. Amid the orange glow something metallic caught my eye. With dull irony, I realized it was the film reel, maybe ten feet away, nestled amid some cactus roses.

I crawled over toward the apparent cause of this mortal pandemic. The cover was off and a good fifteen feet of the film lay unwound on the sand, but most of it was still spooled. I held the celluloid up in the firelight—I had nothing left to lose at this point.

I stared at a few frames, concentrating on the dimly lit characters. It was what Helen had said—two nude women dancing with several men. None of the figures were identifiable in the faint light, but one resembled her sure enough. My first impulse was to toss the damn thing in the fire, but then I decided I could use it to strangle Frank.

I dropped my head and exhaled heavily. Another bout of nausea hit. I vomited on the sand, then closed my good eye and sat mostly still, waiting out the racing heartbeat and sweating brought on by the shock response, the only movement the small spasm I made each time I drew in a breath.

~

In a couple of minutes I was good to go. I stood up on wavering legs, surveying the site. The logical path would be from the back of the aircraft toward the city lights—pretty much where I was standing.

As I looked around, I saw something that confirmed my fears: two sets of shallow footprints in the sand, one substantially bigger than the other, leading off toward Palm Springs. It was possible they had been made at different times, or by different people. It was also possible that I was Flash Gordon. I set right off, hastily rolling up the film and shoving it in my jacket pocket as I went in pursuit.

I followed the shallow trail, shadow-lit by the moon, calling Helen's name out every few steps while dodging the razor spikes of cholla and ocotillo. She never answered but I staggered on, wooziness and the uneven terrain dropping me to the ground several times.

After a good twenty minutes, I reached Highway 111 where the footprints ended abruptly. I crisscrossed the road, walking fifty yards in either direction, but that was the end of the trail. My heart sank as I realized that they must have hitched or strong-armed a ride. Helen was gone—again.

I stood alone on the blackened roadside, whipping winds caking blood on my face. I dug down deep, trying to grasp what was happening, praying for some help, struggling to hold myself together as my world spun further and further down out of control.

53

Within five minutes a truck appeared, heading east. I flagged it down, waving off the cloud of swirling road dust that mushroomed out from its wheels as it ground to a halt on the shoulder. As the sand settled, I made out the sign on the passenger's door:

OLYMPIC FREIGHT FORWARDING, ATHENS, GA.

I rubbed my chin, entertaining a very old suspicion, then dismissed it with a shake of my head as I climbed up on the running board.

The driver did a double take when he saw me, letting out a whistle.

"Jee-zus, son, what happened to y'all? Anybody else hurt?"

"No, just me, had an accident. Can you drop me off in town?"

His eyes kept getting wider as he looked me over. "Sure, feller, sure. Wouldn't y'all rather go to the hospital? You look like hell."

I nodded. "It's all right. They've got a doctor where I'm going. We can be there in ten minutes if we hurry."

"Okay, son," he said, reaching to unlock the door. "Hop in."

I climbed in and he took the next exit at Indian Canyon, driving south into the valley. Along the way, I started to think about what I'd been through. The more I thought about it, the more torqued I got. There was a hell of a lot more going on here than just some amateur stag film gone missing—and everyone seemed to know but me.

By the time the driver stopped at the address, my boiler was lit and making plenty of steam. I thanked him for his assistance, climbed down to the road, and slammed the door behind me, muttering out loud.

He eyed me a long moment, perhaps assessing my sanity, before putting the truck in gear and rumbling off down the road, leaving me alone in the cool, still desert night.

I turned to face the property, clenching my bloodstained fists.

54

Frank Sinatra's home in Rancho Mirage was commonly referred to as the "compound" by friends and strangers alike. The ten-acre property at Tamarisk Country Club had eleven buildings, two tennis courts, a swimming pool, and several train cars—none of which meant jack shit to me at that moment.

I walked down to the service gate and forced it open, ducked a security guard, then stole quietly across the open lawn, making straight for the still-illuminated main house and marching up to the front door.

I tried the handle, but the door was locked. I stood there a moment trying to decide whether to kick in the glass panel or ring the bell. Frank's valet, George, happened to walk past the door at that moment, making my decision easier.

I rapped sharply on the glass with a bruised knuckle. Then I saw George peering out at me. A second later the ornate door opened inward. He looked me up and down a moment then declared, "Good Lord, Joe, what happened to you?"

"Pack of bobby-soxers mobbed me. Frank up?"

"Yes, in the living room, but he's—"

I brushed right past him, storming toward the center of the house.

"Can't wait, George. He'll understand," I said over my shoulder as I went.

I stopped at the entrance to the living room in the darkened hallway. Frank was in the center of the room, speaking to a group of men. The sharp smell of cigarettes peppered the air, the smoke clouding the room. Through the haze I made out the faces of Peter Lawford, Frank's business manager Hank Sanicola, and none other than Johnny Roselli. There were two other nondescript thugs just hanging around, probably Johnny's guys.

In any other setting it might have been highly unusual, but in Frank's house it was just another late-night cocktail party. Then I noticed that no one was drinking.

Frank was speaking to Lawford in an uncompromising tone. "Of course I understand the gravity of what we're talking about here, Peter, but we've got to keep this under wraps a little while longer. Joe's on the case and he always gets results."

Lawford responded, "Well, Frank, if that's so, why haven't you heard from your ace boy all day?"

"How the *hell* should I know?" he thundered. "But he's never let me down—he'll get that film. I need another day, that's all."

I stepped forward, into the room. "*This* film, Frank?" I said, grinding my teeth. As I did, I held up the canister, a foot or so of footage trailing beneath it.

All eyes turned toward me. Their faces hit bottom. No one spoke for several seconds. Finally, Frank said, "Joe . . . mother of God . . ."

"He's got it, Frank," Lawford exulted. "He's got the movie!"

I paid him no attention whatsoever, asked, "How well do you know the Palm Springs police chief, Frank?"

"Kettman? I own him. What's that—"

"Because my plane is a bonfire in his desert. And because Carmine Ratello's body is out there with it. And because Helen is missing again. You're gonna need one helluva cover-up job to keep *this one* under wraps," I said, quaking with rage.

Frank stared at me, his face screwed up in confusion. "Joe, did you find Lilah? Is she all right? And why did you call her Helen?"

"*Please,*" I said tiredly, "can we stop calling her that? Her name is not Lilah DeHart—it's Helen Castano. And she's not from New Orleans, she's from East Troy, Wisconsin. And before she was your girlfriend, Frank, she was my fiancée. I had her, but now she's gone again, kidnapped by some half-assed wingnut of a mobster."

He just looked on at me, pupils dilating.

"I've been arrested, beaten up, blackjacked, shot at, crash-landed, and generally jacked around for three days running. And it's all allegedly over *this* film," I said, hoisting the canister over my head, "which is a load of shit!"

Then, in measured words I spat out, "So I would like to know right now just-what-the-*fuck*-is-going-on-here!"

As I spoke, I wound up my arm and hurled the metal can across the room, rifling it into the sliding glass door behind Frank. It struck hard, cracking the glass on impact, a vitreous crescendo filling the room as fractured shards fell to the floor and shattered on the terrazzo.

The film popped out of the canister and rolled away, celluloid spooling out like railroad tracks in front of Lawford's feet. The reel came spinning to a stop in front of Frank, rattling as it oscillated down on the polished floor. Then it went quiet.

A charged silence fell over the room.

Like gunfighters in a standoff, Frank and I sized each other up, no one moving. The others appeared to be paralyzed by the sight of my swollen face and bloodstained clothes, but Frank just glowered at me, his eyes burning blue embers. I could see him absorbing the shock of what I'd just said. He took the blow, then fired a return volley.

"Hey," he shouted, "do you have any idea what this is all about? Do you know who's on that film?"

"It's a little hard to see by firelight with half your face smashed in. Why don't you tell me, Frank?" I asked, my voice rising. "Then you can thank me for getting it for you. Then you can call the police so we can start tracking down Helen and Spazzo. And then . . . then you can go fuck yourself!"

I shouted the words out, making myself dizzy and hoarse in the process. While I was yelling, Lawford bent over, picking the loose footage off the floor and holding it up.

Frank took a step toward me, the muscles on his neck bulging.

"Well, I'll tell you, Joe. That's a movie featuring Marilyn Monroe, Judy Campbell, and Senator John *FUCKING* Kennedy of Massachusetts! You may have heard of him, he's running for president of the United States." Now he was shouting. "And you can bet your *ASS* they're not discussing the New Frontier! Now do you get it? Do you have any idea the harm that film could have done if it had gotten out?" he screamed, a thin spray flying from his mouth, sparkling in the light.

"How?" I asked. "But Helen said it was . . . I saw it . . . there wasn't any . . ."

I could feel my brain locking up from confusion, pain, and just plain exhaustion. It all just hit me at once, the weight of everything— the poundings, the deceptions, the plane crash.

The dizziness increased. I put a hand to my head, my good eye blinking involuntarily. I could feel my legs going as I began to sway.

Then Frank was racing toward me, calling, "George! Get the first aid kit, and get Dr. Rosenbloom over here—now! Hank! Get Joe a drink. Let's help him to the couch."

Then he was next to me, his arm under my shoulder, helping me stand.

"Slow down, dago, the rest can wait. Let's get you taken care of first. I'll explain everything, I promise."

Peter was holding the film in his hands, examining the frames against a lamp. As I collapsed onto the couch, I could hear him squawking, "It's not here, Frank. This isn't the one. It's not fucking *here!*"

~

I sat back on the couch for several minutes while George cleaned up my face, the ice pack stinging almost as much as the iodine he put on the cut above my eye.

Hank held a glass of whiskey in his paw and handed me a sip every so often. The smell of burnt rye was a welcome relief after the chemical pungency of the antiseptic. Frank sat next to me the entire time, arm across my back. There are Elks Club meetings with less male chumminess.

Lawford sat opposite us in a chair, head in his hands, fretting, "What are we going to do now?" over and over.

Roselli and the thugs sat quietly, saying nothing.

Frank finally said, "You on the level, Joe, she's from Wisconsin?"

"Yeah," I nodded. "Small-town girl. Big-town trouble."

"And how. You have no idea. You were engaged to Lilah, no shit?"

"Helen. Yeah, back in '55. We dated about a year. Didn't take, in case you hadn't guessed."

"Why didn't you tell me?"

"I was going to tonight. I found her on Catalina, we were coming straight here to see you. Couple of goons intervened, screwed the pooch."

"Yeah. Just a little. Sanjee said you called, thanks. How'd you find her?"

I took a sip of the whiskey, glanced over at him. "I just had to figure out where she'd go."

"And that was where?"

"Where only the lonely go. You should know that one, Frank."

His eyes darkened with suspicion. He could see it coming now. "You bet I do, that's my song."

"But it was our place."

That might have been a little too candid for the moment, but it was the truth.

His eyes met mine. "I see," he said, crossing his arms. "It's like that, huh?"

I nodded slowly. "Yeah. It's like that."

He winced silently, the new reality of Helen and me breaking like first light in his mind.

I changed gears. "Suppose you bring me up to speed now, Frank. There's some mighty big pieces missing from this puzzle, and I'm thinking you have a few of them."

He just looked at me for several seconds before answering. "Finish your drink, buddy. I'll get you a cigarette. I got a story to tell you . . . and it's a humdinger."

～

Frank explained that Jack Kennedy and the girls made the film while they were staying at the compound several months earlier. When he found out about it, he begged Kennedy to destroy it, but the senator wanted him to keep it to amuse himself the next time he came out. Frank hid it among a few other stags, later coiling it inside the unmarked film of Helen and Lana Turner. The best Frank could offer was that Helen might have taken it unwittingly when she made off with the other one, but there was little faith in his words. The scales were tipping in my mind, too.

I told Frank everything that had happened in L.A. and Catalina, Roselli watching like a hawk from the other couch the entire time. After that, there was nothing more I could do; they knew as much as I did.

Dr. Rosenbloom came rushing in a few minutes later and tended to me like I was Franklin Roosevelt. He demanded that I go to the hospital immediately. Frank demanded that we bring the hospital to me instead. Two nurses were ordered up and promised within the hour, as was a portable x-ray machine.

The doctor said I might have a slight concussion, but it would be okay to grab some shut-eye. I wasn't going to be awake long anyway. Hank and Frank helped me off to a bed, then Hank left the room.

Frank stopped at the doorway before leaving. "Thank God you're alive. A nurse will be here when you wake up. I'm going to take care of everything else, brother, okay?"

"Frank?"

"Yeah, Joe?"

"Find Helen. We've got to find her."

He nodded. "We will, paesan, we will."

Then he flipped off the wall switch and shut the door, stillness falling over the dark space around me as his footsteps faded down the hall.

55

The dream came again, as it always did.

A dogfight by Picasso—navy blue and silver aircraft streaking across a gunmetal sky in angry hornet swirls, some melting into brilliant orange-yellow smears and fading from view, black ribbons billowing in their wakes. Tracer fire whistling by in surreal, phosphorescent streams—white, yellow, green. Warped voices making slurred sounds on cockpit radios, calling across time.

Sometimes it was abstract, burning men and faceless corpses spread across a dark tableau like lost shades in the underworld. Other times it was more lucid, and I'd see Pete's face or hear his voice.

Fire and war and Pete calling my name. Me searching for him endlessly, diving over and down, over and down, over and down across the black waste of an empty sea.

~

I awoke in a darkened room, my face damp. I lay there in solitude, time-worn memories flickering by, each one a razor cut of sadness and shame.

"Pete . . ." I whispered, "I'm sorry."

Lieutenant J. D. Petersen—"Pete" to the guys in the squadron. My XO, my wingman, my best friend. I loved him like one of my brothers.

And I left him alone to die in combat.

We were in the Philippines, late '44, just kicking the Japs' asses sideways. He and I swapped planes on a bet that day, went up on strafing run together. We pasted the harbor pretty good on our first pass, then I put a burst into a stray dive bomber we caught out in the open as we climbed away.

Pete called for a second pass, but I was bucking for triple ace so I broke away to finish off the cripple. I'd never done that before. Still don't know why I did.

I got my fifteenth kill, but some enemy fighters caught Pete during his solo strafing run. I could hear him calling for help over the radio, but I couldn't find him in the haze and clouds.

Then there was nothing. No cry. No scream. Nothing. Just static on the airwaves.

Sick inside, I circled down to the water, calling out his name. I kept searching for him, oblivious to the battle around me, but there was no trace of him or his plane. Nobody saw him go in, but he never came home.

Because of me.

I just let go after that, became the navy's reaper. I bagged 'em in scores, going out on patrol every day, seeking absolution through killing, trying somehow to undo what could never be undone. Nothing mattered to me any longer—I couldn't feel a thing. The downward spiral began.

I rode it down a long time, smacking the bottom in Cuba before finally bouncing back that night in '52 when I saved Frank from that hit attempt. I've been trying to make things right ever since.

It's a long journey home.

56

I heard the voices of two women somewhere, one an angel, the other a harpy. They were discussing Dr. Spock. That tore it. I rolled over and pulled the pillow over my head, praying for the sandman to come back.

But it was no use. After a minute or so I stirred, and two blurry faces atop white cotton balls turned to face me. I figured them for the nurses Frank promised.

The closest one said, "So you're finally awake," as if I'd been keeping her from her bridge game.

I squinted at her. Focus came slowly and did me no favors when it arrived. She was a plump fifty and hard as slate. Hair like Lucy, face like Viv. Could've been a guard at Tehachapi. I couldn't help grimacing at the sight of her, something she didn't miss.

"Mr. Sinatra says you had a terrible spill on your motorcycle last night," she declared, rolling her eyes in disbelief.

I propped myself up on an elbow. "Yeah," I managed, "hit a coyote, went ass over teakettle."

"Poor thing," she said, emitting the faintest trace of sympathy.

"Thanks."

She peered down at me, dark eyes narrowing. "The coyote."

The other gal floated over. Could've been Angie Dickinson's kid sister—strawberry blonde, beautiful, maybe twenty-four. The top two buttons of her off-white uniform were undone, one fold hanging carelessly open.

She looked at me a moment. Then ruby lips parted, curving voluptuously beneath sapphire eyes that gleamed in the soft light.

It was good to be alive.

I drank her in. Ten seconds maybe. Finally, I asked, "What time is it, Angie?"

"Six fifteen," she said, still smiling, "but my name's not Angie."

"A.m.?"

"No, silly, p.m. You were out over fourteen hours. How about a sponge bath?"

I shot Lucy a sidelong glance. "Who's giving it?"

Angie smiled again, shaking her head. Lucy glared at me awhile, then left the room.

"Okay, darling, mark me down. Frank, er, Mr. Sinatra, home?"

"Yes. I believe he's in the living room talking with the gentleman from Lake Tahoe."

"Tahoe?"

"Yes. He's called Momo, I think. Wears glasses."

"Bath's gotta wait, Angie," I said, sitting up. I noticed then that I was in boxers and a wife-beater T-shirt. "Any pants around here, my dear?"

She chuckled, pointed out some pajamas on a chair. Said her name still wasn't Angie but she'd wait outside.

She went out and I pulled on the bottoms, feeling the pain in my ribs as much as I had the night before. I didn't even bother with the top—that contortion would have dropped me.

I took a look in the wall mirror—and almost turned away. A large bandage covered half of my forehead, surgical gauze protruding from the ends. My left eye was still closed and a deep purple discoloration stained the flesh below it. A raised red knot stood out prominently on my cheek where I took the punch. My hair was matted and sweaty.

I looked like the wreck of the Hesperus, but it was no time for reflection. I grabbed a roast beef sandwich from a platter, tore a chunk out of it, and headed toward the front of the house.

At the edge of the living room I pulled up and leaned in. Late-afternoon sun was flooding in through the sliding doors, bleaching the color from the room. Everything had a yellow hue to it, even the cigarette smoke zephyring by in lazy curls.

I had to look down in order to see, but I made out three figures in the glare.

This time it was just Frank, Peter, and Sam Giancana, the big boss of the Chicago Outfit. He was one of those people for whom Frank had an irrational and dangerous affection. We'd all told him repeatedly to steer clear of those guys, but he saw that as turning his back on his own kind.

Frank saw me and waved me in.

"Gentlemen," he said, "the indestructible Joe Bones, back among the living. Whatsamatter, didn't have any coins for the ferryman?"

He gave me his best wink. I had to smile at that one, but it hurt when I did.

Frank came over and kissed me gently on both cheeks. "Glad you're still with us, buddy," he whispered.

Then he said aloud, "Sam, Joe, you guineas know each other. Sam came down from the Cal Neva up in Tahoe to help us out here. And Joe took one for the club last night, but he'll bounce back."

I nodded to the others and slowly took a seat on one of the sofas without shaking hands.

Giancana's getup looked like a hit job: white loafers, black slacks, the requisite white belt, and a garish black-and-red silk shirt. That alone would have gotten him kicked out of my house.

"*Madonn'!*" the mob boss declared. "You look like someone took a baseball bat to you all right, Buonomo."

"Couple of punks—Maris and Mantle. Anything on Helen, Frank?"

He shook his head. "No. Not a word. I sent some guys out to your plane before the police got over there. Jesus, they said you did a number on Ratello."

I shrugged, gave him a shruggy look.

"The boys combed the area. No sign of Lilah—excuse me—Helen, I guess it is. They brought a few of your things back. Your flightsuit, sunglasses . . . some other stuff."

"My gun?"

"No."

"Your film?"

He paused several seconds, exhaled. "No. We're in Shitsville here, buddy. That film could end any chance Jack Kennedy has of winning next month's election. Can you imagine what that creep Nixon would do with that thing?"

"Let me guess, returning it discreetly is probably not an option?"

He shook his head, smirking bitterly. "There's a better chance the *Lusitania* will float up off the bottom of the Atlantic. Look, the Republicans will ruin him if they get their hands on it—the presidency of the United States is at stake here."

"And there's been nothing from Helen or Spazzo, or anyone else?"

"Not a goddamn thing, but they gotta be together, dontcha think?"

I nodded once. "Yes, I do. Thought we'd have heard from one of them by now."

Frank growled a sigh. "This is one hell of an opera we have going here. A missing girl, a missing mobster, and a missing film—all of 'em together. Joe Kennedy's boys *will* find them, and when they do, Spazzo and the movie are going to disappear forever."

"And Helen?"

He crossed his arms and gave me a leaden stare. "You're going to have to find her first."

"Count on it, pal."

Frank picked up a cigarette from a tray, Peter thrusting out a bejeweled lighter and putting flame to it for him. He took a deep drag, flashed a Bogart grimace, then gestured with his hand, spinning curls of gray smoke into the already foul air.

"So what do we do now?"

I stood up and planted my hands on my hips, frowning impassively. "We wait, Frank. We wait until we hear from them. There's nothing else we can do."

Across the valley, the sun was slipping below the tops of the Santa Rosas, a thin orange corona shimmering above the wrinkled mountains as the day hung on by its fingernails.

I watched it go, lost in thought, trying to make sense of the last four days and my complicated relationship with Frank—and now Helen.

The others left the room, one by one, leaving me to my ruminations. I drifted over to the enormous wall of glass facing west, standing before it in silence as an aching drumbeat began pulsing in my temples.

Outside, purple shadows crept down the hills as evening stole across the desert, wrapping the sands in her long, cool embrace as she enveloped the day, the eternal battle beginning anew.

57

We waited.

All that night. And all the next. Then into the following day. It was just as well since I could only see out of one eye for the first two days anyhow.

The Palm Springs PD went ahead and interviewed me—three times. I told them what I knew: Ratello was a bad guy. He pulled a gun on me. He was a big target.

I gave them my feelings about Spazzo, too, and his new nose. I also described the woman he had with him—but I didn't say she was Frank's girlfriend.

The L.A. boys took a ride out, too. They had a big powwow with the Vegas and Palm Springs detectives. Frank's lawyer handled that one. I got to stay out of the cooler, but each department told me not to leave town. No one ever said in what order, though.

Frank canceled all his appointments, staying inside mainly, taking occasional walks around the grounds. His only meals came out of a Jack Daniels bottle. He asked me a thousand times if I had any ideas. I gave him the same answer a thousand times—we had to wait, Spazzo would contact us.

Late afternoon of the third day, he did.

A telegram came to the house. It read simply: *Have girl. 100k ransom. Details to follow.* It had been sent from somewhere in Mexico, but the sending exchange had been omitted, no doubt at the sender's request.

It was better than knowing nothing.

Frank convened a meeting that night. Roselli came back up from L.A. with two of his boys. Lawford came across town from Vista Las Palmas. I came from the swimming-pool patio where I was resting.

We assumed our usual positions in the living room. Frank began speaking about the ransom request and how he was going to scare up the money. Roselli said he could help. Peter mentioned his father-in-law, Joe Kennedy, as an option. He got told *no.*

Then Roselli suggested an armed intervention. Peter mentioned Joe Kennedy as an option again. He got told *fuck no.*

I sat quietly while this went on, summing up each of the players and calculating his motivation. Frank wanted his girl and the film, but I knew him well enough to know that he'd be okay in the end without either. Roselli wanted the film for his own purposes and didn't give a damn about the girl. Lawford needed both, however, because without the film, Kennedy might not become president, and if he didn't, Frank would have no use for him. And that would put a washed-up actor like Peter in a very lonely place.

I listened to them dicker around a little more, then I cleared my throat aloud and said, "Frank?"

The conversation fell away, and they all looked over at me. Frank said, "Go ahead, Joe."

"Our main asset here is surprise. We don't need money and we don't need an army if we can sneak up on Spazzo."

"But we don't even know where he is."

"Yes, we do."

He crooked an eyebrow. "Where?"

"Mexico."

"It's a pretty big country. Should we start in Mazatlán and just work our way north?"

I shook my head. "I've got somewhere else in mind. I'm going to need some help, though."

Frank put his hands on his hips, his face puckered in curiosity. Roselli looked on with a grin favored by tiger sharks. Lawford stared at his shoes.

"I can leave tonight. I'm pretty much in one piece again—most of the purple in my face has faded to a lovely light green. I can do this, but I could use a couple of guys."

"Who?" Frank and Roselli asked in unison.

"Them," I said, pointing to Roselli's two men outside on the patio.

"Done," said Roselli.

He stood there smiling at my brass as I mused, *Here you go, Joe, another Mexican holiday. Hope it ends better than the last one.*

58

Within two hours, we were rolling south in a station wagon of un-known provenance toward the border at Mexicali, outfitted like three guys on a fishing trip. Rods, reels, tackle boxes, binoculars, brass knuckles, handguns—the usual stuff. Me and Vito and Lino, my two new best friends, just getting away from it all.

The truth is I didn't have any choice. What I needed was four or five crack guys I could trust with my life, an airplane, and Helen's pre-cise location. What I had was two mobsters, a Rambler wagon, and a wild-ass hunch. But there wasn't any time to waste if we were going to get the drop on Spazzo.

Vito and Lino wouldn't have been my first choice—or second or third—but at least I knew they were good enough to be Roselli's body-guards. That meant they were street smart—and tough.

I'd met Vito before and liked him. He was from the old country, and I'd spent some time over there—that gave me an in with him. Lino was Vito's friend. That didn't hurt, either. Under the circumstances, I liked my hand.

We drove south on 111, past Indio and the wine-dark surface of the Salton Sea, a forty-mile-long testament to man's stupidity. One of the guys asked about it, and I told them its history.

Around 1900, engineers had diverted the Colorado River for irrigation, but the water jumped the dikes and poured into a dry seabed. It took two years before they could stop the water flow. When they finally did, the poor town of Salton lay submerged forever beneath sixty-five billion gallons of water.

To me, it was a metaphor for the whole week—human carelessness creating an uncontrollable, spreading disaster—all of it preventable.

Vito said he hoped that we'd have better luck than those engineers. I told him luck struck me as a piss-poor thing to pin your hopes on, adding that I'd rather heed Virgil's advice: Fortune favors the bold.

~

We made Calexico in two hours, stopping on the American side for gas and to double-check the weapons we'd stashed in a hollowed-out area of foam in the backseat. Lino kept the attendant busy while Vito made sure the guns were still secure and well hidden.

I walked away from the pump to burn a Lucky, stopping at the edge of the service station, just out of the light. I lit my cigarette and gazed into the wasteland, where the gravel faded into brown dust and midnight.

A warm breeze was blowing across the open desert, tumbling brush and spinning up tiny dust devils that danced like pocket tornadoes across the arid plain. Those annoying green crickets were chattering away somewhere in the darkness. I hoped there was a spider waiting for each one of them out there.

The lights from a couple of squad cars winked in the darkness. They were parked along the side of the intersecting road several hundred yards away. Some policemen were walking around in the dark, sweeping the ground with their flashlights, the beams bouncing off the dirt, making sinuous shadows on the surrounding scrub brush and cactus. I watched them while I smoked, wondering what in hell they were rooting around for out there.

I finished my cigarette, stepped on the butt, and walked back to the car. The police were forgotten by the time we hit the border, another ephemeral moment buried forever in the dunes of memory.

We got lucky with the Federales. Three "fishermen" with hard faces—one of them wearing a hat pulled down low—crossing the border at midnight usually invites a little scrutiny. Maybe they bought our story, or maybe it was the twenty bucks Lino slipped the agent when he handed him his driver's license.

We took Highway 2 west toward Tecate. Lino did all the driving while Vito and I sat in back and shot the shit. He'd been in the United States ten years, but the *H* in his vocabulary apparently didn't make the crossing. Other than that, he spoke well, and intelligently. For a guy involved with the Mafia, I found it hard not to like him.

He grew up in Italy, near Montese. Hill country. I had relatives there on my father's side. We knew some of the same places, probably some of the same people. We switched back and forth from English to Italian. It was a nice conversation, the kind they have in *Vanity Fair*. I almost forgot what we were doing in Mexico.

I dozed off awhile. When I awoke, Vito was drinking from a hip flask. He smiled, his teeth matching the shock of white hair above his tanned face, as he offered me a drink.

"*Che cos'é?*" I asked.

"*Aquavit' di Montese*," he said. "Try it."

Aquavita. The water of life—*grappa*. I grabbed the little cask, took a belt. It was strong, burned a little. But it was good.

I took another swig, let the fire roll around in my mouth, chugged it. The swirling flames lit my furnace all the way down. I was having a shitty week, but the booze was a tiny oasis of comfort, if only for a moment.

"*Grazie*," I said as I handed the grappa back to him. When he reached for it, I noticed a nasty scar on his chiseled upper arm that looked like a bullet wound.

"Take that one for Roselli, Vit?"

"Dees? German sniper. In the hills near Vignola. I was with the Tenth Mountain Division when dey come up from Roma in '44."

"No shit? You were in the American army?"

"No, I was *partigiano*. I 'elp you guys through the *montagne*. I know 'em like back of my hand. We kill a lotta them fucking Nazis, let me tell you. I hate those blue-eyed jackals." He grinned broadly, then drank.

Yeah, I thought as he handed the flask back to me, *I like this guy.*

59

From Tecate we took Highway 3 south through the mountains. We made the coast about three a.m., then stopped at the first big town. The boys looked surprised when I told them it was our destination, but of course, that was the first time I'd told anyone other than Frank anything.

Spazzo didn't want his location revealed when he sent the telegram, so he had Western Union omit the transmitting exchange. It was a smart move, but it told me something—Spazzo didn't have the muscle lined up or the logistics in his favor to make a ransom transfer go smoothly. Even in Mexico, it takes a few days to line up the local authorities and direct bribes to all the appropriate parties. I figured he was playing for time while allowing Frank the necessary few days he'd need to secure the hundred grand in greenbacks he'd be sending down to *La Frontera*. Clever.

But I was smarter than Johnny Spazzo on my worst day. That dumb bastard could never have dreamed that I knew that the six-digit code on the front of a telegram indicated the exact exchange from which any telex message was sent. Western Union used it as a kind of zip code to confirm senders and recipients.

It was a fairly new technology, but I'd read about it in the Long Beach paper some time back. God knows why it was in the paper, but it was the kind of thing you file away in the back of your head when you run with the crowd I do.

It took me about five phone calls, but I finally got someone who was able to tell me the exact location of the sending exchange—Ensenada—about two hours south of San Diego on the Baja coast.

Ensenada had a storied history of prostitution, blue movies, and hard drinking going back to the days of American Prohibition. It wasn't as wide open as Tijuana, but it was farther down into the Mexican Frontera, a place where brass balls bought more than American dollars—exactly the kind of place a simp like Johnny Spazzo might go when he was in a spot. I still didn't have anything close to a position fix, but as far as dead reckoning goes, it wasn't bad.

The Western Union in Ensenada was the only one south of TJ for a hundred miles. It was a fair bet that Spazzo would return there to send his next message. And if it turned out that he had moved farther on down the line, at least we were already in Mexico on the hunt.

I was gambling as usual, but for once I had the loaded dice.

60

The telegraph office was just off Plaza de Agustín, two sloping blocks up from the waterfront. It didn't open until nine so we grabbed a couple of rooms at the Hotel Bahia and knocked off for a few hours.

At nine a.m. sharp, I was standing outside the office, the first—and only—customer in line. Around 9:15, a clerk appeared from the back room with a sheaf of papers in her hand. She ignored me. I waited an impatient minute, then knocked lightly on the door.

The clerk looked up, raised a pair of cheaters to her eyes, and gazed out at me with Latin indifference. I looked at her and she looked at me for a moment, then she broke into a grin and disappeared under the counter. She reemerged a moment later, heading toward me. The lock clicked and then the door swung open, the little bell tinkling gently as the clerk motioned me in with a sweep of her hand.

She was dusky, maybe thirty, with a predator's eyes and breasts like ripe mangos bulging from the top of her low-cut blouse. "*Buenos días, señor,*" she said, in a singsong cadence.

"*Igualmente,*" I replied.

I kept my eyes on her as I followed her to the counter, the second act every bit as good as the first. She popped up behind the counter, leaning over toward me as I neared, her ample charms on full display. I decided to forgo the formalities.

"*Señorita*," I said, fishing a ten-peso note from my pocket and holding it up, "I have a couple of questions and I was wondering if you might be able to help me?"

"*Claro que sí, amor*," she said, giving me a look that would have gotten her knuckles rapped in Catholic school.

Without breaking eye contact, she took the note from my hand, running her fingers gently across mine. Then she buried the money slowly in the abyss between her breasts and adjusted them for my benefit. I tried not to look down her blouse as she did, but there was just so much to not look down at.

We leered at each other for a second, and then I asked her name. She said it was *Esperanza*, Spanish for Hope. I laughed out loud when she said it.

I flirted with her some more to gain her confidence. It was pleasant enough work, and I needed the practice anyway. Then I looked around outside and asked her about any telegrams sent in the last few days, particularly one sent by an American with a broken nose.

She said she didn't recall anyone like that, but a shifty-eyed local had come in the day before and sent a telegram to the United States, requesting that the sending station be omitted.

In her opinion the man was probably employed by one of the area *jefes*, or warlords, since he had a gun clearly visible in his waistband. She added that it wasn't that uncommon in those parts.

I handed her another ten pesos and thanked her for her help. She told me I could always find her at the telegram office by day and at El Faro bar in the evenings, just down the street. I was pretty sure I knew what she did at her second job.

I leaned in close, into the fecund air around her, said, "*Gracias, amor. Nos vemos*," winking for effect.

I was laying it on with a trowel, but I knew my audience.

～

I met the boys back at the hotel. Spanish was a snap for all of us due to it being a cousin of Italian. They had asked around and gotten the skinny on the Frontera. Baja was a fairly lawless land, even by Mexican standards, with a number of crime kings of various enterprises slicing up the region.

Ensenada was apparently more or less neutral ground where the various *jefes* could come and go as they pleased. But that didn't mean they could waltz around without bodyguards. To do that would be to invite a hit. There were, of course, local police and Federales, but they were just so many palms to be greased. It reminded me of the Chicago I grew up in, when Capone ran the show and Mayor Thompson did everything in his power to stay the hell out of the way.

Outside Ensenada, a number of small towns were flung out along the coast and into the mountains to the east. Some of the warlords were said to live in these villages or in fortified haciendas nearby. The whole setup was almost medieval.

It was going to be tricky going around asking about Spazzo without drawing attention to ourselves and incurring the wrath of one of the barons. Then again, so much slime oozed through the streets of Ensenada on any given day that a few more questionable players drifting into town might not even register with anyone. We were fishermen anyway, after all.

Toward that end, we grabbed some coffee in the cantina across the street, making loud talk about all the fish we were going to catch, even asking a few questions of the waitress about who we might see to charter a boat down at the wharf. We did our best to look like dumb Americans down for a little recreation, libation, and sensation. It wasn't that much of a stretch for two of us.

After we ate, we ambled down to the waterfront and found a nice lonely place by the fishing boats to talk. It stunk of dying fish and brine, but we had it all to ourselves.

I sat down on an ancient overturned dinghy, scoping the piers for any signs of trouble. Vito strolled onto the nearest dock, hands on his sturdy hips, marking a weathered black freighter with his piercing stare as it limped out past the breakers. Lino just leaned back against a gullshit-stained piling and pulled out a cigarette, handing another to me.

I sized up Lino. Maybe five seven, with a center of gravity just above the ankles. Broad through the beam and low on the waterline, he had the look of a longshoreman—hands to match. He seemed comfortable down on the dock, a muscle guy all the way. Lino didn't talk much, but his silence told me enough.

They were a funny pair—Vito gregarious and brutally handsome, Lino quiet and just brutal. I needed them both, but they answered to Roselli, who didn't need me at all or even particularly like me. I never let that thought leave my mind.

When my smoke burned down, I tossed the butt in the water, stepped up on the splintering boat, and signaled Vito over.

A pelican went knifing into the harbor a dozen yards away, disappearing with a *sploosh* beneath the gray-green water. I watched to see if he came up with anything, then launched into the game plan.

"Guys, the ransom telegram was placed from the office here in Ensenada—but not by Spazzo. When Ratello went down, that mammaluke Johnny knew he was out of friends and out of his league, so he scatted on down here where he probably has some protection. If we play this right, we can make him or his accomplice when they place the next telegram, tail 'em right to their hideout. With that advantage, we've got a pretty good chance of getting Helen out of there without firing a shot."

"What happens if we don't see nobody?" Lino asked.

"Then we probably have to pay the ransom, but I don't like that one bit, not down here. I don't see any reason why they wouldn't just kill all of us once they have the money. Spazzo knows he's a dead man if he ever shows up in Vegas again, so he's got nothing to lose by greasing a couple of Roselli's men and some no-name pilot."

"And the *signorina*, Joe?"

A gull screamed overhead and swooped by in a dirty white flash.

"Something happens to her, there'll be no place on earth for Spazzo to hide. If not me, then Frank, but somebody will make sure he dies. I don't think he'll hurt her, though. Frank Sinatra can afford the money, so as long as Helen comes out of here alive, Spazzo's in the clear."

Lino scrunched up his face, said, "But I . . ." then stopped.

"Go ahead," I said.

"The money . . ."

"Yeah?" I could see the gears spinning toward high rev in his mind, practically smell the grease as they overheated. His eyes darted toward Vito, then back to me.

"Nothing," he said. "Nothing."

"I don't think we'll see the money down here before late tonight. Frank and Johnny were sorting that out when we left. I imagine someone's coming down with it from TJ or Mexico City. Probably won't wire it in, too many tracks in the sand."

"Okay, Joe, now what we gonna do?" asked Vito.

"Let's head back. One guy watches the telegram office, the other two guys can ask around some more, see if we can get anything on Spazzo. We'll meet back at the hotel after the Western Union closes. *Capisce?*"

"*Sì*," they said together.

We walked back up the cobblestone landing toward the plaza. I thought we'd covered our bases pretty well, but Lino's asking about the money threw me a little. It seemed like he knew something I didn't.

Slowly, and very subtly, I began to feel like a guy taking a walk down a dark alley. We were only seventy miles from the United States, but it felt like a thousand.

61

We stopped in front of the telegraph office on the way back and I rapped out a greeting on the window. Esperanza looked out through the blinds at me, shook her head, and said, "*Nada*," then gave me another one of those obscene looks. I matched it while zigzagging a finger between the boys and myself to indicate they were with me.

Lino took a seat on a shaded bench in the plaza close enough to keep an eye on the office. Vito and I walked on. He said he'd work the waterfront, where there was never a shortage of cons in the know. I decided to work the nightclub district a few blocks away, no bastion of moral rectitude, either.

Spazzo was probably off the radar in Ensenada, like us. That would make him difficult to find, but it also meant he wouldn't warrant any particular loyalty from anyone who did know of him—just another gringo grafter, either way. Five bucks American from me was as good as it was from him. Money always talks—especially in places like Ensenada, where virtue and vice were turned upside down.

Armed with this heartening take on humanity, I waded into the dirty streets of Ensenada, an open sore of a town in a diseased region. Barefoot children played games with sleeping drunks in alleyways, and disheveled women in flimsy dresses watched me impassively from crumbling bar fronts as I passed through the neighborhoods, ever watchful for anything, anything at all.

I stopped in every bar and cantina, inquiring about a dark-haired American woman and a guy with a broken nose. I got a lot of shrugs, a dozen flat-out *no's*, two offers of all the pleasures I could imagine and one, "Why don't you go pound sand?" I didn't know they had that one in Spanish.

On Helen and Spazzo, I got bupkes.

I took five for a smoke, had a short discussion with myself, wondering just how in hell I'd ended up in another no-win deal in another dead-end town. *Last time, Buonomo, last time,* I told myself. I flicked the butt at a cockroach and moved on to the next dead end.

About noon, I decided to grab a bite—any taqueria would do. At the next corner, I spotted a passable walk-up taco joint just across the intersection.

Avenida de las Águilas was a major boulevard and actually had a light and enough traffic to make a guy on foot respect it. When the light changed, I stepped off the curb. At once, all my senses fired off in danger mode.

It rose up fast in my peripheral vision—a large dark limousine—coming on like a charging bull, the driver laying on the horn as if he were the best goddamn mariachi in the whole world. Instinct took over.

I jumped back on the curb as the limo whooshed past me and on through the intersection without slowing a bit—might have missed me by two feet. Before I could muster a curse, another identical limo shot through behind it. Then another. There were five in all—each one zipping by at fifty miles an hour. I rubbed my chin a few times in curiosity while my reflexes retired from battle stations.

The cars were all late-model American, with dark windows and no markings. I didn't make them for government since they didn't have a police escort or the usual garden of federal, state, and regional flags blossoming off every fender. I turned to a man standing next to me on the curb, asked him who it might be.

He looked carefully both ways before responding, curled his lips and said, "*Ese puerco*, Mario Bravo."

Then he spat onto the sidewalk as if the words were venom in his mouth. It took me a second to place the name. He was one of the crime bosses in the area that Vito had reported on earlier. It occurred to me then that I no longer had any business standing on that corner.

"Taxi!" I shouted, stepping back into the street. "Taxi!"

62

I had no particular reason for following Bravo, not even a death wish. The only thing I knew about him was that he was some sort of big shot in the Baja rackets, if there was such a thing. But then again, I didn't have anything else to go on and there was always the chance I'd spot a better restaurant while following him.

He did me one better. After just a mile or so, the flotilla of cars pulled up in front of an impressive three-story white stucco building with vented pink awnings and a sweeping terra-cotta staircase in front. The stairs were faced with colored Mexican tiles and flanked by huge iron lanterns on either end. Doormen in gold jackets swarmed down the fancy steps, buzzing around the limousines parked under a script neon sign that spelled HOTEL CORTÉS in bright salmon letters.

A few other dark limos were parked alongside the hotel, with men who looked a little too serious to be drivers loitering around them. The joint was apparently the cat's pajamas for Ensenada's dice and vice set. I was intrigued.

I let the cab pass by the hotel, then told the driver to stop at the corner. I didn't recognize anyone as we passed, but I saw a burly man in a white suit brushing off a brace of obsequious types who surrounded him. That was probably Bravo.

By the time I'd gotten out of the cab and paid the driver, the swarm of bodies had gone up the staircase, but I caught just a fleeting glimpse of a woman's dress in the crowd as she disappeared into the building. I was a little more intrigued.

I had no idea who the woman was. Maybe it was Bravo's grandmother or sister, or a nun, but I doubted it. Didn't matter, the dynamic was different. A woman changes everything.

A group of bad guys is a group of bad guys, but throw a woman into the mix and you've got a whole new game. Sex, or maybe romance, a curbing of brute behavior at the least, chivalry at best, that charge in the air, that iron taste on the tongue, those unchecked and impossible thoughts in the minds of those who should know better. A woman changes everything—and seldom for the better.

I decided to take a closer look.

63

I played it straight, walking right up the stairs and into the hotel. Some guy in a gold jacket even held the door for me.

I stepped inside, surveying the lobby for a moment, noting the two men in front of the closed wooden doors on the far side of the room. A mustachioed concierge met my glance, smiled, and came forward to meet me in the middle of the lobby, his rose jacket gliding across the room like a low-flying flamingo.

His skin was a perfect brown, bereft of imperfections, and where it was pulled back around his pink gums, an army of ivory white teeth stood at attention to face me. His hair was jet black and crisp, and parted so lovingly and perfectly that I was sure I'd find a level and a tape measure in his pocket if I checked. A vaguely floral scent permeated the air around us. He was one hell of a dandy, this guy, right down to his white bucks.

I measured him coolly with my eyes, said, "*Buenas tardes, señor.* I was wondering if I might have some lunch today."

He grimaced ever so slightly, as if he'd just swallowed a tiny sliver of glass. "I am terribly sorry, señor; any other day and I could offer you the finest dining in Ensenada."

"But today . . . ?" I asked, lingering over the words, knowing the answer to come.

"But today the dining room has been rented for a private engagement." He made a wonderful faux smile, his waxed mustache rising perfectly at each end of his mouth.

"Ohhh. Too bad," I said in mock dejection. "Mind if I look around the lobby? It's a lovely place, I might want to stay here tonight."

"Certainly, sir. There is no finer place on the Frontera. We would love to have you."

Fine. Fine. Everything was fine with him. It was fine with me, too. I said so. We spent an awkward moment admiring each other, then he excused himself to cut across the polished marble toward an English couple that had come down the grand staircase dressed for a coronation.

I moved off slowly, smiling at him once more when he eye-checked me, then slipped around a corner when a throng of people passed through the lobby.

I didn't really have a plan, just wanted to get a better look at Bravo. Maybe Spazzo was with him. There couldn't be that many full-blown bad guys in Ensenada, and none of the others were likely to drop into my lap the way Bravo had. Sometimes you get lucky.

I was due.

The restaurant's name, *El Jardín*, Spanish for "The Garden," was painted on the wall above the wooden doors where the two guards stood. I'd seen places named that before and they were typically courtyard affairs with open-air dining amid small palms and potted plants—the sort of place where everyone has a perfect smile and a chauffeur, and it never, ever rains.

The doors were large enough to suggest a good-size courtyard. That meant the best vantage point would be from above. I wasn't going to get very far trying to pass myself off as the busboy anyhow.

At the end of the hallway I took the narrow side staircase up one flight and slowly pushed the door at the top open. The hallway was empty and the doors all closed. I figured that I was about halfway down the courtyard, so I knocked lightly on the door of the guest room closest to me. No one answered. The knife trick worked again—I can't remember when it hasn't.

The room was made up and well appointed, but I wasn't staying. I cut across the floor to the window and pulled back the curtain to have a look. The view opened onto a courtyard as I suspected. Leaning forward toward the window, I put my nose to the glass and looked down.

A short, tiled roof ringed the courtyard beneath the guest room windows, a dozen or more people visible below it. They were seated in the middle of the open space at long dining tables arrayed in a box pattern. On the far side of the courtyard, I could see just the legs of a man facing me, the end of a pistol tight at his side. The roofline blocked his upward view, but also cut off a good deal of my visibility of the activity below.

I wanted to see who was present, but I didn't have a reason to take any further risk. It appeared to be some bad guys having lunch, nothing more. Maybe it was their annual awards ceremony, or a company picnic, but it really wasn't worth getting shot to find out who won for Best Supporting Gunsel.

And then I saw her. The woman in the dress appeared suddenly from beneath the overhanging roof as she leaned forward to pick up her wineglass. I stooped down low, squinting tightly as I strained to focus on her. But I needn't have bothered.

It was Helen.

64

I stood up, let the curtain fall, and slumped numbly against the wall as I tried to make some sense from this latest inexplicable twist. There she was, not a prisoner but a lunch date. The whole thing was now profoundly absurd.

Who *was* this woman? Who was she with? And what the hell was I doing there? A hundred other questions ping-ponged across my mind, the preeminent one being: How in hell was I going to get her out of there?

I took several deep breaths and thought it over. Bravo didn't know me, wouldn't recognize me, but Spazzo would—and that would be game over. If Helen was there, it followed that the zoot-suit king was, too, probably just out of sight.

Surprise, a key element in any engagement, was mine, but firepower and numbers overwhelmingly favored the other side. This was a fight you walked away from all the way—if you were looking for a fight. But all I wanted was to get Helen out of that room without firing a shot, without making a sound.

I thought of a way, but it required me to get her attention, and it also depended on her not being so startled she gave me away. I had total confidence in one of us.

65

The wood creaked just a little as I slid the mesquite frame open, but not enough for anyone to notice. Fortunately, the window and most of the lower roof were still hidden in the shade from the overhang above me, but the line was creeping backward as the sun arced past the midday point. The lower foot of the roof was already in bright sunlight, so I had maybe twenty minutes of cover.

Slinking out slowly until my waist was even with the sill, I leaned out the window, raising my feet as a balance. Then, placing my hands on the adobe tiles as a brace, I slid down as low as I could get. The tiles were still cool, but they would heat up quick in the sun. The position was awkward, and hurt like hell, but it afforded me a clear view of the principals at the facing table below.

The big fellow in the white linen suit sat in the middle. He had some Spaniard in him, his fine brown skin several shades lighter than that of his companions. It was offset by a textbook desperado mustache, so heavy and sharply angled that it must have been shaped with a chisel. His hands were large and adorned with gold rings just buckling from the weight of their gemstones. On his wrist, he wore a chunky gold bracelet that rivaled a small mine's entire annual output. A pistol butt protruded from beneath his jacket.

I couldn't see his face clearly, but he seemed raffishly handsome and given to rousing bursts of laughter. I heard someone address him as Señor Bravo.

Helen had gone native. She wore silver bracelets and a pale-blue cotton dress of local origin, indigenous designs ringing the white border around her bust. She sat as distantly from Bravo as she could while still being in the same room, seemingly bored to death by the conversation, which was in Spanish. Her face was blank, her mouth a slit. She didn't touch a bite of the fried lobster or avocado salad in front of her, but sipped occasionally from a glass of sangria, a cigarette smoldering softly between her fingers, wisps of smoke backflipping into the balmy air around her.

Several lieutenant types bracketed them, engaging in casual conversation with unseen parties across the table. On either side of the tables, I made out the legs of standing men who were almost certainly guards, their bodies cut off at the thighs by pink sun umbrellas. The guard across from me was now visible to chest level but his head was still out of sight. I didn't see or hear Spazzo anywhere.

I was way out on a limb in a very real sense, but I had to shimmy down just a little lower to get Helen's attention. Flattening myself as much as possible against the warming tiles, I stretched out toward the edge of the roof.

The Baja sun above blazed down upon me as it edged past the overhang, radiating heat tendrils on my neck and arms. Sweat began dripping off my forehead, making tiny splashes on the baked clay roof as I crawled forward.

From nowhere, a raven suddenly fluttered down onto the tiles just a few feet away, flapping his big wings several times as he settled in.

He hopped about on the roof edge a bit, looked over at me once, and then turned his attention to the courtyard diners. He regarded the men below then began a mischievous cawing.

One of the men looked up, straight at the bird, for the longest time.

I froze in fear, waiting for the shouting to begin, but nothing happened. I could tell by his squinting that the sun was almost directly in his line of sight, blinding him to anything above the ledge. After what felt like minutes, he looked away.

Inching forward into the light, my face pressed flat against the steaming adobe, I finally reached the edge of the roof, maybe thirty feet from Helen. Then I waited.

Periodically, she or one of the banditos would look around or up, but with the sun still relatively high above me, I remained lost in the shadows and streaming light. Lunch went on and on, the conversation about drinking and whoring and some poor son of a bitch who found his way into mother earth for a power play gone wrong.

The sun beat down, sweat drenching my shirt, and the raven stayed on, watching the diners, but Helen didn't look up. Still I waited.

Finally, she propped an elbow on the table and laid her chin upon it, dialed out of the whole situation. Bravo said something to her but she didn't respond.

Just then the raven finally took flight, flapping off with a final, noisy caw. Helen's eyes rolled upward toward the bird, toward me.

I took my chance.

Gently but deliberately, I raised my right hand and waved it side to side a few inches above the roofline. She paused, then cocked her head. I could see her eyes focusing on my shaded figure. She made one of those dull faces people make when they're trying to cipher something.

I lifted my head just a little more, pulling my lips back in an anxious smile. A bead of sweat rolled into the corner of my eye, but I stayed locked in.

Then it hit her, the recognition that it was me. Actress or not, her reaction betrayed her, green eyes doubling in size as her face turned bone white. Her mouth fell open just a crack as she mouthed my name.

I shot her a tight smirk; she was due a surprise of her own.

Helen raised a hand to her face and she dropped her head slightly, then she didn't move at all for several seconds. I visually checked Bravo and the others. They hadn't noticed—they were too busy telling stories about dead men and yukking it up.

When I looked back at her, she was still gawking at me, an incredulous look on her face she shielded with her hand. I pointed to her, then made a hit-the-road gesture with my thumb, repeating it several times.

"Get out of there," I said in a minute whisper, accentuating my facial movements for emphasis.

Helen's eyes interrogated me, but her face was a mask. The mask slowly melted into an *I'll be damned* smile, and she closed her eyes and made a subtle nod. Then she turned toward Bravo and spoke, pointing toward the front of the hotel as she did, probably telling him she was going to the ladies' room. He nodded and gestured to one of his men. She stood up, then walked languidly out of sight, followed by the gunman.

I pushed myself away from the ledge by degrees, fading slowly back into the retreating darkness. Slinking backward up the wall, I slipped into the room, watching the men below the whole time. I paused a moment as the pieces of my spine popped back into place, grunting a little as each grudging bone locked back in.

There was no sign that anyone below had seen me. I grinned in self-congratulation just a little as I closed the window and pulled the curtains shut, planning a very speedy checkout from the Hotel Cortés.

When I turned around, a mustachioed man in a gold jacket gave me a big, broad smile.

Then he stuck two pistols in my face.

Smiling back at Gold Jacket, I said, "This room won't do, thank you, I don't much care for the view."

He was not amused.

I went to my trick bag. Sweeping my hands upward, I tried to deflect his weapons away with my forearms. I got the left one, but he was too quick with the right, bringing it down hard across my chin, dazing me.

He was behind me in a flash, tripping me with a shove and a raised boot. The floor came up quick and then I was done, sprawled forward with Gold Jacket on my back, both of his guns jammed against the base of my skull.

"*Adelante*, gringo," he growled, just begging me to make another move.

66

Mario Bravo watched me walk, the conversation in the courtyard falling away as I approached the table, a trickle of blood running from the corner of my mouth and a pair of handguns pressed to my ribs.

Another gunsel leaped to his feet as I passed, gratuitously smacking his pistol against my temple hard enough to make me wince. He was a sawed-off little shit with a low widow's peak and pointy yellow teeth that he kept baring at me. I think he was actually drooling a bit with excitement. He was bucking for tough hombre, but he looked more like a teen vampire. Must have been a helluva sight as the three of us marched toward the head table: the mysterious stranger, the pistol-packing porter, and Pocket Dracula.

Gold Jacket stopped me ten feet out and shoved half his arsenal under my chin, grinding the muzzle up tight against my skin. Bravo put his fork down, dabbed a canary yellow cloth napkin to his mouth, tossed it away with an insouciant flip, and then leaned back into his curved wicker chair.

He put an elbow on the chair arm, resting his chin in the crook between thumb and index finger, studying me as he might a zoo exhibit as I stood before him, his dark eyes dancing with curiosity.

Several of his men had drawn their weapons, but he never so much as blinked.

Gathering his lips in a mirthful grin he asked, "*Quién es este hombre?*" in a baritone that was rich and full and majestic, the words wrapped in a flawless Castilian accent that flowed from his mouth like molten gold.

"Joe Buonomo," I said before anyone could answer. "*Y yo hablo español, Señor Bravo.*"

This positively delighted him. He sat straight up and wet his lips, looking directly into my eyes for the first time. He took the measure of my face, leaned back again, and crossed his arms slowly across his chest as if he were Cuauhtémoc at a war council.

As he sat there in bemused reflection, Gold Jacket approached him and whispered into his ear for several seconds. Bravo arched one eyebrow while he listened, his face dipping down into a stony glare.

"Señor Buonomo," he began in a Stratford-upon-Avon accent, "my associate here says you have placed yourself in a highly untenable situation. Please, sir, pray tell, what might you have been doing on that rooftop? And let me caution you that your life may depend on the answer you furnish me."

"I've come here to take the girl away from you."

Surprise flooded his face, his pupils dilating. "Is that so?" he asked, incredulity coloring his voice. "And how did you intend to accomplish that? Might you be in the vanguard of some army of liberation?"

"It is so. I intended to go out through the bathroom window. And there's no army—just me."

He was completely at a loss for words for several seconds, his mouth forming a little donut as he grappled with his astonishment. Finally, he managed, "Have you any idea of who I am, sir?"

"No. All I know about you is that the man who told me your name called you a pig."

Bravo just stared at me a heavy minute, eyes narrowed. Then he broke into an immense grin and erupted with laughter. He translated my words for all and then roared some more. All the men broke into loud, derisive guffaws, their howls raining down upon me, echoing across the courtyard, Bravo laughing loudest of all, the ivory handle of his pistol gleaming in the fullness of the sun.

Then he signaled Drac, and something hard came down on the back of my head. I sank to my knees, then took a low punch in the belly from Gold Jacket. I grunted from the pain, air bursting from my lungs. A locomotive roared through my head, its whistle on full blow as I knelt doubled up on the terrazzo, clutching my bucking stomach. My eyes dimmed, but I didn't fall.

Bravo told the two men to take me away. Far away.

The little guy reached down, grabbing for my arm. I popped him a good one in the chops, the blow knocking him sideways on a drunkard's reel. He took two woozy steps, then fell on his ass as I struggled up on one knee. A dozen guns clicked in the still courtyard. No one was laughing anymore.

Then a woman shouted, "Don't kill him!," in steel-edged Spanish.

Heads turned toward the courtyard entrance. The woman was Helen, a hand thrust in the air, her features flint hard.

"Don't kill him," she repeated. "And keep your hands off him, you little animal!" she ordered, pointing toward the half-size gunsel.

I knelt there, astonished. *Now you speak Spanish?*

Bravo shifted in his chair, casually casting inquisitive eyes upon Helen.

"Frank sent him," she declared, marching toward us. "He's here to bring you the ransom money, Mario. Don't lay a finger on him or you'll scotch the whole works. *Sabe, muchacho?*"

"My dear," said Bravo, "if Mr. Sinatra sent him with the money, why is he here trying to ferret you away like a *guajiro* stealing a teenage bride? Surely he wouldn't condone such a dishonorable act."

"Why should I pay you if I don't have to?" I said, spitting scorn. "It's not like you're making an ethical proposition in the first place."

Helen cut in before I could do any more harm. "Just let him go. Never mind his cracks. Let him go, and . . . and . . . I'll do what you asked."

A part of her spirit left her when she uttered those last words. I could see the defeat filling her eyes.

Bravo, preening like a champion peacock, looked over at me, then back at Helen, smugness spreading over his mug. "Get him out of here," he said, fluttering a hand at me.

I stood up and flexed my swelling knuckles, glowering at the men around me.

"Señor Buonomo," Bravo said, "Mr. Sinatra will be told where and when to deliver the money. If you are still in his employ, then we shall meet again. But I caution you, any more Errol Flynn chicanery will be dealt with in the most expedient way possible, and with very permanent results. Do not cross me again . . . *vaquero*."

Drac and Gold Jacket walked me out, shoving me several times as I looked back toward Helen. I managed a final malevolent glare at them, then watched Helen, Bravo, and the whole gang disappear behind the twin doors as they slammed home with a heavy thud.

She was still right there, but I was flat out of options at the moment—I didn't even have a gun. I had to walk away, helpless and defeated.

So I left the Hotel Cortés, trudging across the marble lobby past the startled dandy, down the tiled stairs, away from the pink awnings and iron lanterns, and out into the hot afternoon streets of Ensenada.

67

I headed off down the main boulevard. Just walking, thinking, trying to get my head around exactly what was going on with that woman. I made several blocks without noticing much of anything, drifting in my own personal dust cloud.

I passed a city park with a circular hub in the open center. Instead of the typical fountain, this one contained a large stone object angled up from the concrete on a dais. It took me a few seconds before I recognized the piece. It was a replica of the Aztec sun disk dug up near the Zócalo in Mexico City in the 1800s.

Several worn benches curved around the stone platform in a semicircle, shaded by some Blue palms. I wanted a smoke, and I needed to sit and think, so I ambled over and grabbed a seat facing the stone slab. A drunk snoozed quietly on the next bench over. Other than him, I was alone.

I pulled out the last nail from the pack and lit it, then crumpled the empty package and banged it into the wire basket next to me. I let out some smoke and gave the stone icon a long once-over. I'd seen the original on a stop in the capital a few years back. A single massive stone block cut into a platform for dueling gladiators, it was immense, intimidating, and an undisputed national treasure.

The replica was smaller in diameter, but accurately rendered, with the same carved-relief skulls, jaguars, snakes, and other figures adorning the surface. Four symbol boxes surrounded a sun god in the center of the work. The god was pissed, or maybe just gassy, but either way the old guy was blessed with some seriously oversized choppers and a waving pointed tongue that stabbed out at a now-indifferent world.

He must have been quite terrifying in his time, but he hadn't been enough to stop Cortés from wiping the Aztecs off the face of the earth. *Chopped the heart right out of an entire civilization. For that he gets a hotel with fucking pink parasols named after him. Go figure.*

I vaguely recalled reading that the boxes around the sun represented the four major catastrophes in man's history. I knew one thing as I studied each—the guy who carved them never met Helen Castano, or there would've been a fifth square on that baby for sure.

~

I continued my smoke, still studying 'ol *chicle* teeth as I mulled the day's developments in my head.

"A magnificent civilization, no?" someone declared in a hearty voice.

Startled, I looked up, into the eyes of Mario Bravo. He'd closed in on me while I was lost in thought. He stood there above me, alone but not unarmed. I had no idea what was going to happen next.

"Other than the ritual sacrifice thing, I'd have to agree," I offered.

Bravo smiled congenially at me. "May I sit down?"

"I can't imagine I'm in a position to refuse," I said, scanning the park for his entourage.

But the only one I could see was Pocket Drac, agitating about in front of the limo parked across the street. I knew he was just itching for a chance to even the score with me.

Bravo sat down next to me on the bench and leaned back, the gun under his arm dangerously close. "Joe, after you left, Helen explained to me who you are. She told some fascinating tales about your adventures."

"Any of them involve Johnny Spazzo?"

"Who might he be?" he asked, his face curling into a question mark.

That threw me off step—Bravo didn't even know Spazzo.

"Nobody," I said, covering, "just another con."

He let it pass, then continued. "If even half of what Helen tells me is true, you are a man to be reckoned with most highly. I'm terribly sorry I had my men rough you up. Is it true, then, you are a close friend of Mr. Sinatra's?"

"Yes, that's true," I said, locking my eyes on his. "How does that figure into this?"

This seemed to please him a great deal. He beamed like he'd just solved the Sunday crossword puzzle. As he did, I eyed his pistol butt just inches from my hand. Bravo caught me looking at his gun, made no effort to move.

"Oh, please, Señor Buonomo," he chided, "you wouldn't make such a rash play now, would you?"

He had me. I shook my head in agreement, flashed him a grin. "You can't blame me for thinking about it; I'm not sure how this thing ends today."

"*Cómo no!* I would have been disappointed if you hadn't, but you are in no danger here unless that drunkard urinates on you. Here, would you like to see it?" he asked, pulling out the weapon. "It belonged to one of Franco's generals. I took it from that *comemierda* after I bayoneted him in El Mazuco."

He placed the gun in my palm. A Mauser, blued metal with gold scrolling, offset by an ivory grip. It was beautifully balanced, just a bit effeminate for my taste, and large enough to command respect anyhow. I turned it over a few times, reflecting on how a German pistol had come to a Spanish general and then a Mexican gangster, ever ready to kill regardless of owner.

"You see, Joe, we are not so terribly different, are we? Yes, it's true, I fought against the *Fascistas* in Spain, and you fought the Japanese in China. We're both idealists to some degree—with a flair for violence."

"Funny."

"What's that?"

I looked over at him, locked eyes. "I'd have figured you for a Franco guy all the way, not a Loyalist."

He forced a bitter smile, looked down, paused before speaking. "I was a better man once."

I handed him the weapon, butt first. "Weren't we all?"

He stowed the pistol, then he produced a small silver case from his coat and popped it open, revealing three Romeo y Julietta torpedoes and a cigar cutter that looked strong enough to take off my big toe. He extracted two cigars, clipped them carefully, and handed one to me.

I pulled my lighter—slowly—then lit his cigar. I chomped down on my own, puffing vigorously several times as the fire scorched its end. The clean, smooth taste of fine tobacco came seeping into my mouth, a pungent tang filling my nostrils. The cigar was excellent. I still wasn't sure if I was leaving the park upright or feet first, but either way I was going to enjoy the smoke.

Our communal act was driving Drac apoplectic. From the corner of my eye, I could see him hopping around in frustration near the limo. I blew some smoke in his direction, just to jack him a little.

"Drink?" Bravo asked.

Fuck, why not? "Sure."

Bravo snapped his fingers above his head and held up two fingers like Winston Churchill signaling victory. Drac tilted his head, hesitated, and then disappeared into the back of the limousine.

I took a long drag on my cigar and surveyed the park, letting the rush of the cigar climb to my brain unchallenged. The setup was more than a bit strange, but I'd learned to go where the night takes me as Roscoe once put it. Hey, if Bravo wanted to drink in a public park, we'd drink in a public park. It was Mexico, after all.

Drac came creeping over, holding two glasses and a couple of bottles of alcohol. He held them up cautiously, asking, *"Todo bien, jefe?"*

Bravo said, *"Sí,"* in a voice so tight and dismissive that the little man almost cringed to death. Drac half bowed, then placed the bottles and glasses on the bench, shooting me a profane look as he did. Then he scurried away, his head bobbing from the inaudible obscenities escaping his mouth.

I looked over the booze. One bottle was a French brandy of some apparent significance. The other a bottle of aged mescal from Oaxaca. Bravo looked into my eyes, said, *"Cual quieres, señor?"*

It was a test, but an easy one.

"Mescal."

ONE FOR OUR BABY

"Bueno."

He poured two stiff shots, held his glass up toward me, and said, *"Salud."*

I raised mine, clinked it against his, and declared, *"Cent' anni,"* marking his brown eyes and matching his stare while we drank the smoked agave down.

We passed a long moment in consideration of the liquor, then Bravo turned to face me.

"Joe, I am many things, but above all, I am a businessman. A criminal, yes, but a business-oriented criminal. What we have here is a simple transaction. Your friend Mr. Sinatra stole something from me that has fallen back into my lap unexpectedly. I no longer want it, but it is morally right that he compensate me for his original transgression."

I held up a hand. "Excuse me, but since when does morality figure into kidnapping?"

"Such a vulgar term, *kidnapping,*" he said, in a voice that would have put a smile on Basil Rathbone's face.

"I don't know what else to call it when someone is held against her will for a ransom."

He frowned. "Everything is not exactly as it seems here, Joe, but please understand that I mean no harm toward Miss Castano or Mr. Sinatra either way. Under the circumstances we have, I think one hundred thousand dollars American is not too high a sum to settle his debt to me and secure possession of his paramour. Wouldn't you agree?"

Bravo hadn't made any mention of the film. Truth was, it wasn't really any of my concern any longer, so I stuck to the business at hand.

"I would not agree, Señor Bravo, but I don't have a hundred grand lying around in last night's pants. In light of the fact that Mr. Sinatra does, however, I will be willing to swap you the money for the woman, but in return, you must agree to buy a copy of all of his albums to date."

"You are jesting, no?"

"I am jesting, yes, but only on the second part. I'll have your money tomorrow. I take you for enough of a gentleman that you won't have me shot dead once you have it."

Bravo's face scrunched up like he'd eaten a week-old anchovy. "What a dreadful thought. Once I have secured the money, the debt will be settled. To harm you or Helen would be highly dishonorable and reflect very badly upon me. Additionally, I would then be the one guilty of a slight against the very man whose apology I am demanding."

"Okay," I said, nodding, "but we'll be doing this in a public place, not at Ciudad Bravo."

"If that is what you wish. Again, my interest here is purely a matter of honor. Let us agree upon this—when you have secured the necessary funds, call me and allow me time to send my men to whatever exchange point you choose in Ensenada. Those are very generous conditions under the circumstances."

He took out a gold fountain pen as he spoke, put a telephone number on a wedge of paper, and handed it to me. "As my *hacienda* is a good distance from here in Ojos Negros, it will take them some time to get back into town."

"Fair enough. But I have a question for you, Bravo."

"Mario."

"Mario. If your interest is only one of chivalry, why do you require any money at all? Surely you make a great deal more than that in your various endeavors here at home. Wouldn't a sincere apology from Sinatra be more valuable?"

I had him there. He said nothing for a while, mulling things over. Then, with an undertaker's gravity he pronounced, "Everything in life comes with a price, Joe. Everything."

We sat there a moment, Bravo's words hanging in the air. I took another long drag on the cigar and blew out the smoke, failing as usual to make a ring with it.

Bravo was watching Drac's histrionics with a contemptuous eye, hashing out some issue in his head. He turned back toward me and said, "We are finished here today, my friend. You are free to go. But I have a small request to make of you."

"Shoot," came out before I could stop it, but he passed on the chance to gibe me.

"I am not a man given to impulsive behavior—but I am a man with an immediate grasp of other men's character. I like you, Joe Buonomo. I like what I heard about you, but I like what I saw today even more."

"You should see me on home turf, I'm a world-beater there."

He smiled tightly. "Please hear me out before you roll out the sardonic flourishes. You may cause me to call my own recently trumpeted judgment into question."

I acknowledged his words with a head tilt and a grin, turning a palm up and shaking it the way my uncle Emilio used to do.

Then Bravo placed a ring-laden hand on my shoulder and issued an entirely unexpected invitation. "After tomorrow's affairs are concluded, I would like to have you as a guest at my *hacienda*."

"What would I do there, teach those *jíbaros* of yours English?"

"No, I have something much more substantial in mind. You are an intrepid man, possessed of a quick wit and no small amount of courage. You speak our language, can pilot a plane, and, from what I hear, are extremely handy with a gun. Look at these *payasos* I have to deal with here." He gestured toward Drac, then waved his hand in disgust. "These men are better suited to herding goats than protecting me. I think you would be an excellent lieutenant—"

"You're gonna have to call me Lieutenant Commander. The navy did, and I'm not taking any busts in grade to work in this backwater."

That caught him off guard. "If you are serious, Joe, I could make you a wealthy man—and a powerful one."

"All right, but I want a corner office with a view, and my own secretary, and lots more of these cigars," I said, holding the torpedo up and admiring it.

He realized then that he'd been had. His perma-smile wilted and his eyes closed ever so gently, as if he'd felt a pain somewhere deep inside. He placed his hands together, fingers spread in a quasi-papal gesture. After a lengthy pause, he said, "Should you decide to consider my offer after our business is concluded, I would still be happy to entertain you for a few days."

"I have considered it, thank you."

He wet his lips, cast eager eyes on me. "And . . . ?"

I shook my head. "I've been down that road, Mario. It's a dark trip, brother."

"Is it money? Girls? Whatever you want, I can get—"

"You can get bent, mister, okay?"

His eyes lit up, the brows curling, his lips pursed in astonishment.

I leaned in close to him, pointing with the cigar. "You may be rich and you may have great power down here, but I know you don't sleep at night, not with the voices of all those dead men calling out to you, not with their eyes on you in the dark. I'm all done with that kind of shit. You're right, Mario, everything does have a price. And yours isn't nearly high enough to buy what's left of my soul."

To my surprise, he took it. Just sat there and took it, looking flummoxed and sad. Then his eyes perked up and his lips slowly parted, a wry smile replacing the frown. "Well well well," was all he said, shaking his head in bemusement.

I gathered that it had been a very long time, if ever, since someone had told Mario Bravo where he could get off. "Thanks for the cigar," I said, rising in front of the Aztec carving, *"y buena suerte."*

"Good luck? For *me?*"

"For all of us."

I turned my back to him, took a final, long look at the totem of a ruined people, then drifted quietly away.

68

I walked back to the hotel, giving myself more time to think. After half an hour, I made the corner of San Augustín and headed for the home stretch, just four blocks or so from the hotel.

Thirty yards ahead, two men were leaning against an old DeSoto, looking as natural in Ensenada as whipped cream on a burrito. They were fair skinned, thin lipped, and well built. Both men had short hair, one of them a California blond flattop. They wore matching Wayfarers, too, as if that would keep anyone from making them.

They hard-stared me the whole thirty yards, taut faces assessing the threat as the distance between us fell, then rose again. I didn't know them from Cain and Abel so I just kept walking—I didn't give a shit what their deal was as long as it didn't involve me. By the time I crossed the next street, they were forgotten.

At Plaza de Agustín, I signaled to Lino and head-nodded him back to the hotel. Vito came in about fifteen minutes later. We took a walk together toward the water. I decided to get their news before spilling mine.

"Lino, what do you know?" I asked.

"*Niente*," he said. "I got nothing. Three customers all morning.

Older señora, some guy in a suit—banker maybe—and some old guy, runs a bakery, I think. *Niente*."

"Vit?"

"I walk around, hit the docks, coupla bars, talk with some 'ookers."

"*Talk?*"

"*Sì* . . . talk."

"Sample anything?"

"I . . . ehhh . . ." He broke into a broad grin. "Maybe."

We all had a laugh. Why not?

"You gotta earn their trust, get close," he said.

"Very close, I imagine." I shook my head in bemusement. "Okay, then, did she tell you anything—other than the price?"

"*Sì*, lots. They got four crime bosses here. Godínez—drug runner—piece of shit, nobody. Perez-Henríquez, he got the restaurants, sports racket. Fat bastard—not too tough. On the waterfront, you got Carrucho. Bad guy. 'ookers, drugs, *contrabanda*, robbery, murder—you name it. But, Joe, nobody knows anything about Johnny Spazzo or the girl. I ask everybody, they just shrug."

"What about the fourth guy, you got anything on him?"

"Yeah, yeah. Bravo, Mario Bravo. He's the *gran formaggio* around this place. Dees is a fascinating guy. 'e starts with money, way back from Spain. 'e imports shit— Serrano ham, olive oil, wine—sends tequila out. Nice life, but 'e don't wanna play it straight. 'e goes with the devil, like we say back 'ome."

"Doing what?"

"He starts with 'ookers, moves up to party girls for rich guys, meets some 'ollywood people, tries to be a movie producer. They laugh 'im outta Los Angeles. So 'e goes to Tijuana, makes dirty movies instead—that's big money. 'e makes 'imself the L. B. Mayer of fucking. Anyway, this guy, 'e starts bumping off the smaller fish over the years till he 'as an empire of pussy—like 'ugh 'efner with a machine gun, ahahahahah!"

He and Lino laughed like kids awhile. I said nothing. Vito looked over at me, still giggling, wiped his eye. The laughter trailed off.

"That's a lot of information from one girl, *amico*. You sure about all that, Vit?"

"Actually, there were two girls. The second one, she confirm what the first one tells me."

More laughter. I threw my hands up.

"What about you, Joe," Lino asked. "How'd you make out? Anything?"

"No, not much. Just had a drink with some guy. He told me a little about things down here."

"Ahh. Anybody important?"

"Dunno. Just some guy name of Mario Bravo. Whaddyathink?"

I brought the boys up to speed, told them we'd make the trade the next day then worry about the film when we knew more. As far as I could tell, it was just Bravo and us. If Spazzo had been in on the play, he'd either been paid off, muscled out, or sent over. Didn't matter to me, he was the kind of guy you wiped off your shoe anyhow.

I told the guys to relax awhile, I was going to check in with Frank and take the Rambler for a spin. Nothing was going to happen until the money came in anyhow. I asked a local where the nearest gas station was. He told me it was just a few blocks off. I figured I'd gas up the car, find a pay phone, and place a collect call to the good old U.S. of A. Besides, I needed a map.

69

"Hi, Frank. It's me."

"Joe, good to hear your voice, buddy."

"I found her."

"Thank God."

"If you want, but I did the looking. Anyway, Helen's okay; she's with some guy named Mario Bravo. Ever hear of him?"

"No. Should I have?"

"Well, he's heard of you, brother."

"I'll send him a glossy. Is he gonna let her go?"

"Yeah. We're gonna need that money, though, Frank. This guy Bravo draws a lot of water down here and we gotta do it his way. He's got the men, the weapons, and the home field advantage. You're gonna have to pony up the hundred large."

"That's no problem, I've got it here." He lowered his voice a few octaves. "We can't wire it down for obvious reasons, but Johnny has two guys who are arriving here in an hour from L.A. They'll be the couriers. They can meet up with you tonight. How soon can you have my baby back?"

"We're set up for tomorrow. We'll head for San Diego immediately.

I want to get the fuck out of this country—a lot of things are not adding up down here, my friend."

"Well, let's not take any chances here. If it's not safe—"

"No, that's not it. Bravo seems legit. He had me in a vise, twenty guns at my head. He let me walk, says Helen will be free to go tomorrow."

"You believe him?"

"I've got to."

"So what's the problem?"

I exhaled deeply, knocked the phone against my temple twice. "We're gonna need to talk when we get back. All of us."

"Okay. First get her home. We'll worry about later later."

"Will do. Oh, Frank . . . one more thing . . . there's been no mention of the film. It's either a separate play or Spazzo's off with it somewhere."

"Shit. Well, that's Jack's bad luck. Just please bring my baby home."

"Our baby, Frank. Call you when the money's here. We're at the Hotel Bahia at Plaza Augustín in Ensenada, just off Via Pacifico. I'm in room number eight if anything urgent comes up."

"I can never repay you for this."

"Stow it."

"Right."

He said good-bye and we hung up.

The attendant had finished pumping the gas and cleaning the windshield. I asked him for a good map of the region and paid him for everything when he returned with it.

I walked over and unfolded the map on the hood of the station wagon. Ojos Negros lay about twenty miles to the east amid rising mountains. Several little villages dotted the map between Ensenada and Ojos Negros. I checked my watch and set out for the first one, maybe five miles outside town.

Bravo had asked me to pick a spot in Ensenada, but that was the last thing I was going to do. He made a strategic error there—one I intended to exploit. I needed a small town, away from his likely police support. A place small enough that I could see his guys coming but big enough to have a safe place to duck into if the deal went bad.

Bravo had the upper hand, but I was going to press every advantage I had. It was the only way I was ever going to get any of us out of

Mexico. If we went missing, no one in the country would be rushing to call Interpol. Two dead mobsters and a freight pilot wouldn't even rate a paragraph in the afternoon paper down on the Frontera.

70

The first town I hit was too small—little more than a village. No cover, no siting, no good. I pressed on.

The second town showed promise. A decent main drag, a central rectangular plaza, maybe three hundred by two fifty, and a large dry fountain anchoring the center.

There were plenty of small shops and just enough foot traffic to keep things honest. None of the buildings, save the church that dominated one end, had a second story to hide a shooter, and the walls were all brick—thick enough to stop a bullet.

A temporary wooden stage sat empty at the west end of the plaza, opposite the church. They'd probably had a show of some kind the night before and hadn't gotten around to dismantling it yet, hardly surprising in Mexico.

I watched the people come and go. *Campesinos* mostly. Worn faces, tired eyes, lean bodies, leathered hands. Not the grafter set I'd seen so much of in Ensenada. They went about their business buying vegetables or clothing without paying me much mind, either not caring about gringos or too busy trying to beat a living out of the day to bother with an outsider.

Several kids plied me with *chicles* and small toys. One tried to boost my wallet. Other than that, they left me alone.

The church bothered me. There was a small offset bell tower that gave out a bad vibe. I was a stranger in churches anymore, but decided I better check this one out. I strolled over to the large wooden doors, scoped left to right, then bowed my head and ducked inside the candlelit interior.

The nave was deceptively large—and predictably dark. I dropped a coin in the donation box, struck a wooden match, and put it to a votive candle that sputtered a few times before flaring brightly.

I wandered over toward the shadowed confessionals off to one side, then made for the darkened stairway beyond. A few worshippers sat in prayer among the pews, but they were all heads down, murmuring to the saints while I was head up, eyeing the stairs to the bell tower.

Holding the candle up before me, I peered into the shadowy archway and then put my foot on the first stair.

A soothing voice behind me inquired in Spanish, "May I help you, my son?"

Startled, I straightened up, spilling hot beeswax onto my hand. I turned around, my eyes falling on a graying man in a brown Franciscan robe tied with a white rope.

The padre was thin but wiry, with a full head of close-cut hair, more salt than pepper, offsetting his angular brown features. He was of average height, yet seemed somehow taller, even though he wore simple flat sandals. He was smiling at me as I looked on at him.

"H-hello, Father," I said. "I was wondering if I might go up to the bell tower."

"You're not from around here, are you?"

"No, Father, I'm not."

I was hunting for a story. He gave me one. "But you speak Spanish very well," he said. "Are you a missionary?"

"Uh, yes . . . sort of." I flexed my thumb, trying to dislodge the cooling wax.

He smiled again, crow's-feet taking flight around his eyes. A lean hand emerged from the folds of the robe. "I am Father Lázaro, pleased to meet you."

"Lázaro?"

"Yes," he nodded. "And I rise from the dead every morning—a dead sleep."

He laughed heartily at his own joke, although he must have told it often.

I grasped his hand and we shook. His grip was firm. He held on a good ten seconds, his sharp brown eyes meeting mine the entire time, the smile ever present on his face.

"Tell me your name, my son."

He had me completely disarmed. I said, "Joe," before I even knew I was speaking. The man just had a way about him.

"Come, Joe," he said, placing his arm around my shoulder and leading me toward the stairs. "Let's have a look at that bell tower, shall we?"

~

Father Lazáro showed me the rotting floor of the belfry, explaining that it was no longer possible to access the tower. When I asked him why they didn't repair it, he said there simply wasn't any money. Then I made the mistake of asking why they didn't petition the great and powerful Mario Bravo for assistance since it was his corner of the Frontera. The padre's features grew tight, his hawk-like eyes narrowing.

"We could never accept anything from him. We are poor people here in Agua Caliente, but it is far better to do without than to be touched by his corrupt soul."

I bit down hard on my tongue.

He led me downstairs then, to a small garden in a courtyard behind the church where we sat on a sun-beaten wooden bench. I kept trying to get away, but he buttonholed me another forty minutes, asking my opinion and offering his own on a range of topics. Among others, we covered divinity, salvation, the islands of the South Pacific, and the deeper meaning of the Pirates upending the evil Yankees in the World Series. We didn't agree on much, but he was an intelligent and intuitive man, and I enjoyed talking with him a great deal.

Finally, I stood up, begging his forgiveness but telling him I had to go. He assented grudgingly, then walked me out through the church to the wooden doors, his arm still around me.

"Tell me something," he said, gesturing toward my bruised face, "you're not a missionary, are you?"

"No, Father, I'm not."

"But you are searching for something, aren't you?"

"We all are."

He nodded, smiling. "Well, Godspeed to you."

"Thank you. Say . . . Father Lázaro?"

"Yes, Joe?"

"Would it be all right if I made a donation to your church?"

"Certainly."

I dug out a hundred-peso note. He looked at it suspiciously, said it was too much money. I told him to start a fund for a new bell tower floor with it.

We shook hands again, exchanging warm glances. Then we parted company.

"Safe journey, my son," he called out after me.

I thought I heard him say something else about a celebration, but I was already halfway across the plaza. Didn't matter, I wasn't long for Mexico anyhow.

I took a final walk through the town hub, then headed back toward the car. It was still there—and not even on blocks.

It took three pieces of the gum I got from the kids to make a bubble, but I managed one, popped it, and then dropped into the driver's seat. I put my new wooden turtle toy on the dashboard, flicked its head, and watched as it bobbed up and down stupidly. It made me smile just the same.

Then I put the wagon in reverse, carved a half circle in the dust and rolled out of town.

Agua Caliente. Nice name—for the capital of dirt nowhere.

It would do.

71

I wasted another hour and a half exploring other towns, but decided to stick with Agua Caliente in the end. I also asked several people what they knew about Ojos Negros, but most knew little, or at least said so. From what I gathered, it was a company town and Mario Bravo was the factory. Whatever went on there was tied to his activities and wasn't much in any event.

His hacienda was said to be impressive and well-nigh impregnable, crowning sloping terrain and backing right up to a sheltering U of mountains that rose two thousand feet above the plain below. Stables, crew quarters, and a garden maze were all said to be contained inside the twelve-foot walls that encircled the property and merged into the steep cliff walls on either side. I got this gouge for twenty pesos from a guy who said he did some construction work on the place a few years back. I wasn't sure I believed him, but he wore the tools of a carpenter and spoke with precision. I filed it away as potentially useful information.

I got back to the hotel around six, just as the sun was slipping into the Pacific. Dark shadows fell across the plaza as the day receded, subsuming the light and etching sinister shapes into the walls the way they do in those RKO pictures.

On a hunch, I stuck my head inside the open doorway of El Faro, Esperanza's bar. The boys were playing cards at a side table, whiskey glasses at hand. Smoke hung in the air around the table, spun softly by a ceiling fan turning at an indifferent rhythm. The room smelled like dirt, was about the same color.

Vito winked at me as I approached. Lino pulled out a chair, waved his hand toward the bartender, and pointed down toward me with a thick finger.

"Bourbon," I shouted out as I seated myself.

Esperanza brought over a chipped shot glass full to the brim with amber liquor and put it down in front of me. She gave me another salacious look then sauntered away, hips moving hypnotically to an inaudible beat.

I raised the bourbon up to the light, toasted Esperanza's contours, then threw it down in one swallow. I said nothing afterward, letting the boys finish their hand, the booze seeping down in my tongue like rain into parched earth.

Lino drew a card, flashed a stiletto smile, then flung his hand on the table with more flair than warranted and said, "Gin."

"*Cazzo!*" Vito griped, tossing his cards down.

A quick chin nod got the boys' attention. I spoke in Italian, telling them the plan I had laid out for the next day, which really wasn't so much as a plan as it was just showing up and making the exchange.

Lino asked me where the swap would be. I drew a bead on his eyes and tapped my temple several times with my index finger to indicate that I was keeping that one to myself. I liked both those guys, but they were still Roselli's boys. The closer I held my own cards, the more likely we all were to see San Diego tomorrow.

The swap itself would be straightforward. We'd meet in front of the fountain and make a nice, low-profile exchange, smiling all the while like captains at the Harvard-Yale game, complimenting each other on our smashing successes thus far this season. Then we could promise to do it again next year, say our good-byes, and run like hell for the U.S. border before anyone had a change of heart.

While I explained this, I realized that I didn't have a plan B, some kind of out for Helen and me if the deal went south. Took me about half a heartbeat to figure out what that would be.

When Esperanza returned, I asked her a few questions in passing about Ensenada. She proudly trumpeted the fishing industry, debunked some local legends, and bragged up the once-a-week air service to the United States from the airport. She even put in a plug for her night job, letting me know that special clients were entitled to preferred rates. A regular Chamber of Commerce, that girl.

~

We burned a smoke and had another drink. Until the couriers showed there wasn't much else to do. A check of my watch told me I had an hour or two to spare. I stood up, stretched, and told the guys I was going to duck out for a bit and would meet them at the hotel a little later.

I started the wagon up and dropped it into gear. Then I made a left at the first corner and headed south toward the far edge of town, toward plan B.

72

El Ciprés airport is roughly five miles south of Ensenada, beyond the tenement warrens and across an open patch of flat, dead earth. It's surrounded by the usual desperate clutch of warehouse buildings and unnamed streets that sprout up near all airports like molehills on the prairie. The airport is a civil/military facility with the airlines and the smaller general aviation planes sharing the runways with the Fuerza Aérea, a common arrangement, even in the United States.

But unlike their American counterparts, the Mexican Air Force was a third-rate flying circus that any five kids with slingshots could take down on a good day. I doubted they had anything more than a few World War II issue fighters dry-rotting away in a dark hangar anyway.

The word *ciprés* is Spanish for "cypress," a pleasant deviation from the usual practice of naming an airport for some general who got his ass shot off in one of Mexico's three-dozen revolutions.

But the cypress tree is also a funerary symbol, denoting grieving as well as the underworld. Branches of the tree have been placed outside the homes of the deceased since ancient times, a tradition that lives on in many quarters, including the homes of the Buonomo clan in Chicago. In light of the fact that there were no cypress trees within a hundred miles of Ensenada's airport, however, I found the name to be a bit disconcerting.

I found a road that led to the general aviation sector and parked in front of a Quonset hut that looked like it had done a tour on Wake Island. The hand-painted wooden sign out front said ARAGON AVIATION and listed Pepe Someone-or-other as the manager. The lights were out, but that was fine by me. I wasn't looking for a job—just a plane I could steal.

Security at small airports is surprisingly lax, not because the aviation community has a low quotient of ne'er-do-wells, but because there just isn't that much of a market for stolen Piper Cubs out there.

I flipped the horseshoe latch on the gate and walked right out to the ramp like I was Pepe himself. Near as I could tell, I had the run of the place.

A dozen odd planes in various stages of decay crowded the Aragon ramp like sick cattle awaiting death. Several tired Air Coupes pined for release at the back of the lot near a blast fence that had maybe one last blast in it. Farther off, a wingless PBY slumped beside a deengined DC-4, castrated testimony to the cruelty of progress and the disproportionate value of aircraft parts versus whole planes.

Scanning past the hulks, I spied a row of large half-moon hangars that trailed off into the night, all dark save one. A flood of light spread out on the ramp from the second one a hundred and some yards away, its doors rolling open with a distant creak. Some airliner had probably just had a gear swing or engine change and was going back into service.

I walked over to a couple of the better-looking planes on the ramp, a sun-beaten Cessna 140 and a Debonair. They were probably available for charter, meaning they flew regularly and didn't have too many car parts on them, but it wasn't like I was going to be picky about it if a carload of *banditos* was bearing down on Helen and me. A pair of wings that could get me the hundred miles to America was worth a helluva lot more than a brand-new Corvette if it came down to that.

I climbed onto the wing of the Debonair and jimmied the door lock with the dummy I carried on my key ring. Almost all airplane keys are mere formalities, serving about the same purpose as parsley on egg salad. I wasn't taking it anyhow—at least not tonight—just checking that it would be ready if and when I needed it.

I pulled the door open with care and slipped into the pilot's seat, then fumbled around for the battery button. When I found the rocker switch, I pushed down on it, snapping it to ON with a small click. I gave the instruments a five-second once-over—gas gauges at full, ammeter good, cockpit lights okay—and pronounced the plane fit for flight. Then I flipped the switch down and climbed out.

As I stood up on the wing, I made out several men standing in a faint fan of light from the open hangar down-ramp. A small twin-engine plane was taxiing at a good clip toward the hangar, but it wasn't showing any lights, not even a taxi light. Mechanics often repositioned the planes for maintenance in breakneck fashion, but not unlit and at night. I scratched the stubble on my chin as I watched the operation unfold.

The hangar lights went out as the plane neared, two men guiding the machine through the half-open doors with flashlights. This was highly unusual and ridiculously unsafe. It wasn't acceptable anywhere in the world to taxi a plane into a hangar, especially a dark one, but that was exactly what the guy at the controls did, running up the engines, spinning the aircraft in a hard, tight turn, and cutting the power well inside the doorway. Even in Mexico, that was a bit *loco*.

Then I heard some of the men shouting in English as the noise of the engines died. Hardly a crime—but pretty strange for working-class guys who should have been speaking Spanish.

I cupped a hand to my ear, leaned toward the sound, and clearly heard a man inside the hangar shout, "Shut those fucking doors— now! On the double!"

It was the kind of talk and tone you heard in the military, but rarely in the civilian world. Now I was genuinely interested in what was going on down there.

With the hangar lights doused, the ramp was completely black. I stood there awhile, deciding whether or not to stick my eye into yet another knothole. The whole operation was ominous, and one thing I'd learned long ago was that bad things tend to be related. It was just easier to assume the worst about something and feel guilty—and alive—later if I was wrong. I threw all my chips in and set off across the ramp, staying closely in line with the parked aircraft to mask my movement.

I made it to the near edge of the first hangar, skulking along in the shadows of the closed doors until I reached the corner. The doors of the second hangar were shut tight, but the lights had been turned back on, their shafts escaping through several open transom windows along the building side. The windows were a good fifteen feet above the ground, so I wouldn't risk detection as long as I was quick—and quiet. I took a breath and shot out into the alleyway, traversing the open space as fast as I dared.

Once across, I crouched down in the dark corner behind a doorframe that extended beyond the brick sidewall. The sound of muffled voices came from inside, but the words were just a jumble. I needed to get closer.

Scanning around for anything useful, I spied several maintenance stands bunched along the side of the hangar, one of them tall enough to afford a look inside through the open window.

Slowly, silently, I wound up the stairs, one by one, until my eyes were level with the bottom of the window frame two feet away. Then I reached out very carefully, stretching my arms across the gap and placing my hands against the wall. Spreading my fingers wide, I braced myself against my hands and leaned in until my nose was pressed flat against the brick. Squinting from the bright light inside, I peered through the one-inch opening between the painted glass and the lip of the steel frame.

What I saw stunned me.

73

In the middle of the hangar floor, several men in dark coveralls were swarming around an aircraft—a Lockheed P-38 Lightning with Mexican Air Force markings. The cockpit hatch was open and a man in a flightsuit with a tight platinum flattop was descending from the wing with a snarl on his face that would have sent Pancho Villa fleeing in terror. If he wasn't the towhead I saw earlier in town, he was his doppelgänger.

Both nose cowlings on the plane were raised, revealing the full complement of four .50-caliber machine guns and a twenty-millimeter cannon, same as when it rolled off the assembly line two decades earlier. The plane the Luftwaffe nicknamed the "Fork-Tailed Devil" was no longer a match for modern jet fighters, but at full power the P-38 could go like a raped ape and was still a highly capable and very lethal aircraft.

Several gray metallic boxes sat on the hangar floor at the feet of two men who were attending to the weapons with the care of surgeons. One of the men unsnapped the latch on a box and hauled out a seemingly endless belt of .50-caliber ammunition, holding it up approvingly in his hands as if it were a newborn baby, the copper jackets gleaming in the artificial light. He said something to the other man and let out a low whistle. Both broke into wide grins, the wicked glare of the bullets reflecting in their eyes.

The aircraft scheme was a typical dark olive shade that hadn't been applied any too recently. Patches of bare aluminum shone irregularly along the plane's leading edges where wind and weather had had their way with the paint. The words *Fuerza Aérea* were clearly stenciled in white letters along the tail boom, and a three-colored Mexican flag adorned the vertical stabilizer. A man wielding a paint can was hastily slathering a fresh coat of olive drab over the air force markings on the side of the plane.

A very bad feeling descended over me as I watched the operation. The men were moving with purpose and precision, skilled technicians intimately familiar with their tasks. But they were all speaking English and had no business anywhere near a Mexican Air Force plane, especially since the military portion of the airport was way the hell down at the other end of the field. And there was no accounting for the men painting over the markings, or putting live ammunition in the guns. This was no air-show prep.

No, the aircraft was either stolen or, more likely, tacitly loaned to this goon squad for a CIA mission or some kind of assassination plot. I didn't know who the president of Mexico was that week, but I guessed that he might very well have eaten his last state dinner.

I picked up fragments of the conversation here and there, but most of the men had their backs to me, the low hum of a generator further cloaking their words in a dull fuzz.

"Arriving tonight," "First light," "Not gonna be anything left standing" were among the words I overheard, the hair on my neck rising a little higher with each phrase.

For half a second I considered whether Frank or Roselli could have ordered anything like this up, then dismissed the thought as wildly out of bounds. Still, the whole scene was bone-deep unsettling, and I was suddenly shot through with an overwhelming urge to get the hell out of there while I still could.

I slithered down the stairs, checked my six, and darted away across the ramp. While I ran, I made a snap decision: if the couriers had made it down, I was going to make the swap tonight. There was way too much bad mojo in Baja. Somebody was going to be in a world of hurt come morning—and I didn't want it to be me.

74

Vito was waiting for me in the lobby when I returned. He gave me a quick chin nod and tilted his head toward the stairs. I went right up, and he followed a few seconds later.

In the sepia glow of the poorly lit hallway, Vito motioned toward Lino's room and rubbed his thumb across his first two fingers several times. His mouth hung slightly open, the dull brown light from the exposed overhead bulb glinting off the silver in his whiskers ever so slightly. Something about the light and the excited gleam in his eyes made him look like one of those rapacious figures in a Caravaggio painting. It amused me, although I don't quite know why.

I rapped lightly against the door, said, "It's Joe," and stood back so what light there was would fall on my face.

A thick, deep voice I didn't recognize leeched heavily through the wood, said, "Who's dere?"

I repeated my name, louder. A muffled voice spoke inside the room. There was a pause, then I heard the slow click of a hammer locking back and the fumbling of a chain.

The door cracked open and a honker the size of the *Andrea Doria* slid out like it was making an Atlantic crossing, trailing a face in its wake that suggested a life of brute physicality. The heavy-lidded, uninquisitive eyes on that face did nothing to refute that suggestion.

Above the simian head I saw Lino looking at me. "Let 'em in," he said.

The beast snorted and pulled back the door. I stepped inside and Vito followed. I nodded to Lino then gave the gorilla a good once-over.

Might have been wider than he was tall, shoulders like a silverback just bulging through his threadbare gray suit. There was a high note of some thin cologne around him, but he still smelled like a slit latrine in a garlic patch. And, Christ, was he ugly—I'd seen better kissers on totem poles. The big man projected immense strength and great stupidity. Never did get his name.

Across the room, a slim dark man lay slouching over the back of a shabby chair, picking his nails with a long, narrow knife with a rehearsed cool that was too cute by a mile.

He looked up from underneath an olive fedora with a pimento feather and gave me a knowing nod he hadn't earned. The hat was nice but looked just plain silly with his cream-and-beige knit sweater and tight brown chinos. Somehow it suited him just the same. The tan-and-white spectators just had to be for irony; nothing else could explain them. He said his name was Tony. Of course it was.

Something across the room caught my eye. There atop the low frame bed sat a beat-up leather satchel, offending neither nostril nor good taste. It immediately garnered my full and undivided attention, beating out the rather heady competition offered by Mighty Joe Young and the Dapper Dagger.

I checked out the bag, shuffling through several bundles of hundreds like a dealer splicing two stacks of cards together.

"It's all dere, a hundred grand," Tony said. "Don't ya trust us?"

I looked into his dark eyes, said, "No."

But what difference did it make? They were all I had, four criminals carrying out orders for another man, here in a lawless land backing me up against thirty or more desperadoes in a world-class sucker play.

I took a long look at my army: a cooze hound, a sphinx, a stiletto-packing dandy, and a gorilla. I wondered if it was too late to surrender.

75

I sent Tony and the gorilla to Agua Caliente and told them to take covering positions on opposite sides of the fountain in the town plaza. There was only one plaza and one fountain, so even they would have trouble screwing up the job.

Their orders were to not do a damn thing. If the deal went down as planned, they were to back us up then head for home. I was sure the Brookfield Zoo was looking for one of them anyway.

After they departed, I told Lino, "I want you to drive, okay?"

He nodded somberly.

"Vito, you bring the money and come with me for the swap. Is it all there?"

"I count it myself, Joe, all there. Ten bundles of ten thousand— hundred in all."

"Good. We'll park close to the plaza. Back the car in and leave it running. Lino, you see anyone sneaking up behind us, you do what you gotta do, okay?"

"Okay."

"Vit, we gotta be cool here. We have to get this lady out alive."

"*Sì*," he said, nodding.

"Nothing crazy here, just the girl for the money—like Hollywood. *Capisce?*"

"But they don't use real bullets in Hollywood, Joe. *Capisce?*"

He smiled a bit when he said it, but not too much.

I drew a bead on him and our eyes met. "*Sì*," I said, clipping off the end of the word.

"There can't be two hundred people in that village," I continued, "and it's Sunday night so the town should be quiet. This thing should be quick and neat. Either of you know the guys who brought the money down?"

They both nodded in the affirmative.

"They okay?"

Vito said, "Yeah, I know Tony a little bit. "e's not as dumb as he looks."

"He couldn't be."

He snickered. "Well, Roselli trust him. And 'e can throw that god-damn knife thirty feet, 'it a man in the 'eart."

"You ever see that?"

"No. But I 'ear it's true."

"I see," I said, noting that for what it was worth. "What about the gorilla?"

"*Il scimmio?* I dunno nothing."

"Lino?"

"Yeah," he answered. "I see him break two guys' heads together in a fight one time. Neither guy gets up. He's one strong son of a bitch."

"Is *he* as dumb as he looks?"

"Yes." He gave me the faintest trace of a smile. "S'alright?"

I gestured with one open hand, tilted my head. "S'alright."

And that was that. We could have spent another week on logistics and two hours briefing it and it wouldn't have gotten any better.

I told the guys to check their weapons, get the cash, and meet me at the car in five minutes. I went downstairs and asked to use the house phone for a local call. It was past the time for being coy, and I didn't want to go track down another phone somewhere anyhow.

The clerk handed me the phone, which I pulled away until the cloth cord stretched taut. I pulled out my wallet and unfolded the scrap of paper that I'd tucked inside it. Then I dialed the number on it.

A man answered on the third ring.

"*Buenas noches*," I said, "Mario Bravo, *por favor*." Before he could ask who was calling, I added, "This is Joe Buonomo."

He asked me to wait. There was a long pause, maybe two minutes, and then I heard the sound of heels clicking on stone, no doubt some fine Carrara marble, polished by hand for the gilded hacienda of Baja's smut king. Someone picked up the receiver, composed his voice, took a breath, and then spoke.

It was Bravo.

"Joe. Hello. I am glad to hear from you again. Shall we make a plan for tomorrow?"

"No. We shall make a plan for tonight."

"But this afternoon we discussed—"

"I know what we discussed, Mario, but I've got the money now and I'd just as soon get this thing over with."

"I'm sorry, it's out of the question. You'll have to wait until tomorrow. Just one more night, that's all."

That wasn't going to work. I tried to force his hand. "Listen, I don't want to spend one more minute down here that I don't have to; this place makes my skin crawl. I've got your fucking money—that's what you want, isn't it? So let's get this done. Tonight!"

A hot voice came back, peppering me through the line. "Just who in hell do you think you are, sir? You are in absolutely no position to dictate terms to me, certainly not in that tone. Do not mistake my admiration for you for any hesitation whatsoever to grind you into the dust under my heel if you continue to vex me."

The baritone was rushed but still impressively turgid, with high overtones of arrogance. But I had his attention.

"Okay, listen . . . I saw something today at the airport, something that doesn't make any sense and scares the hell out of me."

"And that matters to Mario Bravo why?"

"Damn it, Mario, something bad is going down out here tomorrow. I saw American commandos prepping a Mexican fighter plane for an assault of some kind."

"I operate outside the realm of government. And what there is of it down here is of no concern to me—I pay them good money to stay out of my way."

My voice tightening, I asked, "And what if that government falls tomorrow?"

"I'm sorry, Joe, you're going to have to do better. Air shows are your department, not mine."

I squeezed a hand into a fist, started to bang the counter with it, caught myself.

"Is that all? Hello . . . Joe?"

I was losing him. Everything inside me told me I needed to get Helen back that night, but Bravo wasn't playing ball.

"Well, good-bye then, Joe. We'll talk tomorrow."

I went for broke. "Mario, wait!"

For a second I thought he'd hung up. But then I heard him sigh on the line. "Yes?" he said, his voice tapering off.

"All right. I'm going to tell you something now that can't possibly benefit me . . . something you may suspect already. I'm in love with Helen. She's in a lot of trouble, but I am not leaving this country without her. I don't know what's going down tomorrow—or where—but I need to get her tonight. Just let me do that. Please, Mario."

He didn't speak for a very long time. What I'd told him was true but unlikely to register in his calloused heart. My better hope was that I'd sown enough concern in him for the well-being of his hundred grand that he'd want to act soon as well. I heard him breathing in low, measured reps as he thought it over.

Finally, he spoke. "I fear there is a great deal about Helen Castano that you may not know. She is a complex and precious woman. I tried to love her myself but she'd sooner love a Gila monster than me. I have no wish to keep her here any longer than necessary—but I have serious reservations about a change of plans."

There was another pause on the line, as he weighed the thing out in his mind again, analyzing my request as well as the possibility that I might be laying a trap for him. I didn't say a word, just let him work it out for himself.

"All right, Joe, it shall be as you wish—tonight—but please do not engage in any irregularities of any sort. The consequences of that would likely be fatal for you and for Helen."

"You have my word, Mario. Have your men meet me at the plaza in Agua Caliente in one hour."

"Agua Caliente? We agreed on Ensenada. I do not think I wish to do that."

I couldn't afford to lose him now. The deal was on, but I needed some protection. I went for his soft spot—his big, fat Castilian ego.

"Mario, Agua Caliente is a nothing little town with one small plaza, a town you must know well. It's right in your own backyard. If you can't control what goes on there, you're not as big a deal as I thought. I'll be there with one man, out in the open. If you want to gun us down, you can. What are you afraid of?"

"I am afraid of nothing," he bellowed, singeing the line again. Then quietly, "All right, fine. You shall have your little meeting, and on your terms. Take pride in knowing you are one of very few men who's ever had that advantage over me—and it's only because I trust you."

"Thank you. It's nine thirty now. We'll be at the fountain in the plaza at ten thirty. Will I see you there?"

"I trust you—but not that much."

I smiled. "Okay, fair enough. Just send Helen and no more than a hundred men. I won't risk her life, you know that."

"I'll send two cars, four men in each. That should be enough to prevent any rash heroism. Good luck, Joe; call me anytime you reconsider your position."

"That's not going to happen. Sorry I won't see you again. You're not a bad guy—for a criminal."

We hung up.

I wasn't sure if I liked him, but I respected part of him. The man had a code. He seemed a bit of an anachronism, even in as back-assward a place as Mexico.

I almost felt bad about lying to him about how many men I had, but if you're not cheating in a game like that, you're just not trying hard enough.

76

We rode in silence to Agua Caliente, the occasional passing car highlighting our tight, lined faces in harsh light. Lino wore his usual expression: none.

All humor had left Vito's face as well. His was the gaze of a stalking panther quietly roaming the night plains. His eyes were narrow and focused as he stared well down the road, locked on something I couldn't see, smoke haze churning upward from the imported cigarette between his still fingers.

The satchel didn't say much, either, just sat mute beneath my elbow. But it sure made its presence felt, a hundred thousand bucks' worth of presence.

I took long looks at my conscripted companions, men who had put their lives up for sale just because their boss said so. I didn't know much about them when you got right down to it, didn't know much about Bravo, either—but you get a feeling about these things.

When you live on the wrong side of midnight, you develop a different set of instincts, and your grasp of people and their motivations becomes much clearer. If it doesn't, you don't see too many more sunrises.

~

We made it to town without any delays, but as we approached I had to double-check the map twice to make sure we were at the right place. Cars and trucks crowded along the roadside the last couple hundred yards, people coming and going from town in big bunches. A yellow-orange corona of light pulsed above the village, and an audible buzz crackled in the air. Mariachi horns blared in the distance, joined by the report of firecrackers.

Lino gave me a stupid look, but I just thrust out two irritated fingers and signaled for him to continue.

I shook my head in utter disbelief. We had arrived for our low-key hostage swap in the middle of a goddamn religious festival.

"Joe, it's a fiesta," Vito declared, wide-eyed.

"No shit!" I snapped. "What are the odds of this happening?"

Actually, they were pretty good. These third-world Podunks didn't have a whole hell of a lot going on, so everybody looked forward to a chance to blow off some steam and skip a day in the fields every month or so. Saint Pepe of the Peyote or the Blessed Virgins of the Taqueria—it didn't really take much to get the people wanting to have a good drink in the name of God and in place of work. Who could blame them with the lives they led?

And it didn't matter a hill of *frijoles* anyhow. We had a meet, which I had set up, and it was still my best chance to get Helen and put an end to this traveling circus of depravity that left behind multiple felonies everywhere it stopped. I also realized that the presence of hundreds of people was likely to keep the shenanigans in check and that we could probably get this thing done quick and right. Maybe it wasn't such a bad night for a party after all.

Lino got us as close as he could to the plaza before the crush of people blocked the street. I checked the time. It was 10:20.

"Okay, guys, new plan," I said. "Lino, just cool it here. If you have to move, take it out a block or so, but stay with the car. Vit, let's go. The crowd's gonna make this trickier, but I don't think anyone's gonna pull any stunts. And for God's sake, let's not have any shooting—there's kids running around all over the place."

"Hey, I got kids, too," Vito said indignantly. "You don't gotta tell me that, Joe."

"Yeah? Sorry, I didn't know. Here, or over there?"

"Over there," he muttered before slamming his door shut. He exchanged glances with Lino, then checked his weapon in its holster and turned to face me, a slight scowl on his face.

For a second I thought he was going to draw down on me, and I recoiled slightly in anticipation. It was the first time I'd been unsure of him—and it was the wrong time for it to be the first time—but then he just tossed his cigarette on the dirt, ground it out, and continued staring at me.

I swallowed down the taste of iron forming on my tongue and said dryly, "Let's go then."

We turned and walked off, weaving in and out of the bouncing throng of revelers as we went.

We entered the plaza from the southwest corner. To our left, at the west end, stood the mariachi stage I'd seen earlier. Opposite that, to the east, the church. The fountain was smack in the middle with low shops ringing the square on three sides. I stopped at the edge of the crowd a long moment, then flicked a finger toward the fountain and we moved in.

The plaza was a beehive of activity. Bright strings of lights criss-crossed the open spaces, bringing a happy glow to the square and the villagers' faces. The smell of cooked beef and roasted corn filled the air, cut periodically by the brusque bite of native tobacco and the tinge of gunpowder from the bandoliers of small explosives the kids were letting off. Hundreds of people frolicked in the formerly deserted space, many of them dancing to the strains of the horns and guitars of the mariachis onstage.

In the midst of the gathering, I spied Father Lázaro, leading a procession. Behind him, several men were carrying a religious icon upon a wooden platform, scattered peso notes pinned irregularly to the lonesome Virgin. I turned my head away so the father wouldn't see me.

Closer in, a man held a pink pig piñata aloft on a wooden pole, circling it around and around his head, the pig dancing and bobbing above the crowd. Vito and I threaded our way through it all to the center, separated, and walked around either side of the fountain, meeting again on the far side, our eyes searching for any sign of our men or Bravo's.

As I surveyed the area, I couldn't believe it was the same place I had walked through just a few hours earlier. Even the fountain was now filled to the top, frothy water spraying up from the middle in a small geyser then falling down upon itself in globs and droplets, splashing off the hands of the children who watched it spatter into the air, their faces bursting with glee.

Watching all those kids, I had a change of heart. I didn't like the scene any longer, not one bit. This was no place for the kind of danger we were courting. I consoled myself with Mario's promise to keep it aboveboard and my assessment of his misplaced sense of chivalry.

I stood with my back to the fountain, facing the church, looking for any signs of anything awry. Vito stood a few feet off doing the same, his head panning back and forth a few degrees at a time. We didn't look anything like most of the revelers, but no one paid us much mind. Here and there, I spied a few gringos in the crowd, mostly groups of the young men who came south for whoring and adventure on the cheap. I hoped they'd get only one tonight.

The church doors were propped open, allowing worshippers to come and go, but the balconies above were vacant, their wooden shutters closed tight. No light shone behind them. The bell tower above was dark also. Considering my relationship with the church, that was about as good a deal as I could expect, but it still didn't feel right.

The mariachi band launched into a two-fisted version of "El Rey," an unofficial national anthem. The delighted crowd began roaring with enthusiasm, pushing toward the raised band platform with gusto. The lead singer picked up on their zeal and stepped forward to the edge of the stage, basking in the adoration underneath an enormous sombrero. His black-and-gold uniform shimmered under the overhead lights as he flung his arms apart and warbled into the well-known tale of a wandering man.

I stole another glance at my watch. Ten twenty-six. My stomach was churning. I desperately wanted to have Helen, but the sheer number of people around and the multiplying possibility for mayhem unsettled me. And I had no idea if my wingmen were in position, either. Subconsciously, I turned my head side to side, muttering, "No, no, no, I don't like this."

I compulsively checked my watch again, but it was still 10:26. I told myself we could just as easily conduct this exchange in the morning. Bravo would understand, he could even call the meeting place if he wanted to—that would square the deal.

My gut made the call. It was time to punch out.

"Vito," I said, almost shouting.

Ever alert, he turned his head, answered, "*Sì?*"

Before I could speak again, a penetrating light shot through the crowd fifty feet away. I turned in its direction, watched as a pair of headlights bored into the throng from the southeast corner, the moving beams cutting the villagers who passed before them into splintered shadows.

Shielding their eyes, the locals darted away from the front of the slow-moving car, leaving a clear space between it and the center of the plaza. The lights came to rest on the only thing between the car and the fountain: me.

Reflexively, I tightened my grip on the satchel, squinting to check the glare as I looked beyond the glowing spheres on the front of the vehicle.

The car was a big, dark limousine—the Bravo Special. It came to a stop, and all four doors swung open. Two men stepped out from either side and stood close by. Behind them, a second set of headlights from an identical car filtered through the wall of people ten feet farther back.

That ended any chance at bailing out—we were taking it all the way now.

77

In the last few seconds I had I eye-checked Vito, still several feet to my left at the crowd's edge, moving him back with a flick of my fingers. He slid off smoothly several feet farther from the fragmented rays of the car lights, fading into the human camouflage.

Once the crowd determined that the limo had stopped, the people began to venture back into the space it had created, first by ones then by tens, like the sea closing in behind a boat wake.

Through the cut glare, I watched four men approach with methodical menace then halt about twenty feet away. None of the men had been at the Cortés in the afternoon, and they were dressed more like workers than mobsters, which was odd. I stared across the open space at the men, scanning their features one at a time.

Their faces were somber and tight, a vague look of angst haunting their dark eyes, leaving me no reason to believe they had come to kiss the feet of some weeping icon. They were Bravo's pawns and they knew it. A guy who handled this job well might move up. One who didn't would certainly move all the way down. Above all, their purpose was to intercept any bullets headed toward more valuable men.

The nominal leader, a thick fortyish man with bowlegs, bad teeth, and a mustache big enough to hide Diego Rivera, spoke first.

"*El dinero. Tiene el dinero, cabrón?*"

I said nothing, raised the bag in my right hand slightly, and gave him my best *fuck-do-you-think?* look. Then I asked, "The woman, do you have the woman? *Tiene la mujer?*" And, in a nod to machismo, I one-upped his insult, closing with, "*cabroncito.*"

He flashed a fractured smile at my brass, lifted his arm over his head, and signaled with his fingers. Several bunches of revelers walked through the space between us then on their way to the stage. After they passed, I saw three men working their way forward behind the front four. Helen was behind them with another man I couldn't see, her face twisted in nervous anticipation, her eyes on mine as she approached.

I marked Vito again in my peripheral vision to give them something to think about, then held the bag up, showed off the hundred thousand iron men bunking inside, and snapped it shut again. Then I motioned for them to send Helen over with one man.

Several villagers caught our gestures as they passed but wisely pressed on. Up on the stage, the mariachis were bringing "El Rey" on home for the crowd, but the words didn't register as I focused on the seven men with guns in front of me.

Several yards away, the pink pig on a stick caromed through the air, bouncing teasingly above the grasping hands of rowdy teens. The piñata man was meandering toward us in wide, circuitous steps. Everywhere the night and the music swayed, the crush of the intoxicated crowd closing in around us.

A brown hand holding a black pistol parted the row of pawns. They stepped aside and Pocket Dracula strode through, one hand on a gun that was too big for him and the other wrapped tightly around Helen's upper arm. He could hardly contain himself as they approached, those yellow teeth glistening in the light.

I started to get that sinking feeling.

Drac cold-stared me, but I looked right past him at Helen. She gazed into my eyes for reassurance, and I returned all I had, but the truth was we were in no-man's-land until she was across that open fifteen feet between us.

Moving forward, I raised my hand upward to reach out for hers. Helen stood there, taut and frightened, but just a few feet away. We were *that* close.

And then I saw it.

A glimmer of light winked from an object above me, not in the bell tower but on the church wall. My eyes followed it to the spot, locking on the form of a man kneeling down on the left-hand balcony. They went wide with shock when they focused on the rifle in his hands.

There was no time to formulate ideas about whose side he was on or what his intentions were. Whoever the hell he was, he was leaning forward with a weapon curled up under his chin—and he was pointing it down at us.

Everything shifted to stop-action, nanoseconds flickering by in frozen frames, my mind processing every movement at high speed.

I heard myself shouting, "Get down!" as I lunged forward, my left hand reaching for the butt of my pistol, my eyes darting toward Helen's.

I dropped down onto a knee as my weapon cleared my shoulder, my arm swinging forward. Helen's mouth dropped open in slow motion as my weapon planed past her face and rose over her head, her eyes bedazzled flecks of jade.

Bravo's men saw me and went for their guns, but they were far too late. By the time they reached their weapons, I was already in firing position.

The shooter was almost two hundred feet away—a miracle pistol shot—but an easy one for a high-powered rifle. I came on with gun drawn, Bravo's pawns falling away like frightened deer, leaving Helen and Drac alone and in the open.

I caught another flash of metal off the rifle scope as the shooter fixed his target.

The powder puff piñata gyrated suddenly into my field of vision, swung aloft on its pole by the dancing man just a few yards away. He was oblivious to his peril, but his pig was perfectly positioned in the sniper's field of fire.

Steadying my hand, I did the only thing I could: I sacrificed the pig.

My first shot blew a leg off into the night. The second struck square in the bacon, the piñata disintegrating like a star shell, a carnation-colored mist showering the plaza with hundreds of pieces of candy and gum and papier-mâché shrapnel.

The report of rifle fire came ripping through the air a millisecond later.

The music jerked to a halt. Someone behind me shrieked, "*Gustavo . . . Dios mio!*" I spun toward the sound.

The lead mariachi, who had just poured his heart into the grand finish of "El Rey," was standing at stage's edge, his giant hat blown off his head. His face was contorted in a demonic mask, marred by the stream of blood coursing from the hole in his forehead. He stood up perfectly straight as if to bow, paused ever so slightly, and then plunged into the crowd below.

One long second of stunned calm followed.

It all went to shit after that.

78

I lunged toward Helen as pandemonium erupted, panicked and screaming people stampeding in all directions. Drac, grinning, checked my path, his weapon pointed down at me.

I flung the moneybag at him and dove away as he fired, a hot rush of air whizzing past my ear. Drac thrust out his hand to block the satchel, releasing Helen's arm in the process. She grabbed his gun hand and leaped away, spinning him off balance into the open center of the plaza.

A brace of rifle shots zinged down upon us from above. Drac took one in the neck.

The little man jerked forward with a violent spasm. He looked at me for a second in bewilderment, his hand reaching toward his shredded artery. Then he bared his fangs one final time and dropped, corkscrewing down on top of me while I was scrambling to my feet.

We went down together in a bleeding heap, Drac sprawling over me crosswise and pinning me to the street. I rolled quickly and kicked away at his body, the blood from the holes in his neck staining my clothes and the cobblestones sangria red.

I got up into a crouch and scanned the crowd at waist level, looking for Helen as rampaging villagers scampered all around me. I turned and a fleeing man flattened me with a knee to the chest, sending my pistol spinning through the air as I tumbled backward onto my can.

I sat up, shook off a few stars, then spotted Helen in the crowd screaming, two of Bravo's men pulling her away toward the car.

Before I could react, more rifle shots came down from the balcony and a pawn got hit in the chest, his hands flying up uselessly as he fell across the hood of the limo.

The other pawns were firing wildly toward the balcony and the fountain. Several shots hit close in, skipping off the bricks around me and ricocheting back into the air.

A runner behind me got hit, staggered sideways several steps, and clipped the low wall, collapsing backward into the water with a *sploosh*.

A hundred things were happening at once and all of them were bad. Gunmen were shooting, terrorized people were fleeing, a village was bleeding—a mariachi was dead. My men were nowhere in sight and I was unarmed, under fire, and unprotected.

The only safe spot I could see was the fountain. In a flash, I spun around, coiled up, and then flung myself through the air, splashing down like a ditched bomber in the cold water behind the two-foot brick wall. My momentum carried me against the far side of the curving interior edge. Spinning on the plaster bottom, I reversed direction and lunged forward, crashing up against the tiled inside wall face-first.

I broke the surface, wiped the water from my eyes, and took a hurried look around. To my left, the runner lay partially submerged, a swirling red film coloring the turbulent water around her body. Vito was next to her, his head against her raised thigh, squeezing off shots between her legs toward the balcony.

There we were, two fish in a giant bowl, with a single waterlogged pistol between us to hold back a sniper and two cars full of pissed-off gunsels. I wondered why we weren't getting any cover from Tony and the gorilla.

The squeal of rubber on brick shrieked through the air as the first of Bravo's cars shot forward, spun around, and raced out of the plaza. I caught a blur of Helen's face underneath a gunman as the limo zoomed by.

The second car followed, then banged a hard U, and pulled up abeam the church, a sheet of fire blazing from its right side as automatic weapons cut loose against the house of God.

Bullets gouged a track up the wall, pranging off the wrought-iron balcony and shredding the plaster beyond. The shooter just disappeared in a haze of pulverized stucco, his limbs flopping out as he flew backward against the wall, the rifle cartwheeling from his hands then pinballing down between the rails to a teetering balance on the edge of the wooden flooring.

The dying man slid sideways, painting a red smear on the wall behind him. Then he twisted around, collapsing faceup on the railing, arms opened wide. The rifle fell a second later, dropping onto the cobblestones below with an empty *clack*.

The second car tore out into the night, leaving me, Vito, and a few stunned survivors a chance to regroup.

The plaza was nearly empty, the only immediate sound the wailing of a woman slumped over the mariachi's body and a few random cries for help. Along the streets that led in, cars were peeling off into the night, villagers trying desperately to leap onto running boards as the cars whipped past.

I stood up, then clambered out of my liquid foxhole, water pouring off me and sloshing onto the bricks below. I signaled Vito to stay back, then crept forward. The shooting had stopped, but I crouched low, making several sweeps of the area before reaching out to pick up my pistol.

I looked down at Drac, who lay dead in the street staring up at the cold moon above. One of his hands reached out into the night, his fingers curling like the tines of a rake. He should've stuck to herding goats.

I was still working off adrenaline. I knew that Helen was gone with Bravo's men, but I couldn't process the totality of this latest disaster. I still had to get myself, my men, and the money out of town before the Federales arrived.

The money. Oh shit. My heart sank even lower.

"Vito," I yelled, "you see the money anywhere?"

"No," he replied, rising up and stepping out of the fountain that was still gushing red water into the air.

I stood there, soaking and drained, fighting off the first shudders of the cool night air, my warm gun shaking in my hand. "Great. We lost the money, too. FUBAR—all the way down the line. You see the gorilla or Tony anywhere?"

He wiped his face, shook his arms hard, flicking water free. "I don't see nobody, Joe."

I spun a three sixty. "And where the hell is Lino?"

"Dunno," he said, "maybe stuck in traffic trying to get to us."

"Well, let's get going over to him," I replied, silently counting bodies in the street. "There's nothing we can do here."

We started a double time out the west end of the plaza toward Lino and the car. After several steps, Vito said, "Look," and pointed toward an archway in a row of shops. "It's *il scimmio*."

Against the wall beyond the stores an unmistakably large man lay slumped down, legs bent crookedly, head down on his chest. Even from a distance we could see the blood soaking his shirt and darkening the stone beneath him.

Vito ran over to check, but the big guy was gone for sure. He came right back and shook his head, drawing his finger across his throat with grim finality.

So much for the gorilla. Tony probably got the same. Somebody had made us—but good. Then Vito looked at me and I looked at him, and we both began running toward the wagon.

79

From a hundred feet out I knew. The way Lino's arm hung out the window, limp, fingers curled. At fifty feet I saw the blood, seeping down his arm, branching off in streaks on the car door.

I stopped running. Vito didn't. "Jesus Christ," I said quietly as he blew past me toward his dead friend.

Drawing my gun, I made several quick turns, checking for unfriendlies. No one was visible in the immediate area, but I wasn't going to wait around for them to return. I gave Vito a few seconds, then walked slowly toward the car. He wasn't yelling, wasn't crying, didn't pound on the roof of the car. He just knelt there in the dirt, hand covering his face, head shaking slowly.

Around the plaza people were beginning to poke their heads out of the shops and from behind the stage. Some general shouting began, people congregating in small, cautious clusters.

"Vito."

He didn't respond. I placed an arm on his shoulder, leaned down. He looked up at me, eyes glazed. "Vito . . . we can't stay."

He nodded, stood up, looked on at the dead man in the driver's seat.

"And we can't take him with us."

He stared at me, but I saw the recognition in his face. "Okay," he said.

I stepped around him, pushed in the button, opened the door. Vito reached down and pulled Lino out. I tried to help him, but he brushed past me, grunting from the weight of the body. He dragged him over to a little shed near the darkened roadside and laid him down as I followed, weapon pointed straight out.

Vito stood beside Lino, looking down in silence at his friend. His eyes were moist, but he showed no other emotion. Wordlessly, he crossed himself then turned away.

I stepped forward and dug into my pockets for change. I found a couple of ten-peso coins and placed them over Lino's eyes. "Safe passage, paesan," I whispered, then turned and made for the car.

Some of the villagers had begun moving our way. A man was pointing toward us, walking in our direction. Another man followed. I climbed in and slammed the door, disregarding the blood-slicked seat. Vito was already seated on the passenger side, pain creasing his face. The keys were still in the ignition. As I cranked the engine over, I spied an object sticking out of the dashboard, sitting low like a half-moon in the darkness. It was a Chinese throwing star. I stared at it in mute disbelief, not wanting to accept the obvious connection: the Ching Hwas were back in the game—and they were pissed.

Down the street, men were running toward us now. Someone yelled, "Stop them!"

I shook off my trance, ripped the shifter into low, and flattened the pedal to the floor. Vulcanized rubber smoked into the air as the spinning tires clutched at the dusty bricks below. Then they dug in and the wagon sprang forward, fishtailing wildly onto the skinny road, surging toward the open edge of town.

It was time to bid *adiós* to Agua Caliente, another box checked on my guided tour of hell.

80

We drove out as we'd come in—in silence—water pooling slowly on the vinyl seat and running back in small streams behind me.

Several police cars passed us moving fast, their sirens wailing—ad hoc funeral dirges dissipating slowly into the night beyond.

I was too numb to think straight, but I knew everything was shot to pieces now. The gunman wasn't mine and he wasn't Mario's, but he could've been Ching Hwa or Spazzo or anyone else. Whoever he was, he was dead now.

But the whole thing was a mess; a complete and total star-spangled clusterfuck. "You got a dry cigarette, Vit?" I asked in disgust.

He fished through the glovebox, pulled out a pack, shook one out and lit it, then handed it to me. He gave me a long, deep stare as he did, his eyes going from the throwing star to mine. Neither of us spoke; there wasn't any need.

I took a deep drag on the coffin nail, shivered a little from the cold, and pushed myself back into the seat, my mind spinning at 5,000 rpm but the clutch not engaging.

~

As the traffic thinned out, Vito asked, "Where we gonna go, Joe?"

"Lemme think. We can't stop by the Bahia, but I'm gonna need to talk to Frank and you're gonna need to talk to Roselli. I can't ask you to do anything else here. Bravo's going to have us measured for boxes if we stay."

"What about Tony?" Vito asked.

"We'll see him at the Resurrection."

He shot me a look.

"I'm pretty sure he's up there on that rail in front of that church, Vit. Who else could've gotten that close to the gorilla—and slit him like that? He's either in with the Chinese gang that did this or died at their hands. And if it wasn't him, he's on his own anyhow. There's no meet-up scheduled and no time for dicking around. We can't afford to be here when the sun comes up."

We both knew we weren't going to make it across the border, not now, not in that station wagon. We'd have to score some other means of transportation to get out.

But there was only going to be one guy leaving. There was no way I was going to desert Helen. Whatever else she'd done, she'd saved my life at the Hotel Cortés. I couldn't leave her to die in that house, not without me alongside her.

81

We parked in an alley a few blocks into Ensenada, near what looked to be a cathouse. At a time like that, you go with your gut.

I poked my head in the door and asked the madam where I could find a pay phone. She gave me the full eyeful—how could I blame her standing there in my soaking clothes and matted hair? But her pink rayon muumuu and purple eye shadow were damn little better. The woman had a private joke with herself, then she smiled and told me there was a phone at the small plaza a block down, next to a peso horse ride for kids. We shared one of those looks, then I thanked her and ducked out.

I decided to leave the car where it was but walked back to let Vito know where I was headed. Then I walked off alone to call Frank. It was gonna be ugly.

I made my way through the shadows to the little plaza a block away. The plastic horse was in the near corner, a white charger with some kick left in him despite having a foreleg snapped off. Pegasus he wasn't, but his face had a certain sneering defiance that resonated.

The phone booth was just beyond. It was tired and unlit, but the hinged door folded easily when I pushed it in. I made a slow survey of the whole plaza before sliding halfway in, having already met my monthly quota for telephone ambushes. Then I placed an international call to a number I'd memorized long ago. George picked up on the third ring, said Frank was anxious to speak with me. I took a few deep breaths while I waited for him to come on the line. It felt like waiting to tell your father you'd been arrested.

"Joseph, what news?" he asked, voice rising in anticipation.

"It's not good, Frank. We got ambushed. Helen's still with Bravo."

"Jeee-zusssss . . ."

"Yeah. People are dead. Couple of Bravo's, couple of ours, some civilians. Somebody tore the roof off the night." My words sounded slow and tired and flat in the wooden booth.

"And Helen?"

"She was okay last I saw her. They dragged her away when the shooting began."

"Oh, is this thing ever a fucking nightmare. Every turn is worse."

"There's more."

"More?"

"Yeah. We lost the money. Bravo got it."

Long silence, deep exhalation, then, "And the locusts?"

"Come again?"

"The locusts, Joe, the horde of locusts. 'Cuz you got everything else to make this a fucking biblical tragedy. I mean it is epic. Ep-ic!"

I closed my eyes, let out some air of my own. "I'm sending Roselli's guy home within the hour. His buddy and one of the couriers bought it, another's missing, but Vito's still here with me."

"Don't do that, pal. Right now he's a dead man. He may just as well stay down there with you."

I pulled away the receiver, gave it a crossways stare. "What the hell are you talking about?"

"The money. The money you guys lost—it's Roselli's, the mob's. That guy shows up without it and he won't even make it home for supper."

"How'd *that* come to pass?"

"Johnny had it handy. You said you needed it fast; he had it. Losing it wasn't exactly part of the plan, you know? Besides, Johnny said he was anxious to pitch in, wanted Jack and Bobby to see how helpful he could be."

"Help? I've told you before, those guys are *not* your friends, Frank. They don't have any friends. I guaran-fucking-tee you the mob wants that film to leverage against the Kennedys—whose problems just got a lot worse." I banged the phone against the booth wall, blew out a deep breath. "You got anything else I need to know?"

"Yes."

"And what might that be?"

"I think there's a bunch of hired guns headed down there."

I bit my lower lip hard enough to draw blood, grunted with suppressed rage. "Aren't you just full of surprises . . ."

Then things started to click together in a horrible way. "How do you know that?" I demanded, my throat tightening.

"Lawford told me."

"Lawford?"

"Yeah. He was acting real squirrelly when we were discussing our options this evening. He didn't want to talk about it when I confronted him, so I slapped him around a little and he broke. Jack told him his old man had contacted Hoover out of desperation about some kind of a commando unit. Do you think he could be serious?"

Everything crystallized. The flattop punks, the P-38, the rifleman.

Joe Kennedy and J. Edgar Hoover, two of the most powerful men in America, both long suspected of nefarious behavior and both capable with a phone call of generating the kind of mayhem I'd seen tonight—and a whole lot worse. Strange bedfellows to be sure, but if enough power was at stake, they'd walk arm in arm down Fifth Avenue in the Macy's parade.

Then I remembered how intently Roselli had been listening to our conversation the other night at Frank's. Commando teams were a little out of his league—but not out of his buddy Momo's.

Hoover. Kennedy. Giancana. One hell of an unholy trinity if there ever was one.

I swallowed hard and slumped against the back of the booth, the words *first light* and *not gonna be anything left standing* cycling through my mind. It was all there in front of me now—they were

JOHN SANDROLINI

going to hit Bravo's place to get the film, to wipe out all record of it. Everyone inside would die.

"Joe? You still there?"

"Yeah, sorry. Listen, I think Lawford could be telling the truth. I'll have to come up with something—tonight. I'll try and call Bravo, maybe I can get him to release Helen. But I'll tell you this, paesan, I haven't heard one word about that film since I got down here. For all we know, Johnny Spazzo still has it somewhere off in Vegas or God knows where."

"*Spazzo?* Where're you getting your news, Pony Express?"

"What's that supposed to mean?"

"Johnny Spazzo is dead, pal. Thought you would've heard from your goombahs down there. Border Patrol found his body down by Calexico last night. Shot three times at close range with a large-caliber gun. Coyotes been eating him for days."

A chill, jet-stream cold, grew in my chest as the words sank in. A grim thought formed in my mind, one I'd been repressing for days but was unable to deny any longer. It had been there all along, this gnawing feeling, awful and growing, seeping down deeper into my consciousness with each passing day.

My stomach bucked once, but I fought it down. "I've gotta go," I said.

"What . . . what are you going to do?"

"I don't know, I really don't know. I'll try to get in touch with you if there's time."

"Joe, wait," he said, his voice pitched with alarm. "Don't take any more chances. This whole thing is way, way out of control. I'll call this Bravo guy myself; maybe I can reason with him. This is my problem, after all. You don't have to do anything else for me."

I drew in some air, held it, let it out. "Frank . . . I'm not doing it for you. Not this time."

He started to speak, caught himself. After a long pause he said, "Well, keep your head down, old friend. Godspeed, paesan." His voice had a dull ring of finality.

I hung up the phone and fell back on the wooden bench in the booth, sweat breaking out on my forehead around the outline of my fingers.

290

My last, and best, chance was to call Bravo and hope he'd listen to me. I dropped fifty centavos into the slot, dialed his number, and took a deep breath. His man answered again, said Señor Bravo wasn't taking any calls. I told him who it was. He said he'd see and walked away.

A minute passed, then I heard shouting in the distance and the sound of breaking glass. Heavy footsteps clicked across the floor in an accelerated gait. A voice came on the line, spewing bile.

"Just who in the hell do you think you are? That was the dumbest elementary-school stunt that anyone ever pulled! And it will be the very last one of your life, I assure you that, Joe Buonomo!"

"Mario—"

"What could you possibly want from me now? If you think there is any way you can save yourself now, you are very badly mistaken. You and everyone in your miscreant army is going to die. You insect! Nobody does that to Mario Bravo! Nobody!"

"That wasn't my man . . ."

"Bullshit!" He was screaming now, pounding on a table or desk near the phone.

"Mario, why would I do that? That shooter was firing at all of us. He's a third-party player."

He wasn't listening. He just continued his rant at fever pitch. "Two of my men are dead. So are several villagers—and a first-rate mariachi. For what?"

"I lost two men, too."

"*Two?* You told me you had one; that proves you are a liar."

"Look, Mario, somebody sold me out, and you better start to realize that they sold you out, too. Haven't you asked yourself why? Do you think you know all you need to know here?"

"This is what I know: In this land . . . I. Am. King," he declared, punctuating each word with a heavy knock. "And I stay in power because people know that my vengeance is swift and absolute. You will see that soon enough."

I waved a hand in the air. "All I want is Helen. You've got the money now—"

"Helen? You are a remarkable man, Joe. Re-mark-able! What elephant has loaned you the balls big enough to ask me that now? You break your word to me, shoot up the Fiesta de las Cabras, and *then* ask for your blue movie star back?"

"Blue *what*?"

"I'll tell you what you'll get. You'll get a lesson no one around here will ever forget. They won't forget because your crucified body will be hanging on a cross in that plaza until the very last buzzard in all of Mexico has picked the flesh from your bones, devoured it, and shat it out!"

"Hold on there—"

"Goodnight, sir!" he shouted then slammed the phone down, an audible *clack* ringing in my ear as the line went dead.

That pretty much ended that. Spent, I pulled myself up and out of the booth, then wiped my face with the back of my hand. I bit a knuckle and sucked wind while trying to come to grips with the latest revelation.

Absently, I reached down into a nearby agave planter, scooped up a handful of native soil, and sifted it through my fingers, watching as a million disturbed grains took flight on the midnight wind.

Blue movie star, I repeated to myself over and over and over, a dull, twisting knife spinning in my gut, tearing out everything left inside me.

82

I walked through an alley that ran off the plaza and cut down the next street toward the Rambler. I crept the last fifty yards as I approached the vehicle, not in the least bit surprised to find it empty.

There was a faint high-low whistle behind me and there was Vito, crouched behind a rusting barrel, hands ready at his sides. I looked behind me once and walked over to his refuge.

"Vito," I said under my breath, "the whole thing's fallen apart. Frank says the money we lost was Johnny's and he'll hold you responsible. Him, Bravo, the Federales, and the Ching Hwas—the Chinese gang who took out Lino—are all going to be hunting for us."

We headed toward the car. When we reached it, I opened the door and stuck the key in the ignition. "Get everything you need out of this heap now, 'cuz it's way too hot to drive. Someone will take this off our hands within ten minutes, I'm sure."

I turned the engine over and rolled down the driver's window. Vito was already behind the wagon, rummaging through the back.

"I know about the money, too," he said. "Roselli told me before we leave. I know what we're up against."

"Good, because we're pretty much fucked six ways from Sunday down here. I'd seek out a quiet place, or steal a car and head up to Tijuana. You can get across the border from there."

I closed the car door and we began walking. Vito cocked his head, turned his hands a little, and made an inquisitive face. "And you, Joe, where are you going?"

"Nowhere. I'm staying here. I've going to get Helen out of Bravo's hacienda."

He stopped walking, pointed a finger down, and said, "Okay. I stay too."

"No," I said, looking into his glowing eyes. "There's a mercenary gang down here, and they're going to finish what somebody started at the plaza. They shot up the place, them or the Ching Hwas—or both. Unless I'm badly mistaken, that posse's going in at dawn to burn Bravo's place to the ground. No sense you going in there along with me."

He swatted my bicep with a light backhand. "Where you want me to go? Roselli, 'e's gonna cut off my *coglioni*, okay? I may as well go with you. You come to get the girl, I come to 'elp you. Nothing 'as changed. Besides, maybe we find the money in there and everything works out."

"That house is heavily defended and set for destruction in, oh, five hours. I don't even have any idea how I'm gonna get in there, and I might just kill the girl myself when I find her."

He chewed on my words a little, said, "It's Bravo's 'acienda, right? Surrounded by *montagne*, Joe—mountains." He carved peaks with his hands to underscore my obtuseness.

Mountains. The dawn broke over me, late but clear. Mountains. Vito, who fought with the Tenth Mountain Division in Italy during the war, might know a thing or two about scaling them. I stared coolly at him as I thought it over.

"One of the 'ookers, she told me that she's been there. That place is right against the rocks in a box canyon."

I'd been told the same thing. That the only approach was from the highway a mile or so below the walled citadel, up a sloping plain. The high ground and the mountains that ringed it on three sides formed a daunting natural defense. If there was a way in, it was going to be from above.

"Think there's any way to drop down behind that place?" I asked.

"I see the 'ills around 'ere today. They're not too 'igh. These people, they are not mountain people. I," he said, tapping his burly chest, "I am a mountain person. I can climb these 'ills."

"I can't ask you that. We have very little chance of getting out of there alive."

"It's more than I 'ave if I go back to Vegas with nothing."

It was impossible to refute that statement.

"Okay, Vit, okay." I smiled and clasped his shoulder. "Guess we'll need some rope."

He smiled back, but then his face tightened up with anxiety. "'ow the fuck we gonna get there? We can't drive past Agua Caliente again. They got Federales from 'ere to the border by now."

He was right. The only road to Ojos Negros ran very close to Agua Caliente and there wasn't enough time to loop around the mountains and come in from the other side. Driving was out. Flying was too—besides the noise there was way too much of a chance of making a smoking hole in the ground trying to land in rocky terrain at night.

Then fortune smiled on me. Peg-Leg Pegasus flashed into my mind and an idea sprouted up. "Vito," I asked, a small smile on my lips, "can you ride, paesan?"

83

Piedras Gordas was the first small town I had checked out in the afternoon. It was no good for my first plan, but it had something else that suddenly made it enormously valuable to me: a large riding stable. It was the kind of thing you don't pay a whole lot of attention to down in Mexico, since they still have plenty of *vaqueros* roping and riding, but now it was a godsend. We could be there in twenty minutes by taxi.

I was holding enough of a roll that I was sure the owner wouldn't mind the late rousting. He would be handsomely compensated for a couple of horses and saddles, and maybe a rifle or two if he had any. Several hundred gringo greenbacks on the barrelhead would speak plenty for us if he was curious. Nobody asks any questions on the Frontera anyhow.

As I expected, Vito said he was a good horseman. That made the decision easy. I was no threat to Roy Rogers, but I was passable. Either way I was in, but it was a lot better to have some help in a deal like this.

It was a good eight miles across open plain from the stable to Ojos Negros. From there I'd have to locate Bravo's hacienda, scale the cliff with Vito, and drop down into an armed compound I'd never seen before. After I'd completed that little warm-up, all I had to do was break

into the house, steal a woman from under the nose of a murderous warlord who wanted to kill me, and then ride off into the hills free and clear.

Day at the beach.

~

A couple of men were still up at the Dos Milagros stable passing a
tequila bottle around when we arrived. They had no interest whatsoever in waking the owner, but they were strangely obliging to our need
for horses and saddles. Something told me the sale went unrecorded
for tax purposes.

It turned out all right, though, as Vito got them to throw in two
hundred feet of rope and some blankets and canteens. I winced at the
price for the Springfield rifle, but took that, too, along with a box of
thirty-aught-six shells.

The horses were both Spanish mustangs, beautiful hearty animals,
strong and spirited. Mine was chestnut, Vito's gray. We saddled them
up ourselves and slung our limited amount of gear on top. Vito made a
makeshift holster for the rifle from a couple of leather straps and slid it in.

The cowhands said it was good riding across the plain and that
most of the fences were low enough to jump. They thought we were
crazy to be heading out into those badlands at night, but they could
see we were well armed—and deadly serious. Their eyes told me they
would be content with killing the tequila and would leave the bush-
whacking to someone else. It was just after one when we set off.

84

We kept a mile or so north of the highway, which ran almost due east toward Ojos Negros. The ground was dark and featureless but the moonlight made it clear enough to trot. The terrain rose gently along the way with only the occasional array of cactus or low fence slowing the horses' gaits. The constant slight *clump clump* of hooves and the random snorts of the mustangs were the only sounds as we rode.

Thirty minutes after we set out, the lights of a small town to the south winked on the horizon. I made it for Agua Caliente, still weeping in the night. I felt it all the way to my bones, shaking my head reflexively at the senseless slaughter.

I looked over to Vito, who was also watching the village, his face somber, drawn.

"Hey," I said, "on the odd chance we get out of this place alive, we should do something for those people."

He just kept surveying the town, thinking perhaps. His head tilted back. "We could give them our 'orses, but then we gotta steal a car. That's no good."

"I've got something else in mind. You okay with the church, Vit?"

"'ow you mean *okay*?"

I waggled my hand. "You know . . . *okay*."

He shrugged. "Yeah. All right, I guess, considering."

"Then you can be the messenger."

He cut me a sidelong glance. "To who?"

"Father Lázaro, the *padre* at that church."

"*Lázaro?*" he asked, his voice spiking.

"Yeah. Lázaro."

He looked on, his face crumpling up in little furrows as he thought it over. "Okay," he said finally.

We rode along in silence awhile. Then he asked, "What's the message?"

"Tell him to get that damn floor fixed."

He shrugged again, made a *s'alright* gesture.

I checked my watch and spurred the mustang, urging it forward. Behind us the lights of Agua Caliente ebbed, then vanished quietly over the horizon. But the angst lingered on.

85

Ojos Negros loomed out of the black around two thirty. Based on the information I had, Bravo's place was a couple of miles outside of town, down a narrow road that ran due north a bit then dog-legged east. It was the only home along that stretch of road for miles. We weren't apt to find too many other walled fortresses out there anyhow.

We crossed a dirt road then took the next one, a paved one-lane highway abeam town. Sure enough, after a half mile, it banked eastward as we traveled on. High hills rose before us, and the terrain became rocky and steeper. I decided to take us off the highway despite the chance of throwing a shoe or cracking a hoof on the rocks. The last thing we needed now was a lame horse, but if one of Bravo's cars spotted us, we'd be between the dog and the fire pole.

Ten minutes later I began to pick up a faint tinge of light as we edged past the outline of a crumbling hill. I raised my hand, signaling Vito to pull in next to me. Together, we nudged the horses forward a hundred feet or so until the source of light was in plain view. It came from a large home high up in the crook between two mountain ridges. The granite walls were better than a thousand feet above the canyon floor with a pretty good drop to them. High, but not insurmountable.

The home itself was a ranch style, but split into three distinct sections, stepping down along the base of the hills. A high, rough-hewn stone wall surrounded the entire complex, running off into the shadows of the adjoining hills. It was ten feet high if it was an inch and lit at hundred-foot intervals by lanterns. A small dirt access road ran from the road up the rock-strewn incline toward the home above, still a good mile away.

I shot a glance at Vito. He was peering intently at the hills through his binoculars, unseen wheels turning in his head. He nodded slowly up and down several times as he brainstormed. I don't know how he could see anything in the dark, but he seemed to have a fix on something.

"What do you think, Vit, can we do it?"

"Yeah," he murmured, dragging the word out slowly across his lips as he mapped a trail in his mind. "The north side is lower, easier to climb. We gotta ride over there," he said, pointing toward the far edge of the mountain, "then we can drop down inside the wall—if they don't 'ave any men there."

"I'd like it better if you stay topside and cover me with that Springfield. Then you can dash on out on Man o' War here if things go to shit—which they probably will. Don't die in this wasteland, Vito. Go back to Italy, see those kids of yours."

"Okay, Joe, it's a good plan. But first, we gotta get you in the goddamn place. It's almost three now. Let's go, 'uh."

"Yeah, we should go. Yippe ki-yay, *paesano*."

"What's that mean?"

"Nothing," I said, half grinning. "Let's go."

86

We rode off several hundred yards and made a wide circle around the front of the hacienda, coming back toward the jutting hills once we'd cleared the broad vista in front of the high ground. The terrain roughed up enough that we had to dismount and walk the horses the last quarter mile. I tied them to a tall ocotillo plant while Vito assessed the incline that towered above us, immense and dark. I shouldered the coiled ropes and hurried over next to him. He had the Springfield in one gloved hand, the binoculars in the other.

He pointed with the rifle toward a natural fold in the rugged surface of the hill several hundred feet up and said, "We can take that cut up this side and around the back. See 'ow it runs almost all the way up? It's a good path."

"All right. I'm ready."

He turned and set off with me close behind. There weren't many loose rocks so the footing was good. The night air was cool, but before long we were both sweating from the effort, even with our coats tied around our waists. My legs were throbbing after thirty minutes, and I slipped a little every so often, but Vito just climbed on as if he was shelling on Waikiki Beach.

Thoughts of what lay ahead forced their way into my consciousness several times. I beat them back each time, focusing on the job at hand. We'd get to that other part soon enough.

~

We made the ridgetop by four and took a blow. Time was short, but the climb had been exhausting. It was better to take two minutes than to go stumbling over the edge of the cliff.

Vito and I scanned for bad guys while we rested, but we had the whole mountain to ourselves, a barren rock under a field of brilliant stars, the panorama below us stretching all the way back to the coast. It could have been a camping trip—but we were no Boy Scouts.

Vito broke the silence as we stood up. "I like what you say—about Italia. I think I'm gonna go 'ome after this, maybe for good. It's time to start over."

I raised an eyebrow. "Now you're cooking with gas. I know a few things about starting over. It's not easy, but reconnecting with your family's gotta beat working for that animal Roselli."

"Maybe I can . . . we'll see," he mused, his words trailing off. Then, "And you, you ever gonna go 'ome, Joe?"

"I don't know. I've been gone a very long time. I don't know if there is a home for me anymore. Ask them, maybe they know," I said, waving a hand at the shimmering constellations above us.

"'ey," he said, grinning, "the gods, they let even Odysseus go 'ome after ten years."

I smiled back as I tightened up my holster. "Yeah, you're right about that, my friend, they sure did. But look what he went home to."

87

The ants moved slowly below me, following an invisible trail as they went about their work. With a thumb roll of the knurled wheel, I tightened the focus of the binoculars, squinting back into them to get a second look.

There were just two of them, weaving back and forth in irregular passes behind the home. Only they weren't ants; they were armed men trolling the wide space between the back of the house and the base of the cliff. Their efforts were indifferent, torpid—like they were asleep on their feet. But that didn't mean it would be easy to slip between them.

The house had too many lights on. They didn't illuminate the area effectively, and they silhouetted the guards for anyone approaching from the hill. An amateur mistake—like the sleepwalking guards—but Casa Bravo had probably never been stormed before.

The learning curve was going to be steep for these guys tonight.

At the extreme left and slightly behind me, the rock wall merged with the cliff. A small wooden gate we hadn't see from horseback was wedged into the nook where the man-made met the mountain. It was well tucked away, and anyone who got anywhere near it from the outside would catch a quick case of dead if they didn't know the secret password. But it was the perfect egress point for us.

I twisted halfway around, made a low *pssst*, and gave a head nod in Vito's direction. The rope around my ankles went full taut as I pushed up from my prone position, hand-walking backward while Vito hauled me away from the overhang I'd been dangling over like a spider in waiting. I loosened the rope, and we crept back over the top of the ridge to confer.

"Vito, there's a jumping-off point almost directly behind the house. The rock shears off completely near the bottom, though. You're going to have to lower me with the rope. It's fifty, sixty feet, no more."

"I can do that, no problem."

"There's a gate at the north corner of the wall, where it meets the mountainside," I said, pointing toward it with my finger. "As soon as I'm down, you bounce down the hill, grab the horses, and meet me at that gate. Will twenty minutes be enough time?"

He thought a second, nodded his head.

"If I'm not out before sunup, or if you hear any shooting, just go. Take your horse and ride—no dicking around."

His eyes met mine for a steely second. He nodded again, said, "Okay."

"Good. Now what's the best way down this hill?"

"We gotta zig-a-zag a little, but the hill, she slopes down easy. I see the ledge you mentioned, we can make that. But, Joe," he cautioned, his stare as hard as the granite beneath us, "don't slip. You slip, you die."

I looked down over the ledge, back at Vito, mulling his words. "I don't know Vit; after so many years of people trying to make it happen, I sometimes wonder if I ever will."

~

It was tedious going down. We had to make our way down the slope carefully, of course, but also in total silence, without loosening any rocks—and against a running clock. We were pretty much the camel going through the eye of the needle at that point.

From the nub of the ledge, I peered down as the guards approached each other. One of them was smoking. Man, were those guys careless. They'd have no shot against whatever ex-OSS guys were probably creeping up the incline now.

Hell, for all I knew, those guys were above *us* on the ridge, looking down in bemusement at our efforts. I tried not to think about that again.

There was no time to get fancy, and we didn't have any gear anyhow, so I drew the rope around my chest, made a highwayman's hitch, and snugged it up while Vito laid out the rope behind him. He doubled it around a large outcropping and tested the base for a foothold. Then he looked at me and nodded that it was okay.

I walked over to him and whispered, "You won't be able to see me once I go over. Just keep playing out the rope gradually until it slackens. I've got four forty. We have less than an hour 'til first light. We need to be way out of here by then."

He held out his hand and I took it, squeezing firmly. "*Buona fortuna,*" he said.

"*Grazie.*"

I leaned over the ledge and waited until I saw both guards cross and march off in opposite directions. Then I gave Vito a final head nod and stepped over the edge.

88

The rope went tight under my arms as I hung there, suspended over the yard below like a side of beef in a meat locker. After a pause, I began dropping down as Vito played the rope out in herky-jerky two-foot measures.

I swung a little with each one, but the descent was clean. Faint grunts came from the hilltop with each drop as Vito tightened his grip on the rope. The smell of wood smoke was on the air, drifting out from the large chimney in the center of the house as it spiraled up and back.

I scanned the yard as I went down, eyes alive for any signs of movement. Everything was still. At fifteen feet I looked down, preparing for the landing. I almost gasped out loud when I did.

Directly beneath me, a man stepped out of the shadows along the tuck-under at cliff's edge. He stood there a moment while he buttoned up the fly on his pants, his rifle braced against his side with his arm, cigarette burning beneath a straw sombrero.

I reached for the knot to release it, but he started to walk off just before I did. Now I was seriously screwed. I could either shoot him and blow the whole thing to hell, or I could drop to the ground and have him pop me while I lay there.

There was one other play, right up there with the ol' Statue of Liberty in terms of viability. But it was fourth and long so I gave it a shot.

Pulling the rope furiously toward me as it dropped, I flung my body backward with all the momentum I could gather. Shifting my weight at the apex of the swing, I swooped down upon the unsuspecting man in front of me.

"*Jefe!*" I hissed as I whipped forward, knees locked, yanking on the release point of the rope as I closed in.

He turned, and got a face full of boot as I collided with him, both of us going down hard with an *Oomph!*

I landed heavily on my back, the soft ground and grass more or less breaking my fall. I lay there several seconds, searching for my breath, then sat up.

The guard lay flat on the turf like a fresh-shot buck, motionless but moaning, his rifle several feet away. I scrambled over to him and drove a fist into his temple. It felt shitty hitting a downed man, but this was the wrong night to be shedding tears for the Marquess of Queensberry's rules.

I looked up, saw what might have been Vito's face looking down, and gave him a wave-off signal. Then I grabbed the guard's rifle, took a hold of his feet, and hauled him quickly into the dark recess beneath the cliff, his small sombrero trailing along by the rawhide choker wrapped around his throat.

Along the base of the rock the ground sloped down into a narrow channel worn by some stream eons earlier. This notch, along with the low weeds and limited light, made a pretty good stash for both of us.

I stripped off his dark wool jacket and threw it on, then checked the pockets. There was a pack of tobacco in one and a nasty little surprise in the other—a small leather bag with buckshot sewn inside.

The hat was too small, but the guard also had a heavy, dark beard and I didn't, so I put it on anyway, scrunching it down as tight as I could and flipping up the jacket collar. Then I picked up the rifle and made for the corner gate a few hundred feet off.

Hugging the rocks, I skulked along the cliff face until I was just twenty feet away. When I was sure I was alone, I darted out of the darkness and pressed myself flat up against the solid oak gate.

Sidling up against the door, I slid out the three-inch-thick wooden batten and laid it on the ground. Then I hauled back on the metal bolt with care and pulled on the door's handle. It took a little effort, but the gate swung inward a couple of inches. I left it that way, slightly ajar, then set off toward the house, hoping that would be the last of my troubles.

It wasn't.

89

Halfway to the hacienda, a shadow grew before me in the darkness. Squinting tightly, I made out the outline of a man, a rifle, and a sombrero, backlit by the houselights. It was the other guard, meandering around in that same, somnambular pace.

I stopped and pulled out a cigarette, turning away from him and holding my hands close together, aping a striking motion several times. He changed direction, ambled toward me.

Reaching slowly into my pocket, I withdrew the leaden bag and hefted it up in a cupped hand, marking the oncoming man all the while from the corner of my eye. When he neared, I asked through clenched teeth and a phony accent if he had a match.

He cocked his head, turning an ear toward me. Then he said, "*Ahh, sí*," digging into his coat and pulling out a box of matches. About five feet out he realized something was wrong, but by then I had him.

I spun a quick pivot and drove my left hand into his startled face, plowing into his cheekbone with my bonus-weight fist. His legs buckled, then he dropped to the ground, straight as a plum line. I snatched his rifle in midair.

He got the grab-and-drag treatment, too, then I hunkered low in the hidden ditch with my burgeoning guard collection, my heart pegged out at max. I've known many men who claimed that they were supernaturally calm while in grave danger—but they were all full of shit.

90

Vito was going to need a little more time to bring the horses around. I hogtied the guards together and stuffed their bandanas into their slack mouths, then thumped them both again just to be sure. I lay there then, still as a sniper in my weed bunker, counting off another five minutes, each one a long, lonely march to the gallows.

I cased the hacienda while I waited, searching for a way in. It was a king's castle for sure, but nothing I would have expected in rural Mexico.

Casa Bravo was a modern post-and-beam ranch, two stories in height, with stacked stone sides similar to the outer walls. Several floor-to-ceiling glass panels ran across the backside of all three wings, divided at regular intervals by stone partitions. The front façade appeared to be nearly all glass from what I could see by peering through the house. The whole complex was anchored in the center by a massive stone fireplace running through both levels and capped by a large, rectangular chimney on the flat roof.

The left wing and the huge center section were built up above flat ground while the right wing was cantilevered out from a rock shelf, seemingly floating over an escarpment that fell away steeply beneath it. Its walls were also glass, with a sleek balcony running end to end.

I'd underestimated Bravo a bit. The man had good taste—or at least a good architect.

The suspended portion of the hacienda was dark, whereas the other two sections had several lights on in each. I made an educated guess that Bravo's sleeping quarters were on the right and the living area was in the middle, with the hired hands bunking on the left.

I checked my watch, the outline of the radium-lined hands glowing ghostlike in the blackness. It was five a.m.—time to move. I took off the jacket and the silly hat and then set out across the open grounds, scurrying toward the darkened section of the house.

I made for the clean steel balcony that ringed the sleeping quarters, but as I neared I realized that there was a pronounced gap between the edge of the steep drop-off and the sleeping quarters beyond. There was no way to reach the balcony above.

That left me two choices: slip into the center of the house through a sliding door, then stumble around from room to room looking for Helen, or jump out onto the metal bracing underneath the quarters, clamber up to the outside edge of the balcony, and then play Peeping Tom. Neither option made me want to break out in the aria from *Carmen*.

There were three bedrooms from what I could see—a large wrap-around end unit, and two others inboard of that. The master had to be Bravo's, so Helen was apt to be in one of the other two. That gave me a fifty-fifty chance—the best odds I'd had all week.

I crept over to the cement retaining wall abeam the extended wing and took a look underneath. There were three large steel poles angling down beneath the edge of the balcony into the concrete foundation thirty feet below. It was about an eight-foot jump to the nearest one—not the hardest thing I'd ever done, but definitely a one-shot deal.

If I made the leap, I'd still have to monkey-climb to the top and find a way in, doing it all quietly enough not to wake anyone. If I missed, they'd be hosing me off the rocks come morning.

Crouching down low, I measured the distance with my eyes as I rocked back and forth to get my timing. I took one final deep breath. Then I leaped into the void.

91

Silently I fell, fingers spread wide, clutching for the pole with both hands as I plunged past.

I grabbed it clean, but it was larger in diameter than I'd estimated and I went skidding around the pole, fingers clawing for a grip on the curving surface as my momentum carried me by.

I twisted around in desperation as I began to slip off, looping an arm over the brace and swinging it down, then locking the other hand on my wrist like a vise grip. The crook of my arm took the brunt of the impact, but I held fast, stifling a grunt as I came swinging to a stop, fifteen feet beneath the bedrooms and a hundred more above nothing.

I hung there, holding my breath, waiting several long seconds to make sure I hadn't woken anyone. When I was sure it was okay, I curled my legs around the pole, hooked them together and began shimmying up slowly toward Bravo's tree house.

In two minutes I made the lower side of the balcony, just barely reaching the lowest of the three rails. Still clinging tightly to the pole, I stretched out the fingers of my left hand, sliding them around the railing and grabbing hold. I exhaled silently, then grasped the steel bar firmly in my right hand and chinned myself up to eye level with the balcony.

I crept over the railing, then sank down flat on the cold cement patio, crawling across the deck toward the bedrooms, hand then knee, hand then knee, trying to remain out of sight. When I reached the glass of the corner room, I rose up a foot and peeked through vertical louvers rustling gently beneath a ceiling fan.

Between the swinging blinds I saw an enormous carved wooden bed in a lavishly decorated master suite. Someone lay in the bed, but I couldn't tell who it was. Swallowing hard, I pushed myself up another foot, then shut one eye and looked toward the bed.

There he was, Mexico's own King Henry, manufacturing Zs under fine linens, a chambermaid under one arm. Bluish light filtered down through a large skylight, falling on Bravo's kisser. Even asleep, he wore a smug, self-satisfied smile.

I eased myself down, glanced over at the other rooms, and then slunk off toward the far end of the deck.

Helen had to be in one of the other two bedrooms. Bravo said she had no interest in him, so she wouldn't be in his room. But he would keep her close, voluptuous little piggy bank that she was, and that meant she'd be in a room down the hall. I just had to decide which one.

Somewhere along the way, the night sky had scudded up, a layer of broken cirrus creeping overhead, blocking the light of the waning moon. This gave me some cover, but it also made it harder to see who was in each bedroom.

I stopped in between them, looking around for any hint of Helen's presence. There was a wooden recliner and a small table a few feet from me, an empty wineglass and a kidney-shaped ceramic ashtray atop the table. Several lipsticked butts littered the bottom of the tray.

Helen had always liked a glass and a smoke for relaxation before going to bed. I zoomed in on the ashtray, noting that the rouged ends all faced the room on the left. It might have been Helen's shade—I wasn't sure—but it was as close to a sign as I was going to get.

Moments later, I was pressing my nose against the glass and peering through the split louvers, just a few inches away from the handle on the sliding glass door.

As my eyes adapted, I made out a woman's form on a bed under a thin sheet that concealed little. Her face was turned, though, and it could just as easily have been another of Bravo's concubines.

I eyeballed the door handle, then the woman, then the other room. If I was wrong, I'd burn. But I was nearly out of time and down to my last card. I decided to shoot the moon.

A gentle push was all it took, the slider floating silently on its tracks, opening up a good foot. Twisting sideways, I leaned in, the blinds fluttering lightly as I brushed against them. Then I slipped into the room, holding the swaying slats until they hung still against the sliding door. There might have been a note of Chypre hanging in the air. Sparked with anticipation, I turned to face the bed.

Cold dark eyes behind a glistening chrome object froze me.

The woman was sitting bolt upright in the bed, as naked as anyone Raphael ever painted—except for the gun in her hand.

92

The gun was a revolver. The woman was full automatic.

Luminous light bathed her beautiful body and finely featured face. Even in my present situation, I couldn't help but appreciate it

Before she could speak—or fire—I whispered, "Helen . . . is that you?"

She didn't answer, just stared at me without recognition, still pointing the .38 at my chest. I began to think that I'd made the biggest mistake of the very short rest of my life. But then I smelled that perfume again. It was definitely hers.

"Helen," I repeated, "it's Joe."

I placed a finger to my lips and moved in a step so she could see that it was me. She didn't lower the gun—but she didn't shoot, either.

Finally, after what felt like a week, the icy stare melted, warming up by degrees to somewhere between astonishment and exasperation. Helen shook her head in disbelief, the revolver dropping down slowly, coming to rest on the inside of her thigh.

I don't want to go chasing all over the world to find you again.

But you would, Joe, wouldn't you?

Bet your life on it, bambina.

In two steps I was across the floor, my fingers pressed against her mouth, my eyes riveted on hers.

"Don't say anything," I whispered. "Just listen. A team of assassins is about to assault this house. Whatever you've done, whatever you want from Bravo, whatever you think of me—it doesn't matter. We have to leave this place right now. Your life depends on it. Understand?"

Her eyes were emerald moons, big and bright and round. She looked up into mine a second, then nodded once.

"Get dressed," I said. "We have only minutes."

She stood, and I looked her up and down without feeling any shame. What I'd gone through to see that again.

As she threw on a dress, I wondered for the first time just how in hell the two of us were going to get out of the house. I briefly considered crawling back out across the balcony and sliding down the pole. No way was that going to happen.

"Is there an easy way out below?" I asked.

She leaned into me, whispered, "Stairs are carpeted, just a few feet away. We can leave through the back patio. I'll go first; no one will question me."

I didn't like that last part, but the plan was good. We were on the razor's edge now anyway, with no time for discussion.

"Let's go."

Helen grabbed a pair of sandals, unlocked the latch, and gently slid the door into the wall. She scanned both ways then darted out into the dark hallway.

She went down the stairs on velvet feet and faded from view. Ten seconds later, she leaned up so I could see her, then waved me down. I pulled lightly on the door to close it, then snuck down the padded stairs, descending past the enormous living room on my right into the lower level.

At the bottom, I made a double head swivel before slinking into a large, dimly lit foyer. There was an enormous glass slider leading to the back patio just a few feet ahead on my left. I moved toward it, then stopped when I didn't see Helen standing next to it as I expected.

I stepped back a few feet and looked around. A large walnut slab door to my right stood halfway open, offering a narrow view into a study or library. At the far end of the room, I made out Helen's candlelit figure in the gloom. She was fumbling with something on the wall.

Dumbfounded, I threw up my hands, then ducked behind the stairs at the sound of shuffling feet from the far side of the foyer.

A shadow rose in the passageway then passed quietly across the open space, disappearing into an unseen hallway beyond.

I waited another twenty seconds behind the stairs, gnashing my teeth into powder.

Behind me, that first very faint orange sliver of daylight began flickering in the eastern sky. We'd hit the zero hour.

My heart racing, I cut across the hall and rushed into the room.

The first thing I noticed was the scent of leather and burnt wood, normally comforting smells, but nothing of the sort at that moment. There was a single tabletop candle burning in a back corner, its yellowish flame the only light in the deep chamber.

As my eyes adapted, I made out thousands of books lining the walls on ten-foot shelves and all manner of horned things springing out from both sides of the room. Large leather club chairs and an immense carved ebony table cluttered the floors already bedecked with lush carpets and animal skins. It really was one hell of a library, but it was no time for the *Good Housekeeping* tour.

Helen was still at the other end of the room, beneath a large mounted panther coiled for attack. I realized then that she was spinning the dial of a wall safe.

We were well past pushing our luck. At that point, we were consciously trying to lose. It was not going to end well.

I stormed over to her, lunging out to grab her arm. As I did, she flung the safe door open with a *eureka!* flourish and shoved her hand in. She pulled it out a moment later, clutching a black cloth bag, her eyes gleaming with excitement in the dim light.

Furious, I snatched her other hand and pulled her toward me, gesturing toward the door with my thumb.

At that moment, for the very first time, I noticed the pungent smell of a cigar in the room along with the other scents. Then a noise like no other in the world clicked in the doorway, its echoes reverberating throughout the library.

A shadow flipped on a light switch. And there stood Mario Bravo, sporting black silk pajama bottoms and a Thompson submachine gun, dark eyes glowing hot above a burning cigar.

Two men flanked him, each with identical khaki safari outfits and mustaches, each pointing another tommy gun in our direction. My heart dropped like a runaway elevator at the sight.

"It would appear," Bravo proclaimed, a malevolent grin spreading on his face, "that for once the mouse has come to the hawk."

93

We were finished.

I had nothing left but scorn. "Tommy guns, Mario? Really? You've been watching too many gangster flicks."

One of the safari twins frisked me roughly, snatching my pistol and shoving me hard to the floor. When I looked up, the barrel of Bravo's machine gun was six inches from my nose. Helen drew her breath in with a gasp.

Bravo looked down at me with sad eyes. "Joe," he began in the voice of a beleaguered parent, "was all this necessary? You gave me your word you'd play it straight at the plaza."

"And you gave me yours. How do I know he wasn't your man?"

"And would he have killed two of my men and risked Helen's life if he were in my employ?"

"Maybe he was a bad shot."

I stood up slowly. Bravo took a step back and lowered his weapon. The twins didn't.

"Well, it doesn't make any difference now. You've seen your last sunrise, Joe Buonomo—and I'm afraid she has, too."

The words came down like anvils. Cold and very, very heavy.

"You've got the money, Mario. Just let us go. If you do, I can tell you something that will save your life. At least let Helen go. She—"

"She nothing!" he shouted, pointing his weapon at me. "She, who has brought all this misery upon us both, she who thought so little of my generosity that she tried to rob me and abscond away in the dark of night? I cannot brook this betrayal of my trust. Killing this vixen will be a service to mankind. Surely, you cannot disagree with that, sir. No, neither of you is going anywhere—except straight to hell!"

Helen broke in. "That's my money, Mario. That was the agreement. What right do you have to renege on our deal? I kept my end of the bargain, you lousy little grifter!"

I just took a number. I no longer had any idea what she'd been up to, if I ever had. The only thing I still knew was that I'd bet my life on another losing horse.

The torches flared behind those green eyes, searing the air around her as she tore into Bravo again. "You made fifty thousand on the deal—free and clear—for doing nothing! I only want what you owe me. And you fancy yourself a man of honor? You're a five-and-dime chiseler—a cheap smut peddler with delusions about Spanish aristocracy. What a laugh! You're as common as corned beef, Mario, and twice as greasy!"

The words came hot and heavy, little pieces of shrapnel zinging around the room, ripping holes into everything they touched.

I hated to interrupt the fusillade, but I had to ask. "Bargain, my dear? What the hell was all this about?"

The great baritone erupted into condescending laughter across the room. "I told you, Joe, there is a great deal about Helen Castano that you do not know. Nor shall you ever."

A smaller fit of laughter book-ended the statement. Even the safari twins got in on the act this time.

I turned toward Helen and gestured with an open hand, interrogating her with my eyes.

"Baby, I'm so sorry," she said. "When the plane crashed, I panicked. I, I was so scared . . . I thought you were dead."

"I get that a lot."

"I couldn't go back to Frank after that, not after I thought you'd been killed. Besides, Spazzo wanted to come down here. He had a gun on me, Joe. He wanted to sell that movie. I figured Mario could help, he's in the business. Baby, I didn't want to hurt anyone; I just wanted to get away. It's the truth, Joe."

"And Spazzo?"

"I slipped away from him down here, took his car when we were at a restaurant. I guess he went back to Vegas."

I made a sad little smile, fatigue and heartsickness pulling at the corners of my mouth. "No, he didn't, honey. Johnny Spazzo died four nights ago in Calexico, the same night we crashed my plane. Shot three times with my gun."

She recoiled a little, shot out a Stanwyck cringe. "Wh-who?" she said.

"You. You Helen. You killed Spazzo."

"Nooooo," she cried. "How could you think that about me, baby? How could—"

"Enough!" Bravo roared. "Confession is over! I don't care who did what. Say your good-byes and your prayers. You two are going to die."

He smiled grimly, then called to his gunmen, "Raúl, Antonio! Shoot them both! Wait—take them outside first. I don't want any blood on my first editions."

Through jaded eyes, I watched as dawn light filled the room, chasing the shadows off into the corners. Then I heard them—the big piston engines of the P-38 echoing off the canyon walls, as clear and as loud as a freight train barreling through a small town at night.

They sounded close. They sounded like death.

Several pistol shots cut the air outside. Men began shouting in front of the house. Other shots followed from multiple guns.

"It's an attack!" Bravo bellowed. "Everyone up!" Then he turned toward me, pointing the Thompson at my head. "All your men are going to die now—while you watch."

"Mario," I said in a low voice, "you're the one about to die. Those aren't my men; they're mercenary commandos. Better throw everything you have at them."

Bravo took me on with a stare, flicking the machine gun once to motion Helen and me toward the doorway. Mario and the twins marched us up the wide main staircase to the living room as several of his men ran past, fumbling with their pants and their guns.

Bravo strode over to the sheer glass wall at the front of the room, fuming like an ambushed general. More men came running half dressed from the far side of the house, rushing recklessly toward the shooting below.

"Everybody out!" Bravo yelled. "To the wall!"

Outside, the winding pitch of a war-bird in a dive grew louder. Helen wrapped her arms around my chest, digging in tight.

"Joe, what's happening?" she asked, her voice high and choked.

I looked up through the glass, saw the Lightning knifing through the breaking skies as it lined up on the grounds in front of the house.

"The end, Helen," I said. "The end."

94

I saw the play as the Lightning dove down. The attackers at the wall were a feint to draw Bravo's men out into the open. The P-38 would cut them down like wheat. I watched as the aircraft hurtled closer, mesmerized by the sight. We all were.

I pulled Helen close, trying to edge away. The safari twins raised their weapons in unison, blocking our path. I stood there helplessly, my eyes brimming with frustration.

"Bravo," I thundered, "let us go or give me a gun for God's sake!"

He cocked his head, then turned and marched toward us. "Here's what I'll do, I'll give this *bruja* a front-row seat of the action."

He jammed the Thompson into my chest, backing me up against the massive floating fireplace in the middle of the room. Then he swung the gun sideways, raking me across the jaw.

My legs buckled beneath me and I staggered backward. Helen tried to catch my fall, but Bravo seized her by the neck and yanked her away. He dragged her off toward the enormous windows in the front of the room as I mushed down against the bricks on legs of boiled linguini, struggling to remain upright. I slumped there, holding my jaw, unable to stand.

Outside, the sound of heavy weaponry I hadn't heard in many years opened up and closed in. It was a singularly terrifying sound—pulsating and mechanical, yet animate and vicious. You never, ever forget it.

I rolled my head around toward the noise then looked on in horror as the attack unfolded.

The Lightning was boring in at high speed, letting fly with all four machine guns and the twenty-millimeter cannon. Flashes of fire pulsed from the nose of the screaming aircraft, sand and rock erupting in dirty plumes amid a gaggle of Bravo's gunmen as the slugs ripped their way through earth and flesh.

Smoke puffed from underneath a wing, and a blur whistled across the compound, disappearing into the left side of the house.

A deafening boom rippled through the air a heartbeat later as the rocket detonated inside, spewing a volcano of glass and fire out the front of the house.

The concussion knocked me off my feet, toppling me over as a wave of machine-gun fire poured into the house, pulverizing the glass walls across the room and chewing parallel ruts across the birch and marble flooring. I covered up instinctively from the flying debris as the Lightning roared overhead in a hard pull-up.

I lay there a second, trying to shake off the shock, the sound of automatic weapon fire from many guns stitching through the air amid the screams of the injured and the dying. The air was rife with the smell of gunpowder, scorched wood, and fear.

I pushed up onto my hands and knees and shook my head several times to chase away the bells that were ringing inside. Ten feet away, a tommy gun lay on the floor. One of the twins was still holding it, but he didn't need it any longer—not without his head.

Bravo was standing defiantly among the shards of the demolished glass wall, laying down a stream of fire with his machine gun and hurling multilingual invective into the morning air. Fire from rocket debris burned below him in several places.

The remaining twin was on the front balcony, firing through the gray-black smoke at the dark figures scurrying forward. Helen was curled up tight behind an overturned end table a dozen feet away. She looked stunned.

I scrambled over to the khakied corpse and wrenched the machine gun out of his hand, then pulled my pistol out of his waistband and grabbed several extra machine-gun magazines from his web belt.

Cocking the weapon as I ran, I darted across the bullet-gouged floor toward the front of the room. As I approached, a hand grenade came wobbling through the air, hit the floor and bounced, then rolled behind Bravo's feet.

"Bravo!" I shouted. "Behind you, a grenade!"

He turned, then grabbed it and threw in one motion, heaving it over the balcony. It exploded below a second later, the scream of an Anglo voice marking the spot.

"Who are these infidels to oppose Mario Bravo?" he raged. "Bring them on, bring them all!" He was spitting now, shaking a raised fist over his head.

Reaching Helen, I bent down, checking her for injuries. I pulled her chin up and pushed back a few random strands of hair from her pallid face. Streaks of blood ran in small trails down her forehead and arms, but she was still in one piece.

"Let's go, baby." I held out my hand to her, but she wouldn't take it. She just sat there staring at me, vacant eyes fixing on nothing.

"Why, Joe, why?" she said in a child's voice. "Why did you have to keep looking for me? I would have come back to you."

She turned her head weakly across the broken room, to the battle outside. Tears began coursing down her cheeks, cutting black trails down her soot-stained face.

As I reached for her arm, a commando in black burst through a shattered glass wall. He hit the floor rolling and came up shooting, plastering the other twin against the railing.

I spun and fired, cutting him down with a burst from the tommy gun. He staggered crookedly, then skittered full on into an ugly standing sculpture, man and modern art collapsing together in a broken heap on the floor.

I advanced toward the shattered front façade, spraying bursts as I hiked forward, pinning down several commandos who were trying to reach the house.

Bravo was on the balcony now, still blazing away with his machine gun. I veered toward him until we were just a few yards apart. Our eyes met for just a second as I tossed him a mag. He might have been smiling.

The airborne whine began anew as the pilot brought the P-38 around for another pass. He had another rocket under the other wing, and I had the awful feeling that one was for me.

The only hope now was to head for the back of the house and flee through the open gate in back.

"Mario," I yelled above the din, "it's all over. Run for it!"

He didn't seem to hear me. If he did, he didn't respond.

I ran back over to Helen, picked her up, and slung her over my shoulder. She didn't resist. Then I ducked down and began to run, zigzagging across the jagged splinters and holes in the floor.

I got about fifteen feet before a white-hot comet tore through my right leg. I lurched, lost my balance, and tumbled down, clutching at the bullet wound in my thigh. We both hit the floor as the scream of the aircraft bore down on us a second time.

I sat up, staring numbly at the blood spreading beneath my fingers.

"Oh God," Helen gasped, looking from me to the dark shape ripping through the sky.

Then she was grabbing me by my belt loops, dragging me to my feet and pushing me forward, shouting, "Behind the fireplace, we have to take cover! Come on, baby, you can make it!"

As I careened forward I saw Bravo, still cursing and firing, as the best weapons platform the Army Air Corps ever had shrieked down and opened up with all guns.

Streams of machine-gun fire laced across the ground toward him, columns of dirt geysering upward in symmetrical wakes. Then the cannon cut loose and a torrent of steel slammed into the house, sawing through stone and timber, shredding the remains of the façade.

The balcony gave way with a wrenching groan, dropping off the front of the house amid an eruption of rock and splinters and flying glass. Mario Bravo rode out like Caesar on his chariot, descending below into the inferno of flame and dust.

Chaos reigned high as Death closed in. Staccato jags of automatic weapons tore through the din of explosions and dying men, sheets of smoke billowing through the devastated house.

I heard the *whoosh* of a rocket launch, then felt Helen's hand on my back, shoving me toward the massive stone hearth. I reached back for her as I fell stumbling to the floor. The last thing I saw was her face.

There was a deafening explosion, and then everything flared blistering white, a searing wave of heat and hellfire devouring the room as the House of Bravo came down around us.

95

The world was black.

The air, the light, the room—all black.

There was no sound, no life.

Nothing.

Everything was shrouded in dense, dark waves of smoke, the air reeking with the acrid smell of high explosives, a bitter, chemical taste stinging my tongue.

My fingers before my face were fuzzy and thick—like warped tubing flexing in a blackened ether.

I half rolled onto my side, saw blue above the roiling clouds of pitch. A heavy shadow lay above me, broad and slanted. I wiped my eyes. The dark form took shape—a support beam, broken and wedged against the mantel above, protecting me from the ceiling that had collapsed around me.

Helen. She dragged me here.

I sat up, trying to locate her, my hands grasping handfuls of emptiness. In desperation, I spun around, peering into the swirling soot and smoke.

The house was a ruin. The roof had split in the center, cleaving down inward from the supporting rock walls, burying the staircase and punching through the floor to the lower level in several places.

Flames danced along the walls, scurrying up exposed posts and across fractured beams, smoke boiling out of a dozen different smoldering cauldrons from all corners of what had been the living room. If that wasn't hell, it was a close second.

I called Helen's name several times, but the discordant hum echoing in my ears was all I could hear.

I grabbed the beam above me, hauling myself up. Stabbing pain coursed through my leg, reminding me that I'd been shot. Gripping the bloody spot on my dungarees, I gave my wound a quick check: it felt like muscle only, no bone. Then I braced myself against the heavy plank and put weight on the leg. I could walk.

"Helen, where are you?" I shouted, panic churning up inside me.

Shapes moved in the distance, converging on the house in several spots.

I retreated several steps toward the back of the living room, the remains of the roof creaking ominously above. A burning chunk broke free near me, dropping through the darkened space like a falling star.

One of the commandos spotted me from outside and opened fire. Bullets whistled by, ricocheting off the stone behind me. A second shooter joined in. My options were closing down fast. I ducked down, hiding in the smoke and wreckage, looking for a way out.

A few feet away, a sagging section of floor drooped down at a forty-five-degree angle, leading into the abyss below. It went from ruin to exit in an eye blink.

Sweeping the room one final time for Helen as I went, I hopped over the jagged wood stalagmites at the fracture point then dropped onto the chipped marble surface amid a hail of machine-gun fire, sliding downward into the inferno's depths below.

There was a hard reception waiting for me at the bottom. I bounced once, banged into a wall, and dropped flat on the marble. Shaking it off, I clawed my way upright along the stones, looking everywhere for Helen in the gloom.

Burning debris and shattered, unrecognizable pieces of stone and timber littered the floor. The whole place was aflame now, above and below.

Even through my concussion deafness I heard a loud snap upstairs, followed by a horrendous moan as the roof remains began to cave in.

Searching frantically for an escape, I spotted a large elk skin displayed on the nearest wall. I ripped it from its hooks and balled it in my fists, then took three hobbling, running steps toward the cracked glass walls at the back of the house.

Just before I hit, I brought my forearms up, then launched myself into the transparent façade. The wall disintegrated on impact, a sheet of green glass spraying out as I burst through onto the cement patio beyond.

I hit the ground hard but kept rolling, spinning myself clear as the remains of the center section came cascading down in a crescendo of fire and rubble.

The cantilevered sleeping wing went next, a one-man teeter-totter without the rest of the house to balance it. It tilted down sharply and collapsed upon itself, sliding off its supports like a ship going down the ways, piling up on the rocks below with a terrible crash.

I scrambled away and stumbled again to the ground. Then I turned and looked back. Two-thirds of the house was a blazing ruin, the rest a junk pile on the slope. Billowing smoke still obscured the air and the deserted back grounds. The only play left was getting out—and fast.

I got up, took several uneven steps toward the gate, and then stopped flat.

She might be alive, trapped inside.

The odds were impossible—I knew that. But I turned around to face the hacienda anyway, ignoring what my instincts were shouting inside me, that last image of Helen's face etched in my mind. Beyond any reason, I drew my pistol and started limping back toward the house.

A heavy hand clamped down on my arm and spun me around.

"Joe, what the fuck are you doing?"

It was Vito, his eyes black daggers glistening in the firelight.

"I've got to go back."

He put his hands on my collar and jerked me forward, his face taut and severe. "She's dead! No one else got out. Forget her, forget it all. We 'ave to go—now!"

We stared into each other's eyes a long second, his words eating through me. But I knew he was right.

332

I exhaled hard, nodded once. "Okay," I said, lowering my head, "okay."

He readied the Springfield, flicked his head toward the gate, and set off. I looked back one last time at the House of Bravo, its shattered timbers glowing orange against the cobalt sky.

"So much for your first editions, Mario."

96

We hit the gate unseen. What the smoke didn't hide, the shadows did. Vito went out first and I followed him, crushing up against the cliff wall as I hobbled on.

I hadn't made it twenty feet before I saw a man lying in the rocks a few feet away. I skidded to a stop and took aim.

Before I could shoot, I realized that he was lying on his back, arms twisted above his head like a discarded marionette. He was as dead as McKinley, dark liquid staining the dirt around him.

Vito saw me looking at him and held up the thirty-ought-six, flashing me a quick half smile. Then he gestured ahead with the rifle and we pressed on, picking our way through the loose stones in the pathway.

We reached the horses in a couple of minutes. Vito helped me climb onto mine then jumped into his own saddle.

"Hold it a second," I said.

I reached under my jacket and tore a long strip from my T-shirt. I wrapped it around my leg tightly and pulled it into a knot just above the exit wound in the front.

"Let's ride," he said. "We'll be clear in a few minutes—they didn't see us. I can clean that out later, wrap it right. Okay?"

"Yeah."

We rode away along the edge of the canyon. We were just rounding the last outcropping before the trail cut back out of sight when I saw something. I whistled and signaled for a stop.

Far down on the road below, a transport plane came rolling into view and slowed to a dusty halt, its propellers spinning at idle speed. I didn't recognize the make, but it was about the size of a C-47 and might have been Russian.

The plan made perfect sense, though. The seldom-used road was a passable battlefield runway. The commando squad could be the hell out of Baja and across the Sea of Cortés in twenty minutes, landing anywhere along the desolate Arizona border for a quick extraction. These guys were pros all the way.

What happened next really surprised me, though, even on a day like that. As we watched, the P-38 swooped in and buzzed over the transport. Then the pilot made a smooth turn, then another, rolling out in the opposite direction with the landing gear down—a standard military overhead pattern. He was making a landing.

Vito saw it in my eyes. He knew what I was thinking. "Let's leave this place. There's only death 'ere."

"Sorry, Vito," I said. "I'm going to have to catch up with you down the trail, my friend. There's someone down there I've really gotta meet."

97

The terrain we were on ran downward toward the valley floor, fanning out along a sloping curve in striated folds. The lowest fold appeared deep enough to hide a man, running within fifty yards of the road before tapering off at the bottom of the fan.

I handed the reins to Vito and dismounted. "I'm going in," I said. "You clear on out of here. There's nothing more you can do."

"What about your 'orse? There's nowhere to tie it."

I looked up into his eyes. "Take them both."

He face tightened in grim resignation. He knew he couldn't talk me out of it.

"Good luck, paesan," I said. "See you in Montese."

We looked at each other for a moment. His hand came out, fingers extended. "You're a good man, Joe Buonomo."

I shook his paw, flashed him a tight smile. "Damn few of us left."

He smiled back, spoke low. "*Arrivederci.*"

Then he turned the gray horse, gave it a little kick, and rode off, the chestnut mare trailing alongside.

I set off down the carved channel. It was rocky, but I moved along pretty well for a guy with a bullet hole in his leg. The ravine was still deeply shaded, but the high ground was plenty bright. I guessed I might have ten more minutes of cover.

Well off to my right, a dozen or so commandos trotted down the hill. They were too widely spaced for a guy with a pistol to do much damage, but I had another plan anyway.

The P-38 driver rolled in low over the transport and banged her in on the road, the swirling props spinning up trailing columns of dust that obscured the air near the ground.

I made my move. Staying low, I juked down the cleft at double time as a mist of fine sand drifted over me. When it cleared, I held myself close to the brown earth, pressed low and flat. The pilot made a crisp turn downroad and headed back toward the transport. A minute later, he taxied past me, spinning another wave of flying camouflage into the air. I pushed forward underneath it.

The pilot brought the plane within fifty feet of the transport, made another tight turn that put the two aircraft tail to tail, and then cut the motors. The top canopy flipped open a moment later, then the side window came rolling down as the pilot cranked the handle. He climbed out of the cockpit and stood on the wing, stretching his back, like a guy who'd had a tough day at the office. Then he pulled an old-style leather helmet and goggles off, rubbing his close-cut blond hair several times.

It was the same guy I'd seen barking orders back at the hangar, and now he was already gesturing angrily to his men to get on the other aircraft. The mission hadn't improved his disposition any.

He appeared to be about my age, and it dawned on me then that he was almost certainly a vet. We might have even served together.

My God, is that what we turned our young men into in that war? Men like him—and me?

The towhead climbed down the small foot ladder at the back end of the wing and ran over to the returning soldiers coming down the hill. It was handshakes and backslapping all the way around. Several of them were reenacting their exploits with their hands. Those guys had battery acid in their veins.

Far above them, the house burned furiously in the early morning light. Two men straggled in carrying a comrade with a chest wound. He was in bad shape, bleeding heavily. They laid him on the ground to tend to him.

Towhead looked over at him, conferred with a lieutenant type. That man raised a hand, held up four fingers. They both looked down at the wounded man. Then Towhead turned back to the other man, his face entirely devoid of expression. He shook his head and held up five fingers.

They spoke some more, then the other men climbed into the plane, leaving the injured man alone on the ground. Towhead walked toward the open cockpit window, twirling two fingers in the air several times. He got a thumbs-up from the other pilot.

My leg was tightening up in the trench. I massaged it vigorously several times then squatted down to stretch the muscle out. While I was crouched down I pulled my weapon, released the safety, and pulled it close to my chest. I could feel my heart pounding against my arm. I took several deep breaths as I waited.

The transport's right engine fired up, then settled into idle. That was good. Now I had cover noise.

I glanced back at the blond devil in charge of those conquistadors. He was standing over the wounded man, looking down at him with a face as stony and gray as that Aztec sculpture in the park.

Without a word, he pulled his pistol and discharged two shots into his comrade, the wounded man's clenched fists flying up, then dropping limply at his sides.

Towhead walked off toward the transport without looking back, without showing any emotion at all. He was a freezer case, that guy, as cold and as distant as a dead star.

My plan had been to put five in him as soon as he got close and let the chips fall where they might after that, but he crossed me up when he climbed into the transport. He exchanged a few words in the hatchway with another man in a flightsuit, then handed him a small bundle. The second man then jumped down from the plane and jogged off as Towhead yanked the door shut behind him. Oily smoke shot out of the left engine a second later as it turned over.

A moment later the transport flapped its flight controls as it rolled down the road, gathering speed for takeoff, legions of dust taking flight behind it. As the dirt settled, I crept up on the other pilot who was making his way toward the P-38, his head down as he rifled through a stack of green bills. As I approached, I realized he was Mexican Air Force, an errand boy sent to help cover the tracks.

When he had one foot on the entry ladder, I tapped him on the shoulder. He turned very suddenly, regarding me with obvious shock.

"*Buenos días*," I said. Then I cracked him in the face with my pistol. Son of a bitch mercenaries.

I rolled him over to the side of the road, his clutch of bills scattering across the plain in the arid wind. Turning, I stole a glance at the departing transport, watching impassively as it lumbered into the sky. There was no hurry to get into the cockpit; it wasn't going to be too much trouble catching up to them anyhow.

98

I had some time in a P-38, but it wasn't much, and I'd gotten it many years before. Still, she was an airplane and I knew I could handle her.

After a short rundown, I switched the fuel pumps on, checked the power to idle, and spun number one. The Allison caught immediately and thundered to life. In thirty seconds, I had both engines powered and the flaps set for a shortfield takeoff. I cranked the window shut, then pulled the canopy down and latched it, giving the road a quick scan as I advanced the power.

The Lightning broke ground in a quarter mile. I kept her level at fifty feet as I brought up the gear, then the flaps. Roaring low across the road, I held the nose down to build up some smash, the airspeed increasing rapidly until I was flat-out screaming across the desert at better than three hundred.

The transport had climbed out heading north while I was running in the opposite direction, but I had a quick fix for that. I took a breath, then hauled back hard on the control yoke. The *g*'s laid on like falling bricks as I pulled the bird into the vertical, the altimeter spinning like a turnstile as I shot through three thousand feet in just seconds. Then I laid the Lockheed on her back and rolled her smartly upright, completing an Immelmann turn. Just like riding a bicycle.

I couldn't see the transport, but I had an easy hundred miles an hour overtake on that crate, and they couldn't have been more than a few miles ahead.

Searching the skies as I sped north, I coolly noted the burning hacienda below. There was no undoing that horror, but this bird was under new management now.

I flew on another minute without picking up anything. The sun was over the distant mountains now, a brilliant white disk arcing toward the heavens. I banked east into the blinding light, holding a hand low to shield my eyes as I bored on.

Then a fleck loomed above and ahead, growing rapidly in the windscreen. I made the coldest smile of my life, turning dead-on for the big plane as a very old feeling arose inside me.

I brought the power up, checked the props at high, and cinched down my harness as I closed in fast on the aircraft ahead, thinking things over as much as you can in half a minute, assessing the weight of what I was contemplating.

These weren't men I was chasing. Fifteen minutes ago they'd come down that hill bragging about how they'd killed other men and women—including the one I'd vowed to save. They left an injured comrade behind to die in the dirt on foreign soil, then did nothing when their commander executed him. And they did it all without any conviction, only for the money.

No, these weren't men. They were something less.

I gave it one final thought as I waited for any hint of remorse to grab me.

Then I charged my guns.

99

I wanted them to see me first.

I came in hot on the port side, chopped the power, and g'd off the excess airspeed with a few quick turns, settling in on their wingtip like I'd been riveted there.

Towhead was in the left seat. He turned with a startle when he saw the Lightning on his wing, then he went positively pale when he made my face. Ensenada, Agua Caliente, maybe the hacienda. He'd seen me somewhere before and knew damn well who I was—and what it meant.

That's right, Towhead, know fear, choke on despair, see Death in my face. Go wherever you want, pray to whoever will listen. You're not going to make it.

And we both know it.

Faces were pressed against the side windows, haunted eyes staring out. That was good. I wanted them to know, too. Wanted them to feel it.

I goosed the throttles, pulled even with Towhead. He beamed hatred at me through dark eyes, his jaw set tight. I gave him a last, cold glance, pointed a finger toward him, held it there.

He rolled into me suddenly, mashing the rudder down and slewing his nose around tight. A blaze of machine-gun fire erupted from the front of the transport, tracer fire arcing past my windscreen in a white blur.

I pushed down hard and cut underneath him, crisscrossing away in a scissor maneuver, avoiding a collision by mere feet.

That son of a bitch had two big guns up front. That was *really* good. Now I had an opponent, not just a duck.

Towhead turned back east and dove to pick up airspeed, trying to shake me in the sun. I gave chase, pushing the manifold pressure up, feeling the superchargers kick in as I closed on the transport like a diving falcon.

I came on dead astern and took aim. Desperate men were firing machine guns at me from waist slots on either side but they couldn't get the angle. They may as well have been throwing rocks.

I fired a short burst for effect, marking the path of the tracers as they passed above and to port of the diving transport. A gentle push on the nose and a small kick on the rudder were all it took to align my fire. Then I squeezed the trigger.

A column of fire shot forth from the nose as the four Brownings erupted in deadly synchronicity. Shards of metal began peeling off the left engine and wing of the transport as my shots struck home. An inspection panel blew off, a silver blur tumbling end over end as it flashed by. A wisp, then a funnel of smoke began trailing back from the damaged powerplant as spewing oil fried on white-hot exhaust pipes.

Towhead pulled up aggressively as I squeezed off another volley. That one missed as I went whistling by underneath him, less than fifty feet away, jacked solid on adrenaline.

I rolled into a hard turn and pulled like hell, damn near curling the wingtips as I muscled the Lightning back onto the six of the smoking transport now two miles ahead.

There was nowhere left on earth for him to hide now, not with that black plume pouring out of his engine. He knew it, too, and he had the big plane laid full out in a dive, no doubt exceeding whatever redline speed the manufacturer had placarded. But I wasn't in any mood to admire his skill.

Sliding up to a high position, I closed in rapidly then went barreling past at full power, checking the transport in the canopy-top mirror as it shrank behind me. Towhead was making for the high mountains, where he could check my superior turning ability. He might have a chance there. It was time to end this.

I streaked ahead, counted off ten seconds, then rolled the Lightning into a 135-degree bank, slicing down in a Split-S, the sun at my back as I zeroed in on him at a combined speed of better than five hundred miles an hour. I brought my ship into firing position at an angle to his nose, forcing him to commit. He couldn't turn away now or I'd carve him up—he had to meet me head-on.

Towhead didn't disappoint. He banked into me and nosed up, bringing his guns to bear. Bright wicks of flame reached out through the sky toward me, wicked steel whizzing by at twice the speed of sound.

I lined them up in the gun sight as they neared but held my finger off the trigger a little longer. I wanted to be close.

I could feel the impact of his bullets striking my own plane, hear the percussive *thump thump* as they punched through the wing, but I bored straight in, not wavering an inch. Closing, closing.

At one thousand yards I let fly.

A stream of metal poured into the center of the transport and swept aft in a wave of destruction, curving indentations sprouting along the fuselage wherever the .50-caliber slugs bit in. Men were dying in the back of that flying tomb.

Then I pushed my nose down a few degrees, squinted into the sight, and toggled the cannon button. I gave 'em the whole nine yards, holding the button down hard until I could feel the weapon clacking emptily in front of me. I could almost see Towhead's face as he profaned me.

The heavy shells rifled forward, tearing into the nose of the transport. There was an odd second where nothing seemed to happen, then the cockpit simply vanished in a gray-green haze, chunks of glass and aluminum blowing loose and pinwheeling into the dirty morning sky.

I pulled up hard as I shot by the shredded plane, throwing my head back in time to catch a glimpse of her through the top of the canopy as she wobbled forward, belching smoke and a swirling tail of flame.

But she didn't go down.

I watched in disbelief from above for several seconds, fairly well stunned that she was still in the air after I'd poured enough lead into her to take down a B-29. Letting out a choice maternal expletive, I banged my fist on the glareshield, then swooped down behind her, prepared to finish the job.

I followed her for twenty seconds, my finger on the trigger, closing in from her six to point-blank range. But I didn't fire. There was something about the way that ship was hanging on, hemorrhaging oil and churning smoke, nosing ever downward, giving up altitude but not the fight. The Sierra de Juárez mountains loomed ahead marking near-certain doom, but they weren't giving up the ghost.

Caution gave way to curiosity. Wary of the waist gun, I pulled forward, banked a little closer, edging toward the crippled aircraft. Initially I couldn't understand why no one was firing at me, but as I got nearer I saw why. A smear of blood marked the blown-out glass of the midship window, an arm flapping in the slipstream, a red spatter trailing aft along the pockmarked fuselage. Inside, I could see another man writhing on the floor, his comrades tending to him. They all looked up as my Lightning loomed into view, the injured man spitting blood as he cursed me in defiance. The others watched me, making no move to raise a weapon, their vanquished eyes telling the story.

I bumped up the throttles, inched toward the cockpit. Towhead was still there, strapped in his seat. But he wasn't a towhead any longer—he wasn't much of anything any longer.

The other pilot was still at the shot-away controls, fighting like hell to keep his ship in the sky, his face and flightsuit mottled with blood. I couldn't tell if it was his or Towhead's, but he looked like he'd been hit. He glanced out at me, exhaustion and fear and the swirling wind clouding his features. I just stared numbly back, dumbfounded by the sudden sympathy I felt for him. There was no denying the raw heroism of his actions.

The scene triggered a memory from the war. During an assault on Rabaul, I'd pulled alongside a Mitsubishi I'd shot up, the surviving pilot sawing back and forth on the controls of his crippled plane, fire blooming on the control panel in front of him. Our eyes met for just a second—he seemed to be looking to me for help even though we both knew he was finished. But I felt nothing for him at that moment. It was a war and they were the enemy, and it was just that simple. I slipped behind them and finished them off with the Hellcat's six fiftys, concerned only with saving my carrier from another possible threat.

Over time, however, that memory began to haunt me, his face appearing again and again in my sleep, the profound sense that I'd somehow wronged him impossible to bury. I don't know why that one affected me so much; the rest of my engagements were just business. There was just something about that look of helplessness in his face and my guilt over denying him the right to finish his hopeless fight on his terms.

I carried that one with me a long time—managing it, locking it inside, suffocating it under my shell—until Pete died and the darkness broke through. They can order you to kill other men, and they can tell you it's your duty, but they can't tell you how to reconcile it, never help you live with it. On that one, you're on your own.

As I replayed that episode, I looked on at those mercenary butchers, those assassins. I knew they weren't the equal of the men I'd fought during the war, weren't entitled to any consideration or pity, flat out deserved to die.

But I couldn't do it. I couldn't execute them like that, no matter what they were, not under those circumstances. Towhead was gone anyway. I'd gotten my pound of flesh from him and then some. If by some miracle they made it now, so be it.

There was nothing I could do for them, though. I flew alongside awhile, jousting with my emotions, watching the struggle play out. Finally, I just eased the power back and drifted wide, falling away, inexplicably hoping to see their plane begin to climb.

The transport crawled ahead, still smoking and losing altitude, the Juárez range closing around them. I watched them go, chastened, dispirited, utterly devoid of any feeling of satisfaction. Then I banked away, leaving them to the Fates as I headed west.

Adiós, Towhead.

100

The state of hyperalertness that combat demands fades quickly. Inside of two minutes I had the shakes. It had been one hell of a morning, and it was barely six o'clock. I reached into my coat pocket for my Luckys and felt an unusual object inside. I pulled it out to see what it was then stopped cold, shot through with a sudden chill.

It was the black bag Helen had pulled out of Bravo's safe. She must have stuck it in my pocket while we were huddled together in the living room.

Holding the aircraft level with one hand and shaking the bag with the other, I managed to loosen the leather drawstring from the eyeholes. I turned it over and dumped the contents on my lap.

There were two things of tremendous interest inside the bag. The first was several bundles of hundred-dollar bills, stacked tall like Dagwood sandwiches—a good fifty thousand easy. I whistled at the sight of all that cabbage.

But the second item was immensely more valuable.

Seeing these things suffused me with a gut-deep sadness as the last image I had of Helen stabbed back at me.

I wrestled the money back into the sack and then stashed the other item in my flight jacket. A flash went off in my head. I nodded in self-approval as I thought it over, then banked toward the towering pillar of black smoke on the horizon.

~

I came in from the north, dropping down to two hundred feet while slowing to one fifty. No one was moving near the fallen citadel, but at the base of the rise I spied a panel truck on the side of the road where the airplanes had been.

I made a sharp bank toward it and swooped in low, maybe fifty feet over the heads of several men who dove for cover as I whooshed by. It took me a few seconds before I made them for Oriental—had to be the Ching Hwas. Then some hero whipped out a pistol and began squeezing off shots at me. That confirmed it; only they would make a play that overarchingly stupid.

I caught myself smiling in the rearview mirror. The Ching Hwas, forever late to the dance and never dressed for the occasion. Silk suits on the Frontera. Whodathunkit?

"This one's for you, Lino," I said as I lined up their truck in my gun sights, half a dozen smallish men fleeing in all directions as I toggled my guns and laid waste to their ticket home.

It was so easy I should have been ashamed, but that didn't make it any less spectacular when the gas tank blew—that truck leaped at least ten feet in the air before landing upside down in a ditch. Must have been some hand grenades on board or something.

The meeting between Sam and the Chings pretty much became a weekend convention after that one.

I kept on going, heading south several miles over the desert toward Ojos Negros, searching for just one thing.

Then below I saw two horses, one gray, one brown, and a single rider, south of the highway and moving fast. The horseman veered off defensively as I approached.

I blew past him, rocking my wings several times while I brought the plane around. When I neared again, the rider was stopped on his mount, pointing a rifle at me. That guy had guts.

I rolled my window down and gave him a vigorous wave as I passed. This time he recognized me, lowering his rifle and holding up a hand as I roared by.

I slowed to one twenty for the third pass. As I came overhead, I dipped the left wing and flung the tightly bound bag o' Ben Franklins out toward the rider below. Then I advanced the power, retracted the flaps, and cranked up the window.

At two hundred miles per hour, I rolled ninety degrees wing low and pulled the aircraft around in a tight turn a hundred feet above the deck. I drew a bead on the rider and made for him, the distance between us fading in a rhythmic blur.

As I neared, I saw Vito, riding hard on the gray mustang, the black bag held high in his upraised hand. He was headed west, toward Agua Caliente.

I gave him another wing rock as I sped by, then I cranked in a turn to the north and pulled the Lightning into the emerging dawn.

As I climbed away, I saw another horse, chestnut in hue, galloping free across the open plain, a trail of dust rising high in her wake.

101

The gas tanks were still half full, and I was less than a hundred miles from the border. I decided to keep her low, duck radar, and sneak across into California. She was a hot ship and I still had a few rounds left, but I didn't want to tangle with any U.S. Air Force jocks in F-101s, not today at least.

With a little luck I could be in Thermal before most folks were even awake. There was an empty hangar there at the far end of the field, and it was plenty big enough to stash a P-38.

I was taking a chance, but I didn't have another plan, and I was pretty sure I didn't give a damn. I was tired and I was bleeding. I needed a cigarette, I needed a doctor—I needed a good stiff drink.

My next stop would be the compound in Rancho Mirage. He would be waiting to hear from me. But that was okay.

Frank Sinatra and I had a great deal to discuss.

EPILOGUE

LODI, CALIFORNIA 1962

I crushed out the Lucky in the ashtray and cold-stared my empty glass. It was well past two, time to be turning in. Instead, I signaled the tender, who gave me a half-interested look.

"One more of these, pal."

He just slid the whiskey bottle my way. I poured a shot, then dug out another smoke and burned it. Some saloon singer was moaning low on the radio, spilling his guts in a bar somewhere. I knew his work.

I took a deep drag on the cigarette and held it in, revisiting the events of *that* week for the nine-hundredth time.

Carmine Ratello's corpse took the rap for Betty Benker and Murray Fine. Nobody gave me a medal for exterminating that rodent—but they didn't charge me with anything, either. That was pretty much a wash.

Johnny Spazzo went down as Unsolved. What difference did it really make?

I kept mum about the Ching Hwas. Sam Woo had the big sit-down with them and everything was kind of, sort of all right for a while. The Coldwater Canyon thing didn't draw too much ink considering, and the Chandlers were just as happy if no one knew that anything like that could happen in Beverly Hills anyway.

Rink Ruggles got a commendation, and a third term as sheriff for his heroic actions. Bendix turned out to be low-rent mob fringe working for Ratello. Rink and I get along better since that night—he even admitted to me that his shot missed Bendix—but I'd already figured that out by then.

Frank offered to buy me a new plane. I told him to stick it. An unnamed party in Nevada traded me a '39 Electra with low-time engines even up for my Mexican Air Force P-38—minus the guns. My new plane looks a lot like the old one, right down to the item stashed in the wainscoting. Roscoe and I do just fine with it.

Kennedy became president, of course. Partly because that film didn't surface, and partly because Richard J. Daley is a very committed Democrat. I never found out if those goons were sent by old man Hoover or Giancana—or someone else—but no one ever said anything to anyone about them.

The election win helped Frank get through his grieving, but he still took it hard about Helen. He locked himself in his bedroom, didn't come out for days. He called one night at four in the morning, asking me if she could have really been that bad. I told him the truth—I didn't know. He bounced back in time, but like I said, he took it hard.

I took it worse. In the time since it all went down, I've gradually put the pieces together. It's hard to accept the facts—but I do.

I didn't start out as Helen's mark, but when things spun out of control, she grabbed for anyone within reach, the way a drowning person does. And she took me almost all the way to the bottom with her. I should have seen it all sooner, but I was in too deep.

Maybe in time she could have turned it around. Or maybe not. It's a fool's errand to try and change people—or save them from themselves. Everybody dies anyway.

They held a funeral for her out here. Her folks came out from Wisconsin, and then they went back. They said they didn't mind burying her on Catalina; they knew how she loved it there.

Of course, there was no body. Officially, there wasn't even a fire. Privately, the Mexican government said nothing was ever recovered from that place: no money, no film, no Bravo—no Helen. Still, I wonder . . .

In time, I went back to the island. I drop into Avalon every now and then, usually when I'm on a run. I haunt the places we shared. Sifting through the ashes, searching for the reasons, trying to rewrite the past.

Sometimes I go by the Casino in the evenings. I sit on the quay and watch for her without knowing why. It's just a sailor's dream of a mermaid—or maybe a Siren. The dark waves roll endlessly by as the sun fades over the mountains and the moon rises quietly overhead.

But she never comes.

Then I take to the night sky. I'm a freight pilot, and there are boxes to move.

END

ACKNOWLEDGMENTS

A very great deal has already been written about the impossible genius and immense contradictions that marked the life of Francis Albert Sinatra. Hey, the man lived big—pal. For me, it has always been about the voice and the passion. Thanks for the music, Frank, it's gonna live forever.

Of all the many, many people who provided material assistance, inspiration, or both in the creation of this novel, the following stand out.

The Professionals:

David Hale Smith, my agent, who took a flyer on this Joe Nobody and greased in a three-point landing. No author is more fortunate than we happy few working with DHS. Thanks for your brilliant moves, ace. Otto Penzler of the Mysterious Press. *The* Otto Penzler. A great man to share a Manhattan with. Rob Hart, my editor, whose deft touch, cheerfulness, and unabashed enthusiasm for this work provided substantial aid and comfort to this rookie. The first-rate crew at Open Road Media, who hit the trifecta with a spot-on proof, period-perfect font, and stunning cover design.

ACKNOWLEDGMENTS

Friends and Aviation Colleagues:

Leslie Rocha from the old 'hood, for her scary-good proofreading and her many kind words of encouragement. Barbara Hoffman, who chaperoned me around Santa Catalina Island, introducing me to its many fantastic characters, herself included. Diana Chen, for her assistance with Chinese language and culture, and for taking me to late-night places where no English is spoken. Lt. Col. Jim "Snake" Daulton, USMC, and Maj. (Ret.) James "Jake" Elwell, USAF, for their hard-earned expertise on aerial combat and gunnery. Marksman Gerhard Gotzmann, for his splendidly detailed intel on the use and terminology of firearms. Captains Jeff Taylor and Kevin Mullen of Jetblue Airways, for buddy-reads of in-flight scenes, and for being stand-up guys. Captain Sean Parker of Jetblue Airways, for his uncompromising and inspirational life as a man's man, for the generous use of his Lake Tahoe home, and for being a great wingman. Speaking of which, I owe a very special debt of gratitude to the World War II veterans at the Palm Springs Air Museum, especially P-38 drivers Blaine Mack and Everett Price. How lucky we are to still have this most vital generation of Americans.

Novelists:

The fabulous Laura Caldwell, author, attorney, and all-around smash, for her warmhearted assistance in the formative days of this work and for the many things she taught me. Writing triple-threat J. D. Smith, for a lifetime of friendship, a valuable buddy-read, and sustained support during the long road to this novel's completion—as well as some very timely visits with Pappy Van Winkle. Bestselling author Henry Perez, whose intensity and drive would bring a smile to Ol' Blue Eyes' face. In addition to three decades of collaborations and thousands upon thousands of hours discussing film, writing, jazz, noir, tough guys, and anything else under the moon, Henry made exceptional contributions to the realization of this work. His hard-nosed advocacy, fearless criticism, and unwavering belief in this project became my machetes as I hacked my way through the writing wilderness. Without his help, this novel would not exist. *Muchas gracias, amigo viejo*, together we are mighty!

ACKNOWLEDGMENTS

Le Donne:

Like most men, I spend my life endlessly beguiled by, indebted to, and eternally grateful for women in general. Three in particular had special influence over me and over this novel's composition. My mother, Mary Jac Sandrolini, who would not have approved of the violence in this book, but whose passionate love of arts and language are its soul. Miss you, Mamma. Enchantress Brenda Castano. Muse. Siren. Force of nature. Baby, the song is you. And, of course, the lovely, irrepressible Nancy Carriero, who hung gasping on every word, believing always in Joe—and in me. Bless you, *bellissima*, for all that you've meant to me. Sleep warm.

Copyright © 2013 by John Sandrolini

Cover design by Mauricio Díaz

Cover photograph of aircraft by Luc Verkoyen

ISBN 978-1-4532-9933-3

Published in 2013 by MysteriousPress.com/Open Road Integrated Media
345 Hudson Street
New York, NY 10014
www.mysteriouspress.com
www.openroadmedia.com

MYSTERIOUSPRESS.COM

Otto Penzler, owner of the Mysterious Bookshop in Manhattan, founded the Mysterious Press in 1975. Penzler quickly became known for his outstanding selection of mystery, crime, and suspense books, both from his imprint and in his store. The imprint was devoted to printing the best books in these genres, using fine paper and top dust-jacket artists, as well as offering many limited, signed editions.

Now the Mysterious Press has gone digital, publishing ebooks through **MysteriousPress.com**.

MysteriousPress.com offers readers essential noir and suspense fiction, hard-boiled crime novels, and the latest thrillers from both debut authors and mystery masters. Discover classics and new voices, all from one legendary source.

FIND OUT MORE AT
WWW.MYSTERIOUSPRESS.COM

FOLLOW US:
@emysteries and Facebook.com/MysteriousPressCom

MysteriousPress.com is one of a select group of publishing partners of Open Road Integrated Media, Inc.

OPEN ROAD

INTEGRATED MEDIA

Open Road Integrated Media is a digital publisher and multimedia content company. Open Road creates connections between authors and their audiences by marketing its ebooks through a new proprietary online platform, which uses premium video content and social media.